SEVEN FACELESS SAINTS

These are uncorrected proofs. Please note that any quotes for reviews must be checked against the finished book. Dates, prices, and manufacturing details are subject to change or cancellation without notice.

SEVEN
FACELESS
SAINTS

M. K. LOBB

LITTLE, BROWN AND COMPANY
New York Boston

This book is a work of fiction. Names, characters, places, and incidents are the product of the author's imagination or are used fictitiously. Any resemblance to actual events, locales, or persons, living or dead, is coincidental.

Copyright © 2023 by Meryn Lobb

Cover art copyright © 2023 by [TK]. Cover design by [TK].
Cover copyright © 2023 by Hachette Book Group, Inc.

Hachette Book Group supports the right to free expression and the value of copyright. The purpose of copyright is to encourage writers and artists to produce the creative works that enrich our culture.

The scanning, uploading, and distribution of this book without permission is a theft of the author's intellectual property. If you would like permission to use material from the book (other than for review purposes), please contact permissions@hbgusa.com. Thank you for your support of the author's rights.

Little, Brown and Company
Hachette Book Group
1290 Avenue of the Americas, New York, NY 10104
Visit us at LBYR.com

First Edition: February 2023

Little, Brown and Company is a division of Hachette Book Group, Inc.
The Little, Brown name and logo are trademarks of Hachette Book Group, Inc.

The publisher is not responsible for websites (or their content)
that are not owned by the publisher.

Library of Congress Cataloging-in-Publication Data TK

ISBNs: 978-0-316-38688-3 (hardcover), 978-0-316-38716-3 (ebook)

Printed in the United States of America

LSC-C

10 9 8 7 6 5 4 3 2 1

Dedication TK

＊

They say it rained the day Chaos fell from grace.
Not in a mist upon a delicate wind, but in a
torrential rush. He fell because his children did: their
broken, mortal bodies trampled in the northern mud.
When he retreated, it was with a scream that shook
mountains. A scream that transcended worlds and
settled in the cracks of every city, holding vigil in the
spaces between light.

His lover, Patience, watched mournfully as he
fell. And though her heart, so like his, was full of
revenge, she did not reach for him. She only waited,
knowing that every war has its end, and every sin
begs a punishment.

Chaos is hasty. But Patience . . .

Ah, Patience knows precisely when to strike.

—Saints and Sacrifice, Psalm 266

LEONZIO

It was just past midnight when the paranoia set in.

Leonzio paced the length of the room, heartbeat so vigorous it was a foreign sensation in his chest. He was hyperaware of the cool air against his skin. The way his tongue—too dry, *too dry*—sat all wrong behind the cage of his teeth.

Unable to stand it any longer, he crossed over to the door, opened it, and peered into the corridor. It stretched out before him like an infinite passage, all but the first few steps consumed by oppressive shadow.

The guard who should have been standing there was gone.

And yet the disciple couldn't bring himself to leave his room, unwilling to navigate the dark Palazzo.

The building had eyes. He'd felt their weight all week: first in the place where he prayed to the saints, then in the council chambers where he met with the other representatives of the blessed guilds. They tracked his every step, and not even the light of the stars could drive them away.

As he slipped back into his room, frustration nagged at the edges of his mind. What had he been doing prior to the fear taking hold? He'd been looking for the chief magistrate—that was it. Had needed to tell the man something crucially important. But *what*?

Leonzio swept a hand across his perspiring brow. The candle he'd lit cast slanting shadows up the walls, soft lines shifting as the flame quivered in the breeze from the cracked window. Staggering to the other side of the room, he shoved the glass pane open wider, letting the wind caress his face as he stared into the night-shrouded gardens below.

They stared back.

Pulse ricocheting higher, the disciple stumbled in his haste to yank the curtain closed. Something was *out* there. Something ghastly and inhuman prowled the Palazzo grounds. He couldn't see it, but he could feel the wrongness, the slimy, shifting weight of it a pressure at his throat.

He twisted his sweat-slick fingers together, muttering a prayer to the patron saint of Death. *His* saint. The one from whom his family was descended, blessing them with the gift of magic. And yet tonight his fervent murmurings brought little comfort, for the more he questioned Death's power, the less he felt the saint's presence.

Help me was the central request of his current plea, though he only grew hotter and felt sicker. Perhaps it was not enough, the disciple thought, to request protection with mere words. Compulsion gripped him as suddenly as the nausea had, firm and unrelenting. He let it carry him. He was a distant spectator, two eyes in a flesh prison.

Vision beginning to blur, he dragged himself to the room adjacent, using the wall as an aid. He imagined he left handprints against the gilded paint, swipes of rusted crimson that would draw the saints to him. As if they were no longer deities, but slavering beasts seeking a fresh carcass.

The saints were merciful. All the stories said so.

But the stories also said they craved blood.

Leonzio dropped to his knees beside an incoherent arrangement of debris he'd collected from the Palazzo grounds. He didn't quite know when or why he'd begun stuffing rocks into his pockets and snapping twigs off bushes like some kind of compulsive pruner. The process had simply felt...necessary.

His hands shook as he knelt on the floor, redistributing the debris into a different shape. The stone beneath his knees grounded him slightly. As the disciple aligned the sticks, he whispered not only to Death but to all the faceless saints.

Then he picked up the knife.

When the first drops of blood fell, it was almost a relief. Stark fear gave way to welcome inertia.

By the time he realized he was dying, it was far too late.

DAMIAN

Damian Venturi was weary of death.

In fact, he was weary in general. The night had long shifted closer to dawn than dusk, and it was increasingly difficult to focus on the dead disciple before him. He adjusted the collar of his Palazzo-issued coat, hoping it might ease some of the pressure building in his throat.

Leonzio Bianchi, former disciple of Death, showed every indication of having been poisoned. His pallid lips were slick with a distasteful layer of foam, and the veins lacing his forearms stood out in stark, bruise-like relief. Despite it all, his expression was peaceful, the curve of his mouth soft, as if he'd resigned himself unflinchingly to death.

Damian leaned away from Leonzio's body, repressing a shiver. The disciple's bedroom was cold, and dim candlelight cast shadows on the gilded walls. Perhaps it was merely situational, but there was something oppressive about the darkness nipping at the edges of that orange glow. Something unnerving about the way Leonzio's face was turned so as to reflect in the mirror across the room.

"Well?"

The chief magistrate's voice interrupted Damian's examination of the body, startling him enough that he lurched away from the bed. Sweat beaded on his brow. Death always brought him back to his time in the war. It made his chest tighten, his blood race, and his feet feel as though they were being dragged through mud.

"I don't know," Damian said, turning to face the chief magistrate. He kept his tone clipped but polite. The chief magistrate's fury was a presence of its own; Damian had felt it from the moment he'd walked into the room. "Is it possible it was a suicide?"

Chief magistrate Forte, a tall disciple of Grace with impeccably combed hair and a thin moustache, peered at Damian over his spectacles. Forte had occupied his position for little more than a year, having been selected by the guilds' representatives to replace his predecessor. It wasn't often one of Grace's disciples fulfilled the role, and Damian wondered if that knowledge had shaped Forte into the sharply uncompromising man before him.

"A suicide?" Forte echoed the suggestion derisively, hands roving the dead man's clothes and bedsheets for whatever they could tell him. Disciples of Grace had a connection to such things: It was what made them expert weavers, able to manipulate fabrics into anything from trousers to tapestries without touching a needle and thread. "How convenient that would be for you, Signor Venturi."

"I beg your pardon?" The reply slipped out before Damian could stop it. As Chief magistrate, Forte was believed to be the saints' earthly voice, but it hadn't made him any more tactful. Damian had been back in Ombrazia barely a year, and already that much was clear.

"Were this self-imposed," Forte continued, "it would mean Palazzo security hadn't failed to protect a top government official." He didn't look at Damian as he spoke, but pulled away from the bed, a frown settling between his untamed brows. "Leonzio certainly died in these clothes, but there's nothing otherwise unusual about them." With a wave of his hand, the bedsheets wriggled free and swept up to cover the disciple's body.

Damian was grateful not to have to look at the dead man any longer, but his relief faded at Forte's next words.

"Speaking of Palazzo security, where were you tonight, Venturi? Is it not your job to ensure this kind of thing doesn't happen?"

Frustration pulsed through Damian's veins, but he gritted his teeth to cage in the retort he wanted to fling. "My apologies, mio signore. I was at the Mercato."

The city's weekly night market was a chance for disciples to sell and exchange their wares. The four guilds who dealt in craft—Strength, Grace, Patience, and Cunning—were the backbone of Ombrazia's economy, and the reason it was the hub of trade. Grace's affinity for fabrics was matched by Strength's affinity for stone, Patience's affinity for metal, and Cunning's affinity for chemicals. As such, their major function was to churn out weapons, textiles, stonework, and all manner of potions to be shipped to other lands.

All disciples were descendants of the original saints, but not all descendants had magic. Sometimes, Damian's father had told him, the revered abilities possessed by disciples skipped a generation or disappeared entirely when the bloodline became too diluted.

Descendants without magic—people like Damian—weren't disciples. They were little better than the rest of the unfavored citizens.

As such, acting as security was the only way Damian would ever be able to attend the Mercato. Crafted items were not for people like him. Mingling with disciples was not an option for those with nothing to offer society. In case the unfavored chose to ignore that fact, security officers were there to keep them away. Damian's occupation was the closest he would ever get to experiencing the life he might have had.

But he knew as well as Forte that, as head of Palazzo security, it was a job he ought to have delegated. Unless he was doing his rounds of the temples, his job was to be *here*, in the Palazzo itself. His number one priority was to protect the disciples elected to represent their guilds.

"You were at the Mercato." Forte's voice was bland as he echoed Damian's statement. "Did you not make your rounds of the temples this morning?"

"Yes." He winced to admit it. "I thought—"

"No, Venturi." The chief magistrate cut him off. "You *didn't* think. I'd say that's abundantly clear." With each word he took a step closer to Damian, jabbing a finger at his chest. "The guilds rely on us to protect their representatives. I rely on *you* to ensure the Palazzo is the safest building in Ombrazia. And yet, on the night one of our disciples turns up dead, you're frolicking around the Mercato?"

Damian swallowed, protestations springing to his tongue. He longed to argue, to say that by no means had he been *frolicking*, but months of experience had taught him it wouldn't make a difference. "Mio signore, I assure you no one could have been in the disciple's room tonight without my officers knowing.

Besides"—he inclined his chin at the body—"there's no injury to his person. Either he had some kind of sudden aneurysm, or he was poisoned. I assure you we keep a very close watch on who comes and goes from the Palazzo."

The chief magistrate's nostrils flared. "Clearly not close enough."

Damian had no response to that. There had already been two unexplained deaths in Ombrazia in a short amount of time: the first a young girl, the second a boy around Damian's age. Their bodies had been carted off to the city morgue, and Forte hadn't bothered assigning officers to investigate. The unfavored fought among themselves all the time, he'd said. What did it matter if a couple had fallen?

But this was different. The disciples of Death had chosen Leonzio Bianchi to represent them in the Palazzo. His sudden demise would frighten and infuriate people.

"It's too convenient," Forte growled. "Targeting Death's representative, so that no one is around to read the body?"

Despite himself, Damian nodded. He'd had the same thought. Blessed with the ability to make contact with the deceased before their souls fled, a disciple of Death might have been able to glean what happened to Leonzio before he died.

Of course, given that Leonzio *was* the Palazzo's disciple of Death, they were likely out of luck. Souls didn't tend to linger very long.

"I'll get someone here," Damian assured the chief magistrate. "Just in case."

Forte drew a hand across his forehead, unappeased. "Fix this, Venturi. We won't be able to keep it from the public, so we'd better have answers for them soon. I'm starting to wonder whether my general made a mistake appointing his son head of security."

He pulled a silver watch from his pocket, as if he had somewhere of great importance to be in the middle of the night. "I let Battista bring you back from the north, and I can have you sent away again just as easily."

The words were scathing, and they cut deep. Damian didn't think he could handle being sent back to war. His nerves were frayed enough as it were.

"I'll figure out what happened," he muttered. "I won't let you down."

Forte leveled him with an incensed look. "You'd better not. Report to me tomorrow. If you suspect poison was involved, I take it you know where to start."

Damian's cheeks burned, but he bowed to Forte as the man slipped out of the room, large form swallowed up by the dark hallway. Another sleepless night, then. Sometimes he wished his father hadn't bothered promoting him after he'd returned.

To keep you busy, Battista Venturi had told Damian at the time. *Because I know what it is to be alone with thoughts of darkness.*

Damian had waited for those thoughts to go away. How was he supposed to get closure when he knew the war was ongoing? The Second War of Saints was stretching into its twentieth year. Men and women had battled in the north for far longer than Damian's two-year stint, but as it turned out, that meant little. Death still stalked his every waking moment. It traced cold, malevolent fingers down his spine and hissed garbled nothings in his ear.

Once, he might have distracted himself with memories. Would have pictured the face of the girl he loved and used her smile to drive away the fear. Now, though, three years on, he couldn't imagine Rossana Lacertosa as anything other than furious.

It was why Damian stayed away from Patience's sector

whenever possible. He'd seen Roz in passing, but they hadn't spoken to one another since his return to Ombrazia. The Roz of his subconscious already knew what sins he'd committed; the reality of telling her would be so much worse. Besides, her magic had shown itself, meaning she was a disciple now. And Damian? He was but a fractured boy playing at commander.

He shook his head to clear it, then raised his voice to be heard outside the room. "Enzo?"

A thin serving boy about Damian's age appeared in the doorway, clad in the slate-gray uniform of Palazzo staff. He'd been standing outside the room when Damian arrived, and clearly hadn't moved. His grimace was animated as he took in the sight of Leonzio's sheet-covered body. "Signore?"

Damian sighed. "Forte's gone. You don't have to call me that."

Enzo relaxed at once, dragging a hand through the inky sheen of his hair. He'd been at the Palazzo less than a month, but he and Damian had become fast friends. "*Merda*," he said, attention still fixed on the bed. "He's really dead, isn't he?"

"So it would seem." An edge slipped into Damian's voice. Enzo hadn't yet spent any time up north, and had likely never seen a dead man. At his age, it was strange he hadn't been drafted yet, but it was only a matter of time. Everyone able-bodied and unfavored found themselves there eventually.

"And Forte expects you to figure out what happened?"

Damian shot Enzo a sideways glance. "You aren't even going to *pretend* you didn't eavesdrop?"

Enzo was staunchly unapologetic. "Hard not to. How can I help?"

The question made Damian's head spin, and he was quiet a moment as he began formulating a plan. "Can you fetch Signora de Luca for me?"

"Sure." But Enzo didn't leave right away, instead fixing Damian with a curious expression. "Are you okay? You look a bit...off."

Damian let his shoulders slump, no longer bothering to maintain an air of confidence. He indicated at the bed. "This is on *me*. I should have been here."

"You didn't know this would happen. And it's not as though you're the only one on duty."

"That's not the point."

Enzo hesitated, looking uneasy.

"Enzo, please. There's nothing else you can do."

"All right." The words were heavy. "I'll be right back."

Damian sank into the dead disciple's desk chair as Enzo's footsteps retreated. His ears rang, the sound shifting into the echo of gunshots. In his head they multiplied a thousandfold, and the cold sweat that followed had nothing to do with the situation in the Palazzo. For a heartbeat he was ankle-deep in mud, head spinning in terror, dragging a brother's rigor mortis–stricken body away from the front lines. How many times had those moments reared their heads in his nightmares?

You're a soldier. The head of Palazzo security. Pull yourself together, you—

"Just in here, Signora."

Enzo reappeared in the doorway, now accompanied by the resident disciple of Cunning. Damian gave himself a shake, rising to beckon Giada de Luca into the bedroom.

"Thank you for coming. Enzo, can you head to Death's temple? Tell the guild to send one of their disciples to the Palazzo. I don't care who it is. I need a read on the body."

Damian always felt a bit strange, ordering his friend around, but Enzo nodded. With another meaningful look at Damian, he melted back into the dark hallway.

Giada swallowed a dry sob as she caught sight of Leonzio's body. She was older than Damian—probably in her midtwenties—but was a slip of a thing, with dark hair and a darker gaze. "It's true, then. He's really dead." She touched her eyelids, then her heart, in the sign of the patron saints.

"So it would appear. I'm sorry to have called upon you so late, but I require your expertise. I need to know what type of poison killed him." As a disciple of Cunning, Giada knew poisons better than anyone. She should be able to sense the chemicals in Leonzio's veins—a partial autopsy with no incisions required.

"How could this happen?" Giada asked hoarsely. "You have officers in every wing of the Palazzo, do you not?"

She didn't say it like an accusation, but it felt like one.

"Some things are outside my control, Signora. If you'd be so kind?" Damian pointed meaningfully at the body, and Giada sidled over to the bed, face wan in the dim.

Her hands moved like pale moths across the dead man's chest. She shoved the crimson fabric of his robe aside, lips forming words Damian couldn't make out. He watched as she tipped Leonzio's head back, prying open his jaw. Teeth glinted in the candlelight.

"Based on the color of his lips, I would guess he spent his last moments fighting for breath," Giada said. "Yet the appearance of the skin suggests the poison was bloodborne, not an asphyxiant....Something vile definitely lingers in his body, though it's hard to say what. It feels a bit like dustweed—kills swiftly once it enters the circulatory system but, when taken undissolved in water, is liable to cause choking."

Damian frowned. "You don't know for certain?"

"*Wait.*" Giada's interruption was the crack of a whip. She shoved the sleeve of Leonzio's robe up further, baring the delicate skin of the inner bicep. There was a mark there, Damian saw: a deep smudge like fresh ink from which black tendrils radiated outward. Giada touched the skin gently with a finger, only to leap back as if she'd been burned. "No, no. It wasn't dustweed."

Damian's teeth came together with an audible snap. "Oh?"

"Dustweed leaves a latticelike pattern and almost no trace at the injection site. But these marks follow the veins from the point of insertion." Giada leaned forward and, without touching this time, used a forefinger to indicate the lines climbing the dead man's arm. "This is something else. I don't recognize the appearance or the sensation of such a poison. And it's too late to draw it out."

Damian's heart sank. If Giada didn't know what had killed Leonzio, it would be more difficult to come up with a list of suspects.

Though he already had one, of course.

"Signs point to him having been dead around six hours," Giada added, oblivious to his discomfort.

"Right." Damian knew what he had to do. He extinguished the candle and reached for the cuffs at his belt. "Giada de Luca," he said heavily. "I'm placing you under arrest for the suspected murder of Leonzio Bianchi. Should you attempt to struggle, your life will be forfeit. You will be subject to questioning forthwith, and thereafter as I see fit."

Guilt roiled within him as Giada blanched, holding out her wrists. He sincerely doubted the soft-spoken woman was responsible, but he had to know for certain. He shackled her hands together before leading her down the stairs. She moved slowly, shakily, not breathing a word. As if she wasn't surprised by the turn of events, but rather disappointed by them.

The dungeons beneath the Palazzo were quiet as a tomb,

currently empty of criminals and deserters. Damian ushered Giada into an interrogation room, all cold stone and grim shadows. She sat, studying him with a mixture of fear and apprehension. Damian remained standing.

Giada folded her shackled hands on the table before her, fingers interlacing, knuckles pale. Her dark eyes didn't waver from his.

"Convenient, isn't it," Damian said, "that Leonzio turned up poisoned tonight, mere days after you two argued over a new policy initiative."

It wasn't much of a motive; the Palazzo disciples disagreed all the time. They had to, in order to come up with policy decisions that would best benefit the city. And despite Giada's skill with chemicals, she wouldn't have been foolish enough to kill Leonzio in such a way. Not when she knew it would make her the primary suspect.

But it didn't matter what Damian thought. Forte's instructions had been clear.

If you suspect poison was involved, I take it you know where to start.

As the Palazzo's top official, both symbolically and in practice, Chief Magistrate Forte was not to be denied. The disciples trusted him. Revered him. They believed he spoke to the saints daily in order to discern their will. He was a fat spider positioned at the center of a political web.

Giada was the first person Damian would question, but she wouldn't be the last. The Palazzo—the *city*—was teeming with people whose motivations he couldn't discern.

Giada licked her lips, a sheen creeping over her eyes. "Officer Venturi, I swear I wasn't behind this. I didn't recognize that poison, and I doubt Leonzio's death was self-imposed. I think..." Her voice trailed off in a whisper. "I've heard rumors, you know, from the other disciples. I think darkness has taken root in the Palazzo."

Damian pressed two fingers to the bridge of his nose, confusion pulsing through him. "What's that supposed to mean?"

A beat of silence hung between them, turning the air cold before Giada finally answered.

"Someone—or something—managed to infiltrate the Palazzo and kill a representative without drawing any suspicion. Without leaving any trace." The words were halting, a desperate note to them. She leaned across the table, fixing Damian with a panicked look. "With all due respect, mio signore, you shouldn't be accusing me of murder. You should be worrying about whether I'm next."

ROZ

Rossana Lacertosa detested crowds.

She hated the unnerving sense of pure anonymity as she waded through swaths of people, giving them a good shove whenever they didn't get out of her way fast enough. Crowds were so infuriatingly *slow*, and Roz did nothing at a languid pace.

She scanned the colorful night market that spilled from the piazza into the side streets. Disciples moved among the stalls in groups, excited voices permeating the night air. Held every weekend from dusk until dawn, the Mercato was one of many things in Ombrazia that catered solely to disciples. There, an assortment of magical wares would be for sale: robes enchanted to repel flame, knives that never needed sharpening, locks that opened only at a specific person's touch. The latter was a thing Roz herself had been working on intermittently for weeks. Given the recent rebel activity, the locks were in high demand, so she and the other disciples of Patience had slowed their creation of wartime supplies to meet it.

In Roz's opinion, that was the worst part about being a disciple: the expectation that one spend so much of one's time creating magical items. She had no interest in using her affinity for metal to support Ombrazia's already booming economy. In fact, she was hard pressed to give a shit about the economy at all. Not when it only benefited a portion of the population.

She cracked her jaw, pushing her way through another group of people. The Mercato didn't consist only of magical wares. There were also regular items: weapons and expensive rugs, hand-carved statuettes and herbal elixirs. All things disciples could create in less than half the time required by someone without a magical affinity. All things that fetched a pretty price when exported.

It was beautiful, this part of Ombrazia, where moonlight gilded the flagstone in spaces the lamplight didn't touch it. Where those descended from the saints could pretend the less savory parts of the city didn't exist.

Across the way Roz could see a disciple of Cunning poised behind a display of vials, opaque black liquid swirling within them. The scent drifted to her, smelling strongly of sugar and iron. She let it draw her over, heeled boots clicking against the cobblestones, and smiled sharply at the vendor. "The usual."

The red-haired disciple's eyes flicked to the scowling man Roz had stepped in front of—the man who ought to have been next in line. But she didn't argue, reaching under the table of wares to procure a vial of shimmering liquid. Roz took it, passing her payment over. "Thank you." To the quietly fuming man behind her, she batted her lashes and said, "My apologies, Signore. I'm in a rush."

She wasn't, but he straightened at her direct address, looking appeased. "No matter."

He seemed to hope she would say more, but Roz only shot him another vague smile before turning on her heel. She shoved the vial into the pocket of her jacket, thumb skimming the wax stopper.

Fire danced in her periphery as she passed a stall manned by a few of her fellow disciples of Patience. Surrounding them was the familiar metallic tang of their magic, and Roz quickened her step, keen not to be spotted. She slowed upon noticing two security officers at the edge of the piazza, and pretended to be interested in a display of silk dressing gowns. As she strained to listen in on their conversation, a third officer joined the duo, dragging a youth along with him. The boy was about Roz's age, with a shock of ginger hair and an upturned nose. His clothes were so dusty they looked gray. The officers ignored his curses as he struggled against Patience-made handcuffs, trying to free himself.

Fool, Roz thought heavily. He should know as well as anyone that the cuffs wouldn't budge for anyone save the officer to whom they'd been issued.

"I'll give you five seconds to answer my question," the third officer snapped, and Roz chanced a furtive look. He was a tall man, unsmiling, with a shock of black hair. A former soldier, no doubt. Most Palazzo security were.

It wasn't *him*, though, and something within Roz eased.

She knew Damian Venturi was around—had seen him from a distance these past six months—but the idea of running into him here always set her heart racing. She wondered what the other

18

officers thought of Damian as a commander. Whether they feared him the way people feared his father. She had no doubt her childhood sweetheart was following in Battista Venturi's blood-soaked footsteps.

The dust-covered boy yanked his bound hands away from the guards. "What, no good-cop, bad-cop act?"

Roz grinned into the dresses as the officer scowled, not condescending to answer. "Why are you lurking around the Mercato?"

"I wasn't lurking!"

"Sure looked like it to me." The officer paused to dip his head at a passing disciple of Mercy before turning back to the boy. "No ring, no entry."

Roz automatically glanced down at the slim band on her index finger that marked her as a disciple. As always, the sight of it made her grimace. She'd discovered her affinity later than most—when she and Damian were tested together at age thirteen, neither of them had shown any signs of magic. Her connection to metal hadn't reared its head until three years later. By that time, Damian had gone off to the front lines, and her father had been killed for deserting them. Roz might've been able to hide what she was, but without Jacopo Lacertosa's meager military stipend, Patience's guild was her only option. She might hate what she was, but at least it was a way to support herself and her mother. When you were a disciple—traitor father or not—you were never left to starve.

The officer's voice recaptured her attention as he asked the boy, "What do you know about the rebellion?"

Now *this* was new. Roz went preternaturally still, adrenaline surging in her veins. As far as she was aware, the chief magistrate and the Palazzo weren't taking the threat of the rebellion seriously.

"I know nothing," the boy snapped.

The officer gave him a long once-over, eyes narrowed to slits. "Hmm." Eventually he relented. "Pay the fine and you can go."

Rather than sag in relief, the boy went even more tense. "I—I don't have any money."

Before the officer could respond, Roz turned and sauntered over, pulling back the hood of her jacket. Her dark ponytail tumbled free, spilling over her chest. She grinned at the three guards in what she knew was a disarming way.

"I couldn't help but overhear. I'm happy to pay the fine, if it means you'll get rid of him." She made a show of wrinkling her nose, hoping the boy didn't take it personally. As if she hadn't done this before. "How much?"

A bland smile replaced the officer's frown, and he backed away from the boy as his gaze dipped to Roz's hand. "Never mind, Signora. You don't need to concern yourself with this."

It was likely meant to be polite, but it felt placating in a way Roz didn't appreciate. She tilted her head, eyeing the man with disdain. "He said he doesn't have the money. Either take me up on my offer, or let him go."

Something in her tone must have been convincing, because the officer unshackled the boy and all but shoved him away from the piazza.

Roz smiled again, less nicely this time. "Mercy is an honorable quality, I'm told." She didn't mention she possessed precious little of it.

While the guards gaped, she redonned her hood and slipped into the dark.

As she walked, the expertly crafted pillars and wrought-iron accents gave way to dreary architecture and feeble wooden gates.

The air turned acrid in her nostrils. There were no streetlamps here, and darkness stretched to occupy every space the moonlight couldn't reach. Ombrazia was divided into six sectors for each of the remaining original saints, leaving the unfavored to build their lives in the spaces between. As such, they had decided to take over the abandoned sector that once belonged to the seventh saint.

Every disciple was descended from one of the original saints: Strength, Patience, Cunning, Grace, Mercy, Death, and Chaos. But every so often, a disciple was born whose power rivaled that of their respective original saint's. When that happened, they were considered a reincarnation—all but a deity in their own right.

History, Roz knew, had shown it was dangerous to have a saint on earth. Seventy years ago, two reincarnations had existed at once: Strength and Chaos. Each vying for power, they had split the country in two. The northern side—now an independent city-state called Brechaat—had lost horribly. They'd rallied behind Chaos, and he had fallen, like each of his predecessors dating back to time's inception. It was for the best, everyone said: Disciples of Chaos were illusionists with an affinity for the mind, and they were simply too powerful. They couldn't risk another reincarnation of Chaos being born. And so his surviving disciples had been destroyed, his likeness struck from all renderings of the pantheon. In Ombrazia—the southern side, and the winning side—merely mentioning the fallen saint was considered heretical.

That had been the First War of Saints.

Now, they were embroiled in the second.

Despite the less pleasant scenery of unfavored territory, Roz felt her tension lift. Her steps echoed across the stone, earning her furtive glances from a couple of passing youths. Their clothes were threadbare, expressions fearful. Roz wondered whether they'd managed to avoid the war draft, or if their time hadn't come yet. She offered a nod that neither of them returned.

"I wouldn't be out this late, if I were you." Roz tried not to make her quiet words a threat, though she wasn't sure she succeeded. "I take it you know what happened to Amélie Villeneuve."

One of the youths blanched, pulling the collar of his jacket closer. The more daring of the two, however, shot her an accusatory look.

"*You're* out this late." He must have been around thirteen, the same age Amélie had been. Roz's answering laugh had him taking a step back.

"Yes," Roz acknowledged. "Well, I'm a lot harder to kill than most."

The boy's face twisted, and his companion tugged wordlessly on his arm. Of course they'd heard about Amélie—who hadn't? The way her body had been found two months ago, cold and abandoned, in an unlit alley down the street from her home.

And no one had done a *saints-damned* thing about it.

"Get out of here," Roz urged the duo, who by now appeared positively horrified. "Go home."

They obliged, all but sprinting away from her, and she watched until they disappeared around a corner at the end of the street. Her stomach was a hollow pit.

Fools. Amélie was freshly buried, and people were already throwing caution to the wind. She wasn't the only victim, either—the other day a young man had been discovered dead on the riverbank outside Patience's sector, his identity undetermined. There was no reason to believe the two incidents were connected, but Roz couldn't help noticing how little effort had been put into tracking down the culprit. In fact, the Palazzo had yet to address the deaths publicly.

They weren't disciples, so they don't matter, Roz thought, and spat onto the street. If she were the next victim, how would she be treated? Would her death make headlines and thrust Ombrazia into a frenzy? Or would the Palazzo know her to be a traitor's daughter and be glad for her loss?

She slowed as she approached Bartolo's, a dilapidated tavern with no sign designating it as such. Three children sat out front—street urchins whose parents had been drafted, no doubt—in hopes the tavern owner might spare them some food. They stared at Roz on her way to the door, eyes enormous in their pinched faces.

Voices emanated from inside the tavern, slurred and uproarious. Roz reached for the handle, braced for the noise that would greet her, only to find herself face-to-face with an exiting drunkard.

The man let out a whistle as his liquor-glazed eyes took her in. "Well, well. Good evening." A hand reached to loop around her hips, but Roz caught his wrist before it made contact. He was shorter than Roz—which many people were—and too slight to be any real threat.

Staring is free," she told him coolly, flicking her knife out in a single, smooth motion. "But touching costs a finger."

The man reared back, ruddy face reddening further, and nearly tripped over his own feet. "Filthy whore." His voice was a slur.

Roz *tsk*ed. "Should I take that tongue, instead?"

When he withdrew a knife of his own, it was with so little finesse she couldn't help laughing. Could she go nowhere in this saints-forsaken city without encountering a man who thought himself entitled to her?

But he was too drunk for Roz to bother with a real fight. So she dragged him by the collar into the street, then kicked him in the stomach with the same boot he'd fouled. He released a huff of breath, taking a stumbling step back before landing on his ass.

Roz left him there, slamming the tavern door behind her.

She stepped into an assault of light and sound. The hazy air was thick with smoke and the reek of various liquors. Bartolo's was often busy, particularly on weekends. Roz blinked as her eyes adjusted, shoving her way through patrons to the bar, where a dark-haired girl waited.

"Nasim." Roz raised her voice to be heard over the clamor. Outspoken and unfailingly loyal, Nasim Kadera was one of the few people she considered a friend. "Where's Dev?"

Nasim loosed an inaudible sigh, tilting her head toward the back of the room, where a blond boy sat alone.

Devereux Villeneuve, grieving elder brother of Amélie, was slumped over in his chair. The table before him was littered with empty glasses, and Roz's chest gave an uncomfortable twinge. Doubtless he had been there all day, and yesterday, and the day before that. It hurt to look at him. He'd been the one to find Amélie cold and unresponsive on the pavement, and they hadn't seen him smile since.

"Well, fuck." Roz propped her elbows up on the bar, motioning at the man behind it to bring her a drink. He did so without needing to take her order.

"Yeah," Nasim agreed, clinking the rim of her cup against Roz's. "*Salute*, I guess."

Roz took a sip. The wine tasted bitterer than usual. "What time did he start drinking today?"

"Too early."

"Just before noon," the bartender cut in gruffly, overhearing their conversation as he swiped a dirty cloth over the counter. "Running up quite a tab, he is."

This time it was Roz who sighed. Nasim's eyes were back on Dev, bottom lip trapped between her teeth. "He's still not making much of an effort to talk to anyone."

"Can you blame him?" Roz said. She remembered the night she'd met Dev. How he'd come across her throwing knives at the side of the tavern after dark, and leaned against the wall with a wicked expression curling his lips. She'd feared him about to proposition her when he said: *You may want to aim at something softer, if you want those to stick.* Then he'd tilted his head at a man exiting the building. *How about him?*

His words had startled a laugh out of Roz, and they'd been friends ever since. Carefree, impish Dev, who wouldn't know solemnity if it hit him upside the head.

Until now.

He'd asked for time to grieve, and Roz had given it to him. But he wasn't getting better, and she'd be damned if she was going to sit here and watch him drink himself into a stupor every day.

She grasped her own drink with more aggression than necessary. "Come on," she said to Nasim, who gave a humorless laugh.

"Maybe you should talk to him alone." Nasim passed her glass from hand to hand, not meeting Roz's gaze. "He didn't want much to do with me earlier."

"I'm sure that's not true."

Nasim peered at Roz from beneath her lashes. "I know when someone doesn't want me around, Roz. It's fine."

It wasn't fine, though. Roz had seen how Nasim and Dev appeared to be drifting closer in a way she couldn't touch. It made the petty, selfish part of her uneasy. After all, who did she have if not the two of them?

Lately, though, Dev's misery seemed to have become a contagious thing. His relationships were fracturing, and Nasim was content to let him pull away.

Roz was not.

Maneuvering among the tables and patrons took considerable dexterity, and she stepped on more than one foot on her way to the back of the tavern. Despite the raucous noise and ever-present stench, the place was a comfort to her. She'd memorized every stain on the wooden tables and noticed every time Piera replaced the art on the walls.

"Dev," Roz said by way of greeting when she finally reached him. "Mind if I join you?"

Dev gave an inelegant shrug.

It was close enough to assent for Roz. She dropped into the chair across from him, shoving the empty glasses aside and setting her own down with a wet *thunk*. "You can't keep doing this."

Dev ignored her statement. His hair was an uncharacteristic mess, and his eyes were half lidded. "Did Nasim send you over to bother me?"

"Nasim doesn't send me to do anything." Roz folded her arms on the tabletop, getting straight to the point. "No amount of alcohol is going to bring Amélie back, you know."

"You don't say?" Dev drawled, raising his cup to his lips before realizing it was empty. "In that case, I suppose I ought to stop drinking for necromantic purposes. From now on, it's purely for fun. Excuse me!" He thrust out a finger in an attempt to summon the nearby waitress. Roz smacked his hand down.

"I know what you're doing."

He blinked dolefully at her. "What's that supposed to mean?"

"You think if you can stay drunk, you won't have to face what happened." Roz knew she was being harsh, but she hadn't seen her friend sober in weeks. "You think it's your fault because you weren't there to protect her. Tell me I'm wrong."

"Don't," Dev said grimly, softly. "You don't underst—"

"I don't *understand*?" Roz gave a disbelieving laugh. She slammed her fist on the table, jolting him into meeting her gaze. "You know what happened to my father. Do you think I didn't want to drown in misery when his head showed up on our doorstep? Or when my mother nearly lost her mind because of it?" Her voice was a hiss, and she made a concerted effort to rein in her frustration.

Dev seemed to hunch in on himself, thin shoulders curving. When he spoke, the words held a vitriol with which Roz was acutely familiar.

"They've done *nothing*, Roz. I know the coroner examined her, but my parents and I weren't allowed to see the report. We still don't know how she died." He flexed his fingers, veins standing out beneath translucent skin. "The Palazzo hasn't assigned security officers to the case. No one's spoken to potential witnesses. Amélie wasn't a disciple, so..." Dev swallowed. "It's like she doesn't even *matter*. At least you know who killed your father."

Roz exhaled, pushing her anger out with the breath. "You're right. I do know. And what difference does it make? He struts around the Palazzo, constantly protected, never to face any consequences."

General Battista Venturi—Damian's father—had given the order for Jacopo to be hunted down and butchered like an animal after he fled the front lines.

A shadow crossed Dev's aquamarine gaze. Harshly contemplative, he drew his index finger over the rim of the nearest glass. "What's the point of anything, Roz, if we can't even get justice for those closest to us?"

That was when he cracked. His face came to rest behind his hands, and his shoulders shook as his breathing grew labored. Roz didn't try to comfort him with futile words; she knew he wouldn't want to hear it. She only sat there, waiting until he'd finished.

"We'll get justice," Roz said quietly. "For my father. For Amélie."

When their gazes met, she saw that Dev's eyes were dry. She hadn't lost him yet, then. They were two sides of the same coin: Both had honed their misery into something vicious. She only had to remind him that vengeance was sweeter than spirits.

DAMIAN

In the end, Damian released Giada.

It was a move his father would have admonished him for. Battista didn't believe in trusting one's gut. He acted on the evidence and asked questions later.

He also felt no mercy. He would have looked at Giada, moon pale in her fear, and been unaffected.

We have a job to do, Battista always said. *When we let our emotions get involved, we're more likely to do it wrong.*

Damian knew it was the truth. He'd seen firsthand what could happen if you hesitated, or gave someone the benefit of doubt. But no matter how hard he tried to remember his father's words, they were beaten down by the memory of his mother's.

You feel for people, she'd told him mournfully, mere days before she died. *That is a skill as powerful as learning how to fire a gun. The world may be harsh, Damian, but don't let it take that from you. Can you promise me you won't?*

Of course he'd promised. How could he not? He wasn't going to sit there, clasping her death-frail hand, and not give his word.

But sometimes Damian wondered whether he'd made a vow he couldn't keep. He'd always thought his father harsh, detached, but how could he not be? When one had seen as much death and misery as Battista, how could you expect them to still be soft? There were times during the war when Damian had wanted to rip his emotions from his chest and hurl them into the cold northern sea.

He hadn't let Giada go because he felt for her, though. He'd let her go because he didn't think she'd done it. There was no real motive. And though he hated to admit it, what she'd said had gotten to him.

You should be worrying about whether I'm next.

Damian didn't have any proof that someone was targeting the elected disciples, but the idea of it was nearly as horrifying as the idea that he was failing at his job.

He passed through the Palazzo's main entryway, lost in thought. The building was quiet, the cavernous hall plagued by shadows. On nights like this, you could taste the Palazzo's secrets in the air. They were so tangible you might be tempted to reach out and grasp them, only to feel them slip like smoke through your fingers. Arched pillars separated the open ceiling from a covered walkway, the tile floors of which were patterned in faded colors. In the middle of the room a small fountain splashed merrily, and upon its platform the faceless saints held hands in a circular formation. Every so often they took a counterclockwise step: a sure sign of being created by a disciple of Strength.

"Where you headed, Venturi?"

Damian hadn't heard Kiran Prakash draw up beside him. A crest bearing a sword on fire was visible on the shoulders of his fellow officer's jacket, marking him as Palazzo security. Despite being taller even than Damian, he was notoriously silent in his movements. His tousled hair curled around his brow, and his face was good natured. Kiran was accompanied by Siena Schiavone, a girl with an easy grin and dark hair in intricate braids. Siena had been part of Damian's platoon up north. He often tried not to dwell on the fact that she appeared to be weathering her trauma far better than he.

Then again, perhaps that was how people looking from the outside perceived him, too. He didn't know the extent of Siena's suffering.

"Hey," Damian said, slowing to allow them to keep pace. "I'm on my way to the crypt."

Siena grimaced knowingly, one hand resting on her belt. "We heard Forte was hard on you about Leonzio's death." She added, "Enzo," before Damian could ask.

Damian groaned. He ought to have known Enzo would tell the rest of their friends. "To be fair, Forte acted more or less as expected. Besides, he's right—I messed up."

Kiran glanced skyward as they made their way outside. Rain was threatening overhead. "You could have sent Siena and me to the Mercato, you know."

"I know. But I wasn't there long. Left just as Matteo started detaining a few unfavored loitering about." Damian sighed. "I needed to get out. Spend too long in the Palazzo, and it starts to feel..."

"Claustrophobic?" Siena suggested.

That was it exactly, Damian thought. As if the longer he spent behind the gilded walls of the city's most opulent building, the harder it became to breathe. "Yeah."

She gave him another measured look. Whatever she saw in Damian's face must've been worrisome, because she said, "You look brutal, Venturi."

"Saints, Siena." Kiran choked on a laugh, shaking his head. A curl of dark hair fell to brush his cheekbone, and he reached up to retie the knot holding it back.

"What? It's true."

Her observation didn't surprise Damian one bit. He suspected he looked brutal most of the time. Ever since he'd returned from the north, he refrained from looking too closely at his reflection, afraid of what he might see there. Afraid that if he'd changed in the ways he imagined, he wouldn't be able to ignore it any longer. He saw how other people looked at him—as though his sins were written plainly on his face.

And they might as well have been. Everyone knew the story of how he'd watched his best friend die on the front lines. How, in mindless retaliation, he'd taken out three enemy soldiers at once. *Heroic*, they called it. But also: *terrifying*.

Realizing Siena still awaited his response, Damian shrugged. "That's what happens when you've been up for two days straight, I suppose."

"You need to sleep. You're going to crash."

"I think he already has," Kiran offered. "Blink twice if you're not fully conscious, Damian."

Damian made a point of glaring at Kiran without once shuttering his eyes.

They descended the Palazzo's tapering front steps and navigated the wide path through the garden. Atop the meticulous stonework of the building, a rooftop gargoyle swiveled to track their progress. Another creation of Strength's disciples.

"You think the rebels had anything to do with it?" Kiran asked, blessedly switching topics.

Damian didn't have to ask what he was referring to. He'd already asked himself the same thing: whether killing Leonzio had been a way for the rebels to express their disdain of the system. "I can't imagine they're that well organized," he said honestly. "Whoever killed Leonzio was clever. No one even knew they were in the Palazzo. The rebels are...messy."

Siena raised a manicured brow. "You mean because a couple of them were caught trying to break into the city prison? I'm not certain that means they're messy. It's the first time we've been able to identify any of them."

"They're only going to grow more restless as more unfavored are sent up north," Kiran said. "Given that they're against the war, and all."

A chill crept over Damian's skin with the wind. Why didn't people understand that the Palazzo existed to protect them? To represent them? As of late, the rebels' main complaint was that the unfavored were being drafted to fight in the Second War of Saints, while the disciples had no such obligation. How could they? Their abilities made them the backbone of Ombrazia's economy. Even Damian understood the difference.

"How can they think the war is a waste?" The question was more to himself than Kiran and Siena. "Brechaat is trying to push into our territory. They're promoting *heresy*."

The enemy city-state still worshipped the patron saint of Chaos. After losing the First War of Saints and splitting off from Ombrazia,

Brechaat had suffered terribly. Their citizens were almost entirely unfavored, and without Ombrazia's economy to rely on, they spiraled into poverty. But nineteen years ago—only fifty years after the first war, and right before Damian was born—Brechaat launched an attack. An unfavored general had roused citizens from their miserable slumber, incited their anger, and convinced the rest of Brechaat they could take back power if they captured enough of Ombrazian land to gain control of key trade routes.

As it turned out, it wasn't that easy. The two city-states had been at an impasse ever since, neither of them backing down. Brechaat had gained some land, but not near as much as they wanted. And if Ombrazia didn't take it back, the chief magistrate was certain the enemy would spread its heretical ideals. So the war went on, leaving Damian to fear it would never end.

"I don't think the rebels appreciate just how much wealth and influence Ombrazia has to lose," Siena said, drawing Damian out of his thoughts. He nodded in agreement.

Kiran kicked the toe of his boot into the hard ground. "What I don't understand is why Brechaat doesn't focus on their own economy. Is it really worth trying to push into Ombrazia, dragging out the war, when they could be focusing on their own state?" He raised his hands defensively when both Siena and Damian shot him a disbelieving look. "I'm only asking!"

"Disciples aren't common in Brechaat," Damian reminded him. "Try as they might, they'll never have as much power as Ombrazia. Their best chance is to overtake us."

"And they won't back down now," Siena said. "Not when they haven't gotten what they're fighting for."

The conversation died as they arrived at the entrance to the Palazzo crypt, all three of them halting.

"Hey," Kiran said, eyeing their location and seeming to deduce Damian's intentions. "It wasn't your fault, no matter what Forte says. You know that, right? And you can examine the body as much as you like, but you won't know more until you get a proper autopsy."

Kiran was probably right. About the latter, that was. Damian blew out a breath. "It's my job to ensure the disciples' safety."

"It's not your job to be everywhere at once," Siena countered. "Forte knows that. He's only worried about the city's reaction when they find out and needs someone to blame it on."

"He said he'd send me back up north if I didn't find the culprit."

They sobered at that. Kiran said slowly, "He wouldn't do that. Your father wouldn't allow it."

Damian nearly laughed. He knew from the stories Kiran shared that he had a large family who adored him, and not only because his position at the Palazzo was their main source of income. They'd been relieved to tears when their son returned from the war in one piece.

Battista Venturi was not like that. Damian had only ever seen his father proud of him once, and it had been on the worst day of his life.

He made a noncommittal sound in the back of his throat. "My father had to do a lot of convincing for Forte to give me this job in the first place. If he wants me gone, I'm not sure anyone will be able to change his mind."

"Siena and I would give it a shot." Kiran gave a crooked grin, elbowing Damian lightly in the arm. "Look, don't panic yet, okay? Forte's harsh, but he's not unreasonable. He knows things like this take time." Kiran gestured at the door to the crypt. "You want us to come with you?"

"No. Thanks, though." Damian needed to be alone, to *think*. To examine the body without Chief Magistrate Forte looming over him. He glanced up at the midnight sky. "Your shift's nearly over, and we need to question the rest of the staff tomorrow. Go get some sleep."

"Pot, kettle," Siena said smoothly, but she was already beginning to back away, dragging Kiran along with her.

Damian took one last glance at the night sky, which remained steadfastly blanketed by a layer of clouds. Tradition taught that stars were the saints' eyes, and if he couldn't see them, it meant no one was watching him, either.

His body felt heavier as he descended the stairs to the crypt, one hand braced against the cold stone wall. As he reached the last step, cool air enveloped him. The ceilings were low, lending the sensation that the walls were closer than they truly were. The only corpse in the room was the disciple's—the rest of the space was empty. It should have relieved Damian, but instead he was vaguely unsettled.

A single sconce was lit, and feeble strains of illumination licked up and down the ivory walls. Damian repressed a shiver as the sight of Leonzio's body struck him all over again. It was somehow worse the second time: The gray tinge to the disciple's skin was unearthly. Damian touched his eyelids, left and right, then his heart. He clenched his icy hands into fists. Took another breath. And then, as if handling a sleeping patient, he rolled up the fabric of the dead man's sleeve the way Giada had earlier.

He examined the faint gray lines that webbed Leonzio's wrists, darkening into a latticework of black as they moved up the arm. He'd hoped a closer look might help him glean something, but he only felt more hopeless than ever. Someone had managed to poison a heavily guarded disciple in his bed. *How?*

Damian had unquestioning trust in his security officers, and yet someone must have gotten past them.

He leaned forward, propping his elbows on the stone altar. It was like resting on a block of ice, but he barely noticed, staring into the middle distance as his head spun. He swore he could feel Death here, admiring the newest member of her eternal cadre.

When will you become accustomed to my presence, Damian Venturi? Her whisper seemed to caress his neck, snatching the air from his lungs with frigid fingers. *You've carried me with you for quite some time.*

He pushed the thoughts away. He was not descended from Death; he had nothing to do with her. How cruel life was, that she followed him so. And yet when Damian cast about for Strength, he came up empty.

With a sigh, he touched his fingertips to Leonzio's eyelids, mirroring the action he'd made earlier.

He jerked his hand away.

Whatever was beneath those thin, purple-veined flaps of skin, it certainly wasn't Leonzio's eyes. The flesh felt unnatural. Too solid. Damian took a breath, wiping away the layer of dampness on his forehead. With a hint of hesitation, he lifted one of the disciple's eyelids.

The shock that passed through him was a sickening thing. Instead of clouded irises, there were only flat black orbs. Some kind of metal, or perhaps glass. They looked horribly *wrong*, set there against the white-rimmed sockets.

Whoever killed Leonzio Bianchi had taken his eyes with them.

Roz

It was dawn by the time Roz returned to Patience's temple. She'd got-ten a few hours of sleep on the sofa in Piera's small apartment—the top floor of the tavern—although Piera herself had remained curi-ously absent. The remnants of wine still moved sluggishly through Roz's veins, though she'd had fewer glasses than she normally would. It was hard to enjoy a drink with Dev's anguished face across from her. His personality had altered completely since his sister's death, and Roz recognized the shift for what it was: survival mode. Her friend was simply trying to move from one day to the next. It was a state Roz knew well, having experienced it herself following her father's death. When grief weighed so heavily on your bones, how could you move? How could you fight?

Together with Piera and Nasim, Dev had helped drag Roz out of despair. She only wished she knew how to do the same for him.

Her chest seized whenever she remembered the little blond-haired girl waving from the window of the Villeneuve family home. Amélie had been so happy, so innocent. Had Roz ever been like that? She didn't think so. Amélie had been a spot of light against a dark landscape. Someone who found joy in the places others didn't.

For the world to snuff that light out so soon struck Roz as unfathomably cruel.

Patience's temple was a dark stone behemoth in the center of the sector, heavily accented with curling wrought iron. Roz had always thought it looked rather like a villain's lair. It was beautiful, she supposed, in the way that expertly sharpened blades were beautiful. A great arch rose above her head as she made for the entrance, framing the dawn for a fraction of a moment before she stepped inside.

She wasn't surprised to find the entryway occupied, even at such an early hour. A few younger disciples hurried by her, likely headed to a tutoring session where they would learn to coax their will into weapons, tools, and all manner of ornaments. Having developed her ability unnaturally late, Roz had been forced to do the same for a number of months. It had been terribly boring, and she was relieved it was over. Not that her current station was much better. She had no intention of spending her life as a glorified blacksmith.

"Roz!"

Someone uttered her name, and Roz whirled, finding herself face-to-face with Vittoria Delvecchio. "Oh. Hey."

Vittoria arched a brow. She was harshly lovely, and exactly Roz's type: tall, muscled, and invariably unsmiling. Her hair was so light a blonde it was nearly white, tumbling in a sleek sheet to her rib cage. Roz was relieved to find she didn't hurt quite so much to look at. A few months after joining the guild, and two years after Damian's departure, she and Vittoria struck up something of a relationship. Stolen kisses in empty hallways, holding hands in the temple's flower-dense courtyard. Vittoria was the only person Roz had kissed since Damian, and Vittoria was confident, heady passion where he had been inexperienced, teenage hesitation.

Every physical moment spent with Vittoria was perfection. Roz could still remember the sharp curves of her body, the cinnamon-sugar scent of her soft hair. The rest, though, was where they'd always had problems.

"I figured you'd be late," Vittoria said. Her gray eyes were searching. "Didn't you go to the Mercato last night?"

Roz shrugged, not about to admit she had only just returned, or that most of those hours hadn't been spent anywhere near the Mercato at all. "The sun woke me."

Vittoria would know it was a lie. It didn't matter. And *that* had been the problem in their relationship: Roz never told the truth. How could she? Vittoria believed in the importance of their role as disciples. She wore her ring with pride and prayed to the saints with sincerity. Roz, on the other hand, didn't care about any of it. They fundamentally didn't understand one another. And so they'd settled into something of a friendship, rarely mentioning what had come before.

"Right," Vittoria said, brushing invisible dust from the front of her gray jacket. "Well, since you're here, you might think about contributing to the Mercato instead of just attending it. I can only cover for you so often."

Her words were good natured, but firm. Roz rolled her eyes,

though she knew Vittoria was right. She relied on the periodic payments she received from the temple to care for her mother. If she kept shirking her duties, she might find herself in trouble.

"Okay, okay." Roz pinched the bridge of her nose. "Let's go."

Vittoria led her over to the wide, curving staircase near the temple's entrance. Its banisters were exquisite wrought iron, the steps marble. Roz eyed the slope of Vittoria's neck as she pulled her hair up into a knot, then mentally smacked herself.

As they descended the staircase, heat billowed up to meet them. Roz felt her face arrange itself in a familiar scowl, and she peeled off her jacket. She *hated* it down here. Disciples of Patience didn't require forges to shape metal, but they had to start somewhere, and you couldn't exactly turn ore and powders into anything of use.

The sheets of once-molten metal, Roz had to admit, were beautiful. Silvery and full of possibility, they sat in the center of the cathedral-like space, ready to be used by the disciples of Patience that milled around them. The warm air was acrid, holding the scent of ash and something oddly sweet.

Vittoria grabbed Roz by the arm, dragging her over to a group of girls at the edge of the room. The air sparked around them, hazy and dense with magic. Roz didn't know any of them particularly well, and would be the first to admit it was for lack of trying. Every disciple wanted to be the best, the most productive, the most respected. Doing so would give them a chance at being chosen to represent the guild at the Palazzo. Roz, of course, had never desired such a thing and thus couldn't relate to them at all. She tried in vain to pull away from Vittoria. "I'll just work by myself."

This was a variation of a conversation they'd had before, and

Vittoria reverted to her default argument. "I can't be your only friend, Roz."

"Sure you can." As always, Roz refrained from mentioning that she *had* other friends—they just weren't disciples. "Besides, it's only a matter of time before they kick me out. You know full well nothing I create is of sellable quality."

"Because you don't try." One side of Vittoria's mouth quirked.

"We can't all be perfect."

Vittoria rolled her eyes, humoring Roz, and said nothing more.

It was true, though. Roz *didn't* try. The rest of the disciples thought her something of a strange phenomenon: blessed by a patron saint, but hopelessly useless at her craft. Roz was content to let them believe it, as long as it meant they weren't bothered by her lack of participation. She didn't care about forging. Working with metal was boring. Of all Patience's disciples, she had to be the least patient, and everyone knew it.

The problem was, Roz was *good* at the job. If she'd wanted to, she could create impeccable items. Somehow she knew that she barely tapped into her potential. The part of her that was descended from Patience longed to do more—so much more—but the rest of her refused to give in to the euphoria her fellow disciples clearly felt when they used their magic. It wasn't fair that she had a comfortable life simply by virtue of being born into it. It wasn't fair that she got paid for doing a piss-poor job of whatever the temple demanded. Not while Dev's and Nasim's families struggled to stay afloat.

And then there was the fact that disciples of Patience were largely tasked with creating weapons for the war. It made Roz sick. Her father had *died* thanks to that pointless, unending war.

"Are you okay?" Vittoria asked, letting go of Roz's arm. Her brow was furrowed, and Roz wondered what her face looked like. She didn't bother feigning a smile.

"I'm just going to work over here."

This time Vittoria didn't bother arguing. Only gave a small shake of her head, going to join her other friends. Roz should have felt guilty, but she couldn't summon the emotion. She wiped sweat from her brow, then deposited her jacket onto the floor. The ceiling far above her head was painted with depictions of Patience—a featureless warrior-woman brandishing a sword— carrying out various acts of godliness. Near the crown molding was the faint outline of a male saint's brawny form: Chaos, Roz knew, had been poorly scrubbed from the scene. All that remained was his hand, still wrapped around Patience's, fire blossoming between them. Words took shape unbidden in Roz's mind.

In the heart of Strength's mountains, Patience called forth heat. It was she who created fire, and Chaos who gave it movement.

Chaos and Patience, the original lovers. Opposites and equals who balanced one another out. Roz was hard pressed to believe they'd truly had a hand in creating the world, but even so, it struck her as rather rude for her fellow disciples to unceremoniously scratch away their saint's life partner. Maybe one day Patience would come down from the heavens to smite them all.

Roz rolled up her sleeves and banished herself to the farthest corner of the room. A metal rod was waiting for her, leaning against the wall. They were supposed to be making gun barrels, and Roz could see in her mind's eye the exact way she would bend the rod to her will. How her fingers would shape the metal like it was clay, and how, when she was done with it, it would only fire for whomever it was issued to.

Her hands grew overwhelmingly hot, and her blood turned

molten in her veins. Power coursed through her, yearning to be released, but she clamped down on it. Refused to unleash more than a slow trickle.

By the time Vittoria came to find her, Roz had little to show for the morning's work.

"Those are terrible," Vittoria observed, cheeks flushed with the healthy glow disciples always seemed to get when they were doing the work they loved.

Disciples who weren't Roz, anyway.

"So they are," Roz said lightly, kicking the useless barrels into a haphazard pile. "Oh well. Shall we go?"

After bidding Vittoria goodbye, Roz walked through the temple's courtyard, following the path that traveled its circumference. Flowers and ivy crept up the balustrade on either side of her, and the air smelled like distant rain. The courtyard provided a shortcut home, but as she emerged on the other side, Roz heartily regretted taking it. Had she been paying attention, she might have recognized the heavy footfalls. The light jingling of keys hitting the end of a baton on an army-issue belt.

There was little Roz hated more than security officers, and she couldn't help the snarl that crept across her lips. Former military promoted to a higher rank, every officer she'd encountered had a superiority complex. They weren't disciples, but they might as well be, brainwashed to believe they existed to serve the saints' descendants. Officers were forever conducting raids in parts of the city occupied by the unfavored, eager to catch them in acts of wrongdoing or else searching for evidence of the rebellion. In doing so, Roz had even heard that they stole from the unfavored citizens' homes.

None of that was why all the air suddenly left her lungs, though.

Of the two officers walking toward her, she recognized one of them. And *that* was the reason for her abrupt inability to breathe.

Damian Venturi.

It was the closest she had been to him since his return from the north, and she studied him with a mix of shock and disdain. He didn't look anything like Roz remembered. For one, he was taller and far more muscular beneath the dark fabric of his uniform. His gold regalia glinted beneath the dawn light, as did the archibugio strapped to his back, and his navy jacket was buttoned all the way up to his chin. The unruly hair from his childhood was gone, now a slightly grown-out version of the typical military style. And though the softness of boyhood was still visible beneath his sharp cheekbones, there was something different about his eyes. They were no longer bright, happy, but watchful. Guarded. As though he were eternally braced for something to leap out of the shadows.

Roz wondered if the world had beaten him down the way it had her. She hoped so.

Saints knew he deserved it.

After Damian's father was appointed to military commander three years ago, he had taken his family north to his new post at the border, where Damian began training as a soldier. By then, Roz's own father had already been at the front for some time, and the foolish, fifteen-year-old part of her had hoped the two men might be able to comfort each other there. After all, Jacopo Lacertosa had been warm where Battista Venturi was not. Once, Damian had even confessed to Roz he felt closer to her father than he did to his own.

It made sense, now that she knew Damian's father to be the biggest snake in all of Ombrazia. Jacopo and Battista had been friends since childhood, and not even Battista's becoming a disciple could sever their bond. But when Jacopo attempted to desert the front lines, Battista Venturi had tracked down his former friend and sent his head home in a box.

Roz had been sixteen at the time. She remembered wanting to vomit at the sight, but her body hadn't betrayed her that way. Instead, as icy, tingling shock spread through her bones, she'd merely stared into that box in absolute silence. That silence had then become an incessant roaring in her ears, demanding bloody justice. Her father's death hadn't broken her—not for long. Instead, it had forged her into something vindictive.

It had shattered her mother, though, and Caprice Lacertosa hadn't been the same since.

Damian hadn't so much as written after that. He'd chosen his side—that was clear. So much for the things he'd said in their youth. He might as well have spat on Jacopo's grave.

Roz had managed to avoid Damian for nearly a year, but now that he was mere steps away, she had half a mind to confront him. Perhaps strike him across the face with the force of her betrayal. Before she could organize her thoughts, though, Damian's companion spoke. It was a female officer about Roz's age, brown skinned with soft features, her braided hair tumbling down her back.

"...not going to be happy," she was saying. "People are going to learn of the disciple's death soon, Damian. Especially with his replacement being chosen this weekend."

Roz tilted her head, suddenly more intrigued than anything else.

"I know." Damian's answer was curt. "The chief magistrate has made it clear this is a priority matter. I took Giada in for questioning, but nothing lines up. I need to talk to my father. He'll know what to do."

"Personally, I'm still not convinced it wasn't a suicide."

Roz bit down hard on her tongue, willing them to pass without incident as the gears of her mind whirled. A Palazzo disciple was dead? The revelation was like a slap in the face. Not because of the death itself—she wasn't too worried about that—but because of what Damian had said.

The chief magistrate has made it clear this is a priority matter.

The ferocity of her anger was sudden and overwhelming. Amélie and the unidentified boy lay in the city morgue, their murders unsolved. The Palazzo hadn't bothered assigning officers to *their* cases. But now that a single disciple had died, it became a priority?

Roz willed them to pass without incident. To assume she was just another disciple walking down the street. But because the world had a twisted sense of humor, Damian lifted his gaze as their paths crossed.

And looked directly at her.

"Rossana." He said the formal version of her name like an accusation. His voice was deeper. Steadier. It held a note of command he hadn't possessed before. When he halted, the female officer copied him, brows drawing down in confusion.

Roz clamped her teeth together hard. She didn't know why she felt suddenly as if she were on display. Maybe it was the way

Damian's bewilderment looked so familiar. Maybe it was the fact that she could picture him at the table in her family's old house, a quizzical smile playing around his mouth as he watched her try and fail to recreate one of her mother's recipes. He'd still eaten it, though. He always had, no matter what she presented him with.

It's the effort that counts, Roz, he'd say, brandishing his fork. *And there's nothing salt can't fix.*

That was before Roz had known there were, in fact, *endless* things salt couldn't fix. It couldn't fix murder. It couldn't fix betrayal. It couldn't fix heartbreak or fill an unending well of rage.

It was a moment before she realized she still hadn't spoken. Perhaps to account for the silence, Damian said, "What are you doing here?"

Roz kept her own gaze steady as she held his familiar one: deep brown and bottomless, framed by black lashes. The pale scar running from the curve of his cheek to his jaw, however—that was new. "I'm walking. That isn't against the law, is it?"

He frowned, bristling against her hostility. "I—no, it's not. I suppose I'm just surprised to see you here."

"And I suppose *you* know I'm a disciple of Patience," Roz said, smug relief trilling through her when the words came out steady. She gestured at the grandiose building behind her. "This is Patience's temple, if you hadn't noticed."

Damian set his jaw. "That it is."

His expression was unreadable, and it caught Roz off guard. She couldn't think of a time when Damian's face hadn't been an open book, at least to her eyes. That was when she understood: This creature—with his muscles, smart uniform, and impenetrable exterior—was not Damian Venturi. This was a man she didn't know. A man who had been to war and come back a copy of his traitorous father.

Roz could still remember the last tour from which her own father had returned. How he'd heaved himself onto the sofa, exhaustion in every line of his weathered face, and gripped the drink Caprice offered him with a shaking hand. *Battista got promoted again,* he'd said. The words had been hollow. Roz knew her father well enough to know it meant he was furious. *He's commander of our unit. The man cares for nothing but climbing the ranks. I don't know who he is anymore.*

At the time, Roz had found this incomprehensible. Now, though, she understood the sentiment perfectly.

There was nothing meaningful to be said with the female officer present. She looked from Roz to Damian, clearly trying to understand the dynamic. "I take it you two know each other?"

"We did," Roz said before Damian could reply. "Once."

His stare bored into her like one of her poorly forged tools. There was a stiffness to his posture, as though he feared she might reveal something to his companion. Roz pursed her lips in contempt. As if she would want anyone to know of their connection.

Damian surprised her, however, when he explained: "Our families were friends when we were younger."

The female officer nodded, but her mouth remained tight.

Roz smiled sweetly. "Yes, they were. Until Damian's father murdered mine."

There was a prolonged silence. Damian's face was a mask, the tendons in his neck standing out. It was a mark of the other officer's training that she digested this information in stride, saying only, "I see."

"Battista Venturi," Roz clarified, as if the girl didn't already

49

know. It was worth it for Damian's reaction alone. "I'm sure you know him."

Damian's gaze didn't waver from hers as he said, "Roz's father was a deserter."

It was merely a fact, of course, but it felt like a most aggressive form of retaliation. Roz fisted her hands, astonished to learn that her fury could peak even further. She let out a harsh laugh. "It's true. But at least he wasn't a backstabbing piece of shit."

The female officer's brows ascended to her hairline. Damian looked as though Roz had slapped him. His lips parted, but no words came out. Perhaps he'd been able to construe she hadn't only been talking about Battista.

Roz might have laughed, but she forced herself to walk away, leaving more silence in her wake. She needed to get the hell out of there before she did something she'd regret.

Her legs carried her homeward without her being conscious of their movement. She felt jittery, a little ill, and angrier than ever. *That* was why she'd been avoiding Damian. *That* was why she tried so hard not to remember.

And yet she could imagine the conversation they might have had if things were different. How Damian would have asked her what she was up to, dragging her heels through the street all alone. How one side of his mouth would tilt up—just a little—the way it did when he was equal parts concerned and amused.

I was walking, Roz would have told him, good-naturedly this time. *That isn't against the law, is it?*

I only asked because you looked sad, Damian would have said, because he would've noticed. He always noticed. *Don't you ever take anything seriously?*

Roz gave herself a shake, bitterness searing through her veins. That version of Damian—of herself—was gone. Dead. Just like her father.

I don't *take anything seriously*, she thought to no one in particular as she slunk around the corner. *Not really.*

And then, an afterthought: *Except vengeance.*

ROZ

Roz was almost home by the time she'd finally calmed down enough to think straight. How *dare* Damian. It was laughable now to consider there had once been a time she thought she couldn't survive without him. A time when she'd gone daily to check the list of names posted at the Basilica, and prayed his wasn't there so hard she feared she would crack.

But she'd survived, and the months had passed, and the only news she received from the north was of deaths that weren't Damian's. Never him. The saints, Roz thought, must have been listening, regardless of the sentiments her father now harbored toward them.

One morning, however, she and her mother received a different type of news.

Then a package on the doorstep.

That was the last time Roz had asked the saints for anything. The way she saw it, there were two options. One: that the saints heard her prayers but didn't have the power to intervene. If so, what was the point of praying to them? Or two: that the saints *did* have the power to change things, yet chose not to.

It didn't matter either way. For as her world came crashing down around her, she knew precisely who to blame. She saw the city of her birth with new eyes, like a shimmering veil lifting to reveal a rotten interior. She abandoned the saints, with their trickery and game of favorites, and never called on them again.

But had there been a patron saint of Fury, Roz undoubtedly would have prayed to him.

The apartment Roz shared with her mother was set back from the sector's main web of roads, small and discreet, though fine in the way disciples' quarters tended to be. Her arms trembled as she pulled herself up the side of the adjacent building, leaping over to the window she used to access the apartment. She preferred not to allow anyone to see her coming or going from the place. Her mother was vulnerable, and didn't do well with strangers. Only Piera, who often delivered food, was an acceptable houseguest.

"Mamma," Roz blurted as she swung herself inside. Caprice Lacertosa was still awake, sitting at the round kitchen table with her gaze fixed on something in the middle distance.

Caprice was a small woman, her dark hair pinned in a messy bun behind her head. She had an angular, solemn face, and shared Roz's tanned skin and blue eyes. But where once Caprice's eyes had been sharp and clever, they now appeared vacant.

She, too, was a disciple of Patience, but she'd left the temple when Jacopo went off to war, and stayed away when he came home convinced of the system's corruptness. Roz had never seen any evidence of her mother's magic, and a horrible part of her was glad Caprice wasn't coherent enough to know her daughter was living the very life she'd abandoned.

"Rossana," Caprice said, trailing a finger over the surface of the table. There was no food before her; she was simply sitting there, shoulders hunched. "Where have you been?"

Roz released her hair from its tight cord. "I had work to do," she told her mother, whose mouth turned down.

"I was looking everywhere for you. I thought you had died."

Saints. Caprice seemed to think Roz was dead whenever she disappeared from her sight for more than a few moments. Perhaps it was the result of what had happened to Jacopo, or perhaps Caprice's memory problems were getting worse.

She hadn't been the same since her husband's death. Roz couldn't conjure another explanation for the decline in her mother's health since the fateful day that box had shown up on their doorstep. Overnight, Caprice became a different person. She didn't remember things. She refused to leave the apartment. She sometimes spoke to people who weren't there and laughed at jokes that hadn't been told.

As Caprice's sanity slipped further away, Roz realized there was no way her mother would be able to support them any longer. And since Jacopo had deserted, they weren't entitled to the same meager compensation other families received when their loved ones were killed on the front lines. So Roz had taken a job at Bartolo's, accepting what little pay the owner, Piera, could offer her. It wasn't enough. Not nearly enough, given how expensive it was to live in Ombrazia. But for a time, at least, Piera had been there to listen. The woman had wiped glasses and let Roz talk as much as she needed, always coming up with a thoughtful reply. She brought Caprice food and didn't expect anything in return. There was no way Roz could have asked Piera for more money, so she resigned herself to struggling.

Then came the day she'd felt it.

A heat in the palms of her hands, almost uncomfortable in its intensity. As it grew hotter and hotter, panic had risen in her throat, and Roz had raced from the kitchens into the alleyway beside the tavern. When the heat gave way to a tingling sensation, she realized what was happening.

Do you possess any extraordinary abilities? a representative of the Palazzo had asked Roz and Damian some three years prior, glancing surreptitiously at his notes. *Have things around you moved without your touching them? Are you particularly skilled with your hands? Do you feel a strong connection to other people?*

Those were only a few of what felt like countless questions, and she'd answered honestly at the time. No—she didn't have any magic. She knew she wasn't a disciple and hadn't been blessed by any saint.

She hadn't realized that would change.

In that alleyway, tears pricking her eyes, Roz had pressed her hands to the cold stone wall, trying to cool them. She was her father's daughter, and Jacopo had been proudly unfavored. For her to be anything else felt like a betrayal to his memory. After all, what was her other option? Patience. Patience, the saint of antithesis, of temperance. The saint who was inexplicably connected to blacksmithing—a craft in which Roz had never had any interest.

She'd reached for her knife, praying to the saints she no longer believed in that nothing happened.

But the metal had twisted in her grasp.

For someone who had long since decided she hated disciples and the system from which they benefited, it felt like a curse. And then, when Roz used it to her advantage, she felt terrible guilt.

She was an anomaly, the man who had tested her years before decreed. An impossibly lucky child who had been blessed far later than most. Presenting herself at Patience's temple had felt like being an interesting specimen under harsh light.

But Bartolo's tavern had given her an outlet for her rage: a place she could be with people *truly* like her. People whose loved ones hadn't returned from the war, or else had come back irrevocably changed. People whose aging parents were driven mad by the loss of their child or partner. People suffering beneath the inequity of the current system. It wasn't fair that the most powerful disciples ran the city. It wasn't fair that they evaded the military draft while everyone else battled Brechaat over religious semantics and resources they barely had the privilege of using.

"I'm sorry I wasn't here last night," Roz said far too belatedly, ignoring the sinking sensation in her chest. "I stayed at Piera's after work."

She cringed as her mother's face relaxed. Caprice thought she still worked at Bartolo's, and Roz couldn't see the merit in telling her the truth. It would only confuse and upset her. Besides, her mother never left the apartment; there was no way for her to find out on her own.

"Always working so hard." Caprice's face lit up. "What would we do without you, tesoro?"

Roz hadn't a clue which "we" Caprice was referring to this time, but she didn't ask, mustering a close-lipped smile. The answer was clear: Without Roz, her mother would waste away to nothing in this apartment. It was why she forced herself to play the part of a good little disciple. In a way, everything she did was for Caprice. Roz needed retribution for her family's suffering like she needed air to breathe.

"I haven't seen Damian in a while," her mother went on, causing Roz to freeze. "What has he been up to?"

How did she *know*? For someone who rarely seemed to occupy the real world, Caprice was eerily perceptive. She always managed to bring up precisely what Roz was thinking about, whether it made sense or not.

"Damian doesn't come here anymore," Roz said, more harshly than she'd meant to. She knew she shouldn't resent her mother's tendency to dredge up the past, but it always managed to hurt.

Caprice's lower lip jutted out. "You smile more with him."

Roz refrained from telling her mother she was as likely to kick Damian as smile at him. Instead, she forced her face into a grin that probably looked more like a grimace.

"You make me smile just as much. Would you like something to eat?" She skirted the round mahogany table on her way to the kitchen. The entire apartment was almost sterile in its immaculacy. Her mother did little else but tidy, scrub, and dust, humming or murmuring to herself all the while.

Caprice shook her head. "I'm not hungry. Oh, I worried myself sick about you last night, tesoro."

Roz pulled a pan out of the cupboard nonetheless. They had come full circle. "I told you I wouldn't be home."

"You did not!"

"I did. Right after dinner, remember? We were sitting there"— she pointed at the forest-green sofa—"and I told you not to wait up for me."

Confusion crossed Caprice's face, and Roz backpedaled, swallowing a curse. Her mother tended to get upset when she was confused.

"Never mind," Roz muttered. "Maybe you're right. Maybe I forgot to tell you."

She went about making her mother a cup of tea, procuring the vial she'd bought at the Mercato and dumping its contents in with the fragrant leaves. The potion was intended to help Caprice's nerves, and Roz had to admit it worked quite well.

She prayed silently for her mother to change the subject, then wished she hadn't. What Caprice said next made Roz's stomach turn.

"We received a letter from your father."

Roz stilled where she was, cracking eggs, gaze flicking to the single sheet of parchment in her mother's hands. Caprice often mentioned Jacopo Lacertosa in the present tense, but never claimed to have gotten a letter from him before. It was rarer still for her to make the trip downstairs to the mail slot.

"That's nice," Roz said, treading carefully. "What did it say?"

Caprice's eyes grew large. Her fingers trembled where she clutched the letter—or whatever it was—and for a moment Roz wasn't sure she would respond. But she waited, making no sudden movements, as though dealing with a frightened animal.

Finally Caprice said, "It was a warning."

Roz relaxed. That was better than, say, a promise from Jacopo that he would be home within the week. She'd seen how her mother reacted when she realized all over again that her husband wasn't returning.

"He wants us to leave the city," Caprice rasped, and Roz's skin prickled. "Something dark dwells in these streets."

"What?"

58

"Listen!" her mother pleaded, scanning the parchment. "*To my dearest Caprice and Rossana: I miss you both terribly. I write to you in warning, for you must leave Ombrazia at once.*"

Roz tensed all over again, unease spreading through her. "Can I see that?" she asked, but Caprice had no intention of being forthcoming. She leapt to her feet in a single abrupt motion, voice rising to a desperate wail.

"It will kill you! It will kill us all!"

"*Hey.*" Roz made the word a threat. She grabbed her mother by the shoulder and shoved her back into the chair. It wasn't difficult; she was muscular where Caprice was delicate. "Calm down. Let's get some rest, okay? I'll bring you some tea."

It took some wrangling and coaxing, but in the end they lay side by side on the bed, Roz waiting for the sound of her mother's breaths to deepen. Only then did she slip out of the sheets and sneak back over to the table.

The letter, as she'd suspected, was blank.

It surprised her nonetheless.

DAMIAN

Damian navigated the halls of the Palazzo in a daze. His chambers were on the other side of the building, and he wanted nothing more than to fall into unconsciousness for the rest of the night. The rest of the *week*, if possible. His thoughts, his heartbeats, were all too loud. He was too aware of his body, as though his earlier encounter with Roz Lacertosa had woken him from a slumber he hadn't realized he was trapped in.

When Damian was up north, he'd found it difficult to imagine a version of Roz beyond the mischievous, dark-haired girl with whom he'd once raced through the streets. She wasn't that girl anymore, though. No—she'd become something harsh and vital, tall enough to look him in the eye without flinching.

She'd done just that, and it had nearly made him wither. She was furious. Damian had known she would be, the same way he knew he deserved it. It was the reason he'd been avoiding her. He was a saints-damned coward.

And yet it wasn't until they were face-to-face that he realized how much he'd missed her. It was as if the dull, constant ache that pulsed at his center had been abruptly wrenched to the forefront. Never had he wanted so badly to pretend nothing had changed. He wanted to wrap her in his arms the way he had when they were children, and lose himself in the summer-sweet scent of her skin.

Unfortunately, there was the small matter of the fact that Roz hated him.

Yes, Battista had killed Jacopo Lacertosa. And yes, it had been horrible. Damian had known Roz would be crushed, but he hadn't realized—perhaps naively—just how mutinous she would be until her parting words.

At least he wasn't a backstabbing piece of shit.

Damian wasn't a fool. He knew Roz hadn't only been speaking of Battista. But what could he do? How could he fix it?

He couldn't. He'd known that the moment it happened. Somehow, they'd both become the people they swore they never would.

Damian could still remember the day representatives from each of the temples had come to test him and Roz. They'd been freshly thirteen. Afterward, he'd stretched out on her bed, and she'd sat against the wall by the window, honeyed sunlight playing in the loose strands of her hair. Damian had thought her the most beautiful thing he'd ever seen.

I don't care if I'm not a disciple, Roz had said matter-of-factly. *As long as you're not, either.*

Damian wasn't. It had disappointed him for a fraction of a

moment, until he'd seen Roz grinning. As long as their results were the same—that was what mattered.

You realize we'll have to go north, then, he'd replied. Back then, it hadn't seemed a real possibility. It was as distant and unfathomable as the war itself.

Roz had shrugged. *Then we go together. Better than having to train in one of those fancy temples, where everyone thinks they're so important.*

People die in war. That, at least, Damian had already been aware of.

Not us. We won't die, and we won't kill. We'll just survive.

They were the foolish words of a child who knew nothing of the world, but they'd comforted Damian at the time. Roz had joined him on the bed, then, resting her cheek against his shoulder. The contact had set Damian's nerve endings alight, and he'd wished vehemently that they could stay like that forever.

In the end, he had killed people. Roz had become a disciple. And that moment of bliss had never felt so far away.

Damian ran a hand through his sweaty hair, releasing an unsteady breath. He needed to stop dwelling on the past. He'd attempted to distract himself for the remainder of the day, questioning the Palazzo staff about Leonzio's death until dusk stole across the sky. Everyone more or less had the same story: They hadn't seen the disciple of Death that night. If an outsider had done it, nobody knew how they'd gotten in.

Noemi, the security officer who'd been patrolling Leonzio's floor, was more infuriated than guilty.

"This is *insulting,*" she'd snapped, viciously enough that Damian was taken aback. "Of course nothing could have gotten past me. I'm not an *amateur,* Venturi. I've been doing this job longer than you. If Leonzio was poisoned, it must have happened earlier in the day. As for whether he was acting strange…I don't know if you noticed, but Leonzio was a strange man. Seemed to get more paranoid by the day. Now, are we done here?"

Damian, his head full of Roz, hadn't relented, and it only got more unpleasant from there. In the end, though, he had little more information than he'd started with.

All of which was to say, he was *tired*. Exhausted in ways he hadn't known a person could be. His eyes didn't seem to be working properly, and every action felt strange, as though he were moving through a dreamscape.

He ascended the stone staircase to the second story, then made his way to the end of the corridor. Night had long since crept into the corners of the building, shrouding the arched ceiling so that the plaster designs grew unfathomable. Damian's door was the last one on the left, and the sheer sight of it relieved him. Fingers unsteady from waning coordination, he tested the handle gingerly.

It was open. Misgiving flooded Damian as though he'd been drenched in cold water. Not because he feared someone had broken in, but because he knew at once who had.

He stepped inside. The room was dark, but he could discern the outline of someone sitting motionless on the edge of his bed.

"Father," Damian said.

Battista Venturi looked as awake and unruffled as always. He had Damian's dark eyes and hair, though he wasn't quite as tall as his son. Not that it made a difference: His presence always filled a room. He commanded attention and respect wherever he went, and the front of his uniform was lined with tiny medals reflecting everything he'd accomplished during the war.

"You're back," Battista said. The general was notorious for

concealing his feelings, though there was a twist to his mouth Damian recognized.

"I am." Damian hung up his archibugio, lit a lamp, and deposited his jacket onto the chair beside the bed. His rooms, though simple, echoed the ornateness of the rest of the Palazzo. The bedsheets were lush, the crown molding intricate. Though it was a morbid thought, Damian wished his mother had lived long enough to die here instead of in a drafty, wood-paneled bedroom up north.

"I've been waiting quite a while. How did it go?"

Damian released his tension in a single long breath. "You heard about Leonzio's death."

"Of course I heard," Battista said, a crease punctuating the space between his eyebrows. "The chief magistrate came to see me. He isn't pleased. Tell me you at least spent the day doing something productive."

Shit. Could this not have waited until morning? Damian could barely stay on his feet. Or perhaps it was embarrassment weakening him as he admitted to the day's failures.

He sunk into the straight-backed chair beside the bed, no longer bothering with professionalism. "Leonzio appeared to have been poisoned, but Giada claimed not to recognize the effects. I took her in for questioning, but didn't get anything useful out of her. Siena and I let the temples know there would be another ceremony this weekend, and then I spent the rest of the day questioning the staff."

"I see."

Damian held his breath, waiting. He'd expected his father to be displeased. Instead Battista seemed...quiet. Reflective.

After Damian's mother had been lost to illness, Battista threw himself into his duties. He'd risen quickly from military commander to general, returning home to oversee the security officers. He now traveled between the city and the front lines, but Ombrazia was where he worked most often. It was only through Battista's status as a disciple of Strength—and his standing with the chief magistrate—that Damian had been allowed to take command of Palazzo security. It didn't matter that Battista rarely made use of his ability. He was a disciple, his magic was powerful, and that was enough to garner respect. If Damian failed to prove himself, it would reflect poorly on his father. He was enough of a disappointment as it was, given that he hadn't been blessed with magic of his own.

"Damian," Battista said finally, heavily, "I've been trying to help you. I advised you on setting up your patrols, and how to play to your officers' strengths. I keep telling Forte to be patient; you simply need more time to get your footing. But I have my own tasks to carry out, and I can only dig you out from a certain depth. Forte is worried. What with the rebel activity, he wants Leonzio's murder wrapped up quickly. I'll hold him at bay for as long as I can, but we need answers soon, or you'll be replaced."

Damian swallowed. Though Forte had already made the ultimatum clear, it was equally unpleasant to hear it a second time. "I can't go back there. I can't go back to war."

He knew it was important for Ombrazia to keep Brechaat and the heretics in check. He *knew* that. But he also knew the reality of war, and how it took no time at all for dreams of glory to turn to ash in one's mouth.

"I don't want you to go back, either," Battista said gently. "But Leonzio's death happened on your watch."

"It was an accident."

"It was a *murder*," his father corrected him. "A murder you didn't see coming. A murder you ought to have been able to stop."

Shame flooded Damian. He wanted to argue, but how could he?

"I understand," he forced out. "I'm sorry. Do you think it won't keep me awake, knowing I should have been the one to save his life? I can't..." He trailed off, running a hand down his cheek. "I can't see these things coming. I don't know how I'm expected to."

Battista sighed, his expression softening. He rose to his feet and braced his hands on Damian's shoulders. Damian lifted his chin. Staring into his father's dark eyes was like looking into a mirror of his future.

"We can't waste time wondering how to do our job," Battista said gently. "We simply have to *do* it. I know you're more than capable. You're my son."

Something heavy settled in the pit of Damian's stomach. Though his father would never say it, Damian suspected his disappointment grew more tangible by the day. The pride Battista exhibited after learning of his *heroism* during the war—saints, even thinking the word made him feel sick—had eroded. His father wanted nothing more than for Damian to prove himself. And hell, he tried his best, but lately it felt like the world was pushing back too aggressively for him to maintain his footing.

He wasn't like Battista. Wasn't able to unthinkingly place his country, his honor, above all else. He knew he ought to be able to—knew it was what his position demanded—but the things he'd done continued to haunt his thoughts.

"What about the other recent deaths?" Damian said, unable to help himself. "Do you think they're connected? The boy found on the riverbank, and the young girl—"

"Forget about them," Battista cut in. "Forte didn't deem them a priority, and the last thing you need right now is to be distracted. Focus on Leonzio's murder and that alone."

Damian paused, caught off guard. Surely his father could see why he might want to canvass all possibilities? Three potential murders so close together was unheard of in Ombrazia. If the same person was responsible for all of them, perhaps they'd left evidence behind at one of the other scenes. He wasn't about to argue, though.

"It has to have been someone already inside the Palazzo," Damian said, circling back to the subject at hand. "Either that, or they helped an outsider sneak in."

Leonzio had been a politician—there were undoubtedly those who stood to gain by getting rid of him. But here, in the safety of the Palazzo, it was hard to imagine who might have had the opportunity.

Battista adjusted the already impeccable collar of his jacket, shoulders straining beneath the fabric. His disciple's ring glinted in the low light. "Whoever you eventually mark as a suspect, you're going to need evidence. I suggest you get another pair of eyes in the Palazzo."

Damian didn't pick up on his father's meaning right away. It must have shown in his expression, because Battista added, "I'm talking about informants. Your officers can't see everything at once. Use the staff you trust to keep an eye out. What about—what's his name? Nico?"

"Enzo?" Damian sighed inwardly. His father made little effort to learn the names of the staff.

"Sure. Enzo. Use whomever and whatever you need. Forte won't hesitate to get rid of you if he doesn't think you're doing your job, and that's the last thing I want." Battista grasped Damian's shoulder again, this time with a single firm hand. "The saints are on your side, boy."

That was easy for his father to say—proof of their favor flowed through his blood. Damian swallowed. Each day he sought Strength out with undying fervor, hoping for a sign from the patron saint. Hoping for *something*. But no matter how much he prayed, he felt no presence save Death's.

"I'll fix things," he told his father, hoping the saints would hear and help him make it so.

One side of Battista's mouth lifted. "I know you will."

Damian watched him go, chest tight. He doubted very much that Enzo was still awake—it was nearing midnight, and the staff generally awoke at an unholy hour—but he knew his restless mind wouldn't allow him to sleep until he checked.

He made his way down the gilded staircase, thoughts churning. The servants' quarters were on the main floor, and sure enough, they were abandoned. Damian hovered in the empty kitchens for a moment, listening to the dull hum of the wind outside. He spread his hands against the cool marble countertop, considering the raised veins extending toward his joints. It made him think of black-laced skin and hollow eye sockets.

Giving his head a shake, he headed back to the stairwell, gripping the banister more tightly than was reasonable. He would speak to Enzo later. He needed to sleep, before his attempt to be vigilant verged on paranoia.

As he stole through the dark labyrinth of the third floor, a faint rattling noise sounded from the end of the corridor. Damian froze, his heart beating so frantically he thought his chest might cleave in two. He squinted through the dim, past the bisecting hallway to where the chief magistrate's office lay.

A shape moved at the edge of his vision.

He stepped forward on silent feet, never dropping his gaze. One hand went to the knife at his waistband. The rattling continued, and it took another moment for the sound to register. When it did, Damian quickened his step. It was the unsuccessful manipulating of a lock.

Someone was trying to break into Forte's office.

He gripped the hilt of his knife and wrenched it upward. By now he was mere steps from the intruder, and he extended his arm in the darkness, directing the point of his blade to where he suspected—hoped—the figure's neck might be. "Don't. *Move*."

The intruder gave a start, backing away from the door. When they turned to raise their hands, Damian's stomach plummeted in horror. "It's *you*."

Chief Magistrate Forte looked from Damian to the knife in his grasp. Confusion settled in what was visible of his face. "This is my office."

Damian hurriedly lowered the blade, cheeks burning, glad for the cover of night. "Forgive me, mio signore. I thought someone was trying to break in."

Forte *harrumph*ed. "No matter. The magic has been faulty lately—it doesn't always seem to recognize me."

"Let me help you."

Forte moved aside to allow Damian space to insert his master key. The lock clicked, and the door swung open with an extended croak. It reverberated through the corridor like a whine.

"Thank you," Forte said. He moved to enter, then paused, brow furrowing as his eyes met Damian's. "How is your investigation coming, by the way?"

Damian swallowed hard. "We've questioned nearly everyone

in the Palazzo. Our next course of action is to look into possible rebel involvement."

"You don't believe any of the Palazzo staff were involved, I take it?"

"It's hard to say," Damian hedged. "Anyone can lie. No one struck me as particularly suspicious, though. I'm going to ask Enzo to keep an eye out for anything unusual."

"You trust him?"

Was Forte questioning his judgment, or simply curious? How typical, for someone like him to think mere servants were unworthy of trust.

"Yes," Damian said firmly. "Yes, I do."

There was a beat of silence. Then Forte nodded, a single dip of his head. "Very well. Goodnight, Damian."

It was only when Damian reached his own room that he realized the chief magistrate hadn't called him *Venturi*.

8

ROZ

When dawn broke the next day, it was a somber thing. The sky was the muted, hazy gray of the blank-faced statues Roz scurried past on her way to Bartolo's tavern. They towered ominously amid the foliage of the neglected gardens—an attempt by the chief magistrate to force some semblance of religiosity into the outskirts. Since no one bothered to maintain the patch of land, greenery had overtaken the benches and crept up the stone saints' carved robes. It was beautiful, Roz thought, in a wild sort of way. An ode to the fact that few in this part of Ombrazia cared to bow before divinity.

She decided to take a slightly longer route, intending to pass by the river where the murdered boy's body had been found earlier that week. She didn't know what she was hoping to discover, only that she was frustrated no information about the death had been disclosed. Had the boy been a deserter, perhaps? Someone who'd leapt from a military ship rather than allow it to carry him to war?

But the last draft had been over a month ago, and the river had been calm lately. It felt like too great a coincidence.

Lanterns illuminated the street at wide intervals, casting a dim glow on the grass embankment that separated cobblestone from rippling water. The clouds reflected in the river's surface, a bleak painting upon a shimmering canvas, cast into abstraction every so often by a passing boat. Roz stood there a moment, heart beating painfully in the back of her throat. When she was young her father had taken her on walks by the riverbank, pointing at the lights across the water and telling her stories of the city long before both of their times, when the disciples hadn't yet held Ombrazia in an iron grip.

These are the things we hold on to, Jacopo always told her, his mint and tobacco scent overwhelming whenever he leaned close. It was a smell that lived in every crevice of Roz's memories. *You must remember the way things were in order to know what to strive for.*

Her father had wanted change as much as she did. Perhaps that was why he'd deserted—Jacopo hadn't been the type to do as he was told.

Roz supposed they were alike in that way.

This time, Piera Bartolo was at the bar when Roz entered the tavern, ignoring the CLOSED sign on the door. With white-streaked black hair and a wiry frame, Piera was a knife blade of a woman, sharp and eye-catching in every way. She looked up at the sound of the door opening and smiled when she saw Roz. It was an edged smile, not quite warm, but comforting nonetheless.

"You're early." Piera abandoned the rag she'd been using to wipe down the counter, brushing hair off her brow with the back of her hand. Behind her a sliver of the kitchen was visible: Roz could see a stone wall lined with wine bottles, and wooden racks upon which herbs and meat hung to dry.

"Yeah." Roz glanced at the few occupied tables. There were only four other people here so far, sipping on what was likely Piera's mixture of coffee and brandy. "I wanted to talk to you about something."

Piera's flinty gray eyes narrowed. "Is it Caprice? How is she?"

"About the same." Roz sighed. "No, it's not her. Listen—yesterday I overheard a conversation between two security officers that I thought might interest you."

The woman inclined her chin, indicating that Roz should continue. She did, lowering her voice. "I'm sure half the city already knows by now, but one of the Palazzo's disciples was found murdered."

Piera's brows shot up so fast it might have been amusing in other circumstances. "Really? *Murdered?*"

"That's what they said."

"They think it was us, don't they?"

Roz shook her head. "They didn't say that, but I'm certain it's a possibility. I thought I should give you a heads-up, so you can let everyone know to keep their eyes open."

Piera scanned the tavern, attention diverted toward a group of newcomers as they entered and claimed a table. Her mouth remained a tight line until she refocused on Roz and said, "That's not all, is it?"

"No." Roz felt her face twist. "According to Palazzo security, investigating the disciple's murder and uncovering the culprit is a *priority*."

Piera grabbed the cloth and wrung it between her fingers, jaw working. She didn't need Roz to explain why this bothered her so much. "I see," she murmured. "I wish I could tell you I was surprised."

Roz wasn't surprised, either. But it didn't make her any less infuriated. "If he finds out—"

"*When* Dev finds out, he'll live." The words were firm but gentle. "I can't imagine he expected anything different."

"He's more sensitive than he seems."

"So are you."

Roz pressed her lips together. She adored Piera, but at times she hated how well the woman knew her. Hated that she'd allowed someone to see her vulnerabilities, so that they might be used against her. Piera would never do such a thing in a way that mattered, but any mention of Roz being *sensitive* felt like a personal attack.

"I'm not," she grumbled, and Piera shot her a look.

"You are, and that's okay. You can handle anything regardless. So can Dev."

Roz opened her mouth to answer, but the next moment saw the subject of their conversation stride into the tavern, Nasim at his side. They made a beeline for the bar, and Piera snatched her cloth up with another meaningful glance.

"Still nothing," Nasim said when she neared, slamming a newspaper—then her palm—against the countertop.

Roz, midway through taking a drink, choked at the force in the action. "Am I meant to know what you're talking about?"

"There's still nothing about the boy they discovered on the

riverbank earlier this week. The second…" Nasim lowered her voice as Dev scowled.

"The second victim," he said flatly. "You can say it, you know. I'm not made of glass. Piera?" He waved at her. "Whiskey, please. Neat."

Nasim gave a guilty wince, but Roz said, "We know you're not, Dev." Then to Nasim: "Do they have his name yet?"

"Doesn't seem like it."

The boy's body would sit in the morgue until someone identified him or he started to rot. It wasn't right. His life should have mattered the same way the dead disciple's apparently did. The more she thought about it, the more rage pooled in her chest like poison flowing from an unstoppered bottle.

She slid onto a stool and leaned against the bar, gaze skimming the room as more people filed in, equally unbothered by the sign deeming Bartolo's CLOSED. Roz knew each one of them. Josef and Zemin, Ernesto and Basit, Nicolina, Jolanda, and Alix…Citizens untouched by divinity and lacking a voice because of it. The ones who had watched as their city was shaped by a system that left them behind.

Piera slid Dev's drink down to him, then doffed her apron and came around to the other side of the bar. Everyone had arranged themselves at the tables so that they were facing her. A heavy sort of expectation swelled to saturate the room, laced with the slightest bit of unease. Piera simply waited, refusing to speak until the soft mutterings had ceased. It didn't take long.

And then the rebel meeting was in session.

"Buon giorno," Piera said. "I apologize for calling you all here so early. But it's important you know our attempt to get Frederik out of prison was, unfortunately, unsuccessful." The corners of her mouth tightened slightly, the only indication that this news had affected her. "Rafaella and Jianyu have been detained. Their fate remains unknown."

A hush had spread across the tavern. Not quite horror, and not quite surprise; it was more a heavy acceptance. Roz's stomach sank, and it only sank further as someone called out, "Who could have ratted them out?"

She felt eyes on her before anyone could voice their suspicions aloud. She'd wanted to be *part* of that attempt, damn it. With her ability, she would have been an undeniable asset. And though Piera knew it, she'd gently told Roz that the other rebels assigned to the task refused to work with her.

Hot beneath the press of the room's attention, Roz shook out her hair, letting it tumble down her back. "Because I know some of you are thinking it," she snapped loudly, "it wasn't me."

Nasim squeezed her hand in solidarity. *Piera trusts you, so I trust you*, she had told Roz staunchly from the start. She was one of only a handful of rebels, along with Dev, to take that stance. It had been almost a year, and Roz knew full well most people didn't want her here. Apparently it didn't matter how useful her position allowed her to be.

Piera had been childhood friends with Jacopo Lacertosa, and thus had known Roz well before she was a disciple. In fact, it was Piera who'd supported Roz's decision to present herself to Patience's temple.

They'll pay you far better than I can, the woman had told her. *And if you're willing, it would put you in the perfect position to be of use to me.*

That was when she'd told Roz about the rebellion, and Roz had leapt at the chance to be part of it. Ever since her father's death, resentment had been stewing in her core—a fire that never truly sputtered out.

Piera had given her a way to use it.

"I don't suspect *any* of you," Piera said now, and her voice held a note of warning. "I do not believe anyone here would have betrayed our plans. It was simply poor fortune that the guards' rotation took place a few minutes ahead of schedule."

A rebel named Alix chewed on their lower lip. "Will we make another attempt?"

"Certainly. But not yet."

There was a beat of silence, and Roz raised her voice again. "Palazzo security guards have begun asking about us. They seem to be posing the question to whomever they detain. I overheard as much when I was at the Mercato the other night."

Now Alix glanced her way. They, at least, were generally polite. "Who was asked?"

"A boy around my age. He didn't know anything, of course."

"So they're taking us seriously," Piera cut in, nodding in satisfaction. A few of the other rebels did so with her. "That's good. They're concerned."

Was it good? Roz hadn't been sure.

"What's next, then?" The question came from Josef, a large man who had lost an arm during his last stint up north. "Do we lay low, or give them a reason to be scared?"

Roz had known Piera long enough to guess what her answer would be. Sure enough, the rebel leader's expression didn't change as she said, "The time for doing things in secret has passed. I'd intended this meeting to be about next steps to recover our missing members, but tonight Roz brought me interesting information."

Ernesto—a rebel Roz knew full well couldn't stand her—threw a disdainful look her way. She tossed him a smug one in return.

"One of the Palazzo disciples has been murdered." Piera let a wry smile curve her lips, leaving space for a dramatic pause as shock rippled and swelled throughout the room.

Nasim's eyes glinted, but Zemin was the first to ask, "Which one?"

"They didn't say," Roz replied when Piera's gaze landed on her, questioning. "Does it make a difference?"

Piera shook her head. "Not particularly. What's important is that everyone should be a little more cautious than usual. I suspect it likely, given what Roz has said, that the rebellion is being suspected. Now, this makes everything we do a little riskier, but if they don't find the culprit right away, it'll make us appear more of a threat than we already are. I can't say I'm upset about that. What's more, Chief Magistrate Forte is doing everything he can to get the disciple's murder solved. This sends a *very* clear message to people like us"—her eyes landed on Dev—"who have lost one of our own and still don't have answers."

A silence draped over the tavern like a heavy blanket, only to be replaced heartbeats later by furious muttering. Jolanda gave a grim shake of her head. Roz, though, followed Piera's gaze to Dev: He didn't appear to even be listening. His stare was fixed unblinkingly on his half-empty glass as if he wished he could drown in the brown-tinged liquid.

"You're kidding." Nasim's brows ascended, and Roz remembered Nasim and Dev hadn't been present for her earlier conversation with Piera. "After they did *nothing* about the dead boy?

About—" she cut off midsentence, and Roz knew it was because she'd been about to say *Amélie*.

There was a beat of awkward quiet, and Roz chided herself for lending to it. Amélie might be gone, but her name deserved to be said. Tiptoeing around the fact that she was dead wasn't doing anyone any favors.

"Amélie Villeneuve," Roz said firmly. "She deserves justice as much as any disciple."

That got Dev's attention. He glanced up, eyes appreciative, and lifted his chin. Roz returned the gesture. They were rebels, were they not? They spoke the names of their dead, and used their grief as ammunition. They dealt with their sadness, their anger, by fighting back.

And if Dev wasn't quite ready to do that, then Roz would do it for him.

"In the meantime," Piera continued, softer now, "I think we ought to scare the Palazzo a little more. Assuming they *don't* suspect us of the murder, security officers must be feeling fairly smug after foiling our jailbreak attempt." Her voice raised as she went on. "That's why we're going to target the Mercato the week after next. I think you'll agree it symbolizes everything wrong with this city. I don't know about you, but I'm tired of being considered expendable. When the Palazzo needs someone to fight in their wars, who do they conscript? *Us*. They don't care if we're dying on the front lines, and they clearly don't care if we're dying in our own damn city."

Roz shouted her agreement with the rest of the rebels. The collective, electric force of their anger was like a drug.

"They may have forced us to accept their saints," Piera said, "but we will *not* accept their rule. Not like this. Not when Roz's father lies headless in an early grave." She gave Roz a nod of solidarity. "Not when Nasim's brother still wakes every morning on the front lines, and when Josef barely made it back with his life." Piera exchanged a glance with each of them, too. "We are *not* expendable. And yet that's how we're being treated, both on the battlefield and off. So let's show the Palazzo we're not to be trifled with. Let's show people the rebellion has their backs." She smiled slowly and deliberately. "Let's burn the Mercato to the ground."

Josef gave a hoot, and a number of the rebels echoed him, roused by the prospect of such a brazen display of rebellion.

"Well," Nasim said once the room quieted and Piera had retreated to the back of the tavern. "That should be fun." She crossed her ankles, mouth tilting in a grin. "Dev, what do you—"

But he was already halfway to the door. His empty glass lay abandoned on the counter, and Nasim visibly wilted as he slipped outside.

"It's not you," Roz said, laying what she hoped was a comforting hand on Nasim's forearm.

Nasim's shoulders slumped, misery etched in her face. "I just feel as though I should be able to make him feel better."

"You're helping by being here for him. He just needs time."

Roz might have added something more, but abruptly a loud, nasal voice she recognized as Ernesto's carried across the tavern.

"...wonder when Piera will stop taking everything Lacertosa says as gospel," he was saying to his friend Basit, the words dripping derision. "Half the things she *overhears*"—this he emphasized with air quotes—"are probably bullshit. She probably told the Palazzo about our plan to get Frederik out of prison, and I bet she'll tell them about the Mercato plot, too." Ernesto saw Roz watching him then, and his lips curled into a grin. "She's a disciple, for fuck's sake. What are the chances she *isn't* a traitor?"

Basit and a few people nearby murmured their agreement. Roz was halfway out of her seat when Nasim grabbed her jacket. "Roz, don't. You know he's only trying to get a rise out of you. If anyone's full of shit, it's him."

With difficulty, Roz turned away. Her teeth were clenched as she met Nasim's wide brown eyes. "People believe him, though. That's the problem. Half the other rebels don't think I can be trusted."

"Piera trusts you. I trust you. Dev trusts you. You have lots of allies here—they're just not as loud."

"I know." Roz couldn't bring herself to say it simply wasn't enough. No other rebel had their loyalties questioned daily. And though she appreciated Nasim's steadfast support, she also knew her friend didn't understand. If the plan to attack the Mercato went poorly, people like Ernesto would think it her fault. If it went without a hitch, they would consider it a fluke. "I just feel like there's no winning."

"I'm sorry," Nasim said, though she was staring at Dev's abandoned glass. Roz let the subject drop. People had bigger problems than she did. There was a *murderer* stalking Ombrazia's streets, for saints' sake.

As she had the thought, ideas began to unfurl in her head. What if Amélie and the unnamed boy's deaths were somehow connected? Roz knew the boy had been found on the riverbank, but no one had said whether he actually drowned. What if, by some miracle, she could solve Amélie's murder? Maybe *both* murders? Dev could have closure. The rest of the rebels would understand once and for all that she was on their side.

"Listen," she said to Nasim, the sudden urgency in her tone making her friend's gaze snap up. "What if the deaths are connected?"

Nasim frowned. "How could they be? We don't know how Amélie was killed, but she certainly didn't drown."

"What if the boy didn't either?"

"He was found on the riverbank, Roz."

"So?" At Nasim's perplexed expression, Roz urged, "Listen. It might not be a coincidence. If I can figure out how they died—and if they *did* die the same way—there might be clues leading to their killer."

"I suppose it's a possibility."

"The disciple's new replacement will be selected this weekend, right? Selection ceremonies are always held on Sundays at the Basilica. That's where the city morgue is. It's off-limits to the public, but I should be able to sneak down there amid all the commotion. I want to take a look at the boy's body. See if I can find out whether he really did drown or not."

Nasim studied her for a long moment. Roz knew nearly everything about Nasim: She lived with her grandmother. She had a younger sister and an older brother, the latter of whom was fighting up north. She hated disciples with a passion, because they were safe while her brother wasn't. She was afraid of dying without leaving her mark on the world. She loved fiercely, but didn't trust easily. And lastly: She valued justice over all else.

"Do you think knowing who killed Amélie would help Dev?" Nasim asked, her soft voice holding a note of hope.

Roz shrugged. "Maybe. I can't see that it would make things worse."

If the morgue was locked, which it might well be, Roz was certain the hardware would have been created by a disciple of Patience. That meant it only opened at the touch of someone who'd been granted access.

Roz, obviously, was not one of those people. But since she'd made more than a few of the locks herself, she could work around it given enough time.

She hoped.

9

ROZ

Roz stood outside the Basilica as the bells chimed.

Her gaze swept the piazza over which the church towered. Voices punctuated the warm air as people swarmed a stall selling freshly caught fish, and somewhere a musician played an organetto. It was nearly dusk—always a busy time in the heart of the city.

There were entirely too many people here, Roz thought as she shoved through the crowd snaking around the exterior of the church. She wondered if Death's disciples were apprehensive about being chosen this time around, given what had happened to the last representative.

The disciples elected to the Palazzo were chosen from a pool of their most powerful peers. They then made decisions regarding policy and, along with the chief magistrate and their advisers, governed all of Ombrazia. Seven people in charge of the whole city—the six representatives plus Forte—and not a single one of them a voice for the unfavored. After the First War of Saints, when the reincarnation of Strength had conquered Chaos, it was he who'd returned to the south and established this particular system of rule. But he'd died of the plague a short time after, the first chief magistrate taking his place. It had been that way ever since.

Roz elbowed a nearby man in the ribs, clearing her path to the Basilica's entrance. The building stood in the center of Death's sector, smooth gray stone carved with artistic intricacies. An enormous archway framed the main entrance, distinguishable by its wooden doors bearing the insignia of Death's disciples: a skull with stars for eyes. Above them was a perfect rendering of the six faceless saints. One for each of the blessed guilds, with a divot in the rock where the seventh had been messily chiseled away. Their heads were bent in eternal prayer, and as always Roz tried not to look too closely at them.

She didn't trust the saints—not anymore. Her father had been right, and she wished he was still alive for her to tell him so. After all, if the city truly *was* descended from the saints, why were only some blessed with magic? And what reason did the rest of the citizens have to worship them? A true deity, Roz felt, shouldn't play favorites. As far as she was concerned, if the saints wanted her veneration, they were going to have to prove themselves worthy of it. It didn't matter if she was descended from Patience or not.

She filed into the pews with the rest of the spectators—mostly disciples. Despite herself, Roz always found it interesting to see the contrast in the different groups: disciples of Grace in their bright blue, and Strength in their typical black. Death in robes of white, and Patience in deep maroon. Mercy with their humorless expressions, and Cunning with their mischievous ones. If Roz had to guess, she would have said about a third of the population possessed magic, though most citizens worshipped the saints regardless. It was common to have statuettes of one's patron saint at home, and both the Basilica and the other smaller temples around the city were well attended by the devout. She had even seen people leave offerings at their doorsteps.

Following the ceremony, there would be only a few brief moments during which she would be able to sneak downstairs unseen. Roz wished she could have done so while the spectators arrived—it would have saved her sitting through the whole event—but whereas people had entered the Basilica in waves, they would leave all at once.

The guild leaders—those who managed the disciples' day-to-day affairs while their representatives sat in the Palazzo—stood at the front of the sanctuary. Beyond them, Chief Magistrate Forte was mounting the steps leading up to the podium.

"Good afternoon!" Forte said loudly when he reached it, clasping his hands together and scanning the audience. A sheen of sweat was visible on his brow, and if Roz hadn't known better, she might have thought it was nerves. "Thank you all for joining us today. It's been some time since the last ascension ceremony, and I know the disciples of Death have put forth some wonderful new candidates."

Roz rolled her eyes. Hardly any time had passed since the last ceremony, and everyone here knew it.

"The saints look upon us today as we send a new disciple to the Palazzo," Forte continued, glancing down at what Roz could only assume was his speech. His voice took on a lilted, bland tone as he read directly off the page. "From this day onward, they will have the honor of contributing to the governance of our city. My advisers and I will work with them to ensure we represent Ombrazia." Forte grew more serious now, gaze drifting up to the elaborate ceiling. "I know many of you have questions, and they will be answered in due course. The accident that claimed the life of a disciple this past week was merely that: an accident. Such a tragedy shall not be repeated."

He adjusted his spectacles with an unsteady hand, and Roz abruptly felt ill at ease. Did the chief magistrate know something they didn't? Was there a reason to be nervous that the rest of them weren't privy to?

"And now," Forte said, taking a breath, "the story you all know well." Atop the podium he opened what could only be a copy of *Saints and Sacrifice* and then he began to read. *"When the world was young, the sun newly alight, Strength cast his gaze upon earth and found it lacking. And so he cleaved it apart to create valleys, and willed it into the tallest of peaks."* A pause as he turned the page. *"In the heart of Strength's mountains, Patience called forth heat. It was she who created fire, and Chaos who gave it movement. But warmth was never intended to be vicious, and so to temper her impulsive lover, Patience also created rain. The rain gave life to all manner of plants and animals, which humankind might use to survive.*

"But man did not yet have the skills, so Cunning gave them knowledge, and Grace gifted them the ability to create. For many years man prospered, but prosperity does not last forever. Creation requires resources, and the earth could only give so much. So Chaos gave the people war." Hushed mutterings filled the Basilica. Roz suspected that, like her, it was the first time they'd heard someone read the story without omitting Chaos's role entirely. Forte brought his finger to his lips, then turned another page. *"Man battled for many years.*

Mercy and Death watched hand in hand, and together they built a solution. When man was injured, Mercy granted them healing and medicine. And when this was not enough, Death granted them peace. A place to rest when their time on earth was ended."

Forte looked up from the tome. "And so, today, we honor six of these saints. Strength, Patience, Grace, and Cunning, each of whom blessed us with craft. Mercy and Death, who blessed us with the deepest understanding of human life." For a breath he looked as though he might say more, but then he merely pursed his lips and beckoned over a woman Roz knew must be the leader of Death's guild.

She was tall and well built, her mouth a humorless line. She handed the chief magistrate a small leather pouch, the contents of which Forte immediately upended. Dozens of tiny slips of paper whirled through the air like pale butterflies. The audience had gone silent, and Roz watched as all but one of the papers settled to the floor. The remaining slip continued to hover in the air, dipping and twirling in wild pirouettes, until Forte reached out and snatched it.

"Salvestro Agosti," he read. The syllables echoed in the expansive space, forming a name unfamiliar to Roz. Applause rang out—first a smattering of it, then a cacophony—as a tall man rose from a pew near the front of the room. His silk suit was an obvious display of wealth, and opulent rings adorned his fingers. He looked like a man ready to embrace power. No, that wasn't exactly right; he looked like a man who *expected* it.

Roz let her mind wander for the rest of the ceremony, tuning out Forte's monotonous drawl. The discomfort was unbearable. Even if she hadn't been surrounded by disciples, she felt an impostor in places of worship. The morgue beneath the sanctuary seemed to call her, reminding her why she'd come, and she didn't hear another word about saints and sanctification.

About an hour later, commotion flared around her, and Roz realized the other spectators had begun to rise and disperse. She leapt to her feet. The rest of the crowd was focused on filing out of the Basilica, and nobody seemed to pay her any mind as she headed for the door in the back corner of the sanctuary.

She slipped through it as though she belonged, and it shut with a softly echoing *click*, sealing her in the stairwell.

Candlelit sconces illuminated the stone walls, and her shadow became a towering thing. She tiptoed down the steps, each breath a fleeting warmth that dissipated on her lips. The world was colder down here. Quieter. The air itself seemed to still, becoming a heavy weight in Roz's chest. She scurried down the hallway—turned left, then left again—until she found an open door. Behind it, she could see, was a long room of white marble.

The morgue *wasn't* locked. Or if it had been, someone was already here.

Heart clamoring in her chest, Roz peeked around the edge of the doorway. She prayed silently for the morgue to be empty as she scanned the rows of metal tables, shaking loose her inherent disgust at the sight of those holding sheet-covered bodies. It smelled like death—a sickly combination of rot and embalming fluids—but none of that was what made Roz freeze.

Someone was standing beside one of those tables. Someone both familiar and unrecognizable, whose presence had her shifting into a defensive stance. Uniformed, he cut an impressive figure: brassy regalia, red-stitched badge like a wound upon his arm, boots polished to an ink-dark sheen.

Roz's apprehension dissipated, and she strode into the morgue with a dual click of her heeled boots. "Damian."

She drew out his name, injecting venom into the syllables, though seeing him again felt like a punch to the gut. Of *course* he had access to the morgue. But what in the world was he doing here?

Damian stiffened, staring at her as though she were a ghost. Then he caught himself, and his face shuttered, a shadow passing over it. To anyone else he might have looked threatening, but Roz wasn't afraid. In her boots she was nearly as tall as him, and his broad shoulders suggested he relied more on strength than agility. She was struck all over again by how different he was from the boy she'd known. The boy she'd chased through the streets and kissed in the dark, once upon a time.

But the main reason she didn't run was written in the lines of his face. If he'd looked exhausted the other day, he looked half dead now. "Rossana."

"It's Roz, as you well know. *Officer.*"

Damian looked uncomfortable. Good. He came to stand in front of the metal table, blocking the body with his own. "Why do you say it like that?"

"Like what?"

"Like it's a dirty word."

Roz only smiled sweetly, and Damian's tired face contorted in a scowl. The look didn't suit him. Almost every memory Roz had of Damian was smiles, one of his incisors slightly, charmingly, crooked. Now, though, she found it difficult to imagine he ever smiled at all. He was the picture-perfect soldier, the archibugio strapped across his back complimenting his expression of distaste. Would he shoot her, Roz wondered, if she dared him? Would he kill with his father's ease, and be glad of her absence?

Roz could scarcely believe there had been a time when she'd begged him not to leave her. A time when she'd clutched one of those veined hands close to her chest and thought, with unshakeable certainty, that Damian Venturi felt so very much like home.

"What the hell are you doing here?" he demanded, crossing his arms and widening his stance. Suspicion twitched at the corners of his unsmiling lips.

Saints, he sounded like Battista when he took that cool, commanding tone. Roz's blood heated. How she longed to part General Venturi's head from his shoulders, and watch Damian's composure falter when she delivered it to *his* doorstep. "I could ask you the same thing."

"Just answer the question."

"Call it academic interest."

He shifted his weight, dark gaze narrowing. "You're a poor liar, Rossana."

Roz closed the distance between them in three swift strides. "I'm an excellent liar," she said, feeling the current of acrimony that pulsed between them, not missing the way Damian's hand twitched toward his archibugio. Bitterness made her rash, and she leaned closer, putting her lips by his ear. He smelled of amber and mint, of childhood and broken hearts. "And *don't*," she added, "call me Rossana."

Damian jerked away. His lips parted as if to frame a retort, but he seemed to think better of it. "I could arrest you for trespassing," he said instead. "You know the morgue isn't open to the public."

"You could," Roz agreed. "But something tells me you're not supposed to be here either."

His nostrils flared, and for a moment they simply stared at

one another, locked in a resentful impasse. It had been a guess on Roz's part, albeit an educated one. Even now she could read Damian like a book. She knew the way he stood just a little too still when he was hiding something. Recognized the tilt to his mouth that signified guilt.

"Unlike you, I have the authority to be here," he said.

"Maybe. But that doesn't mean you *should* be." Roz cocked a brow, waiting.

There was a pause. When Damian's response came, it was short.

"I'm trying to solve a murder. Multiple murders, in fact."

Now this was interesting to Roz. "Surely you don't mean the two unfavored found dead recently. Shouldn't you be focused on finding the disciple's killer? I hear that's a priority matter."

His nostrils flared. "I have reason to believe they might be connected."

"And what reason is that?"

"None of your concern."

Roz tossed her ponytail over one shoulder, frustration smoldering in the pit of her stomach. "It is, actually. You see, I'd like to know who's murdering people in the streets. Especially since the Palazzo isn't inclined to do a damned thing about it."

Something slammed into place behind Damian's eyes, lending them a distinct coldness. He worked his jaw. Tugged at the tight collar of his uniform. "Regardless of what you might think, I'm not like my superiors. I want justice for everyone who's died. Not just disciples."

"Do you, though?" Roz said, icily soft. "Do you want justice for my father, the man who treated you like his own son? What about my mother, who opened the door for the morning paper and found his head in a box?"

Damian went very still. The coldness melted away, and the column of his throat shifted as he swallowed. "I didn't—I didn't know know about that."

Her answering snort was so loud it echoed off the morgue walls. "Right."

"Rossana, I'm not lying to you."

"Really? So there was a *different* reason I never heard from you after my father's death?"

Silence.

"That's what I thought." Roz snarled a laugh. "Save it, Venturi. Why don't you tell me what you've learned, instead?"

Damian made a disbelieving sound in the back of his throat. "Excuse me?"

She gestured at the body beside which he was hovering. The sheet had been cast back, revealing the bloated, graying flesh of a young man's face. "This is the boy they discovered on the riverbank, right? Do you know how he died?"

"Rossana, if you think I'm going to divulge the details of a Palazzo investigation—"

"We both know the Palazzo doesn't care about this boy's death," Roz snapped before she could stop herself. "You were told not to bother with him, weren't you? That's why you looked so guilty when I came in." At his rueful expression, she added, "Let me help you, and I won't tell a soul."

She hated Damian, but she knew he wasn't lying when he said he wanted justice for the dead. That was simply the type of person Damian was, even if his honorable intentions hadn't extended to her father. She could *use* him. Could use his privileged information and the ease of access that came with his uniform. He wasn't in this morgue by accident: He had a lead. One that, for some reason, he wasn't supposed to be following. That was why he was here rather than in the Palazzo crypt, where the disciple's body would certainly have been taken.

Roz had that much on him, regardless of how often he threatened to arrest her.

Besides, Damian wasn't the only one who wanted justice. Roz wanted it too, and she wanted it *more*. For Amélie. For Dev. For everyone deemed unimportant in this city.

She wanted the justice her father had deserved.

"Why would I let you help me?" Damian said, skepticism punctuating the words.

"First," Roz held up a finger, "I have sources your government men don't. Being a disciple, and being a security officer… They both get you different kinds of access. You'll do better with my help." She paused, careful not to reveal too much. "And second, because of what I just said. You let me help you—telling me *everything* you learn—and I don't get you fired."

"That's blackmail."

"It's a bargain."

Damian stared at her for a long moment, some inscrutable emotion tugging at the corners of his mouth. Down here, the shadows carved out hollows beneath his cheekbones, and Roz was forcibly reminded of someone trapped in time. All his mannerisms were familiar, associated with the boy of her youth, but connected to the face and body of a man who had already seen too much.

"You owe me," Roz hissed, her voice barely audible. "You *owe* me."

Damian's expression fractured. They both knew she wasn't only talking about the circumstances surrounding her father's death. He owed Roz for what happened afterward, when he'd chosen sides with his silence. The silence that had stretched for months and *months*, until the day Roz saw him on patrol in Patience's temple, and realized with a jolt that he hadn't told her he was returning. Hadn't told her he was alive at all, in fact.

How could she forgive him that?

"I really don't understand why this is so important to you," Damian said, equally softly. "But fine, Rossana. You have yourself a deal."

10

DAMIAN

Each beat of Damian's heart sent guilt flooding through him. He watched as Roz examined her flawless nails, then lifted her gaze to recapture his. Those blue-gray eyes were damning.

I'm sorry, he should have said. *I'm sorry you didn't hear from me when I knew you would be expecting to. I'm sorry I allowed you to suffer alone. I'm sorry I didn't tell you I was coming back, or that I was still alive. There was too much of me that felt I didn't deserve to be.*

His pride didn't allow him to say any of it.

Damian knew he had done everything wrong. Telling Roz as much wouldn't change that—not when she was so clearly determined to hate him.

He knew better than to think Roz didn't have some sort of plan up her sleeve. She was always scheming. Coming up with ways to win. When they were young, he hadn't minded, mainly because he loved to see the pure glee on her face every time she bested him at something. Seeing her smile, perhaps even feeling her lips against his cheek, had been far more satisfying than winning.

He was just so *conflicted*. Jacopo Lacertosa should never have been so willing to abandon his fellow soldiers, but that didn't mean Damian had wanted him dead. And if what Roz said was true, and her father's head really had shown up on her doorstep... Well, that was another level of horrific. He couldn't imagine Battista had condoned it.

Furthermore, what did she *want*? To solve the murders, obviously, but why? There had to be reasons she hadn't told him.

"Excellent." Roz's voice speared through his thoughts, and it took Damian a beat to recall that she must be referring to their deal. She extended a hand.

He stared at it, knowing his hesitation was obvious. Roz tensed, the tendril of hair that had come loose from her ponytail brushing her jaw. He yearned to sweep it away. To skim his knuckles against the curve of her cheek and whisper apologies in her ear until he went hoarse.

Instead, Damian took her hand. It felt tiny in his grasp, cool and smooth. Less familiar than he might have thought. Roz wrenched it away the second they'd shaken.

"Okay. Here's how this is going to go. We don't have to be friends—in fact, I'd rather offer myself up to the killer as bait." She glared unblinkingly at him. "We'll try to find the culprit, and in the meantime keep an ear out for any other suspicious deaths. Should one occur, you bring me with you to the scene. We tell each other everything we learn, and share any ideas we come up with. Once we have a suspect, you use your fancy Palazzo resources to ensure they get what they deserve, and then we can go back to never interacting again."

Damian chewed that over. "Fine," he said eventually. "But we're doing things my way."

"What's that supposed to mean?"

"It means we're going to be smart about it."

"Who's to say my way isn't smart?"

He waited, unamused, until Roz capitulated with a furious sigh.

"*Fine*. Tell me then, Officer Venturi, genius among men— what's our first course of action?"

Damian tugged the sheet covering the dead boy farther down, revealing mottled arms and a torso. He'd been examining the body before she arrived. "Well first of all, this victim didn't drown."

Roz gagged at the stench. Neither the cold nor the preservatives chased it away entirely. "How do you know?"

"See those dark lines on the skin? That's not decay." Damian pointed without touching them. "It's poison. The dead disciple's body had the same markings."

Roz grimaced. "I assumed that was some type of...postmortem phenomenon. You know, blood coagulating in the veins, or something like that."

"I didn't realize you knew so much about medicine."

"I don't. We learned a bit at the temple, though. Just the basics."

Right. He'd nearly forgotten she would have been subject to some sort of training. It was still strange to think of Roz as a disciple. "I was surprised, you know," Damian said, "to find out you were blessed. I still remember the day we were tested."

Roz visibly stiffened, the column of her spine straightening. She leaned away from the body, glaring at Damian as though he'd committed some cardinal sin by bringing up the past. "I don't want to talk about that."

"Why not? It's amazing. It's like Patience realized she ought to have given you magic and rectified her mistake."

Maybe he was wrong to allow that note of wonder into his voice, because Roz tensed even further. "Yes, yes. A fucking miracle, and all that."

Damian didn't quite know what to make of her anger. "I'd give anything to be blessed," he said softly. "Anything to know the saints cared about me."

"You think it means the saints *care* about me?" Roz gave a laugh that couldn't have been less genuine. "Yes, I've been feeling *very* blessed. Besides the murdered father, and all that." She shook her head in bitter bemusement. "Anyway, I said I don't want to talk about it. What was the poison? That killed the disciple, I mean."

If whiplash could be a person, Damian thought Roz might just fit the bill. Her response had intrigued him, but since it was clear she would entertain no further questions, he answered hers. "No idea."

"Helpful."

Damian ignored her jibe. "I don't see a connection between the victims. And yet..." He bent over the corpse, careful not to breathe in, and peeled back one of the boy's eyelids.

Roz bit down on a gasp, recoiling. "What the *hell* is that?"

Where there should have been a fleshy orb, there was only opaque black. The boy's eyes had been replaced with something that looked like shards of obsidian. Damian had suspected as much upon seeing the ink-dark pathways of the poison, and he hadn't quite decided whether he was happy or not to be right. A heaviness seemed to settle on his chest. He could feel the comparable weight of Roz watching him, gauging his reaction. It was foolish, the fact that he was comforted by her presence. It made the creeping cold of the morgue less oppressive. She had always been a light, but now she was a veritable fire: the chocolate spill of her hair gleaming in the sconce flame, the jut of her collarbones sharpening as she crossed her arms.

She was distracting enough that he barely cringed as he hooked a finger into the boy's eye socket. The orb came free with a horrible squelching noise, and Roz watched, vaguely disgusted, as he pocketed the thing. Despite the frigid temperature of the corpse, it was oddly warm.

"The disciple's eyes were replaced as well," Damian said in response to her unasked question. "We're definitely dealing with the same killer, then."

"So it's true," Roz said, a little eagerly. "These deaths…they're all connected."

Had the female victim been poisoned too, her eyes also removed? It was impossible to know, since she was already buried. But if the same person had killed both the disciple and the nameless boy, it certainly seemed a possibility. Damian almost said as much, then caught himself. It was, after all, mere conjecture.

"I can't confirm that."

"That's such a security officer thing to say," she scoffed. "Just admit I'm probably right."

A relatively new part of him—a part, certainly, that hadn't existed when they were younger—bristled at her tone. "Remember when you agreed to do this my way? We need evidence before I admit anything of the sort."

The eagerness died in Roz's eyes, something cold and hard slamming down to replace it. *Ah.* That was why Damian had so rarely argued with her. He pressed his lips together, stopping himself from uttering the apology he knew she wasn't owed.

He was braced for a scathing retort, but Roz only said crisply, "Let's find some evidence, then."

Lucky for her, Damian knew exactly where to start.

"I need to know if any disciples of Death got to the bodies in time to do a reading," Damian explained to Roz as they headed back into the Basilica's sanctuary, led by what little light streamed in from the narrow windows high above their head. "It's not likely, seeing as nothing was reported, but…"

Roz finished for him. "But it's possible they didn't think it important enough to report, because who cares about the unfavored, right?"

Her voice was falsely cheerful, and it was enough to bring Damian to a halt at the door to the sanctuary. He turned in one smooth motion, finding her closer than he'd anticipated. They locked gazes. Roz lifted a defiant chin, and Damian fought the urge to take it in his hand.

"You can stop trying to taunt me, Rossana. I already told you—we're on the same side. I don't want *anyone* dead. I don't want anyone else in danger, either. You can think whatever the hell you want about me, but I'm not a monster."

The words came out more fervently than he'd meant them to, even as the last few snagged in his throat. Could he truly say he wasn't a monster?

Hell, he hoped he wasn't a monster.

Roz's full lips parted. Then, cutting as ever, she said, "It sounds as though I'm not the one you're trying to convince, Venturi."

Even now, she read him far too easily.

Ignoring the way his hand shook on the door handle, Damian turned away from her and shoved it open. The sanctuary had mostly emptied, but a few disciples still milled among the pews, their guild leaders congregated at the front of the room like saints in their own right. The chief magistrate, Damian noticed, was already gone. Depictions of the saints surrounded by various flora and fauna covered the walls and the ceiling—*frescoes*, Siena had told him they were called, because she knew more about art than he did. The piece that caught Damian's eye was of Death, a veil covering her face and a skull in her right hand. Even featureless, she managed to convey an air of cool judgment.

As an officer, he had learned never to let your subject walk behind you. You kept them where you could see them. Perhaps that was why he felt so unsettled, walking toward the pulpit knowing Roz was on his heels. Or perhaps it was the near silence of her footsteps, an incomprehensible feat given her heeled boots. Regardless, his spine was stiff as he navigated the space, his shoulders relaxing only when they reached Mariana Novak—the guild leader who'd handed Forte the pouch of disciple names—and Roz drew up beside him.

"Let me do the talking," he growled to her, and she shot him a withering look that he chose to interpret as agreement.

Mariana was in quiet conversation with a man Damian didn't recognize. She broke off when Damian approached, nodding in grave acknowledgment before bidding her companion wait for her outside. Mariana was a beautiful woman of around fifty, curvy and round-featured, but as serious as her expression suggested. She'd been a respected Palazzo representative in her younger days, and now had taken on the role of guild leader, which meant she over-saw her guild's day-to-day functions. Damian knew her smiles to be rare, and was unsurprised when he wasn't offered one.

"Officer," Mariana said, recognizing Damian at once. "We meet again." Her hazel eyes snapped to Roz. "And you are—?"

"She's assisting me with some elements of my current investigation," Damian said smoothly before Roz could respond. "Would you mind answering a few questions, Signora?"

He heard Roz's huff as Mariana beckoned them away from the other disciples, out of earshot. It struck him as fruitless—surely anyone else would guess the topic of their conversation—but he followed her politely nonetheless. Gray-tinged sunlight filtered into the sanctuary as clouds outside the window shifted, illuminating a section of the stone floor.

"As I'm sure you're well aware," Damian said, getting down to business without needing to be prompted, "Lilah wasn't able to glean anything from Leonzio's body."

Mariana's mouth tightened at the mention of the disciple Enzo had brought from Death's temple the night of Leonzio's murder. "I take it he had been dead too long."

Damian nodded. Disciples of Death could make contact with the souls of the dead, could apparently see images of their last moments, provided those souls hadn't already fled. "Approximately six hours."

"Hmm," Mariana intoned. "Frankly, I'm not sure what help you think I can offer you, then."

"The other bodies," Roz cut in before Damian could stop her. Her voice was hard, her stance unflinching. "The two unfavored who were found dead. Were any of your disciples able to read them?"

Now Mariana looked uncomfortable. "No."

Damian shot Roz a glare, hoping she could feel the heat of his displeasure. He ought to have known she wouldn't be able to keep her mouth shut. To Mariana he explained, "We're wondering if the recent deaths might be connected. It's only a theory—one that doesn't leave this conversation. Do I make myself clear?"

He wondered if it was the first time anyone had dared speak to Mariana so. She appeared taken aback, and then something in her face twisted. But she only said, "Yes."

"She's lying," Roz said without ceremony, and Damian turned to face her.

"What?"

"When I asked if her disciples were able to read the bodies. There's something she's not telling us."

Mariana glared at Roz, affronted. Roz glared back. Damian prayed for one of the saints to smite him where he stood.

"Signora, please forgive her," he said to Mariana, and no sooner had he spoken then did something like guilt flit across her face. Hell below. She *was* lying, wasn't she? Roz was right, and now he would never hear the end of it. "You are, however, required to answer my questions honestly."

Mariana went very still. When she spoke, her voice was no longer cool, but edged and precise. "I cannot share guild secrets, even with you."

"Well, start now," Roz said, too pleasantly.

Damian held up a hand, bidding them both be silent. "*Enough.* Signora, if you know something, you must tell me. All of Ombrazia may be in danger. And trust me, the last thing I want to do is detain you for interrogation." It wasn't a lie. It would look bad, taking a guild leader into custody. He wasn't sure Forte would support it, even for the sake of the case.

So his relief was palpable when Mariana squared her shoulders and said, "Very *well*, Officer. If you must know, we cannot read a body without eyes."

"What?" Damian and Roz said in unison.

She sighed. "We read a body through flesh memory. Before a soul departs, there's a short window during which those memories linger for the taking. Without the eyes, although we may still be able to make contact, it's impossible to see what happened. For obvious reasons."

Damian felt his mouth twist. It made sense once you thought about it, but he never would have guessed. "Why doesn't every murderer remove the eyes, then?"

"I told you, it's a guild secret," Mariana snapped back. Then she wilted, suddenly looking very small in the large room. "Nobody's supposed to know, or every murderer *would* do it. Whoever killed those people must be close to one of our members."

That wasn't quite where Damian's mind was. *No*, he wanted to say. *I'd say it means that whoever killed those people* was *a disciple of Death*. Watching Roz's mouth twist in vague amusement, he would have bet she was thinking the same. "Well, you have the Palazzo's thanks, Signora. You'll be one of the first to know when we learn anything else."

Mariana gave an impatient nod, murmuring vague niceties before sidling away from them.

"Well," Damian said. He ran a hand through his hair, releasing a breath. "That certainly was interesting."

Roz didn't answer. She merely smiled, and it was all teeth.

11

DAMIAN

Roz looked like a dream, silhouetted by the gold-tinged dusk outside the Basilica.

It was hard to believe she was real. That she was brilliant and tangible, not a memory or a figure in the distance. Emotions warred in Damian every time he looked at her, clawing his chest apart from the inside. He wondered what was going on in her head. Her expression was neutral as they drew up to the street, the mournful sound of an organetto still echoing somewhere in the near distance. It was strange, knowing she hated him. Damian had expected her to, of course, but it hit differently when he was staring her in the face.

And then there was the knowledge that, if he was only honest with her, he could make her hate him more.

Damian wondered if this version of Roz would kill him.

No sooner had the question crossed his mind then did she strike, turning to position herself in front of him. Her next question was a poisonous barb seeking skin.

"Did you really not know about my father?" Roz forced his gaze to hold her guarded one, ponytail lashing against her shoulder in the wind. "What happened to him after, I mean."

Damian went rigid. She wondered if he was lying about not knowing Jacopo Lacertosa had been beheaded. He wasn't, but what did it matter? It wasn't as though she'd believe him. With her hands on her hips and an edge to her voice, she was out for blood, not reconciliation.

"I was on the front lines when I found out," Damian told her finally. "That he'd deserted, I mean, and that he'd been killed for it. I didn't know my father had given the order, but..." He trailed off, shaking his head. Frustration took root in his stomach. "Everyone knows what happens when you try to leave, Rossana. Do you think your father was special? That he should have been excused from having to fight? The rest of us didn't want to be there, either. We woke up every single day and faced death. On the particularly bad days, we woke up and *hoped* for it. But we stayed, and we fought, and we watched our friends die. Because it was what we'd been ordered to do, and we sure as hell weren't going to abandon them in the northern mud."

He said all this very quickly, surprised by the intensity of his own vitriol. The thoughts had been there for quite some time, he realized—he'd just never said them aloud. And perhaps he shouldn't have, forced as he was to watch as Roz's brief understanding gave way to fury.

"Did I think my father was *special*? No. I think he was a man trapped by a system that treated him as expendable. Did you ever look around, up there in that northern mud, and wonder where the fuck all the disciples were?"

"Rossana, *you're* a disciple!"

"Well spotted," she spat. "Doesn't it bother you? Doesn't it make you angry that you had to go to war while people like me stayed home, safe and comfortable? That you, too, were deemed expendable? Just like my father, you didn't have a choice." She scrutinized Damian witheringly. "Right?"

Of course he hadn't had a choice. Battista was an army commander. A disciple of Strength, at that. "I did what my father asked of me."

Roz shook her head slowly, incredulously. "Saints, Damian. How do you get through life being so utterly *passive*?"

He chose to ignore that, though something twinged beneath his rib cage. "Why do you care so much? You said it yourself— you'll never have to worry about being drafted."

"You don't have to be part of the group being mistreated to know what's happening to them is wrong."

"I'm surprised you care what happens to anyone at all."

He said it harshly, the words intended to cut, but Roz didn't falter. Her lips pulled back over her teeth. "My father was murdered for deserting. In cold blood. Just because I'm unlikely to share his fate doesn't mean I'm *over* it. You don't get over shit like that, Venturi. You should know."

There was a silence. Damian swallowed, hard. "I do know."

"Good." Roz stared at him for a moment, as though she might say more. But then she seemed to think better of it, turned on her heel, and was gone.

Not so much as a *good night*, and frankly Damian hadn't expected one. He only stood there, reeling in the aftershock of her fury.

The moment she disappeared from view, though, he followed her.

Darkness unfurled across the sky as Damian tracked Roz's lean shadow toward the river. The water was wild, the wind coaxing it to lash against the rocks. A light sweat broke out on Damian's skin, tracing a line down his temple, and he found himself shoving his sleeves up. A few unfavored citizens passed him, not even bothering to conceal their fear. He didn't miss the way they pressed as close as they could to the edge of the walkway, then scurried down the nearest side street as if expecting to be arrested on the spot.

Damian had grown accustomed to that reaction. Security officers existed to defend Ombrazia and the disciples before all else. Despite military higher-ups—like Battista—being disciples themselves, regular officers were often unfavored. Protecting the saints' chosen was as close as they would ever get to divinity. It was an honor. But though Damian hated to admit it, not all officers exercised their authority in good faith. Upon being promoted, his first course of action had been to fire those he perceived were doing the job for the wrong reasons. That said, he still couldn't blame people for being wary.

Roz appeared to be taking a shortcut through the outskirts, which were more miserable than Damian remembered. Children too young to be unsupervised ran barefoot across the stones, or stared wide-eyed from the shadows. Windows were boarded up, and the air held the distinct tang of smoke. Someone had painted a phrase in dripping crimson on the side of a crumbling building: *In loco hoc moriemur.*

This is where we die.

A woman in a tattered skirt leapt in front of Damian to snatch one of the frolicking children. He expected her to avoid eye contact, but she looked directly at him, something like hope in her tired face.

"Are we finally getting security here?" she asked in a hoarse voice, barely audible over the sound of her child's disgruntled screeching.

Damian didn't miss the way she angled her body away from him. For a heartbeat he wasn't sure how to respond. "I—no. I mean, not that I know of, Signora—?"

"Just Bianca," she murmured.

"Bianca, then." He glanced past her to the end of the road just as Roz broke into a run. "My apologies. I'm here on other matters, and I really must be going."

The woman's expression fell, and Damian gave an apologetic nod before skirting her. He wouldn't have thought the unfavored would *want* security. Perhaps the murders had rattled people more than he'd realized.

Damian continued to follow Roz, willing his boots not to make a sound on the uneven cobblestones. His exhausted body protested at the exertion. He'd barely slept since Leonzio's death, only managing to catch a few hours here and there. When he did sleep, he dreamt of blood and death and the north. What was he doing, racing through the streets like a common criminal, when he could have returned to the Palazzo to unwind? He ought to have grabbed Roz and demanded to know the real reason she wanted the murders solved. But that would only infuriate her, and arguing with Roz was like trying to navigate a boat across choppy seas: dangerous and unpredictable.

He was relieved when Roz led him to Patience's sector. She passed the temple, rounded a corner, and hurried down a side street. In a moonlit intersection at the end of the road, Roz came to a sudden halt before a small apartment building. She scanned the street in both directions, ponytail swinging behind her like a whip. Almost as if she knew someone was following her. Damian's heart gave a jolt. He ducked behind an exterior stairwell, peering through a crack between two steps until ascertaining she hadn't spotted him.

Then, to his surprise, Roz gripped the stone wall above her head and began to climb.

Damian stepped out of his hiding place and squinted up at her. She had clearly done this before: Her movements were quick, hand placements deft. He watched as she pulled herself around the side of the building and swung through a second-story window.

What in the world?

Damian approached the building, craning his neck to peer up the wall. What now? He couldn't very well follow her inside. For a moment he paced in a circle, unsure what to do, but when his pacing took him beneath the open window he heard Roz's voice.

"I'm fine. Everything is fine." Her tone was soothing, clear as day.

A woman responded, speaking too low for Damian to catch. He could tell she was crying, though, and he pressed more firmly against the wall.

"No," Roz was saying. "Just eat, please. Piera made it." A pause. "I *know*. But I'm busy." Her voice changed, turning harsher, as if she'd erected an emotional barrier between herself and whomever she was speaking to. "You have to trust me, mamma."

Roz was talking to her *mother*? Damian hadn't realized Caprice

Lacertosa still lived in the city. He'd never seen her around—never even heard her name mentioned. He certainly wouldn't have guessed Roz still lived with her. Roz was too...independent. Unrestrained. The woman Damian remembered would never have allowed her daughter to run around on her own. In fact, a number of his childhood memories were permeated by the sound of Caprice yelling at them to *be more careful.* Perhaps that was why she and Roz were arguing.

Except Damian couldn't imagine Caprice crying. Not for the life of him. She had always been stoic and confident, a little intimidating. Just like her daughter.

Spurred by sudden curiosity, he curled his fingers into the spaces between rocks and hefted himself up the wall. It was difficult—more so than Roz had made it look—but he managed to maneuver his body over to the window as she had. Transferring his grip to the ledge, he executed a kind of modified pull-up, muscles quivering as he peered into the apartment.

Roz's back was to him, hands on her hips. She appeared to be addressing the woman sitting at the far end of a worn dining table. The woman's face was gaunt and lined, her wispy hair pulled into a haphazard knot. There was a blank quality to her gaze, as though she hadn't slept in many days. Where was Caprice?

The woman lifted her gaze to the window. When her familiar blue eyes met Damian's, she opened her mouth and screamed.

Damian let himself fall, heart beating wildly with a combination of adrenaline and horror, and he understood. He pressed his sweaty back to the wall beneath the ledge, letting himself slump against it as Roz's voice drifted outside.

"There's no one there, mamma. You're imagining things again."

Again. As though it were commonplace for Caprice to see people who weren't there. Damian put his head in his hands as Roz's earlier words came back to him.

And my mother and I deserved it when we opened the door for the morning paper and found his head in a box?

This was why she was so furious, wasn't it? She'd lost not only her father but her mother, too. That hunched, lifeless woman upstairs was nothing like the Caprice Damian remembered. Under any other circumstances, he wouldn't have recognized her at all.

Another question rose unbidden to his mind, one he didn't want to look at too closely. Had his father really given the order for Jacopo Lacertosa to be killed in such a barbaric way? The Venturi family had known the Lacertosas for years. Battista and Jacopo had been friends even before Battista became a disciple. When Jacopo first got drafted nearly two decades ago, Battista had opted to go north with him. A rare choice. Upon getting promoted, however, Battista's duty had to trump his friendships.

Once Damian had admired his father for being able to put his job first. But if Battista could have Jacopo tracked down and killed, who was to say he hadn't sent Caprice her husband's head?

For a long moment he stood lost in thought, an unquenchable horror gnawing at his insides, his finger running over the black sphere in his pocket.

He needed to speak to Battista.

DAMIAN

The whole way back to the Palazzo, Damian distracted himself from thoughts of Roz by remembering what Mariana had said.

Her information only served to make things more confusing. The murderer stalking Ombrazia's streets had known removing their victims' eyes would make them unreadable to a disciple of Death. Logic indicated, then, that the murderer likely *was* a disciple of Death. In which case they would have known Leonzio, which suggested his murder had been personal. But what about the other two victims? What reason would a disciple have had to kill them?

It simply didn't make sense. Other than the manner in which they'd been killed, Damian couldn't see anything that connected the victims at all.

He dragged himself to the weaponry, where the night shift

would be getting geared up. Indeed, as he passed the rows of polished boots and archibugios, he saw Kiran, Siena, and a handful of other officers chatting in the dim light. Kiran paused midway through stowing a pistola in his belt, glancing up at Damian's approach.

The other officers quieted. Even Noemi, who Damian knew was still offended by his questioning of her the other day. She crossed her arms, staring at him expectantly.

"Evening, all," he said, keeping his voice pitched low. "I'm sure by now you're aware Death's new representative is in the Palazzo—Salvestro Agosti. Obviously he won't be staying in Leonzio's rooms, so he's been given a suite just down the hall from the disciple of Mercy. I want extra patrols of that corridor at night. Anything strange, you report it to me at once. I don't care if I'm off duty. Do I make myself clear?"

Heads nodded.

"Good. Noemi and Kiran, you're at the main doors. Matteo and Siena, the grounds. Everyone else, decide among yourselves which areas of the building you're going to take. I frankly don't care who's where." Damian ran an agitated hand through his hair before dismissing them, placing his archibugio in the nearest rack. From the corner of his eye he saw Enzo stroll into the room, as he always did around this time of night, to wipe down the weapons.

Perfect. Damian beckoned Enzo over, not realizing Siena was already at his side until she spoke.

"Where've you been, Venturi?"

Kiran detached himself from Noemi's side across the room, coming over to join the conversation. He reached them at the same time Enzo did, and Damian was suddenly, unpleasantly aware that he had three pairs of eyes trained on him.

"What?" He stifled a yawn. "You all need to stop looking at me like that."

Siena pointed at her own face. "This, Venturi, is called *concern*. You know you're allowed to sleep, right?"

"I'll remember that, now that I've gotten your permission."

This he said good-naturedly, but Enzo's brows shot up from where he leaned against a tall cabinet, Kiran at his side. He often hung around the officers when they were off duty, and looked as comfortable here as the rest of them. "Did you go to the selection ceremony?"

"I did," Damian said, gratefully latching on to the explanation. He'd nearly forgotten about the ceremony itself—it felt as though it had happened days ago. Everything in his recent memory was *Roz, Roz, Roz.* "It was fairly boring. Nothing unusual. Well, apart from Forte," he frowned, remembering that particular fact. "He was a bit...off."

"Off how?" Kiran asked, but Enzo interrupted.

"Never mind Forte. What's the new representative like?"

Damian shrugged. "I didn't speak to him. He certainly seemed confident, though. I think he'll be a good fit."

Siena nodded. Kiran, though, said, "And the murder? Have you learned anything more about it?"

Damian checked to ensure no one else was listening; the rest of the officers, he saw, were already filing out of the armory to head to their respective positions. "I spoke to the leader of Death's guild after the ceremony. She told me something that makes me think the murderer might be one of Death's disciples."

He left out the part where he went to the morgue and ran into Roz. The part where he'd decided to solve all three of the murders, despite what his father had said.

"What did she say?" Enzo asked, eyes wide with interest.

Damian trusted the three people before him more than anyone else in the Palazzo, but he wasn't sure he should tell them. Not if it was meant to be a guild secret. "I can't say quite yet. I'm more hopeful than I was yesterday, though."

"That's something," Siena agreed. "Are you going to talk to her again?"

"I suppose I'll need to, but I have to go about it delicately. I don't want to offend an entire guild." Damian made a helpless gesture with both hands. "Speaking of which, how did questioning the rest of the staff go?"

"Fine." Kiran shrugged wearily, Siena mirroring him. "With Noemi and Matteo's help, we managed to get through everyone who remained. Our notes are on your desk. None of them struck us as overly suspicious, though. They're all just frightened."

"Great," Damian sighed. He almost hoped the murder was an inside job, if only so that he could track down the culprit more quickly. "Well, thanks for doing that. Sorry I wasn't around today."

Kiran waved his apology away. "We didn't need you. And I mean that in the nicest of ways."

"Sure you do." Damian couldn't help letting one side of his mouth tilt up in a grin. "Anyway, you two had best get going. Noemi and Matteo will be waiting."

Siena nodded, giving his arm a squeeze. "*Sleep.* And if you ever need to talk to someone, you know where to find me." She released him, making her way to the door through which Kiran had just disappeared.

"Siena?" Damian said, and she turned.

"Yeah?"

"The same goes for you."

She blinked at him. Then she smiled, a tight-lipped, sad little grin. It was a grin of mutual understanding.

"Thanks, Damian."

He watched her go, kicking himself for thinking for one second that the war hadn't affected her the way it had him. They were all just doing their best, weren't they?

"It sounds like you're getting somewhere, at least," Enzo said, cutting through Damian's epiphany. He hoisted himself onto one of the weapons tables, leaning back so that his hair brushed the wall. "Is there anything I can do to help?"

"Actually, there is." Damian's station might have been far higher than Enzo's, but he didn't have the kind of access Enzo did. Serving boys could go anywhere in the Palazzo without being questioned. Even when seen, they were largely ignored. "I've been wanting to speak with you."

Enzo straightened, looking at him in worried curiosity. "About what?"

Damian waved his concern away. "My father thinks I should be asking someone in the Palazzo—someone who's *not* an officer—to keep an eye out for anything unusual. I know a lot goes on that I can't see, and seeing as I trust you…"

He trailed off; Enzo was already nodding as though he knew precisely what Damian was trying to ask of him. "Of course I can do that. I mean," he added, "I already am, to an extent. Keeping my eyes open, that is. It's hard not to."

"Fair enough." Damian chuckled weakly, then sighed. "Thanks. I appreciate it." He thought of Leonzio lying motionless in the candlelight. Of the frigid crypt air twisting his lungs. "Be careful, though."

"Always am," Enzo said, but he wilted a bit, the soft curve of his jaw tightening. "You know, this is going to sound pathetic, but I hate thinking it might not be safe here. This is the only home I have."

Damian gave a slow nod of his head. "It doesn't sound pathetic." He knew Enzo's parents were out of the picture; he had asked about them before and gotten a rather noncommittal answer. After that, Damian hadn't wanted to pry. But he understood the sentiment Enzo spoke of now—the Palazzo was his only home, too. Shortly after arriving back in Ombrazia, he'd walked by his childhood house purely out of nostalgic interest, and realized there was a new family living there. He shouldn't have been surprised. Roz's house, too, was occupied by someone else. But it had still made him ache in places he couldn't name.

"I'll help however I can," Enzo said. "Just say the word."

"Thanks." Damian meant it, though the word was heavy in his mouth. He dragged a hand down the side of his face. "Forte made it clear it's on me to find Leonzio's killer, or he'll send me back to the north."

Enzo winced. "I'm sure he's bluffing."

"I suppose I'll find out."

"Hopefully it doesn't come to that."

They were both silent a moment, separately introspective. Damian's mind was back on Roz. He'd planned to reexamine Leonzio's room tomorrow, just to see if there was anything he'd missed— perhaps he ought to invite her along. To show her he was willing to take this partnership seriously. Besides, she was a disciple, and sometimes they could pick up on things a regular person couldn't.

"You know," Damian said abruptly, "there is something else you could do to help me. If you wanted."

Enzo fixed him with an inquisitive gaze, lashes shadowing his dark eyes. "Sure."

Damian went over to a stack of supplies in the corner of the armory, shoving bits of parchment around until he procured a clean sheet and a pen.

The Shrine. Tomorrow. 1900 hours, he wrote messily. *Don't be late.*

Roz would know who it was from. Surely she remembered his penmanship. After all, Damian remembered hers. Just in case, though, he added a *D* to the bottom of the page. Then he folded it in half and handed it to Enzo.

"There are some old apartment buildings in Patience's sector, four blocks west of the temple," Damian said. "It's right across from the river, with a black door and a few missing shutters. Do you think... Would you mind delivering this message there? Don't knock; just shove it through the mail slot. It's not a sensitive matter," he added, because Enzo appeared vaguely bewildered. "It's personal."

"Oh." Enzo cracked a smile as understanding crept across his features. "I see. It's *that* kind of letter."

Damian swatted his friend's thin arm. "Whatever you're thinking, you're wrong."

"Sure I am."

"Can you deliver it, or not?"

Enzo waved a hand, still grinning. "Of course I can. But if things don't work out, it's not on me."

Damian groaned. The thing of it was, Enzo wasn't too far off—he was as anxious as a preteen boy sending messages to the girl he desperately hoped would give him a chance. "Don't make me regret asking."

When Enzo was gone—albeit not without a suggestive wink—Damian felt suddenly, painfully alone.

He had spent a single handful of hours in Roz's presence, and already his life, his every thought, had become about her. How was it that only two days ago he'd been patrolling the streets as normal, having resigned himself to pretending she didn't exist? A single conversation, and she'd wrenched him from that place with more force than Damian had thought possible. He felt as though he'd awoken from a deep sleep, and was suddenly looking at the world around him with brutal clarity.

It didn't matter how much Roz hated him, or how infuriating she was.

Damian was in danger.

ROZ

It had taken considerable wrangling to get away from Patience's temple that afternoon. Vittoria had shaken her head in resigned dismay when Roz told her she wouldn't be attending the evening service—a short but weekly event intended to honor Patience alone. It was a horribly boring affair, and besides, Roz had attended the last few, if only in an attempt to prove that she was putting in the effort.

Distracted as she'd been, Roz was certain her apology to Vittoria had rung false, but she couldn't be bothered with that just then. There was a rebel meeting to attend, and afterward she would be meeting Damian at the Shrine. Connected to the Palazzo, it was where the representatives went to worship their patron saints. It was only open to the public for a few hours a day. As such, Roz hoped to hell Damian had a plan to get her inside. His letter had been on the doormat early this morning, and Roz had scanned it once before shoving it down her shirt to keep Caprice from noticing.

But Damian hadn't provided much of an explanation as to why he wanted to meet. In fact, he hadn't provided an explanation at all. And how had he known where she *lived*?

The rebel meeting had only been a matter of updating everyone on where their captured members were—second floor, eastern wing of the city prison, according to Piera—but they still didn't have a solid plan of rescue.

Now, Roz stood from the table at which she'd been sitting with Dev and Nasim, glancing at the clock in the corner of the tavern. Only half an hour until she was to be meeting Damian. "I've got to be going."

"Huh?" Nasim stared over the rim of her glass, eyes a little unfocused. It wasn't often she let loose, and Roz was loath to miss it. "I thought you skipped service. What else could you possibly be doing that doesn't involve us?"

Dev chuckled softly, the first he'd done so in days. A flush stole across Nasim's cheeks, and she trailed a hand down the length of his arm. He was in a better mood today: His smiles were still rare, but at least he was cracking jokes the way he used to. Roz wanted to bottle his laughter and stow it somewhere safe.

Dealing with grief doesn't follow a linear path. Few knew that as well as Roz. But she was more accustomed to being the griever than the supporter, at least where anyone apart from her mother was concerned. She only knew one form of comfort, and that was tough love. At least Nasim was there for the rest.

Roz let her hair out of its ponytail, massaging her temples with her fingers. If she and Dev had been alone, she might have told him the truth. He wouldn't judge her for working with a security officer, as long as it helped her get closer to finding his sister's killer. Nasim, though, Roz wasn't so sure about. She had an uncompromising set of beliefs. It was surprising enough that their friendship had flourished despite Roz being a disciple.

I believe someone can't help what they are, Nasim had told her once. *You didn't choose to be a disciple. As far as I'm concerned, you're just as much a rebel as the rest of us. Anyone who heard you talk about how much you hate the Palazzo would understand that. They just haven't given you a chance.*

Nasim also knew how much Roz hated security officers; Roz complained about them every time she returned from the Mercato. How, as unfavored citizens themselves, officers should have been supporting their fellows instead of lording over them and taking advantage of them.

No, Nasim wouldn't react well to Roz working with Damian. She was certain of that. At best, Nasim would try to talk her out of it. At worst, she would call Roz a traitor and claim she was wrong to ever trust Roz in the first place.

She wouldn't be able to blame Nasim, either. She'd dug this hole herself. Hanging around Damian would contradict everything she'd ever told her friend.

Then there was the matter of Dev. Roz didn't want to tell him she was looking into Amélie's murder until she was certain she and Damian could solve it. Giving him false hope would only end up hurting him more.

She exhaled past the sudden pain in her chest. "I'm meeting a friend, that's all. I'll explain later."

Nasim pursed her lips.

"That," Dev said, pointing at Nasim, "is the face of *What do you mean, you have friends who aren't us?* And frankly, I agree."

Roz *would* explain, eventually. Just not tonight. Not before she knew whether her partnership with Damian would even last. She checked the clock again, then stood, arching her back. "Tomorrow," she told them firmly. "We'll talk tomorrow. I've got to go."

"Fine," Nasim said with a dramatic sigh, waving her away and taking another sip of her drink.

Dev's glance was meaningful. "Be careful."

Roz nodded at him, then patted her hip where she always stowed her knife. Though she understood his concern, part of her bristled at it. She wasn't Amélie. Wasn't an unarmed child, unattuned to any potential danger.

But she shot him a tight smile before ambling out into the street, enveloped at once by the cool evening air. She'd taken barely a step before she saw a familiar shape leaning against the tavern's exterior, silhouetted by the fading sunset.

"Roz," Piera said, noticing her at the same time. She beckoned Roz over.

"I can't talk long," Roz said, though she heeded the gesture nonetheless. Her heart squeezed at Piera's distant expression. "I'm on my way to meet a friend."

Every night, Roz knew, Piera stepped outside to watch the sun set over the river. It was a ritual she'd shared with her husband from when they first opened Bartolo's, before he'd been lost to the war. It must have been horribly sad, carrying on a tradition without the person you loved at your side, but Piera always said it made her happy.

It's a bittersweet sort of happiness, she had told Roz once. *It hurts terribly to be without him, and yet this is when I feel closest to him.*

Roz could understand that. She felt the same way whenever she went through her father's old things. It was as if a leaden weight had dropped into her stomach, stealing her breath, but at the same time grounding her. Allowing her to remember that he'd been real.

"A friend?" Piera crooked a half smile. "That's different."

Roz bit down hard on her tongue. She didn't want to burden Piera with her problems, but at the same time, she was the only one who would understand. Piera had known Damian as a child, too. Had known him when he and Roz were still best friends. "Perhaps *friend* is a stretch," she hedged.

Piera waited, but didn't pry. She never pried, but let Roz reveal precisely as much as she chose to. She understood grief, and heartbreak, and fury, and the way your insides could ache and hunger for something unnameable.

Roz blew out a breath. It had started to rain lightly, a cool mist that turned the evening fuzzy. She moved farther away from the tavern door as a group of men made to enter, drunk bellows echoing down the narrow street. "It's Damian Venturi."

Piera didn't look surprised. She only nodded slowly. "I had wondered when you two might reconnect."

"We're not *reconnecting*. He's supposed to be solving the disciple's murder, and he's looking into Amélie's death as well. I had already intended to find out what happened to her, and when I happened to come across him..." Roz trailed off, squeezing the bridge of her nose with a thumb and forefinger. "He's letting me work with him. I think he feels as though he owes me, for... well, you know." Piera was quiet, and Roz grumbled, "This is where you tell me I'm a fool."

Piera laughed, the sound quiet but genuine. "You're not, and have never been, a fool. You loved him once, and that doesn't just go away. But," she went on, voice heavier, "he's the Palazzo's man now, Roz. Take what you can from him, but don't trust him. You know better than that."

126

This was the Piera that Roz knew and needed. Someone to be straightforward with her. To tell her that it was okay to feel the things she was feeling, but to remind her what was important.

"I do."

"Good." Piera turned back to the sunset. "Then you should also know you don't have to prove yourself to the other rebels. Regardless of whether you can solve Amélie's murder, you're where you need to be. Anyone who doesn't trust my judgment can come to me about it."

"That's not the only reason I want to find out what happened to Amélie," Roz insisted, heat settling in her cheeks. Piera could read her too easily. "Dev deserves to know what happened. I don't think he's going to get better until he does."

Piera gave a hum of acknowledgment. She stared out across the horizon, her face awash in golden light. "Once you have known true grief, you don't *get better*." The words were firm, but gentle. "You don't recover—you only grow stronger. You learn to bear the things that seemed unbearable. You find a way to rebuild yourself, even with crucial pieces missing." Now, finally, she looked at Roz again, a pointed glint in her eyes.

This time Roz was the one to avert her gaze, blinking hard against the dying sun. "I need to get going," she muttered, sliding away from the tavern. "I'll see you tomorrow?"

Piera nodded, and though she disappeared swiftly from view, her words followed Roz into the dark.

The Shrine was enormous. Dome-roofed with turrets jutting skyward, it had always looked to Roz like the Palazzo's subdued shadow. It was a uniform shade of slate gray, its curved walls bearing intricate carvings of the saints. Not being remotely devout, Roz had never been inside, but she'd dressed for the occasion. Her black dress was low cut and shot through with silver, complementing her heeled boots perfectly. It looked fantastic, and would have the added bonus of infuriating Damian.

Rossana! She could already hear him saying, aghast. *You can't wear that into a temple.*

"Rossana!"

A voice emanated from the Shrine's pillar-framed entrance, so in line with Roz's thoughts that for a moment she wondered if she'd imagined it. Once she squinted, though, she could pick out Damian's broad figure. He stepped into the last vestiges of sunlight and beckoned her over.

"You came," he said as she neared, audibly surprised.

"You told me to."

"That's why I figured you wouldn't."

Roz sniffed. "It'd be difficult to work together if I ignored all your correspondence."

Damian opened his mouth, then closed it as he noticed her dress. His eyes widened, and he directed them upward, evidently deciding not to comment. "I...uh, I'm glad you're here. I have a proposition for you."

Roz waited, heart pounding in her chest. She wished she could reach inside and squeeze it with a fist, forcing it into submission.

"I need to do another examination of the dead disciple's room. Since I promised to tell you everything I learn, I figured it might be easier if you simply come along. Besides, I know disciples can sometimes sense—er, *things* the rest of us can't."

Roz knew what he was referring to. Magic *felt* a certain way.

But in a city full of disciples, it was hard to differentiate one type from another. She wasn't about to tell Damian that, though. Not if he was willing to get her into the Palazzo. The idea both intrigued and disgusted her: She couldn't deny she wanted to know what it was like, this place where only the most powerful disciples resided, but she also preferred to stay as far as possible from what she considered to be the root of Ombrazia's corruption.

Damian watched her as she digested this. He was so still it was a bit unsettling, and Roz cast around for a reply.

"You have disciples in the Palazzo already," was what she settled on.

"They wouldn't be very helpful in this instance."

"Because you're doing something you're not supposed to be?"

Damian's lips thinned, and Roz studied the strain in his neck. The ever-present shadows beneath his eyes. Though he was broad, upon closer inspection she could make out the wiriness of his forearms, as if he didn't eat quite enough to sustain their musculature.

"Do you want to come, or not?" he said sharply. "Because if you don't—"

"I'll come." Roz cut him off, flashing her most pleasant smile. "But if anyone gives us trouble, I won't hesitate to sell you out."

That muscle in his jaw ticked, as if he were having some internal argument with himself. Perhaps he was already regretting inviting her. Roz wondered if he'd seen her face when he closed his eyes last night, the same way she'd seen his. She wondered if he'd wanted to scream into his pillow the way she had.

"Trust me," Damian said, "I know."

He stepped past her to run a hand over the burnished lock of the Shrine's door, and it opened without a sound, recognizing his touch. He moved aside, indicating that Roz should go first. It was doubtless meant to be gentlemanly, but she shook her head, a laugh bubbling in her chest. "I don't think so."

There was a moment of tension during which Damian seemed to be weighing the merits of arguing. In the end, he must have decided it wasn't worth it, because he led the way, leaving Roz to shut the door. The moment she did, it sealed them in a wide tunnel. More carvings climbed the stone walls: faceless, larger-than-life figures with halos upon their brows; abstract designs that, when you looked closely enough, appeared to contain eyes within their repetitive motifs. The ceiling arched high overhead, mimicking the dome outside. It wasn't what Roz had expected.

"The temple itself is underground," Damian said, answering her unspoken question. His words echoed through the space, the last syllable hanging in the air a beat too long. "From there, a second tunnel connects directly to the Palazzo."

"I'm right behind you, Officer," Roz said, hand brushing the knife stowed in the front of her dress.

Damian tensed, as she'd come to realize he always did, at her use of his title. She said it to remind herself of who he was—or rather, who he *wasn't*. Interesting that he didn't seem to like it.

"Rossana," he said quietly, pausing less than a step away from her. She could have shoved her blade between his ribs. She could have wrapped her arms around him.

"Yes?"

Damian turned, the fathomless depths of his eyes rendering her immobile. She hadn't a clue what he was going to say, and yet, for some reason, she was afraid to hear it.

But he only said, "I know you have a knife. Don't even think about using it."

Then he headed into the tunnel, leaving Roz to follow. She exhaled through gritted teeth before doing so.

As they descended deeper underground, the passage became narrower. Quieter. Once, they might have raced gleefully through such a space, spurred on by the promise of the dark unknown. She remembered darting through the streets one particular midnight, Damian's hand in hers, their steps slightly unsteady. It was the first time their parents had allowed them more than a single glass of wine, and Roz remembered thinking, as she grasped Damian's fingers, that being drunk was feeling the world narrow around you. For her, that meant being more aware of Damian Venturi than she ever had. It was the heady scent of him, the giddy breathlessness of wanting. It was the fear of doing everything wrong, and the courage to do it anyway.

That was the first night she'd kissed him. The first night she'd kissed anyone, in fact. She was certain, afterward, that she hadn't done it wrong. Not given the way he'd responded—as though she were a reckless flame, and he all too willing to burn with her.

The memory faded, leaving her hollow as the passage finally widened. Beyond it, a wide arch gave way to an enormous, cathedral-like room. Roz followed Damian out onto a platform from which gradually widening steps descended, eyeing the cast-iron candelabras on either side. The trios of lights flickered as if in some nonexistent wind, turning Damian's face gaunt and formidable.

"Interesting," Roz muttered. She tilted her head to squint up at the vaulted ceiling, which had been painted in shades of deep blue dotted with cold silver. The crown molding at its edges was labyrinthine. Only once she'd torn her eyes away did she notice what was at the other end of the room, far enough away that *room* felt an inadequate descriptor. "Are those supposed to be the saints?"

"Yes." Damian's reverential reply was barely audible. The stone walls of the Shrine swallowed every noise with greedy haste, only to spit them back out as muted echoes.

Roz's footsteps clicked on the dark marble as she approached the statues. They were arranged in a semicircle, a shroud tossed ominously over the one at the far end. Disciple made, Roz assumed, though they showed no signs of movement. Their heads were bowed and hooded. On the floor in the center of the statues, different shades of marble formed the shape of a seven-pointed sun—the original symbol of the saints.

Roz examined each of the saints in turn, pausing when she reached Patience. Even in the dark she could see the statue's hands splayed out wide, small touches of humanity protruding from sleeves that seemed to billow around the sword at her waist. Patience's palms faced skyward, and to Roz it appeared as though the saint were drawing something up from the earth. The realism of her robes was astounding, the folds and wrinkles perfectly mimicking the sheet covering the statue to Roz's right.

Chaos, she realized. It was uncommon to see the seventh saint concealed rather than removed.

She heard Damian approaching, but she didn't turn. People killed and died for these saints. These statues. They came here and knelt before them, seeking imagined guidance. Because that was the central function of faith, wasn't it? To act as a stand-in for one's own agency. To be pointed to when other explanations faltered. How could people believe in the saints' blessings when outside this place so many people suffered? Where was the proof these long-dead ancestors even *cared*?

"The entrance to the Palazzo is over there." Damian's voice

came softly from Roz's left shoulder, an obvious attempt to spur her into moving.

They glared at one another, dark gaze warring with blue, until the sound of a door slamming thrust them aggressively back into action.

"Shit." Damian took Roz by the shoulders, pushing her into the shadows behind the statue of Grace. His body pressed against hers, warm and firm, turning her blood molten in her veins. "Someone from the Palazzo's coming."

"Don't *shove* me," she hissed, but then froze. Damian was right. She could hear voices growing louder as they approached, accompanied by the uneven beat of footsteps. Damian pressed a finger to his lips, an action that struck Roz as both demeaning and futile.

But she said nothing. If she wanted him to share information with her, she realized, she needed him to trust her. And that meant not making it quite so obvious she wished he would drop dead.

"It's the chief magistrate," Damian mouthed.

Roz peeked out from behind the statue and saw that he was right. Forte was immediately recognizable, and the man with him could only be a disciple. It was, she realized after a beat, the man she'd seen selected as the new representative of Death's guild.

"Signor Agosti," Chief Magistrate Forte was saying, "you'll learn that although we make decisions in the council room, the real work is done here, before your patron saints. Their guidance should always inform your choices. Nothing is more important than your connection with the divine." His voice grew urgent as he extinguished the candelabra flames, enveloping the space in darkness. "Remember that you are chosen. You are blessed. But also remember that we are all mere instruments."

Roz cast another look at Damian, disgusted to see his face transformed by something akin to...yearning?

The chief magistrate paused in his monologue, glancing around in what looked almost like suspicion. Had he heard them? Roz held her breath, and Damian, sensing her tension, ran his thumb over her bicep where he still gripped her arm. It was clearly an absent reaction meant to be calming, but Roz's body stiffened further. Time passed in skittish leaps. She felt Damian's heart thudding against hers, felt his short breaths ruffle her hair, but she didn't dare twist away. Her skin was on fire as they stood together, immobile, until Forte and the disciple finished praying.

"All right. Let us go." The chief magistrate's voice raised goose bumps on the back of Roz's neck. She peered out from behind the statue to see his face smudged against the dim, an eerie vacancy in his gaze. He was staring, Roz saw, at the shrouded statue of Chaos. As he did, the bottom of the sheet rippled as though someone had brushed by it. Her heart stopped, her mouth going dry.

If he noticed, Forte didn't so much as blink. He only turned away, so slowly that Roz felt sure he must have known she was watching.

But he didn't say another word, merely clapped a hand to the new disciple's back, and then they were gone.

14

DAMIAN

Death spoke to Damian as he left the Shrine. She whispered to him in the dark, and her voice carried a single name.

Michele.

His brother, if not in blood, then in something just as potent. The best friend he'd watched die, shifting from man to monster to meat. Monster, because war had changed something fundamental within him. And meat, because... well. Damian had seen enough death to know what humans looked like when they reached it.

Michele had saved him. Kept Damian whole when he was fracturing too quickly to collect all the pieces. As a disciple of Cunning, Michele hadn't been drafted to fight—he'd *chosen* to go north, just as Damian's father once did. He'd believed *that* strongly in his duty as a citizen of Ombrazia. He was unfailingly honorable, and optimistic in a way Damian could never seem to manage.

After some time on the front lines, one of the older soldiers, Jarek, had told them when they arrived, *your pistola starts lookin' real good pointin' the wrong direction.*

Damian had understood what the man meant, but he hadn't believed it. Not until the night he woke drenched in sweat, shaking from nightmares that would only continue the moment he set foot outside, and laid eyes on the pistola beside him.

But he was shaking too ferociously to move, and regardless threw up over the side of the bed before he could try, waking Michele. As his friend leaned close, Damian muttered three words: *Jarek was right.*

Michele slapped him so hard his ears rang until morning.

Would he have done it that night, if Michele hadn't been there? Damian wanted to think he would have been strong enough to push onward. He wasn't certain, though, and that was the worst part. The fear that he might one day feel that way again was more terrifying than any nightmare. It was a hopelessness, a misery so deep that, should he ever find himself back there, he didn't trust himself to make it out a second time.

"Are you listening to me?"

Roz's voice yanked Damian back to himself, and he heaved a breath. "I—no. I mean, yes."

They were in the tunnels leading from the Shrine to the Palazzo, and he'd all but zoned out, allowing the dark to trap him in memories. He flexed his unsteady hands, allowing himself a brief prayer to the saint he'd left behind. *Give me a sign*, he entreated Strength, picturing the hooded, cross-armed statue. *Give me any small comfort.*

But there was nothing.

Roz slowed to keep pace with Damian, her sharp features contorted in a scowl. "What's wrong with you?"

Where to start? "Nothing. You can go on ahead."

"I can't, actually, seeing as I don't have a clue where I'm going."

She had a point. Damian dropped his gaze, taking another deep breath. Just looking at Roz for too long was overwhelming. How many times had he pictured her face to get himself through the darkest moments? At first it had been near constantly. There wasn't a second during his waking hours his mind wasn't occupied by her, and sometimes she showed up in his dreams, too. But as the years passed, the thoughts grew less frequent, until he no longer bothered conjuring up Roz's face for fear it might not look the same.

It did, though. Less round, and certainly harsher, but her startlingly blue eyes were the same. The way her grin was always a little mischievous... That was the same.

Though he'd tried to push it away, the younger version of Roz was still stark in his memories. Every so often, Damian played back the night she'd kissed him for the first time. How his wine-addled thoughts refused to cling to anything that wasn't her. He'd known he loved Roz from the time he was twelve—at least, he was as certain as one could be at that age—but the fear of ruining their friendship was always sobering enough that he'd never acted on it. If they were best friends forever, that was fine. He would take as much of Roz as he could get.

That night, though, she had dragged him down an alleyway, breathing hard between laughs. She'd been beautiful in the moonlight, dark hair swirling around her, thick-lashed eyes wide and endearing. Damian had wanted to tell her. As she'd pulled him to where she leaned up against the alley wall, he could think of nothing else. It was foolish to love Roz Lacertosa—she burned so brightly, whereas his colors were muted. Steady grays and deep blues. Her glow would obliterate him.

Roz, was all Damian managed before she'd brought her lips to his.

He was content to burn, then.

"Venturi, you look like you're gonna hurl. If you are, tell me now, because I don't want you getting it on me."

Damian gave his head a shake, adjusting the collar of his shirt, which had begun to feel restrictive. Roz was staring at him, brow furrowed. What was he *thinking*? Why had he allowed himself to remember that?

Even now, four years later, he wished he'd kissed her first.

"I'm fine," Damian said curtly. "We turn up here." He motioned at the curve in the tunnel up ahead, and together they mounted the wide steps leading out of the passage. Roz didn't say another word until they emerged into an empty room adjacent to the Palazzo main entrance. The space functioned only as a transition to the tunnels, which was why Damian had decided to come this way.

Roz looked around, taking in the shimmering arches and polished floor. Her hair glistened beneath the starlight from the open ceiling, matching the metallic sheen of her dress. She was beautiful in an ethereal way. Untouchable. For the span of a breath Damian forgot she hated him. Forgot he didn't trust her.

When he remembered, the weight of it crushed him.

Roz lowered her gaze from the night sky. Damian thought she was about to make a snide comment about the interior of the Palazzo, and he braced himself for the unpleasantness that would surely follow. Instead, though, she said, "Why did you come back?"

The question caught him off guard. Roz's voice was soft, as if someone might overhear. Damian decided to be mostly honest. "My father got promoted not long after my mother passed. As general, he oversees training and recruitment, so he decided to work from Ombrazia most of the time. He got Chief Magistrate Forte to offer me a job in the Palazzo."

Roz's mouth formed a thin line. "I didn't know your mother had died."

"Oh." A jolt shot through Damian's chest. "Yeah, a couple of years ago. Illness from the cold air. It went to her lungs, and even Mercy's disciples couldn't save her."

It sounded so simple when he said it like that. But he remembered the way the disciples had moved their hands across his mother's chest, mouths set in grim lines. Their frantic hollers for more supplies, and the detached mask of Battista's face as he shepherded Damian out of the room. The way he'd lain awake all night, heart fluttering in fear against the tight-fitting prison of his rib cage, and heard the very moment it all went silent.

He'd known, then. But he hadn't moved, hadn't cried, until his father came to get him the next morning.

"I see," Roz said, and then she was silent. She'd known Liliana Venturi for years, of course, and Damian wondered if she was going to offer her condolences. But she didn't, because this was Roz, and besides, she was probably glad his family had been torn apart the same as hers.

"Yeah," was all he could think of to say. "Can I ask you something?"

"Fine."

"When did you find out you were a disciple?"

"*Ugh.*" Roz rolled her eyes. "Anything but that."

Right. Damian had gotten that impression last time he raised the subject. But he was still struggling to reconcile Roz the disciple with the Roz he'd known three years ago. He wanted to know everything he'd missed. What had happened between then and now. "Why not?"

"Being a disciple isn't fun, you know," she said. "You gain countless privileges, don't get me wrong, but it's just so *boring*. Suddenly your temple owns you. They teach you how to use your ability, and even then you're only learning how to make stuff. Your role is decided for you, whether you like it or not." Roz said this all very quickly, as if she couldn't keep the words in any longer. "And the worst part is, most disciples seem to love it. They feel special, powerful, and strut around like they own the damned world. Because," she gave a short laugh, "let's face it—they kind of do. I just don't...fit."

Damian couldn't wrap his head around the idea that someone could be a disciple and not enjoy it. "But Patience blessed you. You have *magic*. Doesn't that make you feel...I don't know. Happy?"

It was a fairly lame adjective to get his point across, but his mind seemed to be running short on words. Roz snorted. "No, I don't feel happy. You think I give a shit about metalworking? Having power"—she procured the knife Damian had seen at her hip, using two fingers to bend the blade as easily as if it were made of rubber—"doesn't mean you're suddenly, magically interested in whatever it is you can control." She bent her blade back into place, nostrils flaring. Damian could feel the warmth from where he stood.

"In the heart of Strength's mountains, Patience called forth heat." He murmured the quote without thinking. It wasn't often he got to see a disciple in action. He knew Strength's disciples used sheer physical force in their craft, and that Grace's possessed incredible dexterity. Roz might not feel she belonged to Patience, but to Damian it made perfect sense.

Roz tossed her hair, managing to make the action appear disdainful. "I think it's silly."

"You think what's silly?"

"All of it. The stories about the saints creating the world."

Damian stared at her. "Where else would it have come from?"

She arched a brow defiantly back. "Where does *anything* come from?"

"Are you telling me you're a disciple of Patience—literally descended from a saint—and you don't believe in them?"

"It's not that I don't believe they once existed. I'm just not convinced they created the world, or that they still rule our lives today. They're dead, Damian. Do you really think they hear your prayers?"

"I don't know," Damian said hotly. "The saints' capabilities are outside our comprehension." It was the explanation he'd heard countless times before.

"That's what everyone says about their beliefs when they don't want to think too hard." Roz didn't say this condescendingly, but rather in a soft, matter-of-fact tone. "It's lazy, and it's cowardly. It's easier than admitting you might not understand the world."

Damian gritted his teeth. He couldn't do this with her. The saints *were* his understanding of the world, and he wasn't interested in hearing anyone tell him otherwise. It was how he'd been raised.

"Forget it," he said. "I didn't bring you here to argue." Avoiding her lingering gaze, Damian made for the corner of the room, picking up the security officer uniform he'd stashed there earlier. He tossed it at Roz, who caught it, staring at the bundle of fabric in disgust.

"What the hell is this? Some kind of role-play thing?"

"Saints, Rossana. No. You can't be walking around the Palazzo in *that*." He waved a hand to indicate her general appearance. The black and silver dress, the plunging neckline, the heeled boots. She'd always been over the top, even in their youth, talking louder than situations warranted and dressing formally for the most casual of occasions. Once Damian had admired that about her.

"Put it on, will you?" he said. "That way if anyone sees us, I can say you're a new hire. Even disciples can't be walking around the Palazzo without a good reason."

"You want me to pretend I'm a security officer? Gross."

Damian felt his cheeks heat in irritation. "Just go change."

Roz wrinkled her nose. But she vanished around the corner nonetheless, only to reappear a moment later in the uniform. It was disciple made, so naturally it had altered to fit perfectly to her frame, yet she'd somehow managed to cinch the waist. She'd also released her hair so that it tumbled around her like a dark halo. Damian gaped for what must have been a full thirty seconds before regaining the ability to speak.

"You can't . . ." But he trailed off, realizing it wasn't worth the fight. What had he been thinking, bringing her here? He needed to get her in and out as soon as possible, before she inevitably caused some kind of mayhem. "You know what? Never mind. Let's go."

Roz grinned archly. It felt like a trap. "Jealous that I look better than you in uniform?"

Damian was trying to form a response that didn't sound foolish when the door swung open, startling them both and revealing a disheveled Enzo. His friend was breathing heavily—he had clearly run here.

"Goodness," Damian choked out. "Are you okay?"

Enzo hinged at the waist, catching his breath. When he straightened, he drew a hand through his hair, fixing Damian with a meaningful look. "I've been looking everywhere for you. I'd hoped to speak in private." Then his attention slipped to Roz. His brow furrowed as he tried to place her before offering a pleasant grin. "No offense intended, Signora. Are you a new guard?"

For the love of all that was holy. Was Enzo *flirting* with Roz? Damian ground his teeth. Before Roz could answer the question, he said, "Can this wait?"

"No," Enzo insisted. "It can't."

Damian widened his eyes pointedly, trying to communicate his displeasure. He suspected whatever Enzo had to tell him was related to his earlier instructions, but he wasn't about to ask with Roz analyzing the conversation.

Enzo, however, stared right back. He was receiving the message loud and clear, Damian realized, and still wasn't about to be dissuaded.

Roz loosed a dramatic sigh. "Whatever you two are *clearly* trying to keep from me, you might as well just come out with it."

Damn it. She wasn't wrong, either; Roz never let something drop when she was determined to get answers. Damian cursed inwardly, turning back to Enzo. "Fine. What is it?"

"You told me to let you know if I saw anything strange. And—"

"Did you?" Roz interrupted. "See anything strange, I mean?"

"I would assume he's getting to that," Damian said dryly.

Roz ran her fingers through her hair, considering the strands in feigned absentmindedness. The frigid weight of her attention shifted to Damian, who suddenly found it difficult to breathe. Enzo, oblivious to this, said, "I thought you might want to know that I just passed the disciple of Death's rooms, and the door was open."

Damian stared. "I'm sure he simply forgot to lock it."

"Not the new disciple," Enzo said impatiently. "The previous one. The *dead* one."

A chill settled in Damian's bones. "Leonzio?"

"Yes. The door has been locked since the night he died, as you well know, but now it's wide open."

Damian shoved the sleeves of his shirt up farther, chewing on this information. Who in the Palazzo would have been snooping through Leonzio's rooms? "I'll take a look. Thanks."

Enzo nodded, shooting another glance at Roz before taking his leave. Damian groaned inwardly: He would be bombarded with questions later, he was sure.

"Well," Roz said smugly when Enzo was gone. "That's good timing. I'll come check it out with you." She angled her chin as if daring him to argue.

Damian groaned inwardly. This had definitely been a mistake. The more he was around Roz, the more he *wanted* to be around her. A foolish, self-destructive part of him wanted to imagine her new edges were a wall she'd build to protect herself, and that they might topple if only he could regain her trust.

144

Then again, Damian had walls of his own, didn't he? He'd changed in ways he didn't quite understand. Sometimes his entire body felt wrong, as though he'd fallen apart and been put back together in a manner that was careless and haphazard. Could Roz tell when she looked at him? Had she noticed his humor was darker, more forced? That he sometimes spent too long staring into the middle distance, braced as if expecting something to stare back?

His sluggish heartbeat pounded in his ears as he said, "Fine. Follow me."

Roz smiled again, and this time it was an excruciatingly familiar thing.

DAMIAN

Just as Enzo had claimed, the door to Leonzio Bianchi's rooms was open slightly. Beyond that, all Damian could see was blackness.

"Is it usually locked?" Roz hissed.

"Yeah."

"Who has a key?"

Damian patted his chest pocket. "Every Palazzo security officer carries a master key. But I can't see why anyone would have been here."

Roz arched a brow, the motion subtle. Damian wondered what she was thinking. Why the curve of her jaw suddenly stretched taut. He'd spent half his life wishing he could read her mind, and apparently the urge hadn't dissipated with time.

But all she said was, "Are we going in, or what?"

Damian swallowed his inexplicable hesitation and, swiping a lantern from the hall, kneed the door open.

The room looked exactly as it had the night of Leonzio's death: windows shuttered, a canopied bed pushed up against the wall, tile floors that yielded a sterile feel. Although he knew it was unlikely, Damian could have sworn the sickly-sweet stench of death lingered. He didn't have a clear memory of the night he'd come to examine the disciple's body—everything was oddly cloudy.

He remembered the false eyes, and his hand flicked to his pocket. The black orb he'd taken from the crypt was still there. Who had touched it last? Why had they left it, and what were they doing with the eyes they'd taken?

"There's no one here," Roz said. She sounded almost disappointed. "So, he died alone? Did you figure out what kind of poison it was?"

Damian turned to frown at her, holding her gaze out of fear his own might inadvertently slip lower. "No."

"I assume you questioned Cunning's representative?"

Irritation surged in Damian's stomach. "*Yes*. It didn't amount to anything. Anyway, this is where we found him." He nodded at the bed, scrubbing his fingers along his jawline. "I did a quick sweep of the room at the time, but then we had to leave it undisturbed for a couple of days, obviously."

You were supposed to leave places someone had died alone for two full days and nights. That was how long it had taken Strength to commence the creation of the world, and as such, that was how long one's spirit had to leave its final resting place. Damian didn't fully understand the parallel, but it was customary, and thus he had never questioned it.

Thankfully, Roz didn't scoff at this. "Right," she said, already tracking a circular path around the bed. The moment she moved, the air around Damian dropped in temperature, all humidity leeching away. He shivered as an icy chill grazed the back of his neck.

"What do you think?"

"It feels strange here," Roz admitted, frowning. "I don't know how to describe it. Not bad, just...something I've never felt before."

Damian's heart sank. He didn't know what he'd expected—that she might somehow sense the killer? Disciples were highly attuned to magic, but then Damian had no proof magic had been involved in Leonzio's death. Trying to solve this mystery felt like walking blindly through a room, ramming headfirst into wall after wall.

He left Roz to her examination, deciding to do his own search of the rest of the space. His steps echoed as he made slow rounds of the bathing room, the study, and the small sitting room adjacent. Nothing appeared to be out of place, and that, more than anything else, made Damian's insides constrict. How was it that someone could be gone, yet everything remained unchanged? A jacket draped over the side of a chair, a worn book open on the desk...Simple things that made up a moment in time. Damian had barely known Leonzio. Hadn't particularly liked the man. But sadness washed over him nonetheless as he stared at what was left behind.

In any case, if someone really had broken into the disciple's rooms, they were gone now. Damian turned away from the study and made his way back to the bedroom, only to stop in his tracks. Roz was nowhere to be seen.

"Rossana?" If she had run off—

"I'm here."

Her disembodied voice sounded from the other side of the room, somewhat muffled. Before Damian could ask, she emerged from the tiny closet by the bathroom, her hair catching the moon's dim illumination through the window. A ghostly figure in a dead man's room.

Then she spoke, and the image shattered.

"There's something in here. Come look."

Damian came around to join her. "What are you..." His words faltered, trailing off into silence. He didn't quite know how to explain what he was seeing.

Arranged on the floor of the closet was an assortment of sticks and rocks. The set up was clearly deliberate, and staining the floor around them was a brownish substance that looked horribly like—

"Blood?" Roz said, too loudly. Too excitedly.

Damian swallowed. It wasn't a lot of blood, but he'd seen enough of it to know she was right. The blood, though, wasn't what bothered him most—it was the eerie sensation that trickled through him when he considered the arrangement of sticks, spread out around the rocks in seven points.

Seven points. He counted again, just to be certain.

"That's a heptagonal sun," he murmured. The symbol of the faceless saints. Had it been there the night Leonzio died? He'd searched the rooms himself—hadn't he?

Roz frowned. "Looks like a pile of twigs to me."

Damian knelt to point at the stones, careful not to touch them. "Seven angles. A circle in the middle. What else would it be?"

"I don't know. Why would there be blood in the center of a holy symbol?"

149

She didn't look afraid, which was more than Damian could say for himself. A cold sweat beaded his brow, and he held his lantern close to the blood. The spots were small, each one about the same size, and not spattered so much as carefully dripped.

"The blood was added after," he realized, pointing to where brown colored the stones. "This was purposeful."

Roz caught his gaze, and Damian found himself enraptured by the curve of her mouth. The sharp cut of her cheekbones. The alluring angle of her eyes. She looked like she knew a thousand different ways to kill a man, and he found it didn't bother him.

"Do you think it's Leonzio's blood?" she asked, kneeling to touch the substance with a fingertip.

Damian blanched, barely managing to stop himself from knocking her hand away. "Leave it alone, would you? I want to get someone in here to examine it."

He might have added more, but a change in Roz's expression brought him up short. She rubbed her fingers together, letting flakes of dried blood flutter back to the tile. It was such a deliberate motion that it made Damian uneasy. Part of him wanted to kick the sticks and stones into disarray, but the more superstitious side of him was horrified at the idea of disturbing the shape. He assumed Leonzio had created the arrangement, but couldn't think of a reason for it. If the disciple had wanted to contact the saints, why not visit the Shrine?

Roz's cheeks hollowed as she blew out a breath, wiping rust-dusted hands on her uniform. "And we're certain he didn't kill himself?"

"We've already established there are too many similarities between his death and the other two murders for that. Even so— yes, I'm certain." Damian heard his own voice grow uneven as a chill passed over him. He tried to attribute it to drying sweat, but it went deeper than that. Cold skittered along the air, filling his lungs each time he breathed. It infiltrated his skin and settled in the pit of his stomach. "Do you feel that?"

She paused where she'd been running a hand up the wall of the closet. "Feel what?"

Across the room, just past the bookshelf, the curtain fluttered against the unopened window.

Damian backed away from the heptagon, pulling Roz along with him. She stiffened, recoiling from his touch, and he let her arm drop.

"Sorry," he murmured. But his fingers twitched, itching to touch the stark angle of her jaw. To trace the heart-shaped curve of her upper lip, even if it curled into a scowl. He needed to get a handle on himself. On his overactive imagination, and whatever the hell was going on below the waist just now.

She rubbed her bicep, ignoring his apology. "What's the problem?"

"I..." Damian took a breath, steadying himself. "I have a bad feeling about this. You don't trifle with the saints. Let's get out of here." Without waiting for her to agree, he stepped back into the short corridor leading to the bedroom.

But the eerie sensation continued to grow, strengthening with each step. He could hear Roz behind him, her breathing labored, and wondered if she was feeling the same. Shadows flickered at the end of the corridor where it widened to join with the bedroom, casting indiscernible shapes up the wall. Or perhaps it was only the designs in the stucco.

Before he reached the end of the hall, however, the shadows consolidated to create the perfect outline of a torso.

Damian stopped short, causing Roz to collide with his back. Ice shot through his veins as the shadowy figure moved along the far wall, disappearing around the corner.

"What is it?" Roz hissed.

He shushed her, muscles tensing as his body shifted into a defensive stance. "We're not alone."

Silently, and before Damian could figure out how it had happened, Roz had a knife in each hand. She looked impossibly wild, and impossibly beautiful—a dark goddess seeking vengeance.

Don't move, she mouthed to him, then continued down the hall. Damian gritted his teeth. Who did she think she was, ordering *him* to stay back? But he pulled his pistola from his waistband and followed.

When he saw his hands, the gun clattered to the tile.

He didn't remember dropping it, but he must have, because all of a sudden he was grasping nothing but air. His whispered name sliced the night as Roz whipped around to curse at him, though her words barely registered.

Damian's hands were covered in blood.

It was fresh, though black in the darkness, cascading through his fingers and dripping to the floor in thick rivulets. His stomach lurched, and a jolt of sheer panic shot through him. His first thought was that he must have injured himself, but he couldn't see a source, and he'd been fine only moments ago. His head spun, trying and failing to fit the scene before him into some measure of sense.

In two steps Roz was back at his side. "What are you doing?"

Damian blinked once before forcing out a reply. "It's not mine."

"What do you mean?"

"The blood." He shook his trembling hands. "It isn't mine." He tried to wipe it on his army-issue trousers, but it continued to ooze warmly between his fingers. His stomach lurched, the tang of iron thick in his nostrils.

"There's no blood," Roz said, nose scrunched up as a sheen of unease flickered over her gaze. "It's in your head." She bent to retrieve his pistola, shoving it into his slick grasp. "We're getting the hell out of here."

Damian gripped the handle of the gun like a lifeline as he followed her to the door. The shadow he thought he'd seen was gone now, but when Roz reached for the door handle, he glanced toward the bed.

Its white sheets were soaked in blood, dark crimson spreading out from the human-shaped stain in the center.

Damian choked, exhaling through his teeth in alarm. The sound caught Roz's attention, and she whirled, frowning at him in what almost passed for concern.

"Get out," he rasped, hurling the door open and shoving Roz through, not caring that he left bloody handprints on her back. The world tilted, making it difficult to keep his feet beneath him. Dizziness sank sharp claws into his skull. With a final glance at the mess that covered the bed, he slammed the door shut behind them.

The corridor beyond was empty. Quiet. Lit sconces burned at equal intervals leading to the stairwell, their glow a sobering thing. It felt like a different world.

"Venturi," Roz said smoothly into the silence, "I don't know what that was about, but next time you push me, I'll detach your arms from your body."

How was she so calm? Damian was covered in blood. The bed

was covered in blood. He didn't know who it had come from, *where* it had come from. Was this Death's way of showing him she knew how much blood was on his hands?

"Are you listening to me?" Roz's voice was a whip cracking through his paranoid musings.

He gave his head a shake, wiping his hands on his trousers for the umpteenth time. "I—can't you *see* this?" He flung his palms out, only to blink in shock.

There was no blood.

Roz slapped his hands away, her earlier concern long gone. "When was the last time you slept? You're hallucinating. No wonder you can't solve a murder to save your life."

Heat flared in the pit of Damian's stomach, equal parts embarrassment and fury. The corridor was suddenly far too narrow, and he wished he could push the walls away.

"I haven't slept *because* I'm trying to solve a murder, Rossana. My father and Chief Magistrate Forte are busy dealing with a fucking rebellion, while also trying to manage the war up north. In the meantime, I'm meant to keep things in the Palazzo under control. Do you understand? I am *this* close"—Damian thrust his hand in Roz's face, thumb and index finger an inch apart—"to being sent back to the front lines. Not that I expect you to care, but I can't do that again." His voice cracked. "I just...can't."

Roz tilted her head, expression unreadable. Damian felt as though she were looking through him. Peeling back his exterior and clawing into his psyche, where all the terrible things he'd done lay in well-organized, threatening rows.

Saints, he was a fool. Lack of sleep really must have been getting to him. Roz Lacertosa hadn't cared about Damian's life for the last three years, and she wasn't going to start again now. She'd made that abundantly clear.

When she finally spoke, there was a mischievous lift to her flawless red lips that Damian neither liked nor trusted.

"We'll find the culprit," she said without a hint of doubt. "Just give it time."

"I don't have time. Not much, at least."

Roz fiddled with the regalia on her borrowed uniform. Damian had never seen anyone wear it with less pride. "Then I suppose this was a waste of it."

He made a sound of noncommittal in the back of his throat. "I'll see you out."

She didn't argue, following him down the corridor and into the maw of a curving stairwell. They passed no one else on the way back to the tunnels—thanks partly to Damian's choice of route and partly to sheer luck. When they arrived, he beckoned Roz through the arched doorway.

This time she went first.

Darkness enveloped them at once, and Damian lit a match and held it to a lantern propped against the wall. When he looked up, Roz was staring directly at him, eyes reflecting the lantern's glow like twin flames.

"What is it?" he asked.

Her mouth was downturned, almost thoughtful, as she said, "Why don't you know more about the disciple's death? Shouldn't a coroner have looked at the body?"

"They did. In fact, I have the report." Damian reached into the pocket of his jacket, flashing a piece of parchment at Roz. He'd been carrying it with him since he'd received it yesterday, scanning it periodically, as if the words might somehow change with each new glance. "But it hasn't been very helpful, since part of it was redacted."

She snatched the paper, brows drawing together at the thick black line that had been scratched through an entire section of the report. "Why?"

"I don't know," Damian told her honestly.

"Who does these reports?"

"The coroner. Like I said."

"No shit. But—"

He interrupted her scathing retort. "A disciple of Mercy from the city morgue came and did an autopsy. Once she finished, she wrote up a report and gave it to Chief Magistrate Forte."

"Does Forte always get the reports?"

"As far as I know."

"So he'll have more somewhere. As in, the ones for the other two victims."

"Well, yeah," Damian admitted, brows coming together. "He keeps them in his office. But it's not like I can just ask for them."

"I assume his office door is magicked to recognize his touch?"

His face twisted in horror. Was she suggesting he break into Forte's office and *steal* the reports? "Every officer carries a master key that bypasses that. Safety reasons. But in case you've forgotten, upsetting the chief magistrate is the last thing I want to do right now."

"It's an option, though. The answers could be right under your nose, and you'd never know."

"Forte would tell me if he knew anything important," Damian ground out. They were partway back to the Shrine by now, and the tunnel felt far too small with Roz at his side.

She gave an incredulous laugh. "Do you really believe that?"

"He wants me to solve this."

"*Does* he, though? Has it never occurred to you that someone in your precious Palazzo might be the murderer?"

"Of course it has," Damian snapped. "Do you think I'm completely inept? We've been questioning everyone, but haven't found anything condemning yet."

Her expression was pure scorn. "I suppose that's to be expected when you conduct half your investigation in secret."

"What's that supposed to mean?" Damian came to a halt. Roz didn't stop right away, but took a few further steps before turning to face him.

"You said yourself Forte only cares about finding whoever killed the disciple. And instead of standing up to him, you're going behind his back. It's pathetic."

"You don't know what you're talking about. It's not just Forte giving me instructions. It's my father, too. And I can't argue with him."

Roz scoffed. "You never could."

"Damn it, Rossana!" Her name ripped free from Damian's throat as anger burned hot in his stomach. The syllables were ragged. "If I disappoint Forte, if I defy my father, I'll be gone like *that*." He snapped his fingers to emphasize the point.

"Maybe," she agreed. "But even if you *could* argue with them, you wouldn't. Because they're not merely your superiors, are they? They're powerful disciples. They think they're better than you. And you believe it."

Damian's knuckles tightened on the lantern until pain spread through his fingers. Her words were like well-placed blows, each one finding their mark. Roz knew exactly what to say to cut through to his core. She pried him apart with little effort, exposing his truth, and wielded each revelation like a weapon.

He should have come up with a retort. Should have given her hell for speaking to him like that. Maybe it was the way the orange light played across the angles of her face, or maybe he was a nostalgic fool, grasping at the remnants of a time long past. Either way, when he spoke, his voice came out hoarse, the words frayed.

"Strength didn't bless me. He blessed my father, and my grandfather before that, but he didn't bless *me*. I don't understand why."

Roz looked at him for a moment that felt like eternity, her lashes thick in the darkness. It was long enough before she spoke that Damian had begun to wonder whether she would respond at all.

"That doesn't mean you're not important."

His heart thudded a painful, frantic beat against his ribs. It was as close to *kind* as he'd seen Roz be, and it did strange things to Damian's insides. He wanted to argue. Wanted to gather her to him. He wanted to tell her he didn't care whether he was important, as long as he was important to her.

He didn't know what he wanted.

"Roz," Damian said, and his voice hitched. But speaking seemed to break the spell, and she furrowed her brow before whirling away from him.

"Get me out of here, Venturi."

He didn't argue. Only led her to the congregation of expressionless statues, the silence between them a deafening thing.

Roz

It had been too late by the time Roz realized she'd forgotten to change.

Damian had clapped a hand to his forehead, then made her promise at least twice to return the uniform the next day. Roz had agreed easily; it wasn't as if she wanted to keep it. But it also meant she was guaranteed to see Damian again soon, when she desperately needed time to recover. The more she was around him, the harder it became to keep her head on straight. To remember who he was, and what he'd done.

Thankfully, he looked just enough like Battista that Roz needed only to stare at him long enough to renew her sense of purpose. Vengeance was set aside while she worked to solve the murders, but that didn't mean she'd forgotten the general. Somehow, eventually, she would find a way to get to him. Damian would hate her then, and the world would right itself.

Roz wasn't expected at Patience's temple the next day, so she wasted the hours of sunlight by reading, thinking furiously of Damian, and helping her mother clean. There was to be yet another rebel meeting that night—Piera had let Roz know when she'd come to drop off food for Caprice—and something in Piera's voice made the subsequent hours pass even more slowly.

The streets were empty as Roz finally made her way to Bartolo's, the moon a bleak sliver against the clouds. The air was still, and tasted of the river lashing in the distance. It was strange, she thought, how the city never seemed to change. These were the same streets she'd walked as a child, her father's hand braced lightly on the back of her neck to guide her. They were the corners at which she'd waited for Damian, heart pounding in her throat. That was the wall against which she'd sat, back pressing into stone, and cried about her mother for the first and only time.

Things shouldn't look the same, though. These streets should have run red with the blood of the unfavored. The air should've rung with the cries of all those gunned down in the Second War of Saints. It was unfair, somehow, that everything remained unchanged. The first war, at least, had left a scar on the city—the bones of what had once been Chaos's sector were proof of that.

These were the things she needed to remember. The things she needed to remind herself of whenever Damian's presence began to lull her into complacency. He was dangerous, that boy, in the way he made her yearn to press her face against him and forget the world. As though everything were forgiven. As if nothing had happened.

How could it be so difficult to hate the son of the man who'd murdered her father? What was *wrong* with her, that she had to remind herself not to soften?

Roz couldn't shake the thought that she must be deeply unhinged. It followed her as she blew into the tavern, startling everyone standing near the door. The familiar dim light enveloped her, grounded her, and the resulting clarity only made her more angry at herself. She strolled over to the table where Nasim lounged with Dev and a couple of other rebels. The latter stood as she approached, sidling away without a hint of shame.

"Right," Roz called loudly after them. "Because that wasn't obvious at all."

With a groan, she slid into the seat across from Nasim, pulling one of the rebels' abandoned drinks toward her. She sniffed it, determining it to be red wine, and grimaced. Not her favorite. But she tossed it back nonetheless, making a face as she swallowed.

"By all means," Nasim said dryly, albeit not without amusement, "help yourself."

Dev was expressionless. He had a drink in his hand and his cap pulled low over his face. Beneath it, his eyes were heavy lidded, and Roz could tell by their lack of focus that he was far from sober. Another bad day, then. His powers of observation must have persisted, however, because he said: "You seem on edge."

Roz ignored that. "How are you doing?"

It wasn't a question she would normally have asked, given how obvious the answer was. But she wanted Dev to know she was willing to listen when he decided to talk. She missed his easy smiles. The way he tipped his cap whenever he heard a particularly good quip.

Nasim shot Roz a pained look over Dev's bowed head, all the while rubbing a hand up and down his arm. He allowed it, which Roz supposed was a good sign.

"I'm fine. I'm gonna get another drink," Dev said softly, beginning to rise from his chair.

Roz stood with him. "Dev, wait."

He turned, questions in the lines of his face.

"I'm close," she said. "I'm so close to discovering who killed her."

Dev's brows came together as he digested Roz's words. "You are?"

She nodded, cleaning her throat. "I think whoever killed Amélie also killed the disciple and the boy found by the river."

Nasim leveled her with a look. "What makes you think that?"

The question brought Roz up short. She still didn't want to say anything about Damian, but yesterday she'd promised them both an explanation. "I'm...in contact with someone who's seen the coroner's reports."

"Who?" Nasim demanded.

Roz bit the inside of her cheek. Even if Dev and Nasim turned out not to mind that she was hanging around a security officer, they'd tell her not to trust Damian's information. Things could get complicated. Messy. Worse, it might upset Dev more.

"One of the coroner's assistants," Roz lied deftly before she could stop herself. She had always been an excellent liar, and it made her feel worse when Nasim nodded. "Anyway," she continued, "he told me the disciple's body and the body of the boy found by the river shared...similarities. Which makes me wonder about Amélie as well."

"What similarities?" Dev asked, his voice harder. More familiar. "I can tell you about Amélie. I saw her before we buried her, obviously."

Roz didn't want to tell him. Certainly hadn't wanted to ask him. "That doesn't matter."

"Roz," he pressed.

162

"I really don't—"

"Please." Dev's hands fisted on the table. Nasim gently pried one of them open, lacing her fingers through his. Collecting himself, Dev added, "Whatever it is, I can handle it. I need to know who killed her."

Silence pulsed in the air as Roz studied him, considering, until she was sure he was telling the truth.

"Black lines on the skin," she said finally. "Eyes replaced by black orbs."

Nasim loosed an audible gasp, shuddering. Dev, though, gave a single nod. *Smiled.*

"That's it exactly." Something like hope shone in his face. "The lines, at least. I didn't...I didn't look at her eyes." He didn't appear concerned about being asked to reflect on his dead sister's body. No—he was *happy.* Because this was a clue, and even a horrible clue was better than none.

Roz understood him perfectly.

"It doesn't make sense," said Nasim, once she had recovered. There was a screech as she pushed her chair back, leaning across the table to fix Roz with a look. "If the deaths are connected, what do the victims have in common? Or if they're chosen at random, why kill someone in the Palazzo? That's like, the least subtle place to commit a crime."

"I don't understand it either," Roz admitted. "I still need more information."

Their conversation was cut short as Piera sauntered into the center of the room, eyes bright and jaw set. She looked very little like the woman Roz had seen outside the tavern yesterday evening. It was one of the things Roz admired most about Piera: She was not ashamed of her feelings, but didn't let them control her.

"I know you were all just here, so I'll be quick," Piera said, more curtly than usual. Her mouth was a thin line as she scanned the room. "Security officers are still questioning people about the rebellion, but I'm not concerned. Nobody knows much of import about us, and I know none of you would be so foolish as to let anything slip if you're ever detained."

If that was the case, Roz wondered, then why did Piera look so displeased? She arched a brow when Piera caught her gaze, knowing the question was clear on her face.

"We've sent another round of demands up to the Palazzo," Piera continued, "promising certain . . . *unpleasantries*, should they continue to ignore us. We're asking for the usual things: a seat at the table for the unfavored, at the very least. But the main reason I called this meeting is because tonight I found out another round of soldiers are set to be drafted up north. More even than last time. And it's supposed to happen by the end of the week."

There was utter silence in the tavern. Then someone exhaled a shaky breath. A shared, unspoken fear hung in the center of the room: Their numbers were going to dwindle. Some of the people here tonight would surely be drafted. If not them, their family or friends. It was impossible to know until the letter came in the mail.

Roz felt the same fear, though not for herself. She was a disciple. And even if she hadn't been, she was still the daughter of a deserter. She would never be granted the honor of fighting for her country.

That was fine by her. But the idea of Nasim or Dev being sent off to war . . .

"What can we do?" Alix was the first to speak, their voice shaky.

164

Piera offered a grim smile. "I have an idea, but it's going to be risky. Potentially disastrous." When no one voiced their opposition to this, she went on. "I promised you a riot. I said we'd burn the Mercato to the ground. Now, though, I think we should take the opportunity to do something meaningful. What if the Mercato is simply a distraction? We all know the inmates at the prison will be sent to fight. That includes our own imprisoned members. And at some point, they're going to have to be transported from the prison to the boat."

Roz knew where Piera was going with this. The plan unfolded in her own mind. "If we raise enough hell at the Mercato, security will be occupied."

Piera nodded. "We'll all need to work together. This isn't a matter of a small group of us trying to break in. We *all* go. We get Rafaella and Jianyu out, along with as many other people as we can. At best, some of them escape for good. At worst, we cause a hell of a lot of chaos, and some of us don't make it home."

Beside Roz, Dev swallowed hard, but his jaw was set. He was in; she could see it. And his desperation to do something, *anything*, mirrored the rest of the faces around the room.

"Do we *want* to free a bunch of criminals?" Ernesto piped up, his question tinged with skepticism. Nasim shot him the dirtiest of looks, but he went on. "I just mean, why don't we get Raf and Jianyu out, then focus on helping young people who *haven't* broken the law? They're going to be drafted, too."

"Some youths want to go north," Dev pointed out before Piera could say anything. If anyone would know, it was him: He'd nearly gone to the front lines himself before he became disenchanted with the saints' religion. "They've been brainwashed into thinking it's their duty. We run the risk of them fighting us, which would be a disaster. Criminals, at least, will want to escape. Not that most of them are even criminals," he added acerbically. "A good portion of them will have been draft dodgers in the first place."

It was more words than he had said in the past week. Piera looked both surprised and as gratified as Roz felt, directing a firm nod Dev's way.

"Roz," Piera said, addressing her personally despite the numerous other bodies in the room, "you're going to be a key part of this. I suspect your magic will help get those prison cells open."

A flutter ignited in Roz's chest, even as rebels muttered around her. Finally, *finally*, Piera was giving her a real chance. She nodded, lifting her chin. "Absolutely. Thank you."

Nasim shot her a supportive grin, and Roz felt heat spread to her cheeks. It was almost difficult to pay attention as the rest of the details were ironed out. The important part was that everyone was willing to participate and would be ready on Piera's signal, no matter how last minute. The rebels had an existing system for ensuring news traveled quickly by word of mouth—it was how they knew when each meeting would be held. This, though, would be a crucial test of efficiency.

By the early hours of the morning, Piera deemed herself confident they had a plan. She dismissed everyone, disappearing up the stairs in the corner. One by one, people began to filter out, but Roz was loath to leave. Her blood was hot with excitement and alcohol. Eventually there was nobody left in the cantina except Roz and Nasim.

"Do you think knowing who killed Amélie will help him?" Nasim asked as they made their way to the door. The night had turned unseasonably cool, and Roz pressed her shoulder against

Nasim's, seeking warmth. She didn't have to ask who they were talking about.

"It would help me, if I was in his situation." It was the best she could do.

Nasim pulled back slightly to fix Roz with a sad stare. "Would it, though?"

"What's that supposed to mean?"

"Well...obviously you know who killed your father." Nasim's voice held a note of apology. "But does that really make you feel *better*? Or does it just allow you to be more angry than sad?"

Roz didn't quite know what to say to that. She thought a moment, then replied softly, "Being angry feels so much better than being sad."

Nasim slowed then. Moonlight played across the smooth lines of her face. She looked more vulnerable than Roz had ever seen her. She looked not like a rebel, but like a girl, young and fearful. It made a protective urge flare up in Roz's chest.

"I think you're right," Nasim murmured. "But sometimes I can't help being sad regardless." She blinked once, twice. "We'll never know peace until this war is over, will we? And it'll never be over."

Roz wasn't about to lie. "Not until there's a clear loser."

"I think there already is," Nasim said, smiling wryly as they reached the corner by the house. She dropped Roz's arm before turning to look back at her. "I think it's all of us."

DAMIAN

An internal war raged within Damian as he moved through the Palazzo. Last night with Roz had been eating at him, bit by bit, until he couldn't stand it anymore. All day his feet had been battling with his mind, and it was the former that ultimately won out. Long after dusk had come and fled, he found himself standing in front of a door that was not his own, and raised a fist to knock.

"Come in."

The sound of Battista's voice emanating from behind the closed door had Damian's stomach in knots. As usual, regardless of the time of night, the general was in his office, the glow of a candle visible from the hallway. Damian inhaled to steady himself before entering, rubbing a finger over the orb in his pocket. Oddly, it had become something of a grounding technique.

He didn't know why he'd come here. No—that wasn't true. He knew exactly why he'd come here. He just wasn't sure it was a good idea.

I can't argue with him.

You never could.

Damian had been angry at the time of his conversation with Roz. But now, in the sobering quiet of his own thoughts, he realized she was right. He never tried to stand up to his father. He rarely attempted to change Battista's mind, believing it pointless to try. This was where that stopped. Tonight, he would make an effort.

Jaw set, he shoved the door open.

"Evening, father."

"Ah, Damian." Battista was shuffling papers at his desk, standing rather than sitting. He lifted his head to offer a tired smile. His face was lit from beneath by a nearly spent candle, nothing more than a misshapen nub in a pool of wax. "I was just about to turn in. I've a meeting with the chief magistrate tomorrow morning. Can this wait?"

"Actually, it can't." Damian adjusted his shirt, then the badge pinned to it. "I wanted to talk to you about the murders."

"Did you take the advice I gave you?"

Damian invited himself further into the room, hovering on the other side of the desk so he and Battista were face-to-face. He needed to be honest. To take his father's reaction—whatever it may be—like a man. "I did. Enzo has been very useful. But that's not why I've come."

Battista, perhaps sensing this conversation was going to be longer than a few words, sank back into his chair. His face was one of open attentiveness—an expression he reserved for his son alone.

It was the face of a father, not a general. The face of the man who had sat up all night with Damian when he'd had nightmares as a child, and read him stories about boys who were fearless. Damian took it as a signal to continue.

"I want to investigate all the murders. Leonzio's, *and* the two victims found dead in the city. I believe they're connected, and I want to treat them as one case. I'd like you to help me convince Chief Magistrate Forte to allow it."

His father's mouth thinned, the good-natured crinkle of his eyes smoothing out. "Damian, your intentions are admirable, but your instructions were clear. Connected or not, the other murders don't concern us."

Damian felt his cheeks heat. "Don't you care about ensuring everyone gets justice? Don't you think the families of the other victims have a right to know who killed them and to see the culprit pay?"

"Not particularly."

This caught Damian off guard. He hadn't expected him to admit it so readily. "How can you say that?"

Battista sighed, the shadows making his features more severe. He wasn't as clean-shaven as usual, and Damian wondered for the first time if his father carried more stress than he dared let show. "I care about *you*. I care about keeping you on track and making sure you follow the chief magistrate's instructions." Battista walked around the side of his desk, coming to brace his hands on Damian's shoulders. His grip was warm, his gaze intense and pleading. "I took a risk, you know, asking Forte to appoint you head of Palazzo security. You're not even a disciple. Do you understand how uncommon it is for someone unfavored to hold such a position?" His hold on Damian tightened until it was nearly as painful as his words. "You know what the consequences will be if you disappoint him."

You're not even a disciple. There it was. Damian knew his father hadn't meant to make it hurt, but the fact was always there, an enduring wedge between them. And Damian would never, ever be able to change it.

He shoved the ache away, persisting. "But if it gives me a more comprehensive view of the case, I could solve Leonzio's death that much faster. Don't you see? It's—"

Battista backed away, dropping his hands. His expression was tired. "*Please*, Damian. Forget the other victims. I don't care if Forte tells you to go down to the city morgue and fling their bodies into the river—you do it. You were not put in this role to ask questions. You were put in this role to obey. *That is your job.*"

Damian didn't know quite what to say. He felt small. Insignificant. A child who didn't understand the ways of the world and had his priorities all wrong. Battista was right: His job was to protect the Palazzo and obey Chief Magistrate Forte's instructions. Why had he let Roz Lacertosa, of all people, get inside his head?

Damian turned to leave, then stopped in his tracks. He had one other question.

"Did you have Jacopo Lacertosa beheaded?"

There was a heavy pause, and Damian immediately regretted speaking the words. But he hadn't been able to stop thinking about what Roz had said the other day.

Did I think my father was special? *No. I think he was a man trapped by a system that treated him as expendable.*

He had seen Roz's grief. Had seen the shell of the woman that was Caprice Lacertosa, trapped in a gray apartment with the ghosts of her past. Regardless of what Damian's father thought

Jacopo deserved, his wife and daughter shouldn't have had to share his punishment.

Battista's gaze narrowed, slicing through him. "Where is this coming from?"

Damian bit the inside of his cheek. He almost wanted his father to deny it. Having a deserter killed was one thing, but sending his severed head to his family? That wasn't justice. It wasn't even retribution.

"I just want to know. You gave the order for him to be killed, right?"

"Yes," Battista said. "When the fact that he was missing came to my attention, it was my job to track him down. I was his commander."

Damian felt his skin ice over. "But you used to be friends."

"He was a deserter." Battista's tone made it clear he wouldn't entertain further questioning. He seemed a man cut from stone, shaped by the hand of his very own saint. "Regardless, by that time we hadn't been true friends in years. Each time I was promoted, Jacopo grew more jealous. He couldn't handle seeing others succeed. It took me some time to realize that about him."

"Right." Damian swallowed. He could see his knuckles whitening where he'd tented his fingers on the desk. "But even then, doesn't the past mean something?"

Battista's gaze was knowing. "Think of it this way, Damian. What if Jacopo had gotten away with deserting? Can you imagine the shame he would have brought upon his family, had he shown his face in Ombrazia again without being honorably discharged? He would have been shunned."

"I'm sure he would rather have been shunned than killed."

That was the wrong thing to say. His father's brows came down hard over his eyes. "The crux of the matter is, Jacopo and

I were friends, and then we were not. The past is the past. What matters is who someone is *now*—not who they were."

The words made Damian think of Roz. *The past is the past.* What was he to do, then, when the past haunted his present? When he was unable to separate the Roz of today from the girl he'd known three years ago? Though he knew he shouldn't, he still felt the same about her. It was as if no time had gone by at all.

It became evident that Battista was waiting for Damian to say something. Damian's confidence evaporated, and he muttered hastily, "I know you're right. I was just wondering."

Battista nodded, and when he answered, the anger in his tone had dissipated. "Forget about the Lacertosas. Jacopo got what he deserved, and his wife and daughter are lucky they don't bear the shame of what he did."

Battista thought Roz and Caprice *lucky*?

Damian, perhaps foolishly, hadn't expected his father to be quite so harsh. Battista had changed since Damian's mother's death, yes—smiled less and spoke more firmly, gave up hugs for encouraging pats on the arm—but Damian had thought that was because of *him*. A consequence of growing older as a boy. Of crossing that invisible threshold where the need for comfort became a foolish thing. Where tears were a weakness, and the ability to dole out death was boastworthy.

He must have stayed silent a beat too long, because Battista waved the subject away with an air of impatience. "Have you quite finished interrogating me?"

"Yes." Damian murmured. "My apologies."

His father grunted, softening once more. "You're doing well, and you'd do even better if you stopped overthinking. Now go to bed, son. You look like hell."

Damian moved to oblige, but he'd barely made it to the door-way when Battista spoke again.

"And Damian?"

He turned.

"I hope you don't regret what you did."

The words crashed down on Damian like a spill of frigid water. He opened his mouth, then closed it again.

"I don't," he managed to whisper eventually. It held the familiar taste of a lie, bitter and nauseating.

His father nodded, eyes already downcast once more, and Damian walked back to his rooms in something of a trance. But he lay awake for a very long time after that, replaying the conversation in his head and staring into the somber dark.

I hope you don't regret what you did.

So preoccupied were his thoughts, it took him some time to realize Battista had never answered the question.

Damian spent the next morning in the training yard, trying to keep himself distracted. The land between the Palazzo and the adjacent river was all boot-flattened grass and dirt, bordered by barracks that housed any soldiers and security officers who happened to be training in the city at a given time. The day was already warm, and the sun beat down relentlessly on the back of Damian's neck. He wiped perspiration from his brow as he barked instructions into the sparring ring, and squinted against the light as he demonstrated the proper way to hold an archibugio at the firing range. The movement, the focus on something that wasn't Roz or his father, helped to unwind whatever it was that had coiled so tightly in his chest. By the time he dismissed everyone, he felt almost normal again.

He took a quick shower and changed from his training gear into his uniform, then made his way to the Palazzo entrance to wait for Siena. She showed up a moment later, collar askew and braids in considerable disarray.

Damian raised a brow at her. "I can guess now why Noemi wasn't at training."

Siena rolled her eyes, then winked mischievously. "She already has perfect aim."

Damian chose to leave that particular statement alone, shaking his head in mock disappointment as they made their way down the path and toward the city center. He tended to leave Kiran in charge while he was doing his rounds of the guilds' temples, bringing Siena with him. She was, however, a little *too* perceptive, and rounded on him as they were leaving Strength's enormous stone temple.

"Okay, what gives?"

He blinked at her. "What?"

"Don't play coy with me, Venturi. You're preoccupied." Siena's knowing expression dared him to argue. "Is this about Forte?"

"What?" The chief magistrate was so far from Damian's thoughts that the mention of his name caught him off guard. "No." He shook his head, then groaned. "Have you ever been in love with someone who hates you? Worse, someone who *deserves* to hate you?"

Siena gave his arm a sympathetic pat, but said, "No. Women adore me."

From what Damian had seen, it was the truth. He dragged a hand along the back of his neck, unable to help a small grin. "Ah, I keep forgetting. Never mind."

But she wasn't done. "I have to say, I'm surprised. I didn't think you were the type to have a crush. You've never seemed interested in anyone."

"I'm not," Damian admitted. "Not usually. I don't know how to explain it, but...I don't feel anything until I know someone well. Really well."

Siena stopped walking, so abruptly that it took Damian a moment to notice.

"Wait," she said. "It's her, isn't it? The girl we came across the other day, outside Patience's temple. The one whose father was a deserter."

Damn it. He had forgotten she'd met Roz. Damian scanned the street as if someone might be eavesdropping, taking in the uneven cobblestones and groups of people entering and exiting the shops. Nobody was paying them any mind. He turned back to Siena, crossing his arms at her expression of glee. "Maybe."

"I *knew* it." Siena punched the air. "What's the problem, then? Tell her you still care about her."

Damian stared. "My father killed hers, and she hates me for it." *With good reason.*

"Ah." Siena winced, tapping her chin with a forefinger. "I'd forgotten about that part. Well, that makes things a bit harder. Have you tried talking to her about it?"

"We've argued a bit."

Now it was Siena's turn to stare. "But have you *talked* to her? Told her you're sorry for her loss, and been honest about your feelings?"

"No," Damian said. It was true: If he wasn't mistaken, he and Roz were entrenched in a game of trying to convince the other that they were fine. But Damian wasn't fine, and perhaps Roz wasn't, either.

"Well then, do that, idiot." Siena said, her tone teasing. She adjusted the archibugio on her shoulder, then inclined her chin—they had already reached the temple of Patience. The sight of it made Damian tense.

"It's more complicated than I made it sound. There are things she doesn't know about me."

Siena's light mood vanished. "War-related things?"

He nodded. It struck him as the simplest response.

"Damian." Siena said his name firmly, coming to stand closer to him. She trapped his gaze with her onyx one. "You did what you had to, up north. We all did. If she can't accept that, then screw her. But at least give her the chance to know you."

"Is that what you do?" he couldn't help asking. "Give people the chance to know you?"

Siena shrugged. "I suppose you could say that." Then she clicked her tongue at him. "But don't change the subject. I'll finish the rounds—go and talk to her."

So Damian, despite his better judgment, ascended the steps of Patience's temple.

Roz

Roz sat in the temple courtyard, surrounded by altogether too many flowers. They made her nose itch, and reminded her of the time she and Vittoria had hidden out here at night, swapping kisses and stories precariously few inches from a rosebush. She was surprised to find the memory didn't hurt anymore. Their bodies might have fit together, but the rest of them certainly hadn't. It had been nice, and now it was over. They were better as friends.

The next thought struck her immediately, relentlessly: *Were* they friends? Friends told one another things. Friends didn't harbor secret fury about the other's tightly held beliefs. If friendship was knowing someone, *really* knowing them, then did Roz have any friends at all? Vittoria didn't know about Nasim and Dev. Nasim and Dev didn't know about Damian. The secrets were piling up around her, all of them necessary, but painful nonetheless.

The sun had disappeared behind the clouds, and the promise of rain hung heavy on the air, but Roz didn't move. She didn't want to go home, and she didn't want to go to the tavern. She didn't want to go *anywhere*. She wanted to sit here and try very hard not to think.

There was the sudden sound of boots on pavement, and Roz nearly leapt out of her skin when she caught Damian in her periphery. His mere proximity was like a swift kick to the face. What was he *doing* here?

"I came to find you." Damian answered her question before she could ask it aloud, settling beside her on the bench. Flowers shivered in the quickly cooling breeze behind him. He looked infuriatingly good: hair a little windswept, face too perfectly proportioned to be reasonable. Roz felt—admittedly somewhat irrationally—as though he were doing this to frustrate her.

Saints, what was it she'd said to him last night? *That doesn't mean you're not important.* It had been a comment on the relationship between disciples and the unfavored, nothing more.

"Did you change your mind about the coroner's reports?" Roz asked, trying to ignore how close his leg was to hers.

Damian shifted. "Not exactly."

"Then what do you want?"

A tendon in his throat twitched, and Roz noticed for the first time that he hadn't shaved in at least a couple of days. He'd never been able to grow facial hair when they were younger, but a shadow of scruff crept across the sharp lines of his jaw and chin. "I needed to talk to you."

She felt oddly apprehensive. Pursing her lips, she bit out, "Go ahead."

But Damian didn't speak for a long moment. He appeared to

be wrestling with himself, perhaps deciding where to begin. Roz waited, not moving even to brush away the strands of hair that blew across her neck. Somehow, she could sense that whatever came next would be profound.

"When I was up north," Damian said eventually, a soft rasp, "I watched my best friend die. Michele, his name was. We were nearing the enemy line, and I told him to follow me. His vision wasn't good, you see, especially at night. His glasses had broken months ago. Trampled into the mud. He relied on me to let him know the coast was clear. I thought I was being careful." Damian drew a hand across his brow, eyes glassy. "I didn't think anything got by me. I told him where to go, and he listened. Didn't even hesitate. But I was *wrong*. I was wrong, and I hadn't seen them in the trees. When they fired, they missed me. But they hit him."

Roz was silent. She wrapped her arms around her knees, heart beating in her throat. Whatever she'd thought Damian would say, it wasn't this. Why was he telling her this story? Did he think it would make her feel bad for him? She wouldn't. Couldn't.

Damian's expression was broken, his lips pale, as he went on. "I lost my mind. I barely remember what happened. I began firing like mad, and I took three of them down. Even when they were dead, though, I kept shooting. I don't know how I didn't get myself killed. Dumb luck, I guess. All I knew was that I wanted to fucking destroy them." His voice cracked. "Some of the other guys dragged me away. They wanted to *celebrate* me, you know, once we got back to safety. I guess the heretic soldiers I shot were encroaching on our border. Michele was a hero, they said. *I* was a hero. But I didn't give a shit about that."

He shoved his sleeve all the way up to his shoulder, baring a vicious, puckered scar. Roz swallowed hard.

"A bullet grazed me, though I didn't feel it at the time. I was so, so angry." Damian's eyes flashed back to hers. "Mostly that it didn't kill me. I would've deserved it."

"I—" Roz began, but he didn't let her finish, continuing so softly she had to strain to hear him.

"After that, for the first time since arriving at the border, I was ready to fight. I was *desperate* to fight. Instead, though, my father gave the order to bring me home. He didn't trust me not to get myself killed on purpose." A humorless laugh. "In hindsight, he was probably right. I'm not sure what I would've done had I been allowed back on the front lines. So I left, a hero to my platoon." Damian's words were twisted by regret, by disgust. "My father needed me back in Ombrazia, he told everyone. I'd proven myself the perfect candidate to head Palazzo security. And for the most part, people believed him. They congratulated me for killing those men. Congratulated me for getting my best friend murdered. Over and over and *over* again.

"I suppose that's why I'm angry at the people who deserted. I know it's not fair," Damian added. "I don't want everyone to suffer the way I did. But it feels like...like abandonment, in a place where everyone so desperately needs solidarity. If you desert, and you get killed for it...well, isn't that the easy way out? It means you're not watching your friends die, or watching your own humanity leech away. It means you're not dreaming about it for the rest of your life. And maybe it's unfair of me to feel that way. But it aches nonetheless." He left his shoulder bared as he glanced to the balustrade above their heads, gaze unfocused.

Roz couldn't help herself. She softened, throat constricting. All these years, she'd pictured Damian turning into the mirror image of Battista. Navigating the war swiftly, brutally, without remorse. She'd never expected to confront this broken man, sharpened by anguish and guilt.

Automatically she stretched out a hand, seeking to brush the scar that sliced the firm curve of his shoulder. As her fingers neared his skin, though, Damian whirled, grabbing her wrist in an iron-tight vise. "Don't."

Roz froze, breath catching at his expression. His gaze was hard, furious, a little wild.

For the first time since she'd seen him outside the temple, she understood how this version of Damian could be dangerous.

They stayed like that for a moment, his breathing labored, hers nonexistent. The wind made Roz's eyes burn, and her wrist began to throb, but she made no attempt to pull away. After a moment— it could have been seconds or hours—Damian appeared to realize what he'd done. His eyes cleared as he released her, confusion flitting across his face.

"I'm..." He shook his head, then angled his body away from hers. He looked as though he might say more, then appeared to think better of it. "I'm sorry. But that's not everything."

What more could there be? Roz had no idea what her face looked like. She cleared her throat. "Okay." It came out sounding like a question.

Damian took an uneven breath. He was preternaturally still. Then he said only, "It was me."

Roz waited, not comprehending. "What?"

"It was me, Roz. I'm the reason your father's dead."

She only stared at him, sheer confusion coursing through her. What had possessed him to say such a thing? "What do you—"

"When Jacopo didn't return from battle one day, I told my father he was missing," Damian pressed on, jaw so taut it was a

182

wonder the bones didn't fracture. He wasn't meeting her gaze. "That was the day he'd tried to desert. I alerted everyone to the fact that he was missing. *I'm* the reason they were able to find him so quickly. *I'm* the reason he was killed."

Roz opened her mouth slightly, then closed it again. Perhaps his words weren't quite reaching her brain, because shock had rendered her utterly empty. Hollow. She felt as though she were watching a conversation unfold between two people she didn't know.

Damian's voice was a whisper as he said, "It was a mistake, I swear it on the saints. I thought he was injured somewhere, or— or maybe dead. I wanted to make sure his body was returned, because I couldn't bear the thought of you never getting closure. I *never* meant—"

"Get out." The command slipped from Roz's tongue, though she couldn't remember intending to say it. Her heartbeat was thunderous in her ears. She couldn't process this properly, not with Damian sitting here. She hated that he had told her this. Hated that he looked so horribly guilty, so that she couldn't even scream at him. If he'd only kept his mouth shut—if he hadn't gone to his father—

Part of her knew she was being illogical. Damian couldn't possibly have known what the consequences of telling Battista would be.

Or could he?

"Please," Damian murmured, looking so wholly, excruciatingly sad. He lifted a hand as though he might reach for her, then dropped it again. "I never—I would never have done it on purpose. I was worried for him. I never thought for one second he might have deserted. I cared about him too; you *know* that."

Roz could feel herself shaking. She wanted to tell Damian once more to leave. She wanted to throw him from the bench and bury her knife in his throat. She wanted him to hold her while she cried until her head hurt and her vision went fuzzy.

"You know why I spent so many years hating you?" Roz rasped. The words tore free like someone was clawing them from her throat. "Not because I thought you played a part in my father's death, even though I know now that you did." She gave a hysterical little laugh, feeling a bit light-headed. Heat rose in her cheeks—part fury, part something she couldn't identify. "Not even because I detested Battista, and felt I ought to detest you by association. No, I hated you because I knew you were *complacent*. You trotted off to war like a good little son, willing to do whatever Battista ordered. I bet you said nothing when he killed my father, nor when he killed anyone else's. You certainly never reached out to me after the fact. You didn't even send a letter."

Roz took a ragged breath. The emotion she'd been unable to identify was *pain*, she realized. She was hurt that Damian stopped answering her correspondence. Hurt that he hadn't reached out to her when he must have known she was suffering. He hadn't told her the truth, hadn't tried to comfort her, and—even worse— hadn't let *her* comfort *him*.

She'd deceived herself by pretending her fury stemmed from anything other than a horrible sense of abandonment.

Roz liked to imagine she didn't need anyone. Not anymore, at least. But she'd needed Damian then, desperately, and he'd let her down.

She wanted to yell at him until her lungs gave out. She wanted an explanation that would make her feel better, yet knew there wasn't one, and the knowing was infuriating.

Damian, empathetic fool that he was, allowed his own expression to shift dangerously close to misery. "You know me, Rossana. I've always tried to follow the rules. How do you think my father would have reacted if I'd written to you after what happened?"

"Who cares?" Roz's voice rose. She knew she probably sounded unhinged, and didn't care. "What has following the rules ever gotten you? You think you do everything right, but all you're doing is whatever people tell you. You go off to war because your father says you will. You pray to the saints because that's what your family's always done. When are you going to think for yourself? How many more people are you going to fucking kill?"

Her words echoed in what was abruptly an unbearable silence. Damian looked like a man staring into the heart of a live explosion. She knew she had hurt him, and she was terribly glad of it.

"I didn't...," he whispered, then trailed off. His throat worked as he swallowed. It looked painful. "I didn't make the right choices. I know that now. Roz, I'm so sorry."

Sorry was nice, she supposed, but it didn't take away three full years of misery. Three years of staring into an empty mailbox, heart in her throat. Three years of wondering whether he was dead.

She was standing, now—when had that happened?—and Damian moved to her side of the bench, lifting his chin to look up at her. So slowly, as if she were a feral animal, he looped an arm around her waist. Pulled her gently over to him.

Roz didn't resist. She didn't have the energy. She put a shaking hand to the back of his neck, letting him rest his forehead against her stomach. Letting him hold her in what was certainly the most awkward, emotionally charged, half embrace of all time. Her father was dead because of Damian. It had been *him*, and he hadn't even meant for it to happen. What the fuck was she supposed to do with that?

This was not forgiveness—not even close. Roz stiffened. She slid a hand around to the collar of Damian's jacket. Smoothed his lapel. Pulled him to his feet.

"Leave," she muttered once more, and this time he obeyed.

She watched him go, clutching the master key, still warm from where it had been pressed against his chest.

BIANCA

Figures loomed in the city gardens, presiding over the silent trees.

The wind skittered across the grass as a woman made her way down the night-shrouded path. Her face was serene, her movements slow but purposeful.

Eyes tracked her progress.

Bianca stopped only when she reached the figures. Six statues, facing east as if holding solemn, eternal vigil for the sunrise. The dusk held its breath as the last tendrils of twilight faded into obscurity, then exhaled. A soft breeze blew the woman's hair away from her face, seeming to whisper a warning she did not hear. She traced a finger over the frigid stone curve of the nearest statue. It was a delicate touch. The kind of touch that might accompany a silent prayer, or tender nostalgia.

She bowed her head as the eyes detached from the shadows and grew limbs.

The moon was a distant, mournful spectator. This was not the first time its cold glow had become a spotlight for some night-drenched atrocity. All manner of vicious things are made more feasible by the dark, are they not? It provides a stage upon which to peel back the mask of morality donned beneath the wretched sun.

The woman turned, saw who approached her, and smiled.

"Buona sera," she said with a polite nod. "I always find myself drawn here when I can't sleep. Are you the same?"

She waited for an answer that never came.

Then she bled.

20

ROZ

Roz spent the night on the too-short sofa, listening to her mother's slow, uneven breaths. She turned Damian's key over and over in her hands, its magic thrumming against her skin, formulating a plan.

It had been almost too easy to take it from him. He'd been racked by emotion, leaning into her as though her body was the sole thing holding him up. Meanwhile, Roz had felt...hollow. Furious in a way that turned her to stone. Though she knew it wasn't helpful, and certainly wasn't healthy, she couldn't stop picturing alternative realities in her mind. Her father, returned home from the north, his escape successful. Her family, leaving Ombrazia and going somewhere Battista would never find them. Her mother, smiling the way she used to.

If not for Damian, her father might have lived.

Her father might have lived.

Yes, Jacopo Lacertosa had still been a deserter. Yes, Battista might still have managed to track him down. But it was the possibility of him staying alive that kept her up until dawn. The mental image of him sprawled across the sofa on which Roz now lay, that familiar, sarcastic smile lighting up the room.

When morning finally came, Roz spent an absurd amount of time standing in front of the mirror, studying the way her face looked protruding from the Palazzo uniform's pressed collar. It was like staring at the girl she could have been. A girl whose parents hadn't been stolen from her. A girl who'd been thrilled to find herself chosen by the patron saint of Patience, and who'd given herself over to a system designed to benefit her.

Roz stared at that girl and hated her with every fiber of her being.

At the very least, it had sharpened her resolve. She would do this without Damian. She would go to the Palazzo today, and she would do whatever it took to get her hands on those coroner's reports. Damian was nothing but a pawn in her game—easily manipulated.

Dawn had begun to slink feebly into day when Roz arrived at the Palazzo. She'd gotten some searching looks on the way, but no one seemed to have recognized her. Or *not* recognized her, in the case of the security officers she'd passed on her way out of Patience's sector.

As she made her way down the path that wound through the Palazzo grounds, she caught a glimpse of the training yard in the distance. The officers taking part were already fully uniformed, regalia glinting in the dim light as they sparred with one another or shot at targets from an incomprehensible distance. She hoped to hell Damian was with them.

She avoided the main entrance, making a beeline for one of the side doors. Standing on guard, she saw, was a boy with dark hair pulled back in a knot. He was accompanied by a severe-looking blond girl whose eyes snapped up as Roz approached.

"Hey!" The boy waved at her, a grin spreading across his face. "You participating in the training this morning?"

"I was," Roz said lightly, because it seemed something an officer would have done. "You aren't?"

He shook his head. "Someone still has to act as security, right?" Then he frowned at her, nose wrinkling delicately. "This your first time?"

Roz shot him a good-natured, gently withering smile. "Don't worry—we haven't met. Venturi just hired me. Extra security given what happened to the disciple."

"Ah. Thank goodness." The boy mimed wiping sweat from his brow, returning her grin with an easy one. "I'm terrible at faces, so I can never be sure. I'm Kiran, by the way, and this is Noemi."

The blond girl inclined her chin. Roz wouldn't have been surprised to learn Noemi had never smiled in her life. But she said, "Nice to meet you" regardless.

Kiran cast his eyes skyward. "She's not much for niceties," he stage-whispered. "Anyway, what are you up to?"

"Venturi sent me to deliver a message to the chief magistrate." Roz fished around in the chest pocket of her uniform, pulling out the folded letter she'd received from Damian the night before last. "Any idea where I might find him?"

"I think he's in a meeting with the general," Kiran said, looking to Noemi for confirmation. "I wouldn't interrupt them if I were you."

"Well, perhaps I can leave it in his office? Venturi didn't say it was urgent."

"Yeah, why not? Third floor, second door on the left. Just slip it underneath."

Roz gave a jerking nod. "That's right. I always mix it up with the general's office. Which is... second floor, third door?"

"Third floor, fourth door." Kiran laughed, and Roz pretended to groan. He moved aside to grant her entry before adding, "Don't worry, you'll get it eventually. Do you need me to come with you?"

No," she said quickly. "That's quite all right. Thanks."

And then Roz was in. At least Kiran had confirmed the chief magistrate wouldn't be around—that would save her some time and stress. She'd planned to create a diversion, if necessary, to get Forte out of his office, but this was far better.

Honestly, she mused, what had Damian been thinking, giving her access to a Palazzo uniform? He was far too trusting. Perhaps that was the cost of never getting a full night's sleep. Or perhaps it had more to do with their shared history.

History. A simple word, Roz reflected, that meant so many things. It was tiptoeing up creaky wooden stairs after midnight. It was standing on the top floor of the Venturi house, silhouetted by the moonlight streaming in the bay window. It was Damian biting his lip, self-conscious as always, and Roz's heart thrumming in her throat as she leaned in to kiss him. It was the way he'd gasped—so softly, so suddenly—when he felt the pressure of her mouth on his, and the way his hand cupped the small of her back to guide her ever closer.

Saints, why was she thinking of Damian's hands? She needed to get it together.

Roz scanned the glistening marble room with some trepidation, but didn't see anyone else around. Attempting to look natural, she made her way over to the staircase. Each echoing step made her wince. Luckily, the stairs carried on directly from the second floor landing to the third. Roz's heart ricocheted into her mouth when she nearly walked into another officer standing guard at the end of the corridor, but she plastered on a bland smile and dipped her head.

"Morning."

The officer frowned, confusion playing around his mouth as he tried and failed to place her face. But in the end he only returned the greeting, clearly swayed by the uniform.

Roz slipped around the corner, pausing when she reached the second door on the left. She scanned the hall, ensuring nobody was around to hear the inevitable *click* of the lock, then inserted the key. She'd created such keys herself—the kind that could open even magicked locks, that was—but they weren't common. They weren't allowed to be.

The door opened.

The chief magistrate's office was dark, the windows shuttered. Roz pulled back a curtain to allow the early morning light to stream in. It drenched the space in a calm orange glow, lending the impression the room had been engulfed in flame. She scanned the ceiling-high bookshelves, which were clearly decorative—everything was covered in a thin layer of dust—and ran a finger along a book's spine.

Opposite the bookshelves were two enormous armchairs and a clawfoot coffee table. Upon the latter was a tome titled *A History of Violence Through Manipulation of Economic Output*, which Roz eyed as she ambled over to the desk. Documents were strewn across the surface of the chief magistrate's workstation, and Roz sorted through them quickly. Mostly the papers appeared to contain information regarding men of military import. One listed a roster of names Roz could only assume belonged to those who had died on the front lines.

There were letters, too, but most struck her as mundane and unimportant: *Thank you for your generous contribution to the war effort.... Your shipment of ammunition is underway.... Please find your invoice enclosed....*

Then the more depressing ones, which had yet to be sealed and mailed out: *It is with a heavy heart that I am writing to inform you of the loss of your son....*

These there were dozens of, and each name was a blow to Roz's chest. There truly were no happy endings for those involved in war, were there? Desert, and you were tracked down and killed. Die in battle, and your family was sent an emotionally detached form letter. The best outcome was that you survived and spent the rest of your life suffocating beneath the memories.

Like Damian, Roz's brain supplied, and she pushed the thought away. She didn't feel bad for Damian, who as the general's son had been discharged early and given a role for which he was barely qualified. He was one of the lucky ones. He was here, living in the gilded Palazzo, while people continued to fight and die in the unrelenting cold and muck of the north.

Roz set the roster aside and yanked open one of the drawers. Inside was a single letter, neither sealed nor stamped. She skimmed the text, then saw it was signed at the bottom by Battista Venturi. Working in such close quarters, Roz supposed, all correspondence between the two men would be hand-delivered by a messenger. She couldn't help but read on:

I'm as disappointed in Damian as you are. I told him I was trying to ensure he wouldn't be sent back to the war, but frankly I'd rather take over the investigation myself. I can only be supportive for so long. I agree more time up north might harden him a bit. In fact, I've arranged for him to be transported with the replacement troops at the end of the week. Assuming he survives the rest of the year, I would ask that he be reinstated as Palazzo security next winter. I admit myself surprised a son of mine would prove to be so soft, but there's time yet.

Roz swallowed, suppressing a twinge of some unidentifiable emotion. Damian *was* soft. He always had been. He may have become muscled and severe, but nothing hid the fact that at his core he was inherently gentle. Thoughtful.

Everything Roz wasn't.

She remembered Damian's outburst the other day, and how panicked he'd been. He clearly didn't know he was already marked to be sent back up north. How long had Battista been plotting behind his son's back?

Whatever. Roz folded the paper in half, shoving it in the pocket of her trousers. She didn't know precisely why she wanted to keep the letter—Damian's problems weren't her own. But she took it nonetheless.

She opened another drawer, then a third, finding nothing of interest. The fourth, however, contained a number of file folders arranged by date. Roz plucked the most recent one, her stomach performing an excited flip. She could tell what it was before she'd read past the name: *Daniel Cardello.*

That must be the name of the dead boy discovered by the river. Roz read on hungrily, but her eagerness faded when she realized the report contained little she didn't already know. It talked about the missing eyes, the black markings, and went into detail about the unnamed poison's effect on the innards. That part didn't make any sense to Roz; it was too technical. What *did* leap out was the fact that an entire line had been redacted by a thick stroke of black ink, just like the report Damian had shown her. Roz held the parchment up to the candlelight, hoping she might be able to make out the raised marks of a pen tip. But no—whoever removed the section had done too careful a job.

She swore, returning the report to the drawer and flipping to the next one. *Amélie Villeneuve*, it read. A jolt passed through her.

Roz didn't have to look far to see part of that report had been redacted as well. But it told her enough to know what she already suspected: Amélie had died in the same manner as Leonzio and Daniel. She'd been poisoned, her eyes removed.

And she'd been a child. Just a young girl.

Roz bent over the desk, pressing her palms into her brow. It was worse, somehow, to see what had happened to Amélie written on paper. It made it more real. More horrible.

I'll find your killer, Roz thought viciously. *Just wait.*

To be thorough, she took a swift peek through the rest of the file. As far as she could see, nothing had been changed under any of the other names. Which meant Amélie, Daniel, and Leonzio were definitely connected, just as she and Damian had thought.

Roz shoved Daniel's report back into the drawer, taking care to arrange it the way she'd found it. Amélie's, though, she tucked into her pocket with Battista's letter. Then she strode over to the window. Far below, the streets of Ombrazia were dark and labyrinthine. The chief magistrate's office was high enough that she could see across the city, all the way to the expanse of darkness that had once been Chaos's sector. Though of course she couldn't make out any details, she knew the buildings were blackened and crumbling, overtaken by nature in the places the unfavored hadn't claimed. After the First War of Saints, the chief magistrate at the time had given the order for the entire sector to be destroyed.

That was what it meant to have power, wasn't it? You could simply destroy that which didn't serve you.

Roz slipped out of the office and back down the stairs, the foreboding in her chest growing ever tighter. One thing was obvious: There was something Forte didn't want people to know about the murder victims.

And she was going to find out what.

21

Roz

Roz sashayed through the long grass, avoiding the main path leading away from the Palazzo. Kiran and Noemi had let her go without ceremony, and although she'd given them a cheerful goodbye, inside she felt jittery. Full of restless energy.

Chief Magistrate Forte was involved in these murders. She knew it with a certainty rooted deep in her bones. His behavior had been odd—she could still remember his unusual anxiety at the Basilica. He wouldn't show the coroner's reports to anyone else, and parts of them had been redacted, likely at his request.

It was a good thing she'd decided to work without Damian. He never would have believed Forte was involved.

To Roz's profound relief, she didn't see anyone save a few unfavored citizens as she headed toward the city center. It was equal parts strange and disturbing to watch how they veered away from her—an instinctual reaction to the uniform she still wore. The soft morning light had faded, giving way to dark clouds threatening to release a torrent at any moment. Roz tilted her chin up as they crept across the sky. She needed to get home.

Tired of being gaped at, and worried she might come across a real security officer, she decided to take the less public route. Avoiding the main roads increased her likelihood of getting caught in the rain, but it was better than coming across someone who might recognize her.

Thunder rumbled in the distance, and Roz quickened her pace. This particular road took her directly past one of the public prayer gardens, but she couldn't imagine anyone would be there given the impending storm. She ducked her head, intending to dart past, then stopped.

Roz had never paid much attention to the statues in the garden, though she knew they were meant to symbolize the six saints. She also knew there was a patch of dead grass where Chaos once stood.

Tonight, however, there was something occupying that patch of grass.

Something that looked horribly like a person, lying flat on their back.

Despite the jolt of panic that shot through her, Roz continued her approach, squinting through the darkness. When she reached the center of the garden, her heart nearly leapt out of her chest.

"*Shit*," she forced out, stumbling backward.

It was obvious the woman was dead. She was too perfectly still to be anything else. Her head was tilted back, as if to look up at the sky, though her eyelids were closed. Roz felt for the woman's pulse nonetheless, unable to help herself.

Nothing. She couldn't have been dead long, though—her color was still relatively normal. With that thought, Roz swallowed her disgust and peeled back one of the woman's eyelids.

She was met with only blackness. Just like the rest of the victims.

She uttered another string of curses. She couldn't leave the woman here—she needed to tell someone. Damian, though, had made it clear he wanted nothing to do with victims who weren't Leonzio. Who did that leave?

Head spinning, Roz backed away from the body, only to step on something that crunched beneath her heel.

Intrigue and hope replacing her dismay, she knelt to pick it up.

It was a syringe. Delicate and empty, though traces of dark liquid beaded against the now-cracked barrel.

"LACERTOSA!"

The sound of her name had each of Roz's nerve endings come to life. She straightened and whipped around, knowing exactly who she would see.

Damian didn't lower his archibugio an inch. The harsh planes of his face were set in fury, and a chill skittered up Roz's spine. She'd much preferred it when he was red from embarrassment.

Saints, she was still so *furious* with him. It was as though she was composed wholly of conflicting emotions. Perhaps Damian hadn't intended to kill her father, but he was so *blind* when it came to his own. There were so many things Roz was angry about, and now *he* was angry with *her*, yet the mere sight of him was like heaving a breath after years of slow suffocation.

"I wondered who Kiran was talking about, when he asked about the new hire," Damian said pleasantly, the tone making him sound all the more dangerous. The top button of his jacket was undone, and the golden ridge of his collarbone gleamed in the gray light. "Impersonating an officer is a crime—did you know that? I could get *fired* for giving you access to that uniform. And then there's this." He gestured at the dead woman before refocusing on Roz. "You're supposed to put your hands up, you know, when you find yourself at gunpoint."

Roz wasn't accustomed to being caught off guard, and found she did not enjoy it in the slightest. The gears of her mind spun, and for a moment she wasn't sure what to do. The guilt-stricken boy from yesterday was completely gone, as though Damian had put him to bed and woken to don his uncompromising officer mask. "How did you know where to find me?"

Damian's mouth thinned. "I saw you leave the Palazzo, and followed to see what else you might have the gall to try."

Damn it all. Roz hadn't even seen him.

"Hands *up*, Rossana."

She huffed a sigh and obliged, letting the syringe clatter to the ground. Damian's eyes followed it.

Still keeping his gun trained on her, he bent to check the dead woman's pulse. After a long moment, Damian straightened. "Turn around."

"Seriously, Venturi?"

"Turn. Around."

She huffed a short breath, but did as he asked, feeling the cold bite of metal against her wrists. "I'll admit, I didn't think this was how our first experience with handcuffs would go."

"What is *that* supposed to mean?" Damian asked hotly.

Roz rolled her eyes. "It's a sex joke, Venturi."

"Pardon?"

"Don't tell me you're unfamiliar. When two people love one

another very much—actually, scratch that, that's the stuffy, traditional version. When two or more people experience fleeting physical attraction—"

Damian's face turned a delicate shade of scarlet. "Would you stop?"

Roz tilted her chin up, watching the storm approach overhead. "Aren't you going to tell me my rights? Oh, wait—you're controlled by a broken system, and I don't have any. I nearly forgot."

"Rossana Lacertosa," Damian said loudly over her, "I'm placing you under arrest for suspected murder. Should you attempt to struggle, your life will be forfeit. You will be subject to questioning forthwith, and thereafter as I see fit."

"You honestly think *I* murdered this woman? Venturi, I don't even know who the hell she is."

Damian put his lips beside her ear, his voice a low growl. "Do you expect me to believe this was a matter of being in the wrong place at the wrong time?"

"Yes, actually."

He came around to stand in front of Roz. "Tell me what happened."

It was obvious he was humoring her, but she wasn't going to waste the chance to tell the truth. After all, for once it was on her side. "I was leaving the Palazzo and decided to take the scenic route. I noticed the body in my periphery when I was passing the gardens, and came over to investigate. She was already dead when I found her."

"You decided to take the scenic route." Damian's voice was disbelieving, devoid of inflection.

"Yes."

"When it's *obviously* about to rain."

"What's it to you?"

Damian pressed his index fingers into the skin beneath his jawline, stoic bravado leeching away. "What about the part where you stole my key?"

"Ah." Roz nearly chuckled. "Right."

He stretched out a hand, and she shrugged, setting the key in his waiting palm.

"You're truly foolish enough to *steal* from me, Lacertosa?" Damian growled, shoving the key back into his jacket. "When I was trying to apologize to you? When I was trying to *comfort* you?" Pain found its way into his expression before the walls were back up. "What the hell did you use it for?"

He really must be angry if he was calling her by her surname. Roz's entire body felt awash in fire. Yet she couldn't help but feel a twinge when she looked into his face, remembering suddenly what his father had written about him.

I admit myself surprised a son of mine would prove to be so soft.

"Does it matter?" she said. "You have it back."

Damian's brows flicked up as if he couldn't quite believe what he'd heard. "Does it *matter*? Of course it matters. You steal from me, manipulate me, and then I find you standing beside a dead body with a syringe in your hand."

Roz said nothing. Her blood was molten—she couldn't deny she found Damian attractive when he was angry. It was something about the way he held his jaw, as if the motion of clenching it was the only thing keeping him from going off the edge.

"I didn't manipulate you," she told him, mouth dry.

"Really?" His eyes flashed. "You pretended to be upset, told me you were upset I hadn't written you back, all so that you could get close enough to steal from me."

That was what he thought? Roz gaped at him, equal parts shocked and angry. "You think I was pretending to be upset?"

"What the hell am I supposed to think?"

The wind had begun to pick up, thick with humidity. "I *loved* you, and you let me suffer alone. I lost my father—thanks to you, I suppose—and had no idea whether or not I'd lost you, too."

The words were out before she could think better of them, and by then it was too late. Yes, she'd loved him. Yes, that was the first time she'd ever said it aloud.

Damian didn't appear to know what to say. Roz, desperate to fill the heavy silence, continued. "And *for the record*, I didn't murder this woman. Check her eyes. She was obviously killed by the same person as the other victims. And if that person was me, why the hell would I be helping you solve the case? I picked up the syringe because I knew it was evidence."

"Right," Damian said with skepticism, seeming relieved to abandon the previous topic. "And yet I'm sure you're more than capable of killing."

"Maybe I am. But at least I haven't actually *done* it."

Perhaps it was going a step too far. Damian's already wan face turned bone white. Roz thought he was going to yell at her, but instead he seemed to hunch in on himself, misery in every line of his face.

That was when Roz knew she'd won. That he didn't truly believe she'd done it.

Damian breathed in through his nose, then exhaled. It was interesting, watching him gain control of himself—there were so many outward signs of the effort it took. "Well, at the very least, I have to take you to the Palazzo for formal questioning."

"Oh? Is this victim a disciple?" Roz asked. "Because otherwise she's not important to you, right?"

Damian's face was stone.

"Do you know what I'd do if I were you, Venturi?" she went on, having come too far to back down now. "I'd stop listening to your father. I'd stop caring what the chief magistrate wants. Did you know they're already working to have you shipped up north? At the end of the week, in fact."

She thought he might accuse her of bluffing, but the sudden shift in Damian's demeanor was palpable. His jaw tightened, the cutting lines of his cheekbones turning more severe.

"What are you talking about." The question was devoid of inflection.

"I have something to show you, if you'll uncuff me," Roz said.

Damian pressed his lips together, eyes wary. "Do you take me for a fool? Tell me what it is."

"Left pocket of my trousers. Two pieces of paper. One is a letter; read it."

He returned his archibugio to its position across his back, moving close enough for Roz to feel the heat of his body. There was a beat of hesitation, and she wondered if he might uncuff her after all, but then he brushed his fingers along her hip bone and slipped them into her pocket. It was obvious he was attempting to touch her as little as possible, but her trousers were tight, and he was forced to extend his hand against her thigh before fishing the letters out. When he straightened, his cheeks were lightly flushed. Roz could smell the amber and musk scent of him as he stepped away.

His eyes flicked up to meet hers, then down.

"Go ahead," she said, a strange apprehension rising in her chest. "Read it."

"This is my father's hand."

"Yes."

Damian was quiet. Roz scrutinized his face as he read the letter. Although his expression revealed little, the lines of his body tensed. He must have skimmed it twice, maybe three times, and when he finally looked away, it wasn't at Roz. His gaze slid to fix blankly on the floor. The silence was so absolute it was almost unbearable. Normally Roz would have found a way to fill it, but for once she wasn't sure how to proceed.

"Right," Damian said after what felt like an eternity, voice hoarse. "Where did you find this, Rossana?"

She didn't bother correcting him on her name. "Forte's office."

"That's what you were doing with my key."

"Yes."

He closed his eyes. "Right."

"You should read the second piece of paper, too."

Damian's fist tightened, knuckles paling as he crumpled the letter into a ball. "Do I *want* to?"

"It's the most important one."

He didn't appear to agree. "Why did you take this?" He shook the fist containing the balled-up parchment. "Why give it to me?"

"I ... don't know."

Damian stared at the piece of paper as though he weren't really seeing it. Then, before Roz could speak, he leaned against the nearest statue and put his face in his hands.

She swallowed hard. An old urge rose unbidden to the surface, and for a fleeting moment it was difficult not to go to him. But this wasn't the boy she'd loved, no matter how much the broken man in front of her looked like him. Certainly she wasn't the girl he'd loved back. It was just that Damian looked so *familiar* in his misery—such a far cry from the detached, humorless creature he'd become.

"What does the second letter say, Rossana?" Damian asked through his hands, slightly muffled. "Just tell me."

"It isn't a letter. It's the coroner's report for Amélie Villeneuve. Can you let me out of these cuffs, by the way?"

He ignored her question, the line of his back curving further. "Why would you take that?"

"Look at it, Venturi," Roz said, becoming impatient. "A line of the report is redacted. The same line that was redacted in Leonzio's, as well as the other victim's. I checked. All were poisoned. All were missing their eyes, so they couldn't be read by a disciple of Death. And all of them shared another similarity—one that's been blacked out by somebody who doesn't want us to connect the dots. Probably the chief magistrate himself."

"He's the one who demanded I *solve* this. It doesn't make any sense."

"Who else could it be?"

Damian worked his jaw. Perhaps it was a product of aging, or perhaps his dark hair was now too short to conceal it, but his bone structure was...lovely. The carved-out hollows of his cheeks accentuated that sudden vulnerability, and Roz could see the shadows of the veins climbing his neck. "Even if you're right, it's not like I can do anything about it. If that letter holds true, I'll be gone by the end of the week."

"So what? You're just going to ignore this?" Roz shot back. "People are *dying*."

"He's the chief magistrate! I don't have any power where he's concerned."

Roz snorted. "Venturi, when you don't have any power, you get off your ass and you *take* some. You can mope around for the rest of the week, and let your father ship you back to war, or you can come with me to the coroner's so we can figure out what the hell is going on. If it turns out Forte *is* involved, then you've got some leverage. A way to convince him that perhaps sending you back to war isn't the smartest move."

"Because that's what you'd do, isn't it?" Damian's voice was acid. "Blackmail people in order to get what you want."

"Yes," Roz said. She wasn't embarrassed to admit it. "You play the hand you're dealt. And I've put the perfect cards right in your lap."

Damian merely stared at her in response. That cold detachment had fallen away from his face. Saints, no wonder he made a poor leader in this administration. He didn't have the natural inclination toward deviousness that most men in power possessed.

"Well, Damian?"

Time stuttered, and Roz realized too late that she'd called him *Damian* instead of *Venturi*. It shifted the atmosphere between them, and she could tell by the stiffening of his shoulders that he'd sensed it, too. *Venturi* was dispassionate. Formal. But calling Damian by his first name felt like acknowledging their shared past. Like admitting she remembered everything they'd once had.

"I can't do that." He shook his head, but there was little conviction in the movement.

Roz lifted a shoulder. "Fine. You'd rather go back to the front lines?"

Damian clenched his fists. He shook his head again, this time with ferocity. When he spoke, it was a whisper, and Roz couldn't make out the words.

"What?"

He lifted his hopeless gaze to hers. "I'd rather die."

A shiver passed over her skin like a current. "Sounds like you've made your decision, then."

Damian unlocked her handcuffs and picked up the syringe. "Let's go visit the coroner."

DAMIAN

The coroner was in Death's sector, directly beside the Basilica. The walk there was tense. Not only because Damian had a corpse draped over his shoulder—he hadn't particularly wanted to leave her in the garden for citizens to stumble across—but because Roz didn't say a word. Was she angry he'd tried to arrest her? She couldn't very well blame him. What was he supposed to do, when he'd found her standing beside the body? Regardless of what logic told him, the circumstances had warranted her detention. At least, that's what any good officer would say.

Damian thought of the syringe, carefully clutched in his free hand. *Was* he a good officer? He'd let Roz go almost immediately. He knew she hadn't done it—had seen the fire in her eyes that first day at the Basilica, when she'd told him she wanted justice—so why did he feel so guilty? His father and Forte were conspiring to send him away. He shouldn't agonize over what they might think if they knew how he'd acted.

But Damian couldn't help it. It was so deeply entrenched in him, he didn't know how to escape.

The thought of the letter made his stomach churn. There was no getting past the fact that it had been written in Battista's hand. If Damian dwelled too long on it, he thought it might crush him.

The Basilica loomed in the near distance, spires jutting toward the clouds as it began to rain. Not gradually, but in a veritable deluge that had Damian blinking water out of his eyelashes. Lightning streaked across the sky, causing the church's gilded exterior to flash silver, and raindrops spattered loudly against the road. Beside him, Roz's hair was a dark mass, tendrils sticking to her neck. Drops cascaded down her cheeks like unrelenting tears.

I loved you, she'd said. *I loved you, and you let me suffer alone.*

It was true. Damian had done just that. He'd chosen wrong, and he would never forgive himself for it.

He wished he'd known back then that Roz loved him. It was a secret hope Damian had always harbored, but he'd never known for sure. If what they'd had was love, then being loved by Roz Lacertosa was like standing in the eye of a hurricane. It was watching chaos reign around you without being touched by it. It was astounding. Debilitating. All-encompassing.

But what was he to have done? How could he have written to her, how could he have faced her upon his return, knowing the extent of his own crimes? He'd convinced himself staying away would save them both terrible heartache.

Of course, Damian had been steeped in heartache regardless.

By reporting Jacopo missing, he'd only been trying to help. Instead, he'd gotten a man killed and been handed a lifetime of soul-crushing guilt.

You didn't recover from a guilt like that. It settled in the body like a parasite, burrowing in your flesh and gnawing at your bones. It ate away at your insides, embedded itself in your brain, until it became impossible to remember life without it. Eventually, you became nothing but a host to the insatiable ache.

And then he'd seen her again.

As they passed the Basilica, Damian was relieved to see the coroner's building up ahead. It was beautiful in the way disciples' houses tended to be, with a small statue of Mercy out front. Unusual for a disciple of Mercy to live in Death's sector, but Damian supposed it was reasonable in this instance. He felt a pang at the sight of the stone saint, and cast a sidelong change at Roz, remembering her earlier words.

They're dead, Damian. Do you really think they hear your prayers?

What if she was right? What if he spent his whole life praying to someone who wasn't listening?

It was his greatest and most private fear. Another species entirely than his fear of failure or of being sent back up north. This was the fear of giving away his soul, and it being all for nothing.

Roz peered through the single window of the coroner's home. The interior was dark, but that didn't deter her in the slightest. She rapped her knuckles firmly against the door, ignoring the brass knocker. A long pause followed.

"Maybe she's asleep," Damian said, but Roz ignored him.

She knocked again, this time with a volume and ferocity that made Damian wince, but a moment later the door was thrust open to reveal a young woman wearing large spectacles. She was small, at least a half head shorter than Roz, but there was a sharp quality to her gaze. She did not, Damian noted, look at all perturbed to see him carrying a corpse.

"Morning, officers. Can I help you?"

Damian didn't miss Roz's wicked smirk at the word *officers*. "I think you can, actually."

But the coroner didn't let her elaborate, inclining her head at Damian's rather unusual cargo. "People tend to bring bodies to the morgue first, not directly to my house."

"We didn't know if you would be there," Roz said. "So we decided to save you the trouble."

Damian was quick to apologize at the weary look on the coroner's face. "I know it's terribly unprofessional. Forgive me, Signora."

"It's Isla."

"Isla, then. I'm Damian Venturi, head of Palazzo security. Could we come in?"

Isla's brows shot up, and when neither of them offered further explanation, she frowned. "Venturi? As in Battista Venturi?"

Roz stiffened perceptibly beside him as Damian said, "He's my father."

At this, Isla nodded. "Fine. But take your shoes off. You'll drip all over my floor."

Stepping aside, she motioned Damian and Roz into the house. Immediately inside the door was a normal sitting room, though she led them past that into what Damian could only describe as a makeshift mortuary. Bookshelves and cabinets lined one wall, with bottles and various objects strewn across a counter stretching the length of the other. In the center of the room was a long table.

On that table, Damian saw with some horror, was an arrangement of bones.

"Oh, that's Gaspare," Isla said, sweeping the bones to one side. They made a horrible clattering sound on the metal surface. "I'm having a hell of a time figuring out how he died, so I brought him home with me. You can put the body here."

Roz's eyes widened. Damian, not particularly interested in knowing more about Gaspare, set the dead woman on the table. Now that he was looking more closely, there was something familiar about her. He couldn't fathom why that might be.

"We wanted to ask you…," Roz began, but trailed off, frowning. Isla was already examining the body, deft fingers peeling back wet fabric. As she did, Damian set the cracked syringe down with a *clink*.

Isla paused at once, looking from the body to the syringe, then back again. Damian could see the minute changes in her face as she connected the dots.

"Oh, saints," she said. "Not another one."

"So you recognize this." Damian gestured at the scene before him.

She nodded soberly. "Of course I do. This is the fourth one in practically as many months. Is that why you've come, then? Everything I know I've put in the reports."

"That's the problem," Roz said, clearly annoyed the coroner was primarily addressing Damian. She flipped her ponytail over her shoulder. "The reports aren't very useful."

Isla turned, nostrils flaring, and Damian was quick to intervene.

"What she means," he said, "is that part of the reports has been scratched out. The same line in each one."

The coroner's shoulders relaxed. She picked up the syringe, sniffing the contents. It mustn't have smelled good, because she pulled a face, nodding thoughtfully all the while. "Ah. Yes, the name of the poison was redacted. Do you know how hard it was to identify it within the short time I was given? I'm not much of an herbalist, but luckily a few of my colleagues have an interest in nonmagical healing. You know, remedies and such. Don't ask me why."

Roz glanced up from where she'd drifted over to the counter, examining a bottle of purple fluid. "What do you mean, you're not much of an herbalist? The poison is a plant?"

"Don't touch that," Isla warned, and Roz put the bottle down, scowling. "Yes, it's a plant. An extremely poisonous one, obviously. It's called vellenium, and it only grows in a cold climate. I believe you can find it near the northern border. Though," she amended, "I can't see why you'd want to."

"So that's what was in the syringe?" Roz demanded.

"Yes. Those black markings on the victims' skin, spreading out from the point of injection? It couldn't be anything else." Isla indicated the dead woman on the table before them, drawing a finger up the length of her forearm with an almost endearing touch. "I've known disciples of Cunning up north to use it, but it's not common in this area. It's not on the list of poisons that Ombrazia is allowed to ship."

Damian pressed a hand to his neck, massaging an ache he hadn't acknowledged until now. "I don't understand. Why would the name of the poison need to be redacted?"

"I've no idea. I only do what I'm told. My job is to find out what killed people, and I've done that."

"*Think*," Roz pressed, a note of urgency entering her voice. It was a command not to be argued with, and Damian was struck by the thought that, if things were different, she might have made a good security officer.

Isla crossed her arms. "If you want to know why that portion of my report was taken out, why don't you go talk to the person who asked me to remove it?"

Damian exchanged a look with Roz. Her gaze had sharpened into something eager.

"Do you mean the chief magistrate?" he asked. After all, the reports *had* been found in Forte's office. He still couldn't see why the man would have killed anyone only to demand Damian track down the culprit, but if Roz's hunch was correct…

"No." Isla's brow furrowed, like she was surprised they didn't already know. "I don't mean the chief magistrate. I mean your father. It was General Venturi who gave me instructions."

Damian's stomach seemed to turn over. Isla might as well have slapped him across the face. His *father* had been the one to demand she remove the name of the poison used in the murders? What reason could he possibly have had for doing that? His gaze slid to Roz's face, unsurprised to find her… well, unsurprised. She was nodding thoughtfully, and Damian could have sworn he saw the gears of her mind spinning, fitting things into place.

"Did my father say why?" Damian asked when he'd regained his composure. "Why he wanted those redactions made, I mean."

"No." Isla's voice was withering. "And I wasn't about to ask him. He's the general. I did as he requested."

"This just doesn't make any sense."

Roz shot Damian a sidelong look. "Doesn't it?"

Damian chose to ignore that. Of course Roz would want to believe his father responsible not only for Jacopo's murder but for every unfortunate death Ombrazia had seen so far. She was biased against him, and always would be. To Isla he said, "Do you know anything more about vellenium? What else can you tell us?"

Isla made her way to one of the overflowing shelves in the room, running a finger along the cracked spines of the books there. It took her some time to find whatever she was searching for, but eventually she plucked one from the row above her head, slamming it down on the counter. Damian caught a glimpse of the title: *Herbalism and Toxicology: Plants of the Northern Region.*

"If any information about vellenium has been published, it'll be in here," Isla said without looking at them. She opened the enormous volume and traced a finger down the table of contents.

Roz cut Damian a sideways glance as Isla flipped through the pages. Her mouth was a daggered line, though her expression wasn't exactly malicious. She looked as though she were gauging his reaction. Watching to see what he would do when he realized she was right, and he was wrong.

Damian forgot his frustration a moment later, when Isla held up a finger. "Yes, here it is. Indellium."

Cold trailed across his skin. "What does it say?"

Roz peered over the other girl's shoulder as Isla read aloud: " *'Indellium is a northern plant characterized by dark green leaves with 'a distinct shine. The number of leaves varies depending on'*—never mind, I don't think we care about that. *'Indellium can be found in the northernmost parts of Ombrazia, though it is considered a native species of Brechaat and the surrounding area, where it is commonly called* Blood of Chaos.' " Isla's brows flicked above the thick rims of her spectacles. "That's quite the name."

"Keep reading," Roz demanded from behind her.

Isla obliged, though not without a sniff of annoyance. *"The plant is so termed because of the characteristic markings seen on the skin when a solution containing its poison enters the bloodstream. These markings are visible even through the epidermis. Indellium is perhaps most infamous, however, for its use in self-sacrifice. Prior to the First War of Saints, disciples of Chaos nearing the end of their lives would purposefully ingest the poison while lying in a prepared grave. They believed that by sacrificing the last of their life force to their patron saint, it would facilitate the growth of his power."*

"That's why part of the report was redacted," Damian said slowly, piecing it together. "Someone didn't want people to learn about the poison's connection to Chaos."

"Someone?" Roz scoffed. "I think we know exactly who."

Damian raked a hand through his hair. He couldn't deny that he saw where Roz was coming from: Battista had lived up north and would have had access to the plant. That said, Damian couldn't see his father wanting anything to do with a poison tied to the patron saint of Chaos.

Isla slammed the book shut. "That's all it says. I'm sure the general knows far more than I do, so I suggest you speak with him." It couldn't be clearer that she was keen for them to leave, and Damian swallowed his embarrassment.

"I'm terribly sorry to have imposed," he told the coroner. "Thank you so much for your help—you've been invaluable." He began backing out of the room, and with a resigned sigh, Roz followed.

Isla said, "Aren't you forgetting something?"

"What?"

She sighed, indicating the body.

Damian halted. "Oh, of course. Right. I—"

But Roz grabbed him by the arm, trying and failing to drag him over to the door. "Come *on*."

He shook free, trying not to revel in the sensation of her fingers digging into his skin. Isla watched them with a bemused expression, then shook her head.

"You know what? Never mind; you can leave the body here. I wanted a cross-section of the affected flesh anyway."

"A happy coincidence," Roz said sweetly.

Damian managed to control himself as they closed Isla's front door behind him. It was only after they strode back into the rain-drenched street that he rounded on Roz, fear and misgiving forming a poisonous concoction in his blood. "Don't look so smug. We have no proof my father had anything to do with this."

Her answering laugh was incredulous. "But you can see why he looks guilty, right?"

Damian blew out a breath. "I don't know, Rossana. I mean, the evidence is there, but it's circumstantial. And I just don't see a motive. Why would he want to kill any of the victims so far? It doesn't make sense. I'm more inclined to believe the chief magistrate sent him to the coroner on his behalf."

"You said it before—Forte was desperate for you to solve the disciple's murder."

"Maybe he was only desperate for me to fail. Maybe he knew I'd never solve it, because I'd never think to blame him, and then he'd have the perfect excuse to get rid of me."

"He's the chief magistrate. He doesn't need an excuse," Roz pointed out. "If he wanted to get rid of you, he just...could."

Damian gritted his teeth. He rocked his weight back into his heels, blinking rapidly so as to see through the rain. "My father was trying to help me, you know. Maybe he *wanted* me to prove it was the chief magistrate."

"To what end?" Frustration laced Roz's tone.

"I don't know, okay? I just can't see why he'd do this."

Roz paused. She seemed to be turning something over in her mind. After a beat she said, "Regardless of who the culprit is, you have to admit there's some connection to Chaos. Using vellenium, when countless other poisons would have been more readily available? That's not mere coincidence. And look at the bodies."

Damian didn't like where she was going with this. "What about them?"

"They were abandoned right where they were killed. That's either a mark of the laziest murderer of all time, or they were ritual killings."

It had been decades since anyone offered up human sacrifices to the saints—those who deserved to die, the Palazzo claimed, did not deserve to be glorified—but Damian still knew enough about it. He gave a firm shake of his head. "Nobody ritual kills anymore. Especially not for Chaos."

"Venturi, they're using the exact poison disciples of Chaos once used for self-sacrifice." Roz peered at Damian as though he were being purposefully obtuse. "Nothing has ever looked *more* like ritual killing."

She wasn't wrong, Damian thought as he watched raindrops trickle from the ends of her ponytail onto the front of her borrowed uniform. Her hands were on her hips, and she stared at him with a fierceness that had him second-guessing whether any of this was worth arguing over. Still, he couldn't help asking, "But what's the point? Who believes in that kind of thing?"

"What's the point of believing in anything?" Roz shot back. "You think a bunch of dead saints hear your prayers. Someone else might think they demand ritual killing. What's the damn difference?"

"One is worse than the other," he said.

"Well, from the outside, they both sound equally nonsensical."

Every part of Damian wanted to be offended—after all, that was how he had been taught to react whenever someone questioned his beliefs. He found, however, that he simply couldn't. He didn't have the energy to argue about things like this anymore. Not when he was growing less and less sure that he had all the answers.

Roz watched him in such a way that Damian wondered if she knew what he was thinking. If she could see the war raging inside of him.

"Come on," she said, voice soft. "I'm tired of standing in the rain."

23

ROZ

Roz led Damian to the bathhouse attached to Patience's temple. It was vacant at this hour, warm and dry, and the sound of water tumbling over stones was a familiar comfort. Damian tensed when he realized where they were, pausing at the entrance.

"I'll just wait outside."

Roz rolled her eyes. "Don't be ridiculous. We're not here to *bathe*. It's a place we can talk freely. No one's ever around, plus it's out of the rain." But she rolled up the legs of her trousers as she spoke. Plumes of steam rose from the surface of the water, and the room was dark save for the blue light emanating from its depths. The rocks lining the pools were imbued with a faint luminescence, and they burned behind her eyelids whenever she blinked.

She settled herself on the edge of the pool, flicking a few drops of water toward Damian. They fell woefully short of his tense frame. "Oh, don't be so uptight." Roz rolled her eyes. "Like I said, no one's going to catch us here."

Damian muttered something under his breath that sounded suspiciously like, *Seven saints, Rossana*, but moved to join her nonetheless. The dark settled in to silhouette him, throwing the lines of his face into sharp relief. Goose bumps rose on Roz's skin in the cool air. She studied the strong set of Damian's shoulders, the way he kept cracking the knuckles of his right hand.

"Sit with me," Roz said, patting the stone ground beside her.

Damian did not. He clucked his tongue at her in feigned displeasure.

"*Sit*," she repeated, and reached up to grab his arm, intending to drag him into compliance. She could feel his pulse beating wildly in his wrist. He made no move to resist her. Even in the blue-tinged light, his cheeks were flushed. He watched her carefully, skeptically, like a man half under a spell. When he cleared his throat, adjusting the front of his trousers, Roz couldn't help her smirk.

She'd intended to bring up Battista once more—to say that it made perfect sense for him to be the murderer. His standing in the Palazzo was high enough that he could do what he wanted. And of course he was planning to get rid of Damian, who was working tirelessly to bring the killer to justice.

But she couldn't bring herself to do it. She watched as Damian yanked off his boots and rolled up the legs of his trousers, somehow managing to look graceful as he folded himself into a seat. He kicked his legs back and forth beneath the glassy surface of the pool, shuttering his eyes, chest rising and falling with each breath. Exhaustion emanated from him, bitter and tangible. For some reason, it made Roz yearn to see him soften.

"You know what?" she said. "I don't understand why your father gave you your position in the first place, if he's not going to trust your judgment. You're a good officer, Venturi, whether he sees it or not."

She could see Damian waging an internal battle with himself, trying to decide whether she was being genuine. He was desperate to believe it, the way he was desperate to believe her the same girl he'd once loved.

He stared at the rippling water, clenching and unclenching his fist, the veins on the back of his hands strained.

I am that same girl, Roz might have said, but it felt like too harsh a lie, even for her.

"You asked before why I don't like being a disciple," she said softly, because she couldn't stand the silence. "I suppose it's because it felt to me like the world was playing some kind of cruel trick. I hated myself when I found out, you know."

Damian cut her a sideways glance. "Why?"

Roz drew her tongue along her top teeth before answering. "My father was sent to war because he wasn't a disciple. Because he wasn't important. I suppose part of me wanted to follow in his footsteps. It was only recently I realized...maybe it's good things worked out the way they did. I was given a privilege, in a sense, and maybe I can use it to create change. That's why I want justice for the victims. I want the people watching—their families, their children, the other unfavored citizens—to know they're important. To someone, at least. Even if that someone is only me."

So many half-truths, layered atop one another. Could Roz truly say she wanted justice, when part of the reason she even wanted to find the killer was to prove to the rebels she could be trusted?

"Roz?" Damian breathed her name into the blue-tinged dark, eyes still closed.

"Yes?"

A beat of silence. Then: "I'm so sorry about your father. I wish...I wish it had been me."

The vulnerability in his voice knocked her out of balance. It was easy to be with Damian when he was frustrated, impatient, or telling her off. It wasn't easy, though, when he wanted her to be genuine. To be vulnerable in the way that came so naturally to him.

Damian Venturi, whether he meant to or not, was going to cause the persona she'd built to crumble.

And she feared she was going to let it happen.

"I don't," Roz whispered, and was surprised to find that she meant it. "I don't wish that, Damian." She tilted her head, letting her hair tumble over one shoulder and down her chest. If she didn't get the words out now, she might never say them at all. "I can forgive you for trying to help my father. For doing what you thought was right, even if it led to his death. I mean, let's face it— he probably would have died regardless. But every day I was terrified that you might have died, too. You could have let me know you were okay. And you just...didn't." She clenched her hands until nails cut into skin, staring into the water, unable to look at him. Her voice was ragged. "How can I forgive you for that?"

Though he didn't move, she heard Damian's sharp inhalation. Saw the faint movement of his throat as he swallowed.

"You can't."

Then, before Roz realized what he was doing, Damian reached out and laced his fingers with hers. Slowly, so slowly, as if gauging whether she would let him continue. She didn't move. She wasn't sure she would ever move again. Damian's other hand came to her neck, stroking the delicate skin there, before tilting her chin up.

"Roz," he said, and his thumb brushed her bottom lip. She shivered. "When I was up north and felt I would lose my mind among the dead... When I thought *I* would be the next to die, and on the worst days, when I hoped I would be... I thought of home. I thought of midnights beside the river, and the way the houses in Ombrazia are so close together, it makes the world feel small. I thought of running through the alleys, of sneaking out to the Mercato, of treading water in the summers. Those memories kept me sane. And you know what?" His eyes were endlessly sad. Dark and infinite. "You were in every single one of them. Everything that reminded me of home—everything that reminded me of happiness—centered around *you*. Every time I looked up at the moon, I remembered when we were nine and I asked what would happen if it fell from the sky. How you laughed yourself silly at me, and said that although space was infinite, the moon never stopped circling earth. How it couldn't stop even if it wanted to. And even back then, I knew which one of us was the earth."

Roz felt her body go numb, all the vitriol draining away as abruptly as the light of a candle being extinguished. Damian might as well have reached out and snatched the mask from her face himself.

The worst part was that, in a way, she knew it was true. Because if she was the earth, then Damian was the moon—steady and unyielding, affecting her from a distance whether she liked it or not. Not minding that she was wild and unpredictable, ever-changing disorder.

"I wanted to be your earth," Damian said, more softly now. "Just once. Just for a moment."

For a moment there was no sound but the soft lapping of the water against the side of the pool. Nothing but the electric sensation of Damian's leg inches from hers. Lit from beneath, the pool looked depthless, as inscrutable as his expression. Roz was enraptured. Chills danced along her skin in unsteady caresses, and her tongue was dry against the roof of her mouth, each successive moment more wrought with tension than the last.

How was it that he didn't realize every bit of her life revolved around him? That it always had? Even the bad parts were painted all over with Damian Venturi.

Roz freed her hand, reaching up to lace both around the back of his neck. The hair there was too short to twine her fingers through, so she dug in lightly with her nails, tipping his face down to hers.

But Damian resisted, reaching out to touch her lips with a forefinger. Stopping her from doing what she so desperately wanted to do.

"No," he breathed. "I've always regretted not kissing you first."

The admittance made Roz's stomach tighten. She blinked up at him, surprised to see him so calm and sure. He replaced his finger with his thumb once more, pulling her lower lip down. Staring at her mouth with such reverence that she didn't know what to do with the rest of her body. This was not the shy, hesitant boy she had kissed that wine-soaked summer night.

Damian took her lip between his teeth for a breath of a moment, then moved up to press his mouth to hers.

Roz slackened against him. In a sense, it was a first kiss all over again: desperate and searching and rendering her weak. But it was also very much *not* a first kiss, because this version of Damian knew exactly what he was doing. His hands were confident as they roamed her rib cage, and his lips were sure as he moved them across her jaw and down her neck. Roz tipped her head back and shuttered her eyes, absorbing the warmth of his hitching exhalations against her throat. His hands came to grasp her waist, to trace the slope of her shoulder.

"I don't think," he murmured into her ear, "that it's possible to get as close to you as I want to be."

Roz knew the feeling. She wanted to hold him and never let go. She wanted to make up for each and every wasted moment of the past few years, and feel his touch against her skin at all times. She needed to know that he was here, that he was alive, and that he still loved her, no matter how messy this thing between them might be.

She had never hated Damian Venturi. A part of her had always known as much. But Roz turned her sadness into anger, her pain into loathing. The feelings were easier to deal with that way.

"I didn't hate you," she managed to force out, arching against him. His roaming hand stilled, and she grabbed it, squeezing his fingers as if they were a lifeline. "I told myself I did, but it was a lie."

Damian's eyes were liquid onyx in the low light. Roz was horrified to find her vision blurring, and she squeezed her own eyes shut, letting her forehead fall to rest against his shoulder. It was firm and warm. The shirt of his uniform smelled like rain and musk.

"It's okay," he whispered, using his palm to make slow circles on her back. His voice was hoarse. "I understand."

They stayed like that for some time, and eventually Roz felt herself relax. She had told him the truth, and he had understood. There were no barriers between them now.

It took her far too long to remember Damian didn't know she was a rebel.

DAMIAN

The high of kissing Roz still hadn't faded by the time Damian returned to the Palazzo.

She'd been vulnerable with him—something he knew didn't come naturally to her. She didn't hate him. After everything, they were beginning to rebuild what they'd lost. And if Damian wasn't mistaken, it might be even better this time around.

There had been something strange about the way she'd withdrawn from him, though. Her voice had been a little too controlled when she suggested they meet up again tomorrow. They would discuss what to do about Battista then, she'd said. In the meantime, she told Damian to avoid his father.

Then she'd left, and Damian hadn't been able to shake the feeling there was something she hadn't told him.

He was imagining things, he told himself as he paced the first floor of the Palazzo, muttering a greeting when he crossed paths with Noemi. Roz had been more honest with him than she ever had. It was why he hadn't been able to bring himself to say he still wasn't convinced Battista was involved.

Yes, his father had the means to carry out the murders. Yes, he might have had access to vellenium when he was up north. And yes, if he was the culprit, Damian might be able to blackmail him to ensure he wasn't sent back to war.

That last one had been Roz's point, and Damian had humored her.

Yet despite the evidence, he couldn't shake the feeling she was wrong.

His head spun, full of questions and fears that only seemed to compound as they cycled through his thoughts. He needed to go somewhere quieter. He needed guidance from someone other than Roz, who would never be able to look at the situation with any kind of neutrality.

When Damian reached the Shrine, he wasn't sure whether the hooded statues made him feel better or worse.

He made a beeline for Strength, kneeling before his patron saint without any kind of hope. How was it that something that had once brought him so much comfort now felt so fruitless? It was as if the imagined light he'd once pictured at the heart of the statue had flickered out. But muscle memory compelled him to try. To bow his head and close his eyes, searching for a place of calm deep within himself.

Please, Damian thought as the cold seeped from the stone floor into his legs. *I need guidance.*

There was no response. He tried to focus harder, tightening the muscles of his jaw, but his mind drifted. He thought unwittingly of Roz's words the other day, when he'd said the ways of the saints were beyond their comprehension.

That's what everyone says about their beliefs when they don't want to think too hard. It's lazy, and it's cowardly. It's easier than admitting you might not understand the world.

As much as he detested admitting it, Roz was right. He didn't want to think too hard, didn't want to look too close, because he was afraid of what he might find. It was so much easier to trust in his own limitations than it was to consider the other option: that no one was listening.

That no one had ever been listening.

He pressed his forehead to Strength's feet. If the six saints were anywhere, it was here. Damian had to believe that. Because if he didn't, then he was alone in an underground temple, face touching cold stone for no reason at all. If he didn't, he would be forced to look back on every aspect of his life and feel foolish.

It was said you would find the saints once you opened your heart to them. So what was Damian doing wrong? He didn't think he could be any more open. Couldn't they hear how desperate he was? He needed a sign—something to show him whether his father could be trusted. He wasn't willing to gamble whatever remained of their relationship without proof. Was he weak, unmanly, if he didn't return to war without complaint? Was that why Strength ignored him?

Lazy. Cowardly.

"Why?" he shouted at Strength's feet, the words echoing in the cavernous room. He wrenched his head up, lifting his chin to the statue's impassive face. When he spoke, the words caught in his throat, choking him. "What am I doing wrong? Why didn't you choose me?"

Something like hysteria welled within him, driving him to stand. He moved like a specter to the other end of the row of statues. Each beat of his heart was an insistent, threatening knock. As if there was something hunkered down within him, fighting to get out.

Damian came to a stop only when he stood before Chaos.

The gray-white sheet fluttered slightly, though the air in the Shrine was still. Damian felt as though he were in a dream, or maybe a nightmare, in which his body moved without his consent. His fingers twitched toward the sheet, but he snatched them back. Removing it felt wrong. Both spiritually and symbolically.

Chaos was evil. He was fallen, and he certainly wasn't present in this place.

But a feeble part of Damian's soul was suddenly certain that if any of the saints were going to respond to him, it was this one. After all, Damian *was* chaos, wasn't he? Perhaps not in his own right, but by association. He let it reign around him without making any effort to staunch it. He had blood on his hands, and not the righteous blood of Death. When Michele died, when Damian shot those men, he'd been gripped by something *other*. Something that thirsted for violence and decay.

"I don't want you," he whispered, vision blurring as he studied the curve of Chaos's shrouded head. He felt foolish, but he needed to say it, just in case. "If you're there, fallen or not—*I don't want you.*"

Nothing happened. Of course it didn't. Chaos had plummeted from grace seventy years ago—Damian couldn't blame his past deeds on the influence of a saint who no longer played a part in Ombrazia's religion. What the hell was he doing? Beneath that ghostly sheet was nothing but a statue. Stone in the shape of a man.

In an effort to reassure himself, Damian reached out and grasped the saint's arm. It was frigid, like gripping fabric-wrapped ice.

But that wasn't why he yanked his hand back.

There was a sound like stone scraping stone, and the wall beside Damian moved.

He froze, heart stuttering as the rock separated and moved aside. Damian watched part horrified, part intrigued, as the wall settled in its new position to reveal a dark tunnel. Automatically—as if in a trance—he took a step forward.

Then he smelled it.

Rot. The putrid stench of something long deceased.

Damian coughed, pressing his nose into the crook of his arm. Nausea rose in his throat. Whether from the reek or the result of his misgivings, he wasn't certain.

There was a secret tunnel in the Shrine, and something in it was dead.

He hesitated. Did he summon backup? What if the passage closed again while he was inside, and he couldn't get it to reopen? Then again, whatever was down there, did he really want to discover it alone?

"Don't be a coward," he muttered to himself. He should at least take a look, if only to see how long the tunnel was. Swallowing bile, trying to inhale as little as possible, Damian grabbed a candle from the nearest candelabra and stepped into the passageway.

The scent assaulted him all over again. He gagged, blinking around. The walls were narrow stone, faded and dirty. It was freezing in here, and yet death still managed to cling to the air. That didn't bode well. Damian held his breath as he moved deeper into darkness. Mercifully, he saw, the passage wasn't long; in fact, a room was already visible at the end of it. He quickened his step, bracing himself against whatever he was about to find.

He didn't know what he'd expected the room to look like, but it was empty, nothing but floor-to-ceiling stone. The smell became overwhelmingly horrible, until Damian swore he could taste it. His stomach gave a lurch as he cast his flame around the space. Its flickering grew ominous, and shadows climbed the walls like swarms of insects.

When he saw the body on the floor, he couldn't help his cry.

The person—a man, Damian thought—had been dead for so long as to be unrecognizable. He had never seen discoloration quite like it. In fact, it looked as though the body were beginning to mummify. He pressed a hand to his mouth and nose, trying not to look too closely at the clear signs of rot. At the skin that no longer looked like flesh, but something sunken and purpled, stretched taut across bone. At the grotesquely disfigured face. The cold had likely helped slow the decay, but not enough. And the *stench*...If Damian had to guess, he would say this man had been dead for at least a week.

That was when he saw the spectacles perched atop the corpse's nose. Recognized the cloak splayed out across the floor.

It was Chief Magistrate Forte.

It was impossible. Entirely so. But the closer Damian looked, the more familiar the dead man became. The shape of the nose. The color of the hair, pulling away from the scalp in clumps. Even the shoes peeking out from beneath the cloak's dark fabric.

Damian stumbled backward, a cold sweat breaking out across his brow. His grip on the candle slackened so that he nearly dropped it.

It didn't make sense. It couldn't be real. He had seen the chief magistrate only recently. Had spoken to him multiple times. This corpse had to be someone else.

But it wasn't. Damian knew it wasn't. The knowledge roiled in his gut alongside the nausea. Both things couldn't be true, though: The chief magistrate could not be both alive and dead. Was Damian losing his mind? Either this wasn't real, or the events of the last week weren't real. And since the latter seemed far less likely, that left the former. Was this a dream? A vision? An illusion?

An illusion.

Damian continued to back away, realization sliding sluggishly into his veins. When two things could not possibly be true at the same time, one of them had to be false. And who falsified reality better than an illusionist?

But the disciples of Chaos couldn't be back. Chaos had fallen, which meant there was no longer any way for them to be created. Damian had to believe that, or nothing else made any sense.

How did anyone know for sure that Chaos fell? his brain supplied, unbidden. *He was a deity. What was the proof?*

"No," Damian grunted aloud, fingers pressed to his temples. He couldn't start questioning these things. Not now. Not when the saints were the only certainties in his life.

The other option, of course, was that he'd completely and utterly lost his mind.

His thoughts spiraled as he backed out of the room, panic clenching his heart like a vise. This was why disciples of Chaos— even the concept of them—were so dangerous. They made you question your own sanity. Were the murders real? The notes Roz had found? Was *Roz* real? Or was someone building false scenes around Damian as though he were a pawn on a chess board?

Despite everything, he needed to tell his father. If anyone

would know what to do, it was Battista. No one was closer to the chief magistrate.

Can my father be trusted? he thought frantically, the doubt searing like a burn.

But another part of him—the part that craved reassurance, that hoped for guidance—said, *go.*

Damian felt as if a stranger had taken over his body. He was hot and cold at the same time, his nose full of death.

He flung Battista's office door ajar. He didn't know what he was going to say, but he would force the words out. The Palazzo, the officers, needed to be on their guard. Something was very, very wrong.

His father glanced up as he entered, surprise flickering across his face. "Damian. What's going on?"

Damian's mouth was dry. None of his thoughts were fully formed. He thought of vellenium, of the notes Roz had shown him. They felt like another, faraway problem.

"I need to talk to you."

"I gathered as much. Take a seat."

Damian did not. He was entirely too jittery. "Something's wrong. I think the chief magistrate is dead."

Battista blinked, perturbed. His gaze narrowed as he took in Damian's harried appearance. "Why in the world would you think such a thing?"

"I saw his body."

There was a pause so long it demolished the line separating uncomfortable from outright awkward.

236

"Damian," his father said slowly, "I met with Forte not two hours ago. Do you mean to tell me you believe he's been killed since then?"

"No. It was a while ago. Or—I'm not sure." Damian ran a hand down his cheek, pulling the skin taut. "Look, do you think...Is it possible the disciples of Chaos could be back?"

Battista rose, the action stiff. Something like concern was beginning to take hold of his features, and the shift in his demeanor coincided with the shift in the air around them. "*Excuse* me?"

"I know it sounds mad. But I've seen things. Things that can't be real." Damian knew mentioning Chaos was a mistake, but he couldn't keep the words from tumbling out. Someone besides himself needed to *know*, needed to do something about it. He thought of the rumors surrounding the fallen seventh guild: Disciples of Chaos could manipulate multiple people at once. They could show you any lie and make you believe it. There were even horror stories of those who had spent so long under a disciple's control, they'd forgotten their reality and died from dehydration.

There was a beat of silence as Battista digested that. When he spoke, it was with careful intonation. "Damian, are you quite well?"

Damian lowered his voice in an attempt to sound less unhinged. "I saw the chief magistrate's body in the Shrine. But it wasn't real, was it? Because you just met with him. Or did you?" He spread his hands wide. "It's impossible to tell! Don't you see?"

His father appeared to have been stunned into momentary silence. He opened his mouth, then closed it again, before shaking his head. "You're hysterical."

"I am *not*," Damian shouted, desperation flooding him. He needed his father to listen, to understand. "Something's not right here. I know you're involved with the murders. I know you met with the coroner to demand she redact the section about vellenium from her reports. Why?"

Battista blinked, managing to look confused. "That is a very strange accusation," he said, too carefully. "Where did you hear that?"

If Damian had the capacity to feel anything other than horror, he might have been disappointed. Why wouldn't his father just admit it?

He watched, wide-eyed, as Battista took a few slow steps toward him, the way one might move around an unpredictable animal. "Damian, perhaps it's best you take a break from the Palazzo. Just for a short while. It appears the stress of the job has finally gone to your head."

His father's face was a mask, and Damian's stomach plummeted. He knew that look. It meant Battista had made a decision. One with which there would be no arguing.

Damian argued anyway. He couldn't help himself. "No." Dread overflowed in his chest. "No, I'm not going back to the war."

"It will be good for you," Battista said firmly. "A man softens when he's away from battle for too long. You'll learn how to better overcome these, ah…delusions."

Damian backed away, edging toward the door. Sweat trickled from his hairline down the side of his face. "They're not delusions. I need you to *listen to me*." He spat the words, agitation making him inarticulate.

In his panic, he didn't hear the office door open. Didn't see his father beckon someone else into the room, and didn't feel that someone's presence as they approached him from behind.

The accusations died on his lips as the world went black.

DAMIAN

The sound of gunfire was a cacophony echoing through Damian's bones.

He was crouched in the mud, his entire body smeared with it, shaking with a cold that went beyond the bounds of regular discomfort. A short distance away, equally dirty so as to be unrecognizable, was Michele. Damian pressed his feet more firmly into the ground. It was too foggy to see properly, and his hands shook where he gripped his gun, finger always frozen just above the trigger. The fear pulsing through him was unlike any he'd felt before. It was fear so stark, so potent, it bordered on numbing. Fear for himself. For Michele. For the other men around him. For the world he might never return to.

The dark figures came over the hill, just like always.

Damian didn't feel the bullet graze his shoulder, just like always.

But he felt the fear. It embedded in his chest, hunkering down beside his frantically beating heart, and never left.

Not even when the world went quiet.

"The general's son?"

"Yeah."

"Why's he trussed up like that?"

"Guess they thought he might try to escape. Leap into the sea or some shit, rather than return to war. I dunno. No special treatment this time, though."

"He's twitching like mad. Think something's wrong with him?"

"Nah. Probably just nightmares, like the rest of us."

Voices drifted to Damian like whispers on a wind, almost too soft for him to make sense of them. It took effort to coerce his eyes open, as if the connection between his body and brain was slower than usual. Sensation flooded back into his limbs. He felt as though he'd been in a fight and gotten off poorly.

"Oi—he's awake."

A moustachioed face entered Damian's field of vision. He automatically shied away, squinting in the sudden flare of light that accosted him. "Put that down, would you?"

The unfamiliar man lowered his lantern. As Damian's eyes adjusted, he saw two men standing before him: one thin and one muscular, both sporting Ombrazia's crest on their military jackets.

"Venturi Junior, is it, then? Welcome aboard. I'm Capitano

Russo." Moustache smiled, though his large companion did not. His voice wasn't friendly.

A pang seared through Damian's chest, quickly replaced by unease when he attempted to move and found he could not. He was in a seated position, he realized, arms bound tightly behind his back. Metal cut into the skin of his wrists, and each time he shifted his weight, something behind him *clang*ed. Was he handcuffed?

"Where are we?" Damian demanded, trying to coax confidence into his voice. He wasn't a fool—he knew what must have happened. He was being taken north, and his father hadn't wanted the inconvenience of a fight, so he'd... What? Knocked him out? Damian had a vague memory of someone entering his father's office, but he hadn't had the chance to turn around before everything went black.

What he did remember, though, was showing his hand to Battista. It hadn't made a lick of difference. Of course it hadn't. Damian wasn't like Roz. He wasn't made for blackmail and scheming. He upheld the law, punished those who broke it, and followed the rules.

It was clear now his father didn't abide by those same rules.

Here in this tomb-like room, with two men he'd never met, his earlier discovery didn't feel real. Damian's memories of the chief magistrate's body were fuzzy. The illusionists *couldn't* be back. Someone would know, wouldn't they? Maybe he truly was losing it. Maybe the horrors in his mind were bleeding into his reality. He'd heard that sometimes happened to those who returned from war and brought their terrors with them.

"Where are we?" Damian repeated, because no one had answered the first time.

Russo exchanged a glance with his companion. It was a glance that suggested he thought Damian was missing the obvious. "We're on *Il Trionfo*. In the hold, more specifically."

A ship, then. That made sense. "Why the hold?"

Russo cackled. "Your father asked me to keep you down here, at least till we leave port. Seemed to think you might make a run for it."

"I'm not going to run," Damian said. Even at this stage, any attempt at escape probably amounted to deserting. And everyone knew what happened to deserters. "Where are the rest?"

Of the soldiers, he meant, and Russo was able to interpret as much.

"Above us on the main deck. We're departing in"—he procured a pocket watch and peered down at it—"oh, about an hour."

Damian's chest tightened. "I'm not going to make trouble. You don't have to do this."

"Ah, but I *want* to." Russo smiled more broadly, and this time Damian could see his mess of uneven teeth. "You know why? Because you're as bad as a deserter. Did you stay and die with your fellow soldiers?" When Damian didn't answer, he continued. "*No.* Daddy took you away and gave you a cushy job you didn't deserve. While *my*"—he slapped Damian across the face— "*brother*"—he slapped him again—"*died*"—again—"*honorably.*"

Damian didn't make a sound as his head snapped left, right, then left again. The blows didn't hurt nearly as much as the realization blooming deep in his stomach. He cracked his jaw, staring Russo directly in the face. "Who was your brother?"

He knew the answer before it came. Russo was an exceedingly common surname. So common, in fact, Damian never assumed two people who had it must be related. In this case, though, he had the disturbing suspicion that—

"Michele," Russo said. "Michele Russo. You knew him, didn't you? You watched him die, and then daddy took you away to protect you from the trauma of it all. But it should've been *you*." The last word was a frenzied hiss, and this time it was Russo's muscular friend who dealt the blow. With his hands behind his back, Damian couldn't attempt to stop it. He let the man's fist hit him square in the side of the face, vision blurring as blood filled his mouth.

Damian didn't spit it out. He let it fall from his lips as he said quietly, "You're right. It should have been me."

Russo watched him in disgust. "There's still time yet. Serino?"

The enormous man—Serino—drew a leg back, then kicked Damian in the stomach hard enough that he bent forward, gasping for breath. Hadn't he told Roz the same thing? That those who deserted the front had left him feeling abandoned? And yet he'd done the same thing. Inadvertently, perhaps, but what did it matter? The outcome was the same.

"I swear on the saints," Damian rasped, "the last thing I wanted was for Michele to die. He kept me sane, up there. I loved him like a brother." Saying it aloud felt like prying his heart into pieces.

"Fuck you, Venturi." Russo drew up tall, shoving his hands in his jacket pockets. "I *am* his brother. And I'm still here, doing my job, because some of us don't have the luxury of running away. You think you know what suffering is?" He peeled his lips back from his teeth. "You have no idea."

Damian tried to inhale, wincing at the ache in his torso. "I swear on the saints—" he said again, "I never meant—"

"Shut the hell up," Russo spat. "As for the saints, you can forget about them. They won't find us where we're going."

Serino's foot connected with Damian's stomach, harder this time. He dropped forward, pulling the chains taut, fighting to draw breath. Distantly he was aware of Russo's and Serino's fading footsteps, but they weren't far enough away from him to miss Russo's parting promise.

"You'll pay for what happened to my brother, Venturi."

Then he was plunged into darkness.

Through the pain, Damian knew Russo was right. Not about him paying for Michele's death—although that was certainly true as well—but about not being a real soldier. The lights behind his eyes gave way to Michele's mischievous grin, soon joined by the deep ache of shame. He *was* as good as a deserter, and now he was as good as dead. He'd never been a real soldier.

A real soldier didn't leave the battlefield until the war ended, or he died on it.

It couldn't have been more than an hour before someone else entered the hold. This time it wasn't Russo or Serino, but a young man Damian didn't recognize. He hauled Damian to his feet, removed the cuffs from his wrists, and merely scowled when Damian asked how far they were from Ombrazia.

"Put these on." The man shoved a military uniform at him. "Quickly."

He was bruised and stiff enough that it was almost impossible to do anything quickly, but Damian did his best, one hand braced against the wall to keep his balance. When he finished, the man collected his Palazzo uniform, threw it into the corner, and gestured to the stairs in the corner of the room. "Go."

It was easier said than done. Damian's chest ached fiercely, and he couldn't catch his breath. But he managed to climb the steps, blinking in dim sunlight. It looked to be dusk, which meant he'd been unconscious for the remainder of last night and part of today.

Damian emerged into a space full of young people dressed in uniform. It was like stepping into the past—it was déjà vu in a way that made him want to scream. And this time he didn't have Michele at his side, the other boy's sunny disposition keeping him afloat.

He remembered all of this. The clusters of youths chatting in their new uniforms, some excited, some afraid, but none of them ready. None of them able to imagine what was to come. How could they? It was impossible to imagine until you'd lived it. Some of them looked around sixteen, the same age as Damian when he'd first joined the fighting. Others looked even younger, their eyes wide, their nerves palpable. It made him feel sick.

He watched the other soldiers interact, all various stages of excited or afraid. At the far end of the ship Damian could picture a younger version of himself standing alone. Could hear a voice in his mind, clear as day.

Is this the best vantage point?

He remembered how it felt to pivot, focus snagging on a sandy-haired boy with glasses and a mischievous smile.

Something like that, he'd said.

Hmm. The boy had come to stand beside him, crossing his arms as he leaned against the wall. *Since I'm not very observant, it's probably best I trick you into being my friend.* Then he'd flashed another grin, showing crooked front teeth, and Damian knew he'd already succeeded. *I'm Michele, by the way.*

Damian desperately needed to sit. To breathe. To stop thinking about Michele and the past.

245

But that left him only with thoughts of the future: about what would happen when this ship docked, and he was once against plunged into the ear-shattering barrage of gunfire. Bile rose in his throat, and the clamor around him suddenly sounded miles away.

Is this what you wanted, father? he thought bitterly. How many times had Battista told Damian he supported him, that he trusted his judgment? And still Damian had failed, over and over, until the man he'd trusted to always be there for him deemed him a lost cause.

He no longer trusted his father. That was what it came down to, and it was a jarring sensation. Damian had always clung to the idea that, even if Battista was harsh, he could be counted on to do what was right. But Roz had known better from the start, hadn't she? Battista couldn't be trusted. At this point, he was the most likely culprit, even if Damian didn't have a clue what his motive might be. How the potential involvement of a disciple of Chaos might tie in. He felt as though he had a bunch of equally impossible pieces, with no idea how they might fit together.

How could he solve murders someone very clearly didn't want him to solve? None of it made sense. His father's evasiveness, the chief magistrate's body, the creeping mania that had flowed into his bones as he'd knelt before the faceless saints. There was a reasonable explanation for it. There had to be. He needed to trust in the things he'd been taught, because they were all he had. A world where Chaos existed once more, a world where Damian didn't have his faith, was a concept he could not fully comprehend.

And yet the more he thought about it, the more he realized even that had changed. Once, faith had sat like a smooth rock in the palm of his hand. A single, sturdy object—easy to grasp on to. Now, faith seemed to flow like sand through his fingers, each individual particle too delicate to hold. All he had were a million tiny fragments clinging to his skin and the fear that brushing up against the wrong questions would cause them to fall away.

But how could he not have questions? Nobody was who he'd thought they were.

Nobody except Roz. Roz, whom he had finally begun to know again, only to be dragged away. Would she learn what had happened to him? Or would she think he had abandoned her once more? The thought was more painful than the stabbing ache in his side.

He didn't know what to do. There was nothing *left* to do.

So he shut his eyes and prayed, not caring whether the saints listened.

ROZ

In the heart of Patience's temple, Roz let heat flow to her fingertips.

Vittoria sat at her side, eyes closed, cheeks rosy. She looked so serene. So comfortable here, in the warm air that hung heavy with the tang of magic.

Roz was not comfortable. She was too hot, too restless. She felt as though her magic was tearing her apart from the inside, hungry for more than she was offering. It had claws and teeth and a mind all its own. What was she trying to create? She couldn't even remember. As the hours scraped by, Roz became less certain she was meant to be here at all. Her head was full of Damian's lips, Damian's hands. The tilt of his mouth.

I've always regretted not kissing you first.

Roz hadn't a clue where this left them. Was he too embarrassed, now, to contact her? After everything, she couldn't imagine that was the case, but she hadn't received so much as a note. And it wasn't as if she could send one his way. They needed to put the kiss aside and figure out what they were going to do about Battista. Could she trust Damian not to have gone to his father already?

"You need to relax," Vittoria said, and Roz looked over to find her staring.

"I guess I'm a little distracted today." She just wanted the day to be over. The metallic walls and dome-like painted ceiling of the temple felt oppressive.

Vittoria shook her head. "You know, sometimes I wonder if the saints made a mistake."

Roz arched a brow, not immediately comprehending. "I thought you believed the saints make no mistakes."

A shrug. "I did. I've just never seen anyone so...disenchanted, I suppose."

Now Roz fit the pieces together. "You think the saints made a mistake blessing me with magic."

"Roz, it sounds horrible when you say it like that. I truly just—"

"No," Roz interrupted forcefully. "You're right. It was absolutely a mistake."

Vittoria blinked, mouth agape. Saints, what must it be like to live in the mind of someone like Vittoria? She asked so few questions, and was content with the answers provided. She accepted everything for what it was. She was a kind person, but Roz would never understand her.

Roz stood. "I can't do this anymore." And it was true. She had a murder to solve. She was about to take part in the rebellion's biggest act of defiance yet, where she would play a key role. Why was she sitting here, hammering out weapons that might well be used against the very group to which she'd pledged her life?

Vittoria stood too, mirroring her. "You can't do *what*?"

Roz pressed her lips together, staring at the girl with whom she'd once thought, for a flicker of a moment, she could be happy with. She'd been fooling herself. Nothing about this life would ever make Roz happy. If she got hell for leaving, so be it. She'd deal with that later.

"I'm sorry, Vittoria. I'm done for the day. If anyone asks, you don't need to cover for me."

And then she walked right out of the temple.

The way to the Palazzo was crossed by spills of light filtering between close rooftops. Roz kept a rapid pace as she passed the river, then the Basilica, skirting groups of people who all seemed to be talking far too loudly. It was only when she neared the towering doors to the Palazzo that she realized she didn't have a plan. Could she just walk right up and request to speak to Damian? She didn't know, but it wasn't like she had many other options.

Inconveniently, the two security officers at the building's entrance were familiar to Roz. One was the tall girl with braids Damian had been with the first time Roz had crossed his path. The second was the handsome boy who'd been on guard the day Roz broke into the chief magistrate's office. Kiran, she recalled.

This might be a problem.

She could have come back later, but it wasn't as if *she'd* done anything wrong. It was Damian who'd given her the uniform, after all. Roz hovered there a moment, considering her options, and then the choice was made for her.

"Hey!"

That was Kiran's voice, and Roz glanced up to see him waving her over. Beside him the other officer simply stared, eyes narrowed as if trying to place Roz's face.

Fuck. Well, at least Roz knew both officers were friendly with Damian. What was the worst that could happen?

She sauntered over to them and up the Palazzo steps. At Kiran's grin, she smiled winningly back. "Hi. Have either of you seen Venturi?"

Kiran shook his head. "Not since yesterday, actually. Aren't you supposed to be on duty?"

Roz winced as the female officer pivoted to look at Kiran, brows drawn together. "On duty? What are you on about? This is Damian's friend. She's a disciple of Patience."

Kiran was equally nonplussed. "She told me she was a new hire just the other day."

They both turned to stare at Roz.

She contorted her face into what she hoped was an apologetic expression. "Yeah, sorry about that. I've been helping Damian solve the murders—er, murder, and he let me borrow a uniform that day. I figured it was easier not to go into it." It was a poor explanation, but Damian was their superior, right? As long as Roz said it was all his idea, what kind of trouble could they get her in?

Kiran's cheery demeanor darkened, but the female officer moved to step on his foot. "Damian's *friend*," she said meaningfully, and Kiran's eyes widened.

"Oh! Right then. Siena's told me about you."

Roz squinted. "She has?"

The female officer—Siena—stepped on Kiran's foot again.

"Damn it," he griped. "Is there anything I *am* allowed to say?"

Siena chose to ignore that, shooting Roz a commiserating look. Roz, for her part, had no idea how to react to any of this. What had Damian told them about her?

"If you haven't seen Damian around," Roz hedged, "I'll just be going."

Siena appeared to be contemplating something, and held up a finger to indicate that Roz should wait. "You know, Damian wasn't at training this morning. I led it for him, then went to his rooms in case he was ill, but he wasn't there. I figured he was doing something for the chief magistrate and had forgotten to tell us."

Kiran shook his head before Siena had finished speaking. "Forte hasn't been around either. He and the general have been busy seeing the boat off."

"The boat?" Roz asked.

"The military boat? To carry more soldiers up north? The first of them arrived last night, and would have just left."

Roz felt the earth tilt beneath her feet. Saints above—she knew exactly where Damian was. Why he hadn't tried to contact her, and why he hadn't shown up to training. It felt as though a chasm had opened in the pit of her stomach. "Damian's on that boat."

"What?" Kiran and Siena said in unison, neither understanding.

Roz dragged a hand through her hair, gripping the ends of her ponytail. She could see it all so clearly: Damian, trusting fool that he was, choosing to confront his father about his involvement in the murders. Battista, realizing his own son had stumbled too close to the truth, deciding to get rid of Damian the very way he'd already planned.

"Listen," Roz said harshly to the officers, "this is going to sound mad, but I'm almost positive Damian is on that ship. His father had already told the chief magistrate he intended to send Damian back to war."

She expected Kiran and Siena to have questions, to ask how

she could possibly know that, but they only exchanged a stricken glance.

Siena said, "That doesn't sound mad at all. They've been threatening him with that since the disciple's body was found."

"We can't let him go back there." Roz tried to keep her voice calm.

Kiran was one step ahead. His mouth was set in a thin line, his expression determined. "Then we go after him. That ship can't have gotten too far."

"And what do you propose we do? Swim?"

It was Siena who replied. "The Palazzo has boats that we use for river security. They're far smaller than any military vessel, so they'll be faster."

Roz lifted her chin. "Then what are we waiting for?"

If someone had asked her earlier that day, Roz wouldn't have predicted that, come evening, she would be sailing in a Palazzo boat with two security officers she barely knew. It was easy to see how deeply Siena and Kiran cared for Damian: The fact that they were willing to break the rules alongside a rogue disciple was testament to that. They had both fought in the war, Roz had learned, and as they'd set off she'd dared to ask if they believed it was a worthy battle.

"Of course," Siena had said without pause. "At this point, Ombrazia can't afford to back down."

"Then why help Damian avoid a second tour?" Roz couldn't help wondering. It hadn't seemed a good time to argue their beliefs, but that was one question she wanted an answer to.

Siena had fixed her with a sad look. "Damian's first tour hit him hard. I assume he told you what happened?" At Roz's nod, she added, "If he goes back there, he won't return. Not all of him, anyway."

Roz hadn't asked Siena to clarify. She wasn't sure she wanted to know. So she just said, "You'd risk your jobs for Damian?"

"We wouldn't even *have* our jobs without Damian." Siena had tossed the words over her shoulder, busy adjusting the boat's sails. "When Battista brought him back to Ombrazia, he let Damian choose a number of soldiers to work with him—to be promoted to officers. Kiran and I were among them. One of Damian's top priorities was making sure the people he commanded wouldn't abuse the power they were given. We owe him for trusting us."

This had surprised Roz. Chewing on her lower lip, she'd hedged. "So the things I've heard about security officers conducting raids of unfavored territory...stealing from the people there..."

Siena had shaken her head. "I won't say it's never happened, but Damian would never put up with that shit." Then she'd smiled. "It's nice you care."

It could have sounded condescending, but it hadn't, and that, more than anything, had made Roz a bit sad. As if Siena didn't expect a disciple to think the unfavored were worth caring about.

"Of course I do," Roz had muttered, not sure what else to say without giving anything away.

Then Siena had stepped away from the sails, drawing a hand across her brow before trapping Roz beneath a serious, knowing look. "Regardless of what he's done, just know that he really cares about you."

The change in subject had given Roz whiplash, but she hadn't needed to ask who Siena was referring to. Did Siena know Damian was responsible for Jacopo Lacertosa's death? Or was she speaking generally? Asking, Roz thought, risked taking the conversation someplace she didn't care to go.

"I know," was what she'd settled on. And it was true.

Sea spray whipped across Roz's face as she stood at the bow of the boat, staring out at the horizon. Dusk would fall soon, and then it would be nearly impossible to track down the military ship. There was no saying how far it might have gotten. Kiran was steering, only partially visible within the cabin, and Siena stood only a few feet from Roz, fiddling with her braids.

"There!" Siena's sudden outburst tore through the air, and Roz's head jerked up, gaze tracking the direction in which the officer was pointing. Shrouded by the mist, waving a flag that Roz knew up close would bear an image of a sword on fire, was the military vessel.

"Hold on!" came Kiran's holler from the cabin, and Roz gripped the railing just in time. The Palazzo boat veered sharply to the right, cutting through the water and sending waves lapping up high enough to soak Roz and Siena. Roz couldn't have cared less. Her knuckles were tight on the railing, the wood slick beneath her fingers. Her breath came in quick gasps, and she worked to slow her heartbeat. Every part of her was certain Damian was on that ship. It was just a matter of getting him off it.

Roz licked her lips, tasting sea salt. They were gaining on the military ship now, and Siena was yelling directions to Kiran over the wind.

"Head for the starboard, close to the stern! That's where the smaller rooms are, remember? They're more likely to be vacant!"

Kiran obliged, bringing them up alongside the much larger

boat. They were close enough that Roz could have reached out and touched its slick, algae-covered side. The ship had a number of windows, and she abruptly felt very exposed. Anyone could be looking out at their trio, whereas it was impossible to see inside.

"There!" she said, pointing to a porthole only a few feet above their heads. Strands of her hair whipped against her face, infiltrating her mouth, and she spat them away. "We'll be able to fit through that window."

"*I* won't," Kiran observed, peering out from the cabin.

"You're staying here, anyway," Siena told him. "You can't leave the boat." She motioned for Roz to give her a boost, and Roz obeyed, using both of her hands to form a foothold. Siena stepped up, her boot immediately coating Roz's fingers in wet grime.

"It's locked!" Facing into the wind, Siena's voice was nearly lost.

"Seriously?" Roz grit her teeth. "Here. Switch positions with me."

She leapt onto Siena's hands, one knee braced against the top of the Palazzo boat's railing. Siena was right—the porthole was locked from the inside. Its frame, though, was brass, and Roz squinted through the mist as she spread her fingers against the frigid metal. Heat pooled at her core, and her pulse racketed up. The scent of burning metal was thick in her nostrils.

"What are you *doing*?"

Siena's yell sounded from beneath her, but Roz ignored it. The porthole was no longer cold beneath her touch. She was dizzy with anticipation, tense with the need to let the full force of her magic free.

For once, she did.

Roz bit out a yell, reeling back as the bolts holding the porthole frame together flew loose. A couple of them hit the Palazzo boat's deck, leaving singe marks in the wood. The rest of the porthole shuddered for a moment, and then the brass frame turned to liquid, dropping into the sea alongside the glass.

Everyone was silent for a moment.

"Well," Siena said, her grip vise-tight on Roz's boot. "That was certainly something."

Roz couldn't disagree. She swallowed hard, her throat dry. She had never seen her magic do *that* before. Sheer damage, that was. Never seen it melt something so entirely. She gave her head a shake to clear it, then peeked into the room on the other side of porthole. "Looks like a medic's office. All clear."

"Good luck," Kiran called, and then Siena shoved Roz up and into the military ship.

DAMIAN

Breath scraping in his lungs, Damian pushed through the crowd of soldiers toward the window. He gripped the sill with both hands, staring out across Ombrazia's familiar skyline. He could still see the gilded roof of the Palazzo. The spires of the Basilica. The shapes of people down by the water, going about their evening. It all looked the same as always. Damian would go north, and he would die, and everything would continue as it always had.

How strange it was, to be alive. To feel at once important and so incredibly insignificant.

He didn't know how long he stood there, letting his thoughts cocoon him, drowning out his surroundings. It wasn't until he heard a voice directly in his ear that he came spiraling back into himself.

"*There* you are."

Damian snapped to attention, blinking at the familiar face before him. Dark eyes, long lashes, and an impatient expression to rival Roz's. He was so caught off guard, he wasn't sure he was seeing things properly at first.

"*Siena?*"

"In the flesh." She put her hands on her hips, and Damian realized she was wearing a medic's uniform. Disciple made, it fit perfectly to her physique. "Get up, would you?"

He gaped, searching for the right question. Eventually he settled on: "What are you doing here?"

She had gathered her braids into a knot at the back of her head, and though the medic's uniform clashed oddly with her tall, officer-issue boots, it was enough to make her look like she belonged. None of the other would-be soldiers so much as glanced her way, save for the odd cursory sweep.

"We came to find you," Siena said. Her eyes flicked around the cabin before returning to his face. "Saints above, I nearly didn't recognize you. What happened?"

"Oh." Damian ran a hand down his bruised face. He hadn't considered how he must look. "I was tied up in the hold. My father's doing, apparently. Turns out the captain of this ship is Michele Russo's brother, and he wasn't happy I survived when Michele didn't." The explanation came out dull, matter of fact. Siena knew about Michele, having been part of their unit, but Damian had never talked to her about his death after the fact. Had never talked to anyone about Michele's death, actually.

Besides Roz, that was.

Siena shot him an apologetic glance. "Well, that explains why it took me so long to find you. I made a loop of the perimeter and hadn't seen you anywhere." Lowering her voice, she added, "Follow me as if you need medical attention."

Damian coughed a hard laugh, then winced as he prodded the swelling along his jaw. "I think I look the part."

"I'd say so." Her glance was sympathetic. "Unfortunately, I'm not a real medic."

It wouldn't have made much of a difference if she was. Only a disciple of Mercy could fix something as superficial as bruising, and disciples didn't go to war unless they volunteered to do so. Rather, those trained in medicine but untouched by a saint were sent to help on the front lines.

Damian grunted as Siena pulled him to stand. "I'm aware of that, strangely. But how did you get here? How did you know where I was? My father—"

"I haven't spoken to your father," Siena said. "It was Roz, actually, who realized where you were. She showed up at the Palazzo looking for you, and when I said you'd missed training, she put the pieces together."

Roz had come looking for him? Damian's heart skipped a beat. His memory skimmed over the past twenty-four hours. The conversation he'd had with Roz might have been weeks ago at this point. The taste of her mouth on his, and the confusing way they'd left things...Hell, he didn't know what to think. But the fact that she'd gone to the Palazzo in search of him and cared enough to involve Kiran and Siena?

"Was it truly your father who sent you?" Siena asked quietly.

Damian grimaced. He couldn't exactly tell Siena what had happened in Battista's office. Not only because of his suspicions regarding the chief magistrate's body but because it was just so...

embarrassing. His father, forcing him onto the ship by rendering him unconscious? For the first time, Damian wondered who the hell had carried him from the Palazzo to the vessel. Whether word had gotten around that he was so much of a coward he'd needed to be sedated.

"Yeah," he said. "Yeah, it was my father."

It seemed to be enough of an explanation. Siena's mouth tugged down at the corners. "I'm sorry, Damian."

"It's fine. I always knew I was in danger of being sent back. I just never thought it would be *him*." But it had been, and that was that. There was no use dwelling on it now.

Damian's heart nearly beat out of his chest as he followed Siena to the other side of the ship. Given how stiff he was from being in the hold, it wasn't difficult to feign a hobble. Together they skirted the groups of new soldiers—most of whom stared at him with either interest or pity—until Siena paused outside an unassuming door marked MEDIC.

"Get in," she muttered, shouldering it open just enough for him to oblige.

The room beyond wasn't much more than a few small cots and a cabinet of medical supplies. A single window—or at least, what *had* been a window—provided a circular view of the gray sea, its waves wild beneath the darkening sky. Air gusted through the hole where the glass had clearly been wrenched clean out of the wall, raising goose bumps on Damian's arms.

And there, sitting cross-legged on a cot, was Roz.

Damian hadn't for a moment considered that she would have come with Siena. That she would be *here*. The sight of her in this place, vibrant and tangible, made everything else feel surreal. He wanted to tell her everything that had happened. She would take it in stride, which in turn might help him make sense of it. He wanted to gather her in his arms and hold her tightly enough that he forget all other sensation.

"Roz," he said, unable to hide his bewilderment.

She leapt off the bed. "Finally."

28

ROZ

Roz might not have recognized Damian at first. He'd traded his Palazzo-issue jacket for an army shirt, and she couldn't help but notice how his biceps strained against the fabric. Mostly, though, he looked as if he'd been through hell and back in the day since she'd last seen him. His cheeks were flushed, and there was a nasty bruise purpling one side of his jaw, which was clenched. He shook his head disbelievingly at Roz as Siena shut the door to the medic's room. "What are you doing here?"

Despite his clear lack of gratitude, relief flooded Roz. Had Damian not been on this ship, she wouldn't have known where to look next. She didn't know what was wrong with her. Why she so vehemently felt the need to ensure he was safe. She'd grown so accustomed to living without him; a single kiss shouldn't have thrust her headfirst back into obsession.

"Last I heard, Venturi, you didn't want to go to war. So I'm making sure you don't have to."

"Why would you do that?"

The question held genuine surprise, and Roz felt heat spread to her cheeks. Had she merely imagined the other night? The way he'd told her *I wanted to be your earth*, and the soft brush of his mouth on hers?

Then again, it wasn't as if she'd given him much reason to be hopeful. Perhaps he had thought their moment of softness temporary—a brief lapse in judgment on both their parts. And perhaps that was for the best.

"Because I'm nice," Roz said in response to his question, already moving toward the destroyed porthole. She couldn't look at Damian. If she did, she was afraid he'd see something else in her face.

"No, you're not." His frown deepened, mouth tightening.

Siena cleared her throat, ear pressed to the door. "Can we hurry this up? I think I hear someone coming."

Roz gritted her teeth and peered through the porthole, trying to ignore Damian's gaze on her back. Water lapped against the side of the ship, lifting the unmarked Palazzo vessel that bobbed alongside it. Kiran waved when he saw her.

Damian followed Roz's gaze, lips parting. He whipped around to address Siena, and anxiety was thick in his voice. "You two could get fired for this. Or worse."

Siena strode between two of the cots and hoisted herself through the porthole, careful to avoid the jagged edges. "We'll have to get caught first." Then she leapt from the side of the ship, lowering herself into the Palazzo boat. The motion caused the small vessel to tip slightly, but it righted itself a heartbeat later, staying atop the crashing waves.

Roz watched Damian worry at his lower lip as he considered the porthole. Siena gestured from down below, braids whipping in the wind.

"Come on!" Her voice just barely carried over the roar of the water. "I'll help you both through."

"If you don't hurry, we'll leave you behind," Roz advised dryly as Damian hesitated. She thought she could hear voices on the other side of the door, but nobody had tried to enter the room yet. She took her pistola out just in case.

Damian shook his head, a jerking motion. "I don't..." He swallowed, then started over. "Listen, I appreciate you coming after me, but...I don't think I can leave."

"What the hell are you on about?"

"I can't come with you. I'm not a deserter."

It took Roz a moment to digest the words. To understand why his expression was so broken, unsure. Anger flared within her, hot and sudden.

"Don't be an idiot. You told me you'd rather die than go back. And given your current track record, you'll end up dead regardless."

Damian's eyes dimmed. "At least it would be an honorable death."

"*Fuck* that." Roz slapped her hand down on the cot. Her fingers trembled, and her fury was a vicious thing, darkening the edges of her periphery. If Damian hadn't looked so forlorn, she might have shaken him. Perhaps she still would. "Those are your father's words, not yours. And they're bullshit."

He recoiled as though she'd slapped him. "Rossana, I don't expect you to understand—"

"Good. Because I don't. Sacrificing yourself isn't honorable, Venturi. It's just stupid. If you aren't through that window in thirty seconds, I'll shove your ass out. That really *will* be an embarrassment."

Damian stared at her for a long moment. He didn't look angry. Only tired. As though he were fighting her because he felt he had to, not because he truly believed it.

"Move," she barked, thrusting a finger at the porthole. *"Now."*

He pressed his lips together, but obliged.

Roz averted her eyes as Damian hefted himself up. Partially because she was too angry to look at him, but mostly because she didn't want to watch the way his tanned forearms flexed with the motion.

He was about to pull himself through the porthole when the door to the medic's room flew open.

Roz's stomach dropped.

"This one's more seasick than most—what the *hell*?" A moustachioed soldier appeared in the doorway, escorting a green-faced youth. He had three stars pinned on his breast pocket, which made him—what? A commander? A captain? He shoved the sick boy aside with a growl, drawing his own pistola as he advanced. "Don't move, Venturi. Or I promise I'll kill you this time."

The soldier's gun was trained on Damian. Roz's gun was on the soldier. It was an uncomfortable sort of impasse. Her fury toward Damian dissipated, replaced by a dauntingly vicious need to protect him. She stared at the soldier over the barrel of her gun, itching to shoot but knowing the sound would draw attention from inside the ship.

From the corner of her eye she saw the youth take off and knew they didn't have long.

Damian and the soldier...they *knew* each other. It was visible in the set of Damian's mouth, in the way his eyes tightened.

"Venturi," Roz muttered, "get out of here."

"Lacertosa," she heard him say acidly, though she didn't dare tear her gaze from the soldier, "I'm not sure you've noticed, but there's a gun aimed at me."

"I'll take care of him."

"No." Damian's voice was thunderous, edged in panic. "Don't shoot him. He's—he's Michele's brother."

Roz started. *Michele.* The boy Damian had been friends with during the war. The boy he'd watched die.

"Don't you dare speak his name," the soldier snarled, knuckles whitening on the trigger of his pistola.

Roz was able to fit the pieces together. This man, this soldier, blamed Damian for his brother's death as much as Damian blamed himself. She wondered if he was the one who'd damaged Damian's face.

If he shot, he would shoot to kill. Of that Roz had no doubt.

So she fired a bullet into the wall directly above his head.

The noise was deafening, and she took advantage of the confusion to flip one of the cots. Footsteps sounded outside, responding to the gunfire, and she heard Damian bellow her name.

"GO," Roz screamed back. Sweat trickled down her brow. Michele's brother fired a shot in return, and she ducked behind the cot as the shelf of medical supplies shattered, spraying her with glass debris. Every inch of her body came alive with adrenaline. Michele's brother tossed the cot aside with more power than Roz would have thought possible, and she leapt to her feet, aiming a spinning kick at the back of his knees. He stumbled, and she took advantage of the moment to shove him face-first into the wall. Somewhere Damian yelled her name again, and Roz spun, watching in horror as he pushed away from the porthole.

"I told you to leave," she gritted out as Michele's brother pulled away from the wall, hand pressed against his nose. He cursed, raising his pistola once more, and this time it was pointed at Roz. She felt the blood drain from her face: a cold, sobering sensation.

Damian didn't hesitate, grabbing the man's arm and yanking it back with a snarl. Another shot went off, burrowing into the wall a short distance from Roz's head. Across the room, Damian continued to grapple with Michele's brother, and irritation shot through her. He could have *escaped*, and instead he'd jumped in to help her.

Damian had gotten hold of the man's pistola, and directed a well-aimed blow with the barrel of the weapon. When he stepped back, bellowing a slew of rather terrible words in retaliation, Damian turned to Roz.

"Get out of here!"

She scowled, but couldn't see a reason not to obey. She launched herself through the porthole right as the medic's door was ripped off its hinges.

She fell hard, hitting the deck of the Palazzo boat and flattening as more shots rang through the air. The bitter spray of the sea misted her face and stung her eyes. She clawed at the wood beneath her, heart thundering in her ears. A breath later Damian had landed in a crouch beside her, far more coordinated than he had any right to be.

"*Into—the—hold!*" someone snarled, and she lifted her head to see Siena half concealed behind a trapdoor. Roz army-crawled toward her, splinters of wood digging unforgivingly into her arms, and catapulted through the square-shaped hole. Damian followed suit, gunfire ringing in his wake. He didn't appear to be injured, thank goodness.

The trapdoor slammed shut.

"You couldn't have used the *ladder?*" Siena's voice said furiously, though she was barely visible in the dark.

Roz panted, testing each of her limbs. Sore, but otherwise fine. "We were busy trying not to get shot."

Beside her Damian was warm and sturdy, his breathing already returned to normal. He snaked an arm around the small of Roz's back, pulling her into him. His hands roamed her torso in the dark, the lightest of touches, fervent in his distress.

"Are you okay?" The question was a hiss.

Roz pushed him away. He was feeling for *blood*. That's why he seemed so desperate to have his hands on her. "I'm fine."

She didn't need to ask the same of him. As soon as Damian had begun to fight back, it was clear Michele's brother didn't stand a chance. There was unrestrained power in those broad shoulders, a kind of animal efficiency Roz didn't usually see from him. She understood, now, why Damian had survived the north.

Satisfied, he turned to Siena. "Will Kiran be okay up there?"

"He'll be fine. The cabin is pretty well protected, and he's not an idiot. Besides, shooting through a porthole isn't easy."

Despite her words, there was an obvious tension in her voice, and Roz felt Damian respond in kind.

In an attempt to distract them both she said, "Venturi, you owe me for sparing that man. He almost killed us."

"Yeah." Damian's tone was curt. Though she couldn't see him clearly, Roz could imagine how his face might contort in a grimace. "Sorry about that. Thanks for not shooting him."

"You knew him?" Siena demanded, and Damian made a noncommittal sound in his throat.

"It was Michele's brother."

Siena gave a harsh intake of breath, then went silent. Roz felt awkwardly as though she were intruding on a conversation that had nothing to do with her. She didn't care whether that man had been related to a boy she'd never met. Michele's brother had tried to *kill* them. Would have shot Damian in front of her, had he gotten the chance. Roz would have been happy to put a bullet in his skull. In fact, she wished she had.

When Siena finally spoke again, Roz was no longer listening.

Kiran got the boat as close as he could to Ombrazia's outskirts before the river narrowed too much to allow it to go any further. Roz, Damian, and Siena had emerged from the trapdoor a short time before. The boat's cabin was peppered with bullet holes, and much of the glass was spiderwebbed or broken, but Kiran miraculously appeared unharmed. Now that they were out of immediate danger, Roz felt too drained to speak. The minutes slid by, crashing into one another as the wind wrapped around her, smelling of salt and iron. She drew her knees up to her chest, traitorous heart thundering in her ears.

Damian had told her to leave him. For a moment there, he'd been willing to stay on the ship. Willing to be killed in the name of honor, even though Roz knew how desperately he wanted to live.

Was this the boy she had chosen to care about? Someone willing to die for the Palazzo, while she was willing to die to see it burn?

Anger filled her, directed both at Damian and herself. She wanted to believe it was because they were painfully incompatible, but deep down Roz knew it was because she couldn't stand the thought of Damian dying. Her own death brought her little fear, but the prospect of losing Damian, and for good this time?

Nothing had ever made her more furious.

Eventually she was forced to direct Kiran as he brought the boat to a halt not far from Bartolo's. Roz knew it was risky, allowing them this close to rebel headquarters, but she wasn't about to risk being seen by disciples.

"Thanks," she murmured, and Kiran turned to her, brows high. The sleeve of his Palazzo jacket was torn, but other than that, he looked impeccable, dark hair held back in a shining knot.

"For what?"

Roz lifted a shoulder, then let it drop. "You didn't have to help me. You could have arrested me."

His grin was a flash of teeth. "Somehow, I don't think you would have made it easy. Besides, I wasn't helping you—I was helping Damian. No offense."

Roz shrugged again, unbothered. It was, after all, what she'd been counting on. Before she could reply, Damian and Siena had moved within earshot, the latter scouring their surroundings with a skeptical expression.

"Are you sure you want to be dropped off here?"

Roz frowned. It wasn't the nicest part of Ombrazia, that much was obvious, but there wasn't anything wrong with it. "I'm sure."

"All right." Siena chewed on her lower lip, turning to address Damian. "What about you? You're not coming back to the Palazzo?"

This question appeared to perplex Damian, and Roz understood why. He was supposed to be long gone. Battista expected him either to die or return a hero all over again. Had that been part of the reason Damian hadn't wanted to leave the ship? Was he truly that desperate for his father's respect?

How can I?" Damian said. He looked out of place here, with his military uniform and the Palazzo's sigil emblazoned on his shoulders. Too stark. Too powerful. The very sight of him would frighten people, especially given the bruising on his face.

"What are you going to do?" Kiran asked.

Damian blinked, and before Roz could think better of it, she found herself saying: "I have somewhere you can go."

"You do?" Damian's expression might've suggested she'd offered him her kidney.

"Yeah. A friend owns a tavern around here. There are rooms above it."

"That would be...great."

It was risky, and frustration still pulsed at Roz's core, but she couldn't very well rescue Damian and then leave him in the street. As it stood, there were really only two places she could take him—the tavern or her house—and she certainly wasn't bringing him home to interact with her mother. Besides, Piera would recognize Damian and know to be a little more cautious.

Damian cleared his throat. "Well." He addressed Siena and Kiran. "Thanks for getting me out of there."

"Don't mention it." Kiran bounced up and down on the balls of his feet, clearly still riding the high of their adrenaline-fueled escape.

Siena lifted her chin, dark eyes flashing. "We're not just loyal to the Palazzo, Damian. We're also loyal to *you*."

Roz saw Damian's throat shift at that, as if swallowing had suddenly become difficult. "Not anymore. Listen, when you get back to the Palazzo, keep your guard up. Something...strange is going on there."

"Strange how?" Kiran asked.

Damian shot Roz a sideways glance before continuing, though

she hadn't a clue what he was about to say. "I think my father had some involvement in Leonzio's murder. He found out I suspected him, and I think that's why he was so desperate to get rid of me all of a sudden."

A seabird shrieked somewhere overhead, making them all start. Roz wanted to take Damian and shake him. It was just as she'd predicted: Somehow he had let Battista know they were onto him. That said, she was bewildered. Had Damian made the mistake of simply asking Battista about it, only to realize to late he ought not to have trusted him? If so, why did he care what Battista thought about his deserting?

Because Damian *had* deserted, hadn't he? After everything he'd said about her father, he'd done the same thing. And he knew it, too.

Was that why he was so upset?

Siena, oblivious to Roz's inner turmoil, said, "You think *Battista* has been poisoning people?"

Damian dragged a hand down the side of his face. Everything about his stance was uneasy. "I don't want to believe it. But given what Roz and I have learned so far, it's a possibility." He didn't go into detail, but instead added, "I just can't see what the motive might be."

Kiran shook his head, letting out a low whistle. "I hope for your sake you're wrong. What evidence do you have?" The question wasn't confrontational—he sounded genuinely interested.

"It's best you know as little as possible," Damian said. "Keep doing your jobs as though nothing has happened. My father can be...dangerous, even to those he considers allies."

Roz couldn't help her soft snort. *That* was an understatement. Luckily, though, no one seemed to hear.

"Once we're sure, you'll know," Damian was saying, and

slid a frustrated hand through his hair. "And be careful around Forte, too, okay? If my father is involved, he's sure to be taking directions."

Roz wasn't convinced—surely Battista could do whatever he liked—but the way Damian's face abruptly became *too* blank made her suspect there was something he wasn't saying. She didn't say a word, however, as Damian gave Siena a quick hug, then reached out to shake Kiran's hand.

"Hell no," Kiran said, and pulled Damian into his chest. "If she gets a hug, so do I."

Roz felt a pang as she watched the easy way Damian interacted with the other officers. They'd had that, once. Far more, in fact. And despite the kiss, it had somehow slipped away. Lost to time and hurt and anger and bitterness.

She didn't know how to get it back. Didn't know if they ever could.

"Roz?"

Damian murmured her name from the edge of the boat, and she lifted her head. His eyes were trained on her, dark and warm and infinite as always. There was a seriousness in his gaze, and all at once Roz didn't think it was the boat's gentle sway that was making her unsteady.

He offered her a hand, and without looking at him, she took it.

Together they stepped onto the dock and watched the Palazzo boat fade into the twilight.

29

DAMIAN

Damian followed Roz through the darkening streets in silence. Roz's step was purposeful, her gaze keen, and Damian was thankful she wasn't reading the panic in his face. Revelations spun through his head in an uncontrollable flurry. He couldn't return to the Palazzo. He was no longer head of security. He would never patrol with Kiran and Siena again. Never wander through the streets of Ombrazia at night, or feel the comforting weight of his archibugio across his back.

What was he, if not a soldier or officer? *Who* was he?

Maybe he'd made a mistake. Maybe he should have stayed on that ship, let himself be carried up north, and fought until he drew his last breath. It would have been miserable, suicidal even, but what if that was his destiny? The saints had created disciples to use their magic here on earth. Perhaps they'd created Damian to fight for as long as he could, then flicker out.

And there was the guilt. Because he had escaped, he was here, and he was safe. How many people on that ship would be dead by the end of the month? By next week? And of the survivors, how many would return to Ombrazia with vacant eyes and heads full of demons?

It took him a moment to realize Roz had stopped outside a three-story unmarked tavern. It wasn't exactly welcoming: The walls were cracked, and grubby children sat on the ground nearby, staring at them with mistrust. Damian assumed this was where he was to stay, but Roz put a hand on the door without entering.

"What is it?" he asked, sensing her hesitation.

When she looked up at him, his breath tangled in his chest. Not only because she was beautiful—which she was, in a way that had always rendered him momentarily speechless—but because the look on her face was the same as the other night at the bathhouse. As if Damian had suddenly cornered her, even though he hadn't.

"Hey." He placed his hand over hers, gently removing her fingers from tavern door. "What are you not telling me?"

Roz arched a brow, her lips parting. "What are *you* not telling *me*?"

Damian thought of the chief magistrate's body. Of the cool stone of Chaos's statue beneath his grip, and all the things he was too afraid to put into words.

I'm afraid Chaos isn't really gone.

I'm afraid I can't trust my own mind.

I'm afraid of loving you.

Instead he said, "I haven't lied to you about anything."

276

Roz let out a hard laugh, yanking her hand from his grasp. Before Damian could say anything more, she had stalked into the tavern.

The wide room was loud, even this early in the evening, its low wood-beam ceiling trapping the sound. It smelled like sweat and a rather pungent mixture of various liquors. Damian was willing to bet not one of the patrons was a disciple, given their rugged appearances and the way they eyed his army uniform in blatant interest. In fact, he found himself shocked this was a place Roz apparently frequented. Every bone in his body was braced for a fight.

"What *is* this place?" he whispered at Roz.

"Come with me if you don't want a knife in the back." Roz slowed to hiss the reply in his ear. "People here aren't exactly trusting, and you're an unfamiliar face. Not to mention the blood."

Damian couldn't see any reason to argue. So he followed her over to where a middle-aged woman was serving drinks at the bar, still reeling. Something was bothering Roz—he just didn't know what it was. Did she regret coming after him? Did she resent having to help him, even though she'd offered to? Maybe she'd thought better of their kiss. He wanted nothing more than for her to be honest with him, but could he do the same?

"Piera," Roz said to Damian when they reached the bar, gesturing at the woman. Piera's thin, sharp-eyed face was familiar, though Damian hadn't seen her in years. She'd been close to the Lacertosas, but never had much to do with Damian's family. Piera relaxed when she glanced up and saw them, giving Roz a smile Damian couldn't help but feel was reserved for her.

Piera put down the glass she'd been holding, gray eyes slipping to Damian as Roz said, "Piera, you remember—"

"Damian Venturi." Piera extended a hand, the warmth fading

from her smile. "It's been quite a while, but I've heard much about you."

Damian shook her hand. "Nothing good, I'm sure."

An appreciative lilt grabbed Piera's mouth, at odds with her otherwise cold expression. "You're self-aware, at least."

"I've been called worse."

Roz grimaced. She was obviously on edge, as though something about the conversation unsettled her. "Could Damian stay here for a few nights? Just until he finds somewhere else to go."

Piera considered, looking at Damian with such intensity he wouldn't have been surprised to find himself spontaneously catch fire. But then she nodded and said, "Second floor, third door on the left. Here." She passed Damian a burnished iron key, which he pocketed.

"How much per night?"

She gave an impassive shrug. "Don't worry about it."

"With all due respect, Signora, I'm not a charity case."

Piera studied him for so long that Damian regretted every word he'd spoken in her presence. "I am well aware of that, Damian Venturi. But I do not want your money."

She said it as though any money he had to offer might be tainted. It stung, but only slightly. Damian offered a polite nod as Roz glanced around the tavern, appearing to shrink slightly when a group of men at a nearby table returned a glare, then muttered something among themselves.

"Come on," she grunted to Damian. She was already weaving toward a stairwell in the corner of the tavern.

He nearly had to jog to keep up. "Who were they?"

"It doesn't matter."

"Do they bother you? I'll—"

She whirled halfway up the worn staircase, brows drawn together. "You'll *what*?" she said breathlessly. "If they were bothering me, I'd take care of them myself."

Damian watched the rapid rise and fall of her chest. The way they were currently positioned, she was half a head taller than him, most of her face shrouded by the darkness in the stairwell. He didn't know how to respond. Wasn't even sure what he'd been about to say. "I was only asking."

Roz didn't deign to reply to that. Damian hovered for a moment, then decided he had little choice but to follow her the rest of the way to the second-floor landing. She stopped outside a door halfway down the hall, gesturing for him to hand her the key. Damian obliged, and the door swung open to reveal a sparsely decorated room with faux-gold accents. A small bed sat opposite a set of wooden drawers, a rather hideous scarlet-and-yellow carpet spread out between them.

"I'll see you tomorrow," Roz said, pivoting to leave, but Damian shook his head.

"Come in."

She studied him for a long moment, eyes slightly narrowed. "I really—"

But Damian had had enough. "I wasn't asking."

"Excuse me?"

"I am *tired*," he said, backing into the room. Roz remained in the doorway, hair tousled by the wind, spots of pink in her cheeks. Disbelief flickered in her eyes, but Damian found he was no longer worried about upsetting her. "I'm tired of not just saying what we're thinking. I hate looking at you and wondering what you're not telling me. I hate second-guessing every word I say." He heard the pleading note in his own voice, and thought it probably took the sting out of his admittance. "Now, I'm going to get cleaned up. If you're ready to talk, stay. If not, then by all means, go home."

Without waiting for a response, he stalked into the bathing room adjacent. Roz would leave, he told himself as he filled the tub with water. She would leave, and his heart would plummet in his chest at the sight of the empty room, but he would be fine. He didn't have any other choice.

Damian stripped off the army uniform and hurled it into a corner. The water in the tub spilled over as he stepped into it, but he barely noticed. He scrubbed himself roughly with soap, using his fingernails to scrape away the dried blood, watching as the water turned from clear to brownish-gray. He let that drain and filled it again.

When he'd finished, he stood before the mirror, staring at his own gaunt reflection. It was the first time he'd done so in months. He didn't like to see the vacant look in his eyes, the shadows beneath them, and the way his cheekbones seemed to cut more harshly across his face by the day. The muscles he'd built up north hadn't faded, but they looked strained, somehow. Like his body was struggling to hold on to them.

Sighing, he threw the uniform trousers back on. Then he rested his elbows on the counter, putting his face in his hands. Heading Palazzo security had been his only distraction for months. It was why he threw himself into the role, avoiding sleep as much as possible. He couldn't bear what he saw when he closed his eyes.

A knock sounded on the bathroom door, and Damian jerked upright.

"Venturi?"

It was Roz's voice.

He shoved the door open, fingers unsteady, and stared at her.

In the short time he'd taken to bathe, the room had gone dark but for the moonlight streaming through the window. It clung to the curve of Roz's cheek, the slope of her shoulder, immortalizing her in silver. Her gray-blue gaze roamed over his bare arms and torso, her lips forming a small *oh*.

"Rossana." Damian made his voice hard. He'd been soft for far too long.

She set her jaw, seeming to search for the right words, and then something within her visibly cracked. "You said you wanted honesty, so you start. What the hell is eating at you?"

When she put it like that, Damian scarcely knew where to start. He blew out a hard laugh on a breath. "Yeah. That. Look, I know you think I'm a fool for telling my father we thought he was involved with the murders, but I wasn't exactly on top form when it slipped out."

Roz's brows drew together. "What is *that* supposed to mean?"

"I think..." Damian pulled a hand through his hair, trying to determine the best way to explain. "I think there's something bigger going on. I don't think the murders are our only problem."

She waited, so he went on.

"After being at the bathhouse that evening"—he felt himself flush just saying it—"I went down to the Shrine. I was feeling a bit...lost, but that's not the point. I grabbed the statue of Chaos's arm, and a *tunnel* opened up. One I'd never seen before."

"Okay," Roz frowned. "And where did it lead?"

"Nowhere. Well," Damian amended, "it led to a room, but that's not important. What matters is that, inside the room, I saw Chief Magistrate Forte. Dead."

Roz's eyes snapped wide open. She moved closer to him, almost automatically. "Someone's murdered *him* as well?"

"That's the part that doesn't make any sense. It looked as if he'd been dead for at least a week. But then, when I got out of there to go tell my father, he said he'd met with Forte only a few hours earlier." Damian clenched his teeth as the confused frustration resurfaced. "I don't understand how that could be. I know what I saw, and I *know* it was Forte. The only explanation I could think of was—"

"Chaos," Roz said at once, and relief flooded Damian, warmth extending all the way to his fingertips. Relief, because here was a person who did not think him insane. Here was someone who did not, for even a moment, entertain the possibility that he'd been imagining things. Roz had come to the same conclusion, and it sounded less impossible coming from her lips.

"That's what I thought," Damian said. "But it can't be, right? Because that would mean he was back."

Roz shot Damian a look that made him feel he was missing something very obvious indeed. "Or it means his disciples were never truly gone."

"A fallen saint can't bless his descendants with magic," Damian said at once, the words escaping him before he even realized it. How many times had he heard that exact sentence spoken? It was regarded as an indisputable fact.

"That's the story," Roz agreed, though there was an obstinate tilt to her chin. "But who's to say all the stories are true?"

Damian wasn't sure how to respond. *Everyone at the Basilica*, he might have said. Or perhaps, *The chief magistrate.* After all, a chief magistrate was supposed to speak for the saints, were they not?

Roz must have seen his thoughts whirling, for her mouth curved in a grim, tight-lipped smile. "I get it," she told him. "If you accept that one thing might not be true, everything unravels."

That was it—that was it exactly. But everything was already

unraveling, wasn't it? It had made Damian uncomfortable, so he'd attempted to simply ignore it.

But he wasn't ignoring it anymore. He couldn't.

"Say you're right," he said to Roz, making his voice firm. "Say a disciple of Chaos is still roaming the streets, and that's why I saw what I saw. Do they have anything to do with the murders, or is this another problem entirely?"

Roz shrugged with more resignation than Damian could muster. Her expression was unsure, and it made her look younger. "I've no idea. I wish I did. Maybe we can start by going back to the Shrine—see if the tunnel and the body are still there?"

"Okay." Damian exhaled. "Yeah, okay." It wasn't much, but it was a plan, and it made him feel marginally better. He managed a weak smile. "Tomorrow's problem?"

"Tomorrow's problem," Roz echoed, her voice leaving no room for argument. "Tonight, you need to sleep. You smell a hell of a lot better, but you still look terrible."

That shocked a real laugh out of him. "I have no intention of sleeping until you tell me what's on *your* mind. Don't think I've forgotten."

Roz lifted a brow, and for a moment Damian thought she might refuse. That, even after everything, she'd tell him he had no right to her thoughts, and they'd be back to square one. She didn't, though. After contemplatively chewing her bottom lip, she took his hand in her small, warm one and dragged him to the bed, gesturing that he should sit.

"I was terrified today, you know," Roz said after what felt like an eternity, face grave. "When I realized you were gone, *where* you'd gone, I thought I was going to lose you again. I didn't care about anything else. So here's what's on my mind, Damian

Venturi: You're a mess, and so am I. Maybe we're not meant to be together, and maybe we'll only hurt one another each time we try. Maybe we had no business kissing the other night." Her throat shifted. "But the truth is, I need you, Damian. I need you like the moon needs the stupid earth, or whatever you said to that effect."

Damian felt as if the universe had frozen. Or rather, he had frozen, and the world continued to spin around him with unrelenting ferocity. His heart pounded in his ears, Roz's words reverberating there. It was everything he had dreamed of hearing her say for years. Even after he'd seen her in the morgue, seen just how hardened she'd become, he'd wanted it still. Her words were a balm to his frustration. A breath smothering a tiny flame.

He didn't know what to say. The idea of fracturing this horribly delicate moment was like a puncture wound to the lungs. Something he couldn't breathe through. Roz was *never* vulnerable, and he wanted to fold her into his chest and keep her there, so the world couldn't touch her and she could stay like this.

"Roz." Damian hooked a finger under her chin, lifting it so that her gaze was forced to meet his. Her eyes were large, impossibly blue, and he was reminded forcefully of the day her father left for the north. The day she'd shown up at his doorstep and simply stared at him, just like this. It was the first time he'd ever seen her cry. "Maybe we *will* hurt one another. Heaven knows we don't have a great track record. But if you want me around, the world is going to have to drag me away kicking and screaming."

Roz flexed her jaw, and Damian watched the tendons in her neck shift. Then she lifted a hand to his face, tracing the bruise blooming along his cheekbone. Her fingers were cool, and he softened into her touch, shuttering his eyes.

"I missed you," she whispered. "I missed you so much I was sick from it."

Damian encircled her wrist, pulling her hand away from his cheek. He pressed his lips to her knuckles. "Tell me how often you thought of me."

Roz stilled, attention traveling down to his chest. His stomach. When she looked back up at him, there was a wicked gleam in her eye. "I thought of you every single day, Venturi." Her hand formed a fist in his grip. "Even when I hated you so much I nearly lost my mind, I thought of you still. I thought of this." Her lips were at his, yielding only the softest brush before they moved to his neck. Damian was frozen, heart pounding a frantic, offbeat rhythm. The world was nothing but her warm breath, her sage and citrus scent.

"I thought of this," Roz murmured against the skin of his throat, nipping him lightly as she positioned herself between his legs. She trailed her fingers down his stomach, pausing just beneath his breastbone. "And this..." Her hands skimmed each ridge of his abdomen until she reached his hips. "And *this*."

Damian felt himself harden against her, though she'd done nothing more than hook a finger in the waistband of his trousers. The implication was enough to send heat rushing to his face, and his blush would have betrayed him if his body hadn't.

"That," he managed, "is a *very* interesting thought to have about someone you hate." A shiver caressed his spine as Roz traced the V of his hip bone. His gaze dipped from her eyes to the hollow of her throat, then down to her chest. Her shirt was low-cut, baring her collarbone, and the sight of her skin had him stiffening further. Saints be damned—he was desperate for her. The only thing on his mind was the electric current between her body and his.

Roz's lips curled into a grin, and then the grin became a soft laugh. "I've always been a rather unconventional lover." She slipped her shirt off, letting it fall to the ground. Damian's blood was fire as she took his hands in hers, bringing them to her waist. "Touch me."

The words made that fire spill from his bloodstream and spread through the rest of his body. Damian pulled Roz close, his hands roaming her chest, her delicate rib cage, the curves of her hip bones. He pressed his lips to her stomach, finding it firmer than he'd expected, and tasted her skin. "You're beautiful," he murmured against her, and her only response was a breathy exhalation. He wanted to know every inch of her. He wanted to love her the way he hadn't been able to for three long years, and make up for every single second he hadn't been able to touch her. Before he could go any further, however, Roz fastened her hand around the back of his neck and tilted his face up.

Her mouth trapped his, tongue slipping inside with careful expertise. A groan built deep in Damian's throat as she ground against him, the smooth pressure of her lips driving his pulse ever higher. He bit her bottom lip gently, overwhelmed by her scent. And then somehow her trousers were off, and so were his, and the sound that emanated from deep in his chest was so feral he might have been embarrassed if he hadn't been so preoccupied.

Perhaps it was foolish, the speed with which they'd gotten here. Damian didn't care. He was tempted never to care about anything again.

"Lie down," Roz murmured, shoving him hard onto the bed.

He obliged, pulling her with him, and the next second she had mounted him gracefully. He grasped her hips, drinking in the sight of her. Saints, if they were really doing this, he might never let her go. He wouldn't be able to bear it. They'd known each other for so long, and yet this was the first time he had seen *all* of her—every indescribably perfect inch. He wanted to imprint it in his mind, so that each time he closed his eyes he would see this. Her.

Damian wondered, perhaps, if the saints had seen fit to let him live for this very reason: so that he could love Roz Lacertosa.

She braced her hands against his chest, and from there every movement was perfectly calculated. Damian clenched his teeth. Gripped her harder. In those moments, in the space between frantic heartbeats, Roz was no longer just his earth. She was his universe, his sun, the atmosphere from which he drew breath.

And when he finally went over the edge, she was right there with him.

PIERA

The restless swell and fall of the sea's waves moved toward shore, the reflection of the city lights fracturing on the surface. By the time the water gathered itself into the winding shape of the river, it had quieted, though not enough for anyone to hear the footsteps.

A short distance away, Piera exited Bartolo's tavern. She loosened an inaudible sigh, shutting the door on the raucous noise that accompanied her, and lifted her gaze to the moon. It was fierce, that gaze. The kind of fierceness the saints admired. And since the stars were out—dim though they were—was it truly so mad to believe they were watching?

Yet she didn't believe it. Not here, where the days bled into one another and the same sun shattered the sky each morning, making a mockery of the mundane.

Piera paused.

She walked over to the river, retrieving two pieces of paper from her pocket. Both were worn and lined, as if they had been folded and unfolded hundreds of times. She stared once more at the stars, then down at the familiar slant of her lover's hand.

The first sheet—a letter declaring his death—she tossed into the river. The second—a note he'd penned to her from the front lines—she kept.

At that moment, Piera shed the last dregs of her sadness for anger. There, on an unremarkable evening, beneath the watchful gaze of the most dangerous type of dreamer.

She was a risky target, but she was also in the way.

As the footsteps neared, Piera turned, tilting her head. Confused, but not afraid. Never afraid. Just like the girl she loved so deeply.

She refused to die quickly.

But like the rest of them, she died nonetheless.

31

ROZ

Roz awoke to find Damian beside her, fast asleep.

He was curled on his side, torso bare and half visible beneath the blankets. His breaths were slow, even, though something in his face was tense. For a moment Roz did nothing but watch him, basking in the memory of his hands on her body. The firm lines of him, and the way he looked at her with an almost hungry adoration.

She trailed a finger down his forearm, but he didn't stir.

"Damian." Roz whispered his name—his real name, not his surname—remembering the way the syllables had rolled off her tongue in their youth. How she'd paired them with a laugh, or released them to the breeze as they ran through the city at night. She remembered dancing by the river, falling asleep shoulder to shoulder, and the way he smiled each time he saw her at his doorstep.

Last night he'd smiled again, in a way Roz hadn't seen for

years. Wide and mischievous and without reservation. It had incited a bittersweet ache within her, and she'd wished she could bottle the way that smile made her feel. It was more enticing than any drug, and the moment it had vanished she'd felt rather bereft.

Damian didn't so much as stir at her touch, and Roz decided she was loath to disturb him regardless. She'd given him one of Piera's sleeping draughts last night—they always seemed to help her mother—and he'd taken it willingly. If past experience was any indication, Damian would sleep a considerable time longer, and little would be capable of waking him.

Besides, he looked so peaceful the way he was now, and Roz feared when he woke it might not last.

Today was the day the Mercato would burn.

Had last night had been wrong of her? Had it been wrong to reach out and steal that quiet, blissful sliver of a moment when she knew there was a chance Damian might never speak to her again? Because she couldn't keep him from finding out eventually. She would do her best, if only to protect everything Piera had built, but at some point Damian would learn the truth. He had to, if they were going to be together.

Later. Roz would tell him later. She had a key role to play today, and nothing was going to get in the way of that. Not even Damian.

At least they'd had one perfect night after all the years of relentless, furious pining.

Roz slipped out of bed and dressed quickly, pulling on her boots and tiptoeing downstairs to the tavern. The business was closed this early, but she knew at once that something was going on. Whispers punctuated the air, and it sounded as though some- one was...crying?

She paused on the second-last step of the stairwell, frowning when she noticed the small group of rebels in the corner of the room. Nasim. Dev. Arman. Josef. Alix. None of them had bothered lighting a candle, and the way they were huddled together piqued her curiosity. What were they doing here already? Had Piera called a meeting without telling her?

Roz cleared her throat. "What's going on?"

No one said a word, but Nasim turned, her face streaked with tears. All sensation fled Roz's body. She had never seen Nasim cry.

Not once.

She stepped toward the group, floating somewhere outside her own mind. She couldn't feel her hands. Her feet. Was she breathing? She didn't know. Dev and Arman turned, and Roz searched their pale faces, eyes wide in a silent plea. She didn't think she could frame the question. She needed someone to say something.

Then her gaze dropped to the floor.

It took a long moment for her brain to process what she was seeing. Her vision unfocused, and suddenly she couldn't get enough air. She clawed at her chest as a soft wail escaped her throat.

It was Piera. The woman was lying flat on her back, face gaunt and masklike. Her mouth was contorted in a grimace, and if her eyes had remained, Roz knew they would have held sheer horror.

She didn't have to ask. She didn't have to go to Piera to know the woman was dead. Roz wasn't the girl who sobbed and squealed and tried to shake a corpse awake. She wasn't the girl who fell apart in a companion's arms, sagging in a half faint as people tried and failed to comfort her. She fractured silently, furiously, and her pain was not a thing that could be assuaged by mere tears.

Some part of her was aware that the others were watching her, fearfully awaiting a reaction. She didn't care. She didn't care that Nasim was crying, that Dev was already sloshed, or that Josef and Arman were as stricken as she'd ever seen them. Roz was—she was—

She grabbed the nearest bottle of alcohol and hurled it to the floor.

Shards of glass flew, and the spray of liquor made Roz's eyes burn. Someone was yelling, but she didn't know who. Didn't know what they were saying. Didn't care. She knocked over the nearest chair with all the energy she could muster, letting the *crash* of wood on wood reverberate through her bones. She did the same with the other chairs at that table, save for the last one, which she picked up and slammed into the wall. Her path of destruction led her over to the bar, and she grabbed glass after glass, flinging them to the floor in rapid succession.

Smash. Nights spent in Piera's company with a warm mug of tea. *Smash.* Talking about her mother while Piera rubbed her back. *Smash.* The smell of Piera's perfume whenever Roz allowed her a hard-won embrace. *Smash.* Piera's soft voice, always devoid of judgment. *Smash.*

Once you have known true grief, you don't get better.

Each ear-splitting ring was short-lived relief. It was something, but it wasn't enough, it wasn't *enough*, and she needed—she needed—

Strong hands grabbed hold of her arms, stopping her as she reached for the next glass. Roz writhed and flailed and fought against them, a flurry of elbows and fists making contact with *who the hell knew what* and filled her with a satisfaction that was altogether *not* satisfying.

"Let—*me*—GO!" she exploded, but she was all chaos and no strategy and it wasn't long before she found herself flat on the floor, glass puncturing her back and alcohol soaking her hair. It was good, the pain of that glass, because it was a pain that was not inside her, and Roz let it hurt and hurt and hurt.

"Don't," Dev croaked, his face looming over her. "Roz, please don't."

That was when she finally cried.

Not hysterically. Not even audibly. Just...brokenly, the tears slipping over her cheeks onto the floor. She made no move to stop them. Spent, she stared up at the wooden beams of the ceiling, vision blurring. Dev became a watery outline, and he loosened his hold on her as she relaxed into the ground. Waited for it to swallow her up.

Roz had failed. She hadn't solved the murders in time, and she had failed. Perhaps she'd missed something crucial along the way. Perhaps she'd allowed herself to be distracted by Damian.

Damian.

His father had done this. Battista Venturi had killed Piera. One by one, he was ripping away the people Roz loved. And yet Damian hadn't wanted to believe it. Had wanted more proof before they did anything about it.

"Let me up," she said hoarsely, blinking away the last of the tears.

Dev studied her, somewhat apprehensive, but seemed to trust whatever he saw in her face. Tears traced silent paths down his own cheeks, and once he ascertained Roz wasn't going to attack him, he slumped to the floor. A broken man.

He had been too late. They had all been too late.

Roz pushed herself to her feet, wincing at the sting of alcohol in the cuts on her back, and gingerly rotated to face the other rebels. She felt as though she were surveying everything through a veil. Nasim appeared almost fearful, and Arman's jaw was reddening, which Roz realized belatedly must be her doing.

"Shit," she murmured under her breath. The single word sounded dead. "I'm so sorry, Arman."

He waved a hand, indicating it was okay, which it wasn't.

Roz bit her lip, hard. Anger surged through her in overwhelming waves, but it was no longer directed at anything in this room. It was bigger than that. It was so big she scarcely knew what to do with it.

"Why do we bother?" Dev rasped from the floor, capturing her attention. "We'll never find happiness here."

She was inclined to agree. But they couldn't simply give up on everything Piera had worked for. What kind of rebellion would they be, if they quit because one of them was lost? Roz blinked back the sting in her eyes. "Everything is in place for tonight's attack. We'll let it move forward as planned. It's what Piera would have wanted."

Everyone nodded save Dev, who stared at Roz in shock. "Are you sure now is the right time?"

"This is a rebellion," she hissed. "It's always the right time to strike." The words tore from her chest. "You know the plan: Everyone will meet at the Mercato at dusk. Cover your faces if you can. Once you get there, I don't care what you do. I don't care what you destroy. Tonight, we're burning the fucking thing down. And when security calls for backup, which they will, the closest officers will have to come from—"

"The prison?" Nasim finished, and Roz nodded.

"Precisely."

Josef added, "That's when we free the draft dodgers."

"Yes." Roz could hear raw sorrow in her own voice, and she clenched her teeth, holding herself in check.

"Tonight, the rebellion strikes," Dev growled darkly. "For Amélie. For Piera."

The others murmured in agreement, the same anguish lacing their voices. Piera was a central part of the rebellion. She always had been. Roz wasn't the only one who had loved and lost her. The rebels loved her, the *city* loved her, and it meant they would fight.

It also meant Piera wouldn't be the only one to die today. But that was why people joined a rebellion in the first place, was it not? Because they believed in something so strongly, they were willing to put their lives on the line to fight for it.

Alix was nodding, their face wan. "What about after, though? What do we do then?"

"Piera had a contingency plan," Dev murmured. His gaze was glassy, either from drink or misery. "Remember?" He rounded the bar, poking at various bottles of liquor until he came across one that, according to the label, was a dark whiskey. Piera's favorite.

Right. Roz, too, remembered Piera mentioning this. The top of the bottle was sealed with wax, and Josef and Nasim—those closest to Dev—took an automatic step back.

He hurled the bottle to the ground. It shattered easily, and in the midst of the shards lay a small piece of parchment. Dev bent to pick it up with careful fingers. He unrolled it and read the message once, then twice, brow furrowing.

"What is it?" Roz demanded.

He swept a hand through his light hair. "She...wants Nasim and me to take care of Bartolo's."

This gave Roz a jolt, but she recovered quickly enough.

"And the rebellion?" Alix asked.

"She wants Roz to take her place as leader."

The room went perfectly quiet.

It was Nasim who finally said, "*What?*"

Dev looked up from the document, gaze locking with Roz's. "Piera wants you to take charge of the rebellion."

Arman gaped, and Josef's eyes were wide. Nasim's expression was eerily blank. For a moment she didn't say a word, and then the silence shattered.

"Are you *kidding* me?" Nasim exploded. "She wants *Roz* to lead? I've been part of the rebellion longer. People trust me. And best of all, I'm not working with a handful of fucking *Palazzo guards.*"

Roz froze, lies springing to the tip of her tongue. She felt as though someone was dangling her off the edge of a precipice, and her stomach was poised to plummet at any minute. Yes, Nasim was the more obvious choice to lead the rebellion, but how did she know?

"Don't look so shocked," Nasim said, her eyes dark fire. "I saw you on the river, Roz. I saw the Palazzo boat. I was going to ask you about it in private, but now *this?*" She gestured disgustedly at Dev, at the piece of parchment he still held. "Regardless of what Piera wanted, you can't lead the rebellion. I'm sorry, but you just can't. Ernesto was right not to trust you."

Roz didn't know what to say. What *was* there to say? The quiet in the room was intense, painful. Her heartbeat felt at once too strong and too fast. She wished the floor would open and swallow her up. "You don't understand—" she began, but this time it was Dev who interrupted.

"Is this true?" He looked from Roz to Nasim, then back again, betrayal etched in the lines of his face. "Are you talking to Palazzo guards? Why, Roz?"

Alix, Josef, and Arman appeared too shocked to say anything. Of all the rebels, they were the only ones apart from Nasim and Dev who had ever been kind to Roz. The only ones who had given her a chance.

"It's not what you think," she insisted. Every piece of her ached down to her soul. There had always been an implicit, unspoken trust between her, Dev, and Nasim. Roz had felt it, even back when they barely knew one another. "I was working with a security officer, yes, but it was only because I wanted to solve Amélie's murder. He was put in charge of finding out what happened to the disciple of Death, and it seemed like all the recent killings were connected, so…" The air around Roz grew heavy. There was nothing but this fragile moment, where words meant everything, yet none of them felt right. "I was trying to use him, okay? I thought if I could figure out what happened to Amélie, the rest of the rebels might start trusting me more."

"So you appealed to the very people we're *fighting against* for help." Nasim's voice was dull. "What an excellent way to garner trust, Roz."

"I screwed up," Roz said throatily, hating how blank the five faces before her remained. "I should have just told you what I was doing. But you don't have to worry—I swear it. None of the officers you saw me speaking to will do anything to compromise our plans. They don't even know I'm a rebel."

Nasim gave a slow shake of her head. Her disappointment was palpable, and it stung with a fierceness that snatched Roz's breath. "You're not. Not anymore. You can take part in tonight's attack, seeing as you already know about it, and then you're done, Roz. I'm sorry."

Nasim stalked to the door, wrenching it open. Her hands were unsteady, but her back was straight. Tall. She was taking charge, doing what she believed to be the right thing. If Roz hadn't been so distraught, she might have been proud of her.

Without hesitation, Arman, Alix, and Josef followed Nasim out into the street.

Dev didn't go right away. He stared at Roz with a sadness so visceral she almost wished he would be angry instead.

"I only wanted to give you answers," she whispered. "So badly."

He shook his head, the corners of his mouth downturned. "I want to believe you. But if your intentions were truly good, what reason did you have to lie to us?"

When he put it like that, Roz didn't know how to answer. She'd only wanted to avoid this exact scenario. But by keeping it a secret, she'd made it so much worse. She knew it looked suspicious—that was the worst part. How could she blame them for wanting to protect everything Piera had built?

When she didn't reply, Dev sighed. Then he, too, turned to leave.

Roz stood alone in the empty tavern, glass crunching beneath her boots, staring blindly at Piera's body.

32

DAMIAN

For the first time since he could remember, Damian slept through the entire day.

When he woke, his head was groggy—probably from the sleeping draught. It took a minute for him to recall the previous night, until he rolled over and smelled Roz's sage scent on the other pillow. She was gone, of course, but he couldn't begrudge her that. By this point it was far past a reasonable waking hour.

Damian hadn't had a single nightmare.

Perhaps his head had been too full of Roz. Her smile, her lips, her body...It felt like a dream. Maybe because Damian *had* dreamed it, so many times. And yet the real thing managed to surpass every single imagining. For a moment it was enough to stop him from dwelling on the fact that he hadn't woken up in the Palazzo. That he wouldn't stumble out of bed and grab his belt and uniform, and that he wouldn't see his fellow officers in the dining room before their shift.

That life was over for him. Once thoughts of Roz faded from his mind, he was left with nothing but that stark realization. It made him feel empty. As if his organs had been replaced by a gaping hole. At the same time, though, his body felt too heavy to peel away from the mattress. But what did that matter? He had nowhere to be. Nothing to do. He couldn't protect the Palazzo anymore, no matter what darkness stalked those gilded halls.

He lay there for a very long time.

Eventually the light outside the window began to dim, and Damian dragged himself into the bathing room. He got ready with agonizing slowness, about to slip on his soiled uniform when he realized someone had left a pile of clothes beside the bed. That was...nice. Perhaps Roz had arranged it.

He slipped them on, finding them a decent fit, and transferred the little black orb into his pocket. He wanted it with him: a reminder of his remaining goal. Then he went downstairs in search of Roz.

The tavern was packed. It was a cacophony of drunken voices and glasses slamming on tables. It was the reek of booze and unwashed bodies, the haze of smoke and dim lighting. Despite all that, though, it looked cleaner than the previous night, as if someone had mopped the floors and rearranged the bottles of liquor. Damian got the sense the patrons were all somehow *together*, and not just because they shared an equally questionable state of cleanliness. It was the way people moved among the tables, yelling over one another, yet not a single fight had broken out.

"Oi!" someone boomed, startling Damian as they pointed out the window. "Dusk's falling, eh? Let's get going, boys!"

He pressed himself against the wall as the tavern's patrons rose to their feet. They hooted and hollered as they made for the door, glasses clanking and spilling in their haste. Damian's heart pounded, but no one paid him any mind in his regular clothes. That, at least, was a blessing.

He kept an eye out for Roz, but didn't see her anywhere. Once the crowd had funneled into the street, he strode over to the bar and slammed his hands down, startling the man behind the counter. "I'm looking for someone."

The bartender furrowed his brow. He was middle aged and balding, a friendly look to his bearded face. "Ain't we all, son. But it's a little too early to find a girl you can pay by the hour."

Damian made his expression a warning.

"Okay." The bartender held up his hands, evidently not blind to the fact Damian was twice his size. "Who is it you're looking for?"

"Rossana Lacertosa. She comes here quite often. Tall, brown hair—"

The man cut him off. "No."

"No?"

"I don't know her."

He spoke too fast, too firmly, and Damian immediately distrusted it. "You don't know her." It wasn't a question. "You don't know the girl who comes in this tavern all the time."

The bartender's face reddened. "Why don't you tell me who's asking?"

Damian cut him with a skeptical look. "Why do you need to know?"

"You kidding?" A single, incredulous laugh. "Answer the question, or get the hell out, boy."

"I'm a . . . friend of hers."

302

Now it was the bartender's turn to be skeptical. "I haven't seen you around here before. You new?"

Did he mean to the area? Damian felt he was engaged in a subtle altercation he didn't understand. "I guess you could say that."

"Well—" the bartender paused, eyes flashing down to Damian's hands. Damian had unthinkingly fished the black orb out of his pocket, rubbing it between his thumb and forefinger as was his newfound habit. "Where the hell'd you get that?"

"Oh." Damian hurried to stow it away, though the bartender couldn't possibly know where it had come from. "It's just a good-luck charm."

He winced as the words left his mouth, and not just because the bartender's eyes narrowed to slits. "What kind of fucked-up sense of humor do you have, boy? There's been enough bad luck round this place today. Owner was found murdered this morning, didn't you hear?"

Damian blinked, taken aback, but the news scarcely registered. "Murdered? I'm not sure what this has to do with—"

"You don't know what you're holding right now, do you?"

Damian tensed. No, he didn't know.

The bartender leaned across the counter, his entire demeanor changing as he lowered his voice. "That there's a metal called chthonium." He jutted his chin in the direction of Damian's pocket. "My grandfather was a special agent in the First War of Saints, see. Dealt with prisoners of war for a good few years. Disciples of Chaos always had chthonium on them, you know, since it let them use their power from a greater distance. Or at least, that was the rumor. In any case, a hell of a lot of that stuff was buried with them." The bartender backed away. "Where'd you say you found it?"

"I didn't." Horror crept up Damian's spine, settling around his neck. His mouth was abruptly too dry to swallow. Chaos's disciples *were* back—or perhaps, as Roz had said, still around. Damian didn't know how, but they had to be. It was the only thing that made sense. The tunnel in the Shrine. The chief magistrate's body.

And then, other realizations that rose unbidden to the forefront of his thoughts: the blood on his hands, and the shadow in Leonzio's room. They'd been illusions, hadn't they? And the murder victims... well, if a disciple of Chaos was involved, it explained how there was so little evidence. But who *was* the culprit? Was it someone Damian knew, hiding in plain sight? Or did they stalk the city in secret, shielding themselves from anyone who happened to look their way?

"*Shit*," Damian muttered under his breath, fear blooming within him. Who knew what Chaos's disciple—or disciples— might be planning? He needed to find Roz as soon as possible. "Thank you, mio signore."

The bartender inclined his head. "Careful with that thing. You could find yourself in trouble if the wrong person spots it."

But Damian was already halfway out the door. He tore through the darkening streets, everyone he passed a blur in his periphery. The night bore down on him, a savage thing, lending to his sense of urgency. It was distressing, not knowing what he was running toward, and it only made him move faster. Roz's name echoed through his head, a ceaseless rhythm. He'd check the Basilica first, then the coroner's. It made sense for her to circle back to one of the places they'd visited, assuming she was still investigating the murders. Why the hell hadn't she woken him? She could be anywhere.

Damian barely noticed the streets growing thicker with people as he neared the sea. He slowed as screams reached his ears, carried on the unrelenting wind. A few citizens bolted past him, eyes wide with panic, tossing glances over their shoulders. Running from...*something*. But what?

That was when Damian noticed the sky.

An orange glow collided with the dark, a dusky haze that blocked the stars. Something nearby must be on fire—the world grew brighter as unseen flames coughed more smoke into the atmosphere. A different kind of adrenaline filled Damian, this time making him calmer. His mind cleared as his confidence surged and his training kicked in. It left no room for hesitation.

By now he was nearing the piazza where the Mercato was held. The screams amplified, and when Damian rounded the corner his heart leapt into his throat.

The Mercato was in disarray. Debris littered the ground from stalls and tents destroyed beyond repair. A number of them had clearly been burned: blackened wooden frames collapsed in on themselves, and the tang of smoke permeated the night air. Colorful fabrics were trampled into the dirt, and shards of glass crunched beneath Damian's feet as he stepped back to avoid a fleeing patron. Officers he vaguely recognized had swarmed the scene, too busy to pay him any attention. They hollered at one another as they attempted to get the flames under control.

Damian's eyes watered as he scanned the scene, gaze landing on a woman as she held her torch to the delicate fabric of crafted robes outside a burning tent. They caught fire at once, save a few that were clearly magicked by disciples of Grace to repel flame. Those the woman ripped from their hangers and tossed to the ground, trampling them with the heel of her shoe. Damian watched in horror as comprehension dawned.

This was a rebel attack.

He didn't have a weapon, but he didn't care. He needed to help. Staying close to the perimeter of the piazza, he sprinted toward the nearest officers. Blood roared in his ears, and there was a crack of splitting wood as a nearby tent gave way and collapsed. Before he reached the other side of the Mercato, however, a man in a loose gray shirt and trousers passed him. His hair was unkempt, his feet bare. Unlike the rest of those fleeing, the man did not look afraid—he looked exhilarated.

Damian knew at once where he had come from.

Whirling, he grabbed the man by his shirt collar, slamming him against the side of the nearest building. "Tell me what's going on," Damian growled. "Now."

The man leered, showing yellowish teeth. "Mass jailbreak, Signor." The title was mocking. "You can't stop us all."

Damian's gut tightened. He tossed the man roughly aside, letting him sprawl on the ground.

Then he ran.

It quickly became clear the criminal had told the truth: The prison was a scene of equal mayhem when Damian reached it a block later. Officers milled around the circumference of the building, guns pointed at gray-clad inmates as they bellowed orders. Some of the inmates ran. Others had their hands raised. A few were already dead, leeching blood into the cracks between the cobblestones.

But there were citizens here, too. Citizens who darted in and out of the prison, snarling at the guards and officers. Citizens with weapons and crowbars and faces half concealed by scarves.

More rebels.

The air was filled with shouting and gunfire. Damian's body vibrated with the need to *do something* as he assessed the situation.

"Noemi!" He hollered the name of the first officer he saw who wasn't engaged in direct combat. She lifted her head, gaze harsh as always, but wilder than Damian had ever seen it. "Give me your pistola!"

Noemi didn't spare a second to question him. She ripped her pistola from her belt with her free hand and tossed it into Damian's waiting grasp. If he'd had time to dwell on it, the action would have warmed his heart. He was no longer the head of Palazzo security, and yet his fellow officers still trusted him.

Thoughts of Roz pricked at the back of his mind, but these officers were his family. He couldn't abandon them. Ombrazia was about to be overrun with criminals, and Palazzo security was the first line of defense. It didn't matter if Damian was no longer an officer in name—he was an officer at heart. It was in his blood. He had to try to help.

Head ducked, he bolted for the prison entrance, firing at a masked man who lunged for him. Inside, the building was in as much turmoil as the grounds. Prison guards wrestled with unarmed inmates, attempting to force them back into their cells. Damian leapt over a guard who lay dead on the floor, a knife protruding from his back. Fury ripped through him like a blade had been buried in his own skin.

A male rebel appeared at the end of the long corridor. Damian clenched his teeth, putting a bullet in the man's leg, and the sound he emitted was ghastly. Damian's own legs shook as he stepped over the fallen rebel, but he pushed past the nausea that filled him. He slunk around the corner, keeping close to the cold stone wall, numb to the cacophony.

A masked figure loomed. A rebel woman, by the looks of it.

Damian pointed his gun as she neared, gaze sharpening, then stopped dead as her long ponytail swung over her shoulder.

Blue eyes lifted to meet his.

No. No, it couldn't be.

Roz.

His gun was still raised, but Damian didn't move. He couldn't move. He struggled to wrap his head around the sight before him, even as the deep-seated knowledge shot to the forefront of his mind—that this made *sense*. Of course it did.

"Rossana?" he said weakly, and she removed the scarf covering the lower half of her face. Her expression was sheer horror, and Damian might have been happy to see it if he hadn't been so horrified himself.

"Damian," was all she said, voice hoarse.

Damian felt emptier than ever, as if Roz had chiseled out what remained of his emotions. He was such a *fool*. It all fit so perfectly. Her hatred of the Palazzo, and her distrust of the saints. How she always spoke of justice, and resented her own power.

He'd had been right all along. Roz was always plotting, and this was nothing but another game to her. *He* was nothing but a game to her.

"Damian, I know what you're thinking, but you have to listen to me," Roz said, approaching him with hands raised. But it was an act, wasn't it? She only wanted him to let her out of here alive. "I wasn't pretending to care about you, I swear it. Everything I said last night was the truth. This is the only thing I've ever kept from you."

Damian merely continued to stare at her, not trusting a word coming from her mouth. All thoughts of the chthonium, of warning her about the illusionists, died on his tongue. He felt detached from his body. The hands stretched out before him might have belonged to someone else. Was this what rock bottom felt like? This violent, unending emptiness? He had lost everything, but at least he'd thought he gained Roz. Now that had been ripped from him, too, and there was nothing left.

None of it had been real. How could it be? Damian couldn't fathom why a rebel would ever want to work with a Palazzo officer. Not unless they were a means to an end.

He couldn't fathom a reason why Roz would love him.

"He killed her, Damian," Roz continued. Her voice shook, and she stumbled over the words. "I was too slow. I failed, and he killed her."

Damian didn't immediately realize who she was talking about, and he was too stunned to ask. "You can't do this, Roz. It's not right."

The misery drained from her face so quickly it was alarming. Fury replaced it.

"It's not right?" She thrust a finger at the nearest cells, and Damian saw some of the bars appeared to have melted away. "You want to hear about things that *aren't right*? It's not right that unfavored citizens—their *children*!—are being sent to fight in a war that has nothing to do with them. It's not right that when they manage to escape, they're treated like criminals. It's not right that a child can be found dead in the middle of the street, or that a boy's body can wash up on the riverbank, and nobody bats an eye." Roz bared her teeth, looking more animal than girl. "Do you know how many of these inmates are draft dodgers? They were here because they didn't want to die. And if that's a crime, you'd better have come to lock yourself up."

Damian felt as if she'd punched him in the face. "You *wanted* me to leave that ship! I would have stayed, but I left for *you*!"

"But Damian, don't you see? Those shouldn't have been your only options!" Roz's voice grew louder as she shook her head urgently. "It's all wrong. Your father, the chief magistrate... Ombrazia doesn't care about anyone but its disciples, and that needs to change. I know you can see it, too."

Damian could barely draw enough breath to form words. "Those are my friends out there!" he rasped, his anger growing more virulent by the second. "Regardless of how the men in power behave, those are just people who pledged their lives to protect this city. Who do you think suffers the most from this little crusade? Not my father. Not the chief magistrate. It's them, Rossana. They're the ones who fight and die and clean up the fucking mess."

Roz's face tightened, but Damian could see his words hadn't swayed her.

"Sometimes that's the price you pay for revolution. People die. Even good ones. That's how change happens."

How could she talk like this? How could she think these things? Damian knew she was cold, but this was beyond what he'd expected her capable of. His father had warned him more than once about radical ideologies, but Damian never imagined he would see the evidence in the woman he loved.

Loved. Saints give him strength, he loved her.

And it was going to crush him.

Damian's grip tightened on the pistola, still aimed at Roz's chest. His fingers quivered.

He knew he had to make a choice, and he knew what his decision would be.

He just didn't know if he could live with himself afterward.

ROZ

Roz hated the way Damian was looking at her.

She'd made her choice, and known what the consequences might be. But it still hurt like someone had shoved a white-hot iron into the cavity of her chest. It was made worse by the fact that she hadn't expected him to be here, fighting for the enemy side. She could tell him that after tonight she would no longer be a rebel—not officially—but what difference would that make? She was still here, now. He would only see it as an excuse.

Roz could see in Damian's eyes that she'd lost him. That, regardless of what she'd said last night, he truly believed she'd never really cared about him.

"I'm sorry," Roz said softly, the anger flooding out of her. It was the second heartfelt apology she'd made today. And though she'd seen this one coming, it hurt just as much. She gritted her teeth to keep her composure. "I'm sure you understand why I couldn't tell you. But this is the only thing I've kept from you, Damian. Everything I told you about the way I feel was true. I know you're furious, and I know you don't believe I've made the right choices, but I would never lie about that."

Damian released a single, emotionless laugh. "This is the way it'll always be with you, isn't it, Rossana? You beg for forgiveness, but we both know the only person you'll ever put first is yourself. That's the way you are. I don't know why I hoped otherwise."

It was an uncharacteristically harsh thing for Damian to say. Roz reached for him and paused, thinking better of it, her outstretched fingers suspended in the empty space he'd occupied seconds before. In the interlude, the space between heartbeats, she saw the tremor in her fingers—slight but there. Her breath knotted in her throat.

"I'm *sorry*," she said again. "I know you don't want to hear it, but I am." Regret pulsed through her. Roz didn't want to lose Damian like she'd lost Nasim and Dev, but it was going to happen nonetheless. How was it that she couldn't hold on to a single person she loved?

"You're right," Damian said. "I don't want to hear it." But he lowered the gun, his expression broken. "Go."

"What?"

"I said *go*."

He wasn't going to arrest her, then. Everything about his body language was resigned. Roz would have preferred it if he'd yelled. Exhibits of rage she could handle, but this... This *empty* man was not someone she knew how to navigate.

And yet he was letting her go. No matter what Roz did, no matter how she hurt him, Damian continued to care for her. She had waltzed back into his life, given him every reason not to trust her, and known all along it wouldn't make a difference.

Being loved by Damian wasn't conditional. It should have been—saints knew he'd be better off—but it wasn't. Him letting her escape only solidified that, and it made Roz feel so much worse.

They loved one another. They likely always would.

But it wasn't enough.

So she went. She didn't have to turn around to know Damian wouldn't follow her. Had the situation been reversed, she sure as hell wouldn't have followed him.

The pain of her guilt, of knowing it was over, was physical. It tightened her throat and sat like a weight upon her heart. She had nothing left. Nothing to lose.

She had nothing left to lose.

Roz had always thought the best way to avenge her father's death was to disrupt the system that had allowed it. When the system fell, the men at the top would crumble with it. She'd known it might take a lifetime, but she was willing to wait.

No longer.

The current tumult was the perfect distraction. Security had congregated at the Mercato and the prison, leaving the Palazzo vulnerable.

Roz thought of Piera's gaping mouth and eye sockets, and her mind was made up. It wasn't like Damian could hate her any more than he already did.

It was obvious from the state of Ombrazia's streets that the rebels had succeeded at organizing themselves. They weren't alone, however—the riots had roused a number of unfavored from their previously passive slumber. The closer Roz got to the piazza, the clearer it became. Committing to a rebellion was one thing, but there was nothing like a crowd to stoke confidence. It was so much easier to take action when you knew you weren't alone.

The dull roar of the wind failed to drown the screams, and the night was laced with fiery smoke. Roz slipped through the crowd, silent and unnoticed, reveling in the pandemonium. The city had let the unfavored down, and now it would burn.

She almost smiled as she slunk toward the Shrine.

It would remain open to the public for twenty more minutes. As such, Roz's timing would be perfect. She let the darkness of the underground corridor envelop her, heart beating a frantic tattoo, a hand on the pistola at her waistband.

There were two robed disciples in the belly of the Shrine, but both were so deep in prayer they were incognizant of Roz's presence. Deaf to the click of her heels across the stone. She crept along the rounded perimeter to the corridor opposite, then darted out of sight. The first time she'd come here, she'd told Damian to lead the way, and had committed every turn to memory. Just in case.

She'd suspected it might someday come in handy.

The door immediately inside the corridor was locked, as she'd known it would be. Luckily the wood was thin, and it splintered when she put her weight behind a forceful kick.

Without checking to see if anyone had heard, she ran.

Left. Right, right, left. Keep going straight. Then another left. Her breaths seemed to thunder in the tunnel, reverberating off the walls. Sweat trickled down the back of her neck. This part—what happened next—could very well be the part where she died. And though her palms were sweaty, and she cursed her body for its traitorous stress, it was unimportant in the face of possibility.

Fear and excitement felt nearly the same, did they not? Often one was indistinguishable from the other.

Roz, then, would feel the one that served her.

She sprinted through the empty hallways. As she'd hoped, the bulk of security officers had been called to the riot, which was audible through the open ceiling in the center of the Palazzo. It all sounded far away, as if it could never touch her in this marble tomb. Roz made straight for the top floor, swerving when she was nearly spotted by a pacing Enzo. His hands were clasped at the back of his neck, his head bowed. Stress emanated from his every movement. How horrible it must be, Roz thought, to be stuck here when everyone else was embroiled in combat, not knowing the outcome.

Stepping lightly, she slipped down a narrow corridor painted in white and gold.

I always mix it up with the general's office. Which is . . . second floor, third door?

Third floor, fourth door, the Kiran of her memories said. *Don't worry, you'll get it eventually.*

Another piece of knowledge locked away, just in case.

Inhaling deeply, Roz called up the unshakeable confidence she kept in the center of herself. Shoved the door open. Pulled out her pistola.

And pointed it at Battista Venturi's head.

Roz

"*Good evening, General,*" Roz said.

She made a slow semicircle around the room, gun raised all the while. Her heartbeats seemed to clamor for precedence in her chest. She imagined slamming a mask into place and stepping into a different version of herself. A calmer version. One that wouldn't execute Battista at the mere sight of his smug face.

Battista leapt up from his desk and lunged for the drawer, reaching for the weapon Roz was certain he kept there. She rotated the pistola in her grip, lowering it. "Hands up."

The general looked different, somehow, now that she was seeing him up close. His trimmed beard was shot through with gray, and he was shorter than she remembered. Or perhaps she'd gotten taller. Either way, he was not the terrifying man Roz always pictured. He was just...a man. A man whose brow furrowed precisely the way Damian's did when he was confused. A man who wore his years on his face, each one adding another layer of exhaustion.

Damian would look like this, someday.

Not that Roz would be there to see it.

Slowly, the general raised his hands. "Signora Lacertosa. I'm surprised to see you here." He licked his lips. "But then again, I'm somehow not."

His face was stone as he studied her unblinkingly. Battista had known Roz as a child, had known her penchant for dramatic, vicious confrontations. Had he known she would confront him about this eventually? Had he expected her to seek him out, to devolve into hysterics and fling empty threats?

But Roz was not that girl anymore. Her rage was a poison to which she had a carefully cultivated tolerance.

She quirked one side of her mouth in a wry grin. "Well, *I'm* certainly not surprised to see *you* here. I figured you'd be in your office, hiding away while others did your bidding. Unfortunately, that didn't leave much in the way of security, did it?"

It was the closest Roz had been to Battista in three years, and the current of hatred that washed over her was overwhelming. She wanted to put a knife to every line of his aging face. Wanted to rip out those expressionless eyes and crush them beneath her heeled boot. The general held her gaze from the other side of the desk, not even having the decency to look uncomfortable.

She sidled farther into the room. She'd worn her tallest boots, and thoroughly enjoyed the fact that they were at eye level. "Do you enjoy it? Letting people die for you? Killing those who aren't good enough for you? Does it make you *happy*?"

"Is this why you've come, Rossana?" Battista's voice was soft, controlled. His eyes tracked her every movement. "To avenge your father? It's too late for that. He still tried to run, you know, even after we'd surrounded him. A coward to the very end."

Red played across Roz's vision, but she shoved her anger down. She waved a hand, indicating the room. "I'll wait for you to see the irony, shall I?"

"What is it you want, Signora Lacertosa?"

Roz tapped her nails against the trigger, watching in satisfaction as Battista sucked a breath. "I want you to confess."

"You already know I was responsible for your father's death. It was never a secret."

"You two were *friends*," she hissed, a familiar pain bubbling in her chest and—*no*. This wasn't why she'd come. She needed to stay focused. "But that's not the confession I'm talking about."

The skin around Battista's mouth tightened. "Then what *are* you talking about?"

"I'm talking about Amélie Villeneuve. Piera Bartolo. Daniel Cardello." It occurred to Roz that she didn't know the name of the victim she'd stumbled across in the garden. Sadness rushed in. This was for her, too, whether or not Roz could name her. "Even Leonzio Bianchi, if I'm not mistaken."

"I don't have a clue what you mean."

Roz closed one eye in a show of aiming the gun at his head. "Wrong answer."

"I'm not lying," Battista snarled. Strangely enough, he looked even more like Damian when he let his fury show. The man Roz remembered from her childhood was nothing like the man before her now. The general had never been soft, and he'd always been intimidating, but he had also been quick to laugh. He'd doted on his wife and been kind to his son. Even thinking back to that Battista, though, Roz could see how this version wasn't such a far leap. It was why she hadn't been surprised when she heard he was responsible for her father's death.

"Are you telling me," she said, "that you didn't kill five victims with the poisonous vellenium, a plant that grows best in the north? Where *you* were stationed for three years? Are you telling me you didn't make a visit to the city coroner and ask her to redact the name of that poison from her reports, lest someone learn about its connection to Chaos? Are you working with a disciple, then?"

"I'll say it again," Battista snarled. *"I don't know what you're talking about."* Each word was clipped, sharply enunciated.

"You can admit it, General. There's no one around to hear you. It's only you and me."

Battista's eyes darted around the room, seeking an escape where there wasn't one. Roz wanted to laugh. He might prance around Ombrazia like a saint, might stand alongside the chief magistrate and preach the importance of a pious existence, but he was a liar. A murderer. A heretic by his own standards.

"I gave you a chance to confess," Roz went on, "but I guess I can kill you regardless." She took a step closer to the general. Then another. Her blood was alive in her veins, fury and anticipation making her wild. Some people said revenge was never as sweet as you imagined—that you saw murder differently once it stared you in the face. That it demanded too much of your soul.

Those people were wrong.

Or perhaps Roz simply had no qualms about giving her soul away.

Because Battista *deserved* this. How many innocent people had he led to sacrifice? How many bright-eyed soldiers had gone off to war with the righteous drive to fight for their country, only to be left rotting in the muck? Or tried to leave and been slaughtered like her father?

The general cursed, and Roz could see sweat beading along his hairline. She was deaf to the slew of excuses that came next. For years Battista had played judge, jury, and executioner. It was her saints-damned turn.

She put her finger on the trigger.

"Roz?" Damian's voice came from behind her, and she froze. So did Battista, shock evident in every line of his face.

"Damian." Roz didn't move the gun as she turned, her stomach bottoming out. Why was he here? She had hurt him enough. She couldn't have him watch this.

Damian raised his hands and stepped into the room. His jaw was taut, his gaze imploring. He was afraid, Roz realized belatedly. Afraid of *her*.

Or, at the very least, of what she would do.

"Roz, I need you to drop the gun."

She did not drop the gun. Rather, she gripped it harder, eyes burning. This was the closest she'd come to revenge. It was everything she had dreamed about for three years. "He's a murderer."

Damian's gaze was entreating. "Maybe he is. But you're not."

Roz snarled. Damian didn't sound angry anymore; he sounded like an officer. A negotiator.

"You're trying to manipulate me."

"I'm not," he insisted. "Please, Roz. He's my father."

"And he *killed mine*!" She spun, the pistola wavering. Tears pricked behind her eyes. "He killed Piera!" Battista watched her warily, as if fearing her sudden loss of temper might earn him a bullet in the brain. He was right to worry—Roz's adrenaline surged too high for anything Damian said to stop her now. After all, she'd already lost him; she may as well put the final nail in the coffin.

"The best time to show mercy is when someone doesn't deserve it," he implored her.

Roz laughed, the sound dark and prolonged. "Thank you, Saint Damian." She jabbed her chin in Battista's direction. "When has *he* ever shown mercy? Tell me that."

Damian pressed his lips together. Roz remembered how he'd looked at her last night, those lips parting as though her touch were a miracle. She'd run her hands down the length of his body as if the feel of him would never be enough. And it hadn't been. She hadn't gotten nearly enough of Damian Venturi. She wanted to measure time by counting his heartbeats, and learn every single thing that made him smile.

But she couldn't. In a way, that dream had died alongside Piera.

"Never," Damian whispered in response to her question. "You're right. My father has never shown mercy. But I'm not asking for him." His throat shifted. "I'm asking for me."

"Damian—"

"Please." His voice was barely audible. "If you ever loved me, don't let it be you."

A pause stretched between them, somewhere between seconds and infinity, and Roz made a decision.

A single shot rang out through the silence.

DAMIAN

Damian's entire body went taut.

She'd done it. Roz had pulled the trigger.

His mind spun, eyes scanning wildly as he looked for blood, for the point of entry, for anything at all. But Battista, head lifting from where he'd bowed it in resignation, did the same. Confusion was etched into his features.

The gun clattered to the ground at the same moment Damian spotted the hole in the wall directly above his father's head.

Roz hadn't shot Battista. Had frightened him, certainly, but there was no doubt she'd missed on purpose. Roz didn't do anything by accident.

Damian's shoulders sagged, relief spreading through him. He had known appealing to Roz's morals wouldn't work. Despite what he'd said about her not being a murderer, Damian didn't doubt she could kill a man and sleep like a baby the same night. So he'd taken a chance, and hoped to hell that last night part of her had been telling the truth. That even if she'd lied, she at least cared enough not to murder his father in front of him.

Roz turned to him, and Damian saw her face had softened. Saw her choose him over vengeance. It was sudden and sobering, like watching a flame sputter out. Had he not shown up, Damian knew she would have done it.

But she cared about him enough not to.

It shouldn't have quelled his heartache, but it did.

When the initial shock had faded, Battista lunged. Whether for the dropped pistola or for Roz, Damian wasn't certain. It didn't matter. He hurled himself into his father, grunting at the force of the impact.

"What the—" Battista panted. "She was going to kill me!" He struggled under Damian's weight, trying to rise.

"I know," Damian said curtly, and watched as understanding flashed across his father's face. The version of the father he knew faded before his eyes, and suddenly Damian was looking at General Battista Venturi.

"You idiot bastard."

Damian ignored the jibe, though he felt himself redden.

"You stopped her from killing me, only to protect her?" Battista's lip pulled back from his teeth. "Why are you even here? *How* are you here?"

He tried and failed once more to rise, and Damian was pleased to note he'd become considerably stronger than his father. Frustrated, Battista managed to twist around, fist striking out at Damian's jaw. It made contact, and Damian, still tender from the beating he'd received on the military ship, growled his annoyance.

He'd never seen his father like this. So angry and...wild. Battista, in his mind, was always calm and collected.

The next moment, Roz was there. She had retrieved her pistola, but she didn't shoot, instead kicking Battista in the ribs. He snarled a word that made Damian stiffen, and he leapt back from his father, raising his hands in a defensive gesture.

"Stop this," Damian huffed.

Battista's fury was a tangible thing, and he beheld Damian with an ugly sneer. "Are you truly so pathetic that you'd side with a traitor rather than fight for your country?"

Roz scoffed. They both ignored her.

"I didn't want to go back to war," Damian said softly. "Not after everything. Not after Michele. I can't apologize for that. But *you*...What you've done with your power is inexcusable. You might think me a pathetic excuse for a son, but I don't care. Given what I know now, I'd be more worried if you were proud of me."

Battista's lip curled back from his teeth. "I didn't kill those people, Damian. I don't know what you two have been on about, but the only death I'll take credit for is Jacopo's."

Something about the way he said it made Damian believe his father. Unease stole over him like a vat of frigid water had been tipped onto his head. "Then who *did* kill them?"

"He's obviously lying," Roz scoffed, at the same time that Battista demanded, "How should I know?"

Damian gave his head a shake, but his thoughts refused to clear. "That's not the point right now. If you're lying, I *will* figure it out. Even if I have to side with a traitor to do it."

"Think of the saints," Battista pressed, jaw taut. "Think of—"

Damian interrupted him. "This has never been about the saints. Everything you've done has always only been about you."

Battista shook his head, the image of false sadness. "Forte told me I was going to regret bringing you home, but I didn't believe him. Evidently I should have. You're too much like your mother."

Damian's heart gave an uneven jolt. He hadn't heard Battista mention his dead wife in years. What would Liliana Venturi say if she could see them now? Would it break her heart, seeing them fight like this? Or would she be pleased that her son was finally standing up for himself?

"I'm glad," Damian said icily. "I'd rather be like her. I always felt I wasn't good enough to be your son. When Forte asked me to solve Leonzio's murder, I thought doing so would prove I was good at my job. But do you know why I was *really* good at my job? Because I cared about people. Because I gave everyone the benefit of the doubt and believed in true justice. Because the rest of the officers respected me. I might not have lived up to your idea of what a security officer should be, but I cared about my work." He took a breath, staring Battista right in the face. "So yes, I'm choosing Roz. And maybe that's the wrong choice. But anything's a hell of a lot better than choosing you."

From the corner of his eye Damian thought he saw Roz wince, but perhaps it was simply his imagination. Battista opened his mouth, face twisted as though he were about to say something harsh, only to freeze.

Footsteps thudded on the stairs.

Roz's gaze snapped to meet Damian's, wide and severe. He looked away before he could get caught in it. She shifted her gun to aim into the corridor, but never got the chance to shoot.

Security officers poured into the room, archibugi raised.

There were at least a dozen of them. They moved with swift efficiency, each one fully armed. Regalia gleamed in the dim light as they took up their positions. Damian's head spun. Whatever was happening here, it was clearly planned. He raised his hands to show he wasn't armed, and Roz copied him, dropping the pistola. Apparently even she wasn't bold enough to think she could take on multiple officers.

"What in the saints' name is going on here?" Battista snarled, showing no indication of standing down. The guns, Damian noted in bewilderment, were directed at his father, too. "I am your *general*. You put the weapons down, or you lose your jobs."

The nearest officer—Damian realized with a jolt that it was Kiran—shook his head. "Chief magistrate's orders. Come with us."

The world tilted beneath Damian's feet. The chief magistrate *was* still alive, then. If that was the case, the body Damian had found in the Shrine was the illusion. But why show him that? What purpose did it serve?

"*Move*," Kiran said tonelessly.

Damian cringed, trying to determine from his friend's expression whether Kiran thought he'd played some part in the rebellion. He couldn't bear the thought of Kiran or Siena thinking he was repaying them for yesterday's rescue by joining Roz's little charade. But Kiran kept his gaze carefully averted, and Damian's heart sank.

The officers spread out to encircle the three of them. Battista continued to rage and threaten all the way down the stairs, but Damian didn't say a word. He was a deserter. Roz was a rebel, a would-be murderer. Whatever was about to happen to them, he was certain it wasn't good. And yet he felt nothing save a vague sense of dread, as though he were watching this happen to someone else.

He couldn't bring himself to make eye contact with any of

the other officers. He was no longer their superior. He meant nothing.

"Thank you," Damian said abruptly to Roz, switching to a different source of misery. "For not killing him."

She blinked, her expression hollow. As if she'd lost something, or perhaps given up. "How many people am I going to have to let him take from me, Damian?"

He hated that after everything, she'd lost Piera, too. And though he was angry at her—how could he not be?—the words she'd said earlier began to ring true. Hadn't they been fighting for the same things? It was only that Roz was willing to fight harder, dirtier, than he was.

"Piera was a rebel too, wasn't she?" he murmured, the realization dawning on him.

For a long moment Roz didn't speak. Then: "She was the leader. She was a mother when mine couldn't be. Now she's gone, and I'm running out of reasons to care."

Damian studied the curve of her neck, the tense line of her mouth. He could understand that. He knew what it was to feel you had nothing left to fight for. "I'm sorry."

They were quiet then, as Battista was dragged off in a different direction. Damian cursed under his breath when he realized he and Roz were being taken to the dungeons. How many times had he guided someone down this dark stairwell? How many times had he heard the ominous creak of the iron gate as it slammed shut, sealing his arrest inside a tiny cell? He'd often considered how terrible it would be to be left alone in the bowels of the dungeon, never imagining he would experience it.

"What's happening?" he demanded of Kiran, who acted as if he hadn't spoken. "Kiran, listen to me, the Palazzo isn't safe—"

The cell door shut with a bang, cutting off his warning. A stone cell, of course; they weren't about to risk putting Roz in one with metal bars. There were various types of enclosures down here for that reason. It was like being trapped in a giant cinderblock, the door a thick slab of reinforced wood with a small window.

The moment they were inside, Damian leaned against the frigid wall of the cell, trying not to think about the last time he'd been somewhere this small and dark. At least he wasn't alone: Roz's hair tickled his nose as she moved closer to him. He heard her release a breath as the officers' footsteps receded.

"What do we do now?" Roz asked as the silence pressed in. "We can't sit here waiting for whatever comes next. You still have allies in the Palazzo, right?"

Their names sent a pang through Damian's chest. "You saw Kiran just now, didn't you? They likely think I've been consorting with rebels."

"You have, technically."

He glared at her outline. "Not quite ready to joke about that."

"Sorry. What about Enzo? I saw him earlier."

"And how do you expect me to get ahold of him? He has no idea we're even down here."

Roz made a hum of acknowledgment, slumping against the wall. "Well then. Who do you think it is?"

"What?"

"The disciple of Chaos. Who do you think it could be? Or do you think it's someone we haven't even come across?"

"I don't know." Damian scraped a hand through his hair. "Part of me still hopes there's another explanation entirely. One that doesn't involve Chaos, or me going mad."

"Well, you're certainly not going mad," Roz said into the

dark. "I believe you saw exactly what you said you did. I know that probably doesn't mean much right now, but it's the truth."

At her words, Damian was catapulted back to the public prison. *Everything I said last night was the truth*, Roz had said.

Right before he'd realized she was going to destroy him.

"I can't believe I didn't guess you were a rebel," he muttered abruptly, unable to help himself. "The whole time I thought I was getting to know you again, I didn't really know you at all, did I?"

She pressed closer to him, her scent chasing away the chill on the air. "You aren't the only one I've lied to, you know, and I can say with certainty it wasn't worth it." A hollow laugh. "I've made a lot of mistakes over the past three years. I won't deny it. I'll never be perfect, and hell, I'll probably never even be *good*. But I can try, right?" Roz's voice was pleading. "I'll try, if you give me the chance."

"Damn it, Roz." Damian dragged a hand across his brow. "What am I supposed to do? Forget about it, until you find another good reason to lie to me?"

She was silent at that. After a pause she said, "I joined the rebellion because I know this city can be better. I don't want us to be divided by those who have magic and those who don't. When a group starts rebelling, it's because they're desperate. It's because nothing else has worked. If I could fix it, I wouldn't send our youth to war. I wouldn't let the guilds dictate how everyone else lives. I want every citizen to have a say, and I don't want anyone to suffer." Roz's voice was pleading. "Are those really such bad goals?"

They weren't. Damian wanted that, too. He just didn't have the vision, and wouldn't know where to start if he did. Roz, though—she said the things he was too afraid to say. Saw the things he tried to ignore. Between the two of them, she had always been the one destined to create change.

He only had to be brave enough to follow her.

"Okay," he said. "You're right."

The moment he said it aloud, he realized it was true. He was afraid of the rebellion because he was afraid of change. Of disarray. But it was nearly impossible to achieve the former without the latter, wasn't it? Nothing shifted on its own accord. You had to go out there and fight for it.

Roz's silence was thick with disbelief. "I'm what?"

"You're right," Damian repeated forcefully. "I'm done ignoring the things I know are wrong. I'm done calling on the saints to do the things we need to do ourselves. If the saints cared about justice, we'd already have it."

She blinked long lashes at him. "But the Palazzo—"

"Has thrown me in this cell," Damian finished. He heard the frustration in his own voice. "You had it right, Roz, and I was wrong. Besides, when you care about someone, their goals become yours."

Her lips parted in shock, and it was clear she didn't know quite what to say. Damian didn't mind. From here on out, Damian would support Roz Lacertosa in whatever she did. If she asked him for the world, he would find a way to get it to her. She held his heart in her hands, whether he trusted her grip or not.

"Thank you," she said, the words heavy with emotion.

"There's nothing to thank me for."

Instead of responding, Roz turned, lifting a hand to skim the side of his jaw. Damian's vision had adjusted enough to see the intensity in her gaze, the soft curve of her upper lip.

This time, instead of letting her guide him, he cupped the back of her neck and pulled her mouth to his.

A small breath escaped her. The heat of it was enough to set Damian alight, and all at once the cold stone no longer seemed unbearable. He pushed her hair back from her face. Lifted her chin. Traced the crescent of her teeth with his tongue, and heard the amused rumble in her chest as she pressed her body closer to his.

The way Roz made him feel, he thought, might be the closest thing he ever found to proof of the divine. For once, Damian didn't care that he was unfavored. Roz's touch was more grounding than a prayer. She was holier than any saint. If she let him, he might just make her his new religion.

Whatever was about to happen, they would weather it together. Before Damian could tell Roz as much, though, an unfamiliar voice rang through the darkness like wind chimes.

"Saints, get a room, would you?"

36

Roz

Roz was certain she was dreaming. There really must be a disciple of Chaos in the Palazzo—that was the only explanation for Nasim's voice emanating outside the cell.

"Who's there?" Damian demanded.

Roz was too shocked to respond right away. It was Nasim who eventually said, "I'm Roz's friend."

Friend. What was going on?

"Oh," Damian said on a breath, though Roz couldn't quite share his relief. "Another rebel, I assume? How did you get into the Palazzo?" But he shook his head before Nasim could answer, backtracking. "You know what, it doesn't matter. Listen, if you head down the hallway behind you, there's a spare master key hidden in the crypt."

Light flared, making Roz wince as her eyes adjusted. Through the tiny window, Nasim stood illuminated by a golden glow, a lantern in one hand and a key in the other. "I wish you had told me that before I stole this."

Damian rolled his eyes, but there was no malice in the action. "Who'd you steal it from?"

"An officer standing guard outside."

"You didn't kill him, did you?"

Nasim huffed. "No. I mean, I'm fairly sure I didn't."

Damian shook his head in resignation. "Well, I can see why you and Roz are friends."

Roz couldn't bring herself to laugh. She felt strangely jittery, and more than a little apprehensive. Her muscles locked of their own accord as Nasim inserted the key, yanking the door open with a wretched creak. None of this made any sense. Nasim wasn't the forgiving type. She wasn't like Damian, who loved Roz more than she deserved. Nasim wouldn't hesitate to cut ties with those she believed deserved it.

Roz didn't follow Damian from the cell, but rather stared at Nasim expectantly, knowing the other girl was about to say something.

"Dev came to talk to me," Nasim muttered, not making eye contact. "Right after I left the tavern."

"Oh?" Roz swallowed, afraid to hope.

"He told me he believed you, and that it made sense you hadn't told us. That the way I'd acted was likely the very reason you'd kept it a secret." Nasim toed the stone floor with her heavy boot. "Once I wasn't quite so angry, I couldn't say it didn't make sense. If I really care about honoring Piera, I need to trust her judgment. So…I'm sorry."

Roz's thoughts whirled in her head. It wasn't what she'd expected to hear. First Damian sympathizing with the rebellion, now Nasim exhibiting some measure of forgiveness? She didn't deserve people like this in her life. People who stood by her side no matter what happened.

She was shaking her head before Nasim had even finished speaking. "No. You're right, I should have told you what I was doing. The longer I kept it a secret, the more suspicious it seemed. I knew that. I just couldn't stand the idea of you resenting me, and I thought once I had the answers about Amélie's death, everything would fall into place. I was an idiot."

Beside Nasim, Damian shifted his feet, equal parts awkward and perplexed. *We have to go*, his body language said, and Roz knew he was right. But Nasim wasn't finished.

"I'm still upset," she admitted. "But Dev said something else that made me think. He said you'll be a great leader, because you could have had everything, and you turned it down. You had all the benefits of a disciple, but you didn't care about losing them, because you were never just in it for you. You cared about making real change happen for everyone. And I knew he was right."

Roz bit her lip. Dev *was* right, though she'd never thought of it as anything more than... well, being a decent person. "I can't live a comfortable disciple's life when I know other people are suffering. That doesn't make me a saint. It just makes me someone who isn't completely terrible." She laughed, and the sound was hollow. "And I don't want to lead the rebellion. You were right—it should be you. You deserve it. Besides, if I took over, everything would go to shit."

Nasim coughed a laugh, acknowledging this. "What if we do it together?"

Roz's heartbeat kicked up a notch. Could they? Could she and Nasim really carry on together what Piera had worked for? Some of the rebels wouldn't be happy about it, but they had no reason to distrust Nasim.

"Okay," she said, and couldn't help a small grin. It hurt, that grin, because agreeing to this meant acknowledging Piera was well and truly gone. But it also felt right. "Let's do it."

Damian frowned at Nasim, leaning against the exterior of the cell. "I'm not even going to pretend I understand what's happening here," he said, "but how the hell did you know where to find us?"

Nasim's face tightened. When she answered, it was directed at Roz. "I was at the Mercato when Alix showed up. They told me you'd disappeared during the prison break, and a few minutes later a bunch of officers were called to the Palazzo. Security breach, I heard them say. I just *knew* it was you, and that you'd done something idiotic." She snorted good-naturedly. "So I went to the side door, knocked out the guard, and stole his key. I saw you two being escorted down here, so I followed, then hid in the dark until I was sure the officers had left."

"You have my sincerest thanks," Damian told Nasim, the words oddly stiff. He no longer looked confused—he must have been able to infer which of Roz's lies Nasim was talking about. "But we should really get out of here."

Nasim nodded, waving his concern away as she turned back to Roz. "I still wish you'd trusted us. But I'll be damned if I'm not going to fight by your side tonight."

"I'll make it up to you," Roz murmured. "No matter how long it takes."

She couldn't lose her friend. In a way, Roz, Nasim, and Dev— three people trying desperately not to create emotional bonds— had formed the backbone of their own little revolution.

They were tenuous, these relationships. Her and Nasim. Her and Damian. For once, though, Roz was determined to strengthen them. That was how people loved, wasn't it? By giving away pieces of themselves, little by little?

For too long Roz had tried to keep all her pieces to herself. But what good had that done?

Nasim paused at the top of the stairs, pressing a finger to her lips. Roz dragged her thoughts back to the present, forcing herself to focus. Damian flattened against the wall as Nasim peered around the corner.

"Okay," she said, relaxing. "The coast is clear."

Damian grimaced. "Before we go anywhere," he said to Nasim, "I think there's something you ought to know."

He was no doubt referring to the disciple of Chaos, and Roz felt adrenaline shoot through her like a lethal injection. They needed to find the culprit before anyone else died. But how did you find someone who could hide behind illusions? How could you fight, how could you win, when you didn't even have reality on your side?

Nasim's brow creased. "What do you mean?"

Damian's gaze flashed to Roz's, and then he began haltingly to explain what he'd discovered. Nasim's eyes widened as he spoke, but otherwise her expression didn't shift.

"You don't look surprised," Roz noted afterward.

Nasim risked another glance around the corner before responding. "Oh, I'm surprised. There's clearly a cold-blooded killer stalking the city—I just hadn't guessed it was connected to *Chaos*, of all things. You really think he's back, then?"

Damian gave a halfhearted shrug. He looked as tired as Roz had ever seen him, a sheen of sweat along his temple. "Either that, or his disciples were never truly gone. I don't know what to think."

Nasim heaved a breath, her face clouding over. "You know what? It makes sense. Did you notice the expressions of the officers who arrested you? It was like they were under a spell."

"It's true," Roz said, remembering. A sensation of foreboding alighted at her core. After all, a disciple of Chaos could manipulate multiple people at once. Multiple people with *guns*. They needed to tread very, very carefully. "Damian, the officers outside the Palazzo were unaffected as far as you could tell, right? Do you think you could convince them to help us look for the disciple?"

Damian was doubtful. "They just arrested me, if you'll remember. A few of them might be willing to hear me out, but that's about it."

"Well, can you try?"

He nodded.

"Good." There was no way they could do this on their own. "Then we'll need to get out of the building. Nasim, you lead the way, since you're the one with the gun. I've a knife in my boot, but it won't do much good unless I can get within close range."

"Why didn't you get that out when we were being arrested?" Damian said accusatorially.

"Was my tiny boot knife going to help us against a dozen security officers?"

Nasim cleared her throat, interrupting their argument. "*I'm* rescuing *you* two. Shouldn't I be the one giving orders?"

"Fine." Roz crossed her arms, feigning offence. "What do you propose?"

Nasim's mouth lifted, the shadow of a grin. "I'll lead the way, since I'm the one with the gun."

Roz snorted, but something within her lightened. That was more like the Nasim she knew. She opened her mouth, prepared to fling a retort, but never got the chance.

Because at that very moment, for the second time that night, a shot sounded through the Palazzo.

37

DAMIAN

In the end, Damian took Nasim's gun, as he was a better shot.

Damian tiptoed down the hallway, Roz and Nasim on his heels, moving into a sprint when he found it still abandoned. He suspected the sound of gunfire had emanated from the Palazzo's entryway; the way it had echoed surely meant the shot was fired in an enormous space.

Sure enough, as Damian skidded around the corner, boots slipping on the marble, he saw two familiar figures.

Framed by the arches of the Palazzo's main entrance was Chief Magistrate Forte, his gray hair silver beneath the moonlight streaming in through the ceiling.

He was standing over Battista Venturi's body, pistola in hand.

"*Saints,*" Roz breathed from behind Damian's shoulder, but he barely heard her. His world slowed around him as he tried to comprehend what he was seeing. For a heartbeat there was nothing but the crimson spreading across the floor, and the silence in his own head. The shot had been perfect, straight through the skull.

Battista had always had an enormous, intimidating presence. Now, though, he was nothing more than a shell. A nothing-creature in the shape of a man Damian had once known and loved. Because he had loved his father, even when it hurt to do so.

The last member of his family, gone. And any possibility of mending their relationship was gone with him, snatched away in a fraction of a second. Their last conversation had been a horrible one, and Damian would never be able to remedy that. Would never know if there was anything left to salvage.

Shaking, he raised his eyes and his gun to the chief magistrate's face. *Why?* was the question he ought to have asked. *Why have you done this?*

But instead he said, "You were *dead*. I saw you."

Damian had been certain the body in the Shrine was the illusion, but now he wasn't so sure. The man before him now looked...wrong. When Forte grinned, there was something unnatural about the way his lips stretched: too slowly, too deliberately. His eyes were wild, a lively spark in them Damian had never seen before.

"Ah, Signor Venturi the younger. Foiled." He didn't so much as attempt to point his pistola in their direction. That, more than anything, made Damian uneasy.

"Drop your weapon," Damian said, trying to keep his voice from cracking.

Forte smiled wider. Then wider still, until his face was no longer human but some heinous, cackling mask. The corners of his mouth split like cheap linen stretched too tight. His body began to convulse, and the gun dropped from his hand to clatter against the marble. His eyes glazed over, rolling back in his head before popping free to dangle against his cheeks. Blood fell in clotted, blackened rivulets, mixing with the crimson already spattering the floor. As Damian watched, Forte shed his skin like an ill-fitting suit.

Nasim let out a scream, and even Roz whimpered softly. Damian swallowed bile, though he knew it was an illusion. It had to be.

Because someone else stepped daintily out from that pile of flesh and bone. Someone familiar.

"No." Damian couldn't breathe, couldn't think, couldn't feel. "No, *no*. It can't be *you*."

Beside him Roz adopted a fighting stance, her expression a mixture of terror and confusion. Nasim was frozen, one hand stretched toward Roz as if she'd stopped midway through reaching for her.

"Why not, Damian?" Enzo said smoothly. "Why can't it be me?"

He was different, somehow: his voice strong, his stance self-assured. Even as Damian stared at him, Enzo's face sharpened, his body thickening. Before long he was handsomer, and years older than he usually appeared. And none of it made *sense*. It didn't—it didn't—

"You're the disciple of Chaos." Roz's harsh voice helped Damian grasp at his sanity. "Aren't you?"

Enzo shot her a withering look. "The First War of Saints may have wiped us out, but that doesn't mean we didn't come back. Do you know what it is to be the only one of your kind? To live in hiding, grappling with the knowledge that your magic makes you an enemy?" He skimmed his tongue over his top teeth. "For a city obsessed with power, Ombrazia certainly is afraid of it."

Damian went cold. Part of his mind still couldn't comprehend that Roz had been *right*. The stories had gotten it wrong. They must have, because if they were true, there was no way Enzo could be standing before him right now. "So what does that mean? Is Chaos back? Or did he never fall in the first place?"

"Do you truly think Chaos could have been felled by mere mortals?" Enzo's tone was mocking, pure silk. "Do you think his lover did not teach him restraint? He lies in wait, but he will return to be the most powerful saint of them all. I intend to ensure it." Enzo bent to pick up the pistola, and as he did, the mass of flesh that had been the chief magistrate disappeared. "It made me sick, watching this place run by a group of inferior disciples who only sit in this Palazzo because they stole it. They stole it from *my* people. They vilified *my* patron saint."

Damian shook his head in an attempt to clear it, unable to fathom what he'd just heard. "What do you mean, Chaos lies in wait?" he rasped. "If that's true, why aren't there more of you? Why doesn't he have more disciples?"

Roz came to stand at Damian's shoulder, surveyed Enzo as though sizing him up before a fight. Her presence made Damian feel slightly more grounded.

Enzo twirled his gun, pointing it at Damian, then Roz, then Nasim. Then back to Damian. A leer stole across his face. "Why? *Why?* Because we have been targeted. Destroyed. We were killed during the war, and now, when children are tested, anyone showing signs of possessing his magic is taken away. Did you know that?" Enzo's eyes grew unnaturally wide, making him appear unhinged. "They're taken away and killed by people like your father. People like your precious Chief magistrate. I've searched for them, you know, to no avail. I've never *stopped* searching."

It was obvious he was attempting to rattle them, and it worked. Nasim gasped, and Roz's lips parted, through no sound came out. Damian felt as if someone had dealt him a brutal punch to the gut. Was Ombrazia really that broken, that *children* were being punished out of fear of Chaos?

"That's why you killed Forte and my father," he croaked. "Isn't it?"

"And Leonzio Bianchi." Enzo wagged a finger at him, looking almost pleased. "Yes. But that wasn't the only reason."

As Damian battled his thoughts, he couldn't stop looking at the boy—the *man*—before him. It was as if his mind simply didn't want to process the sight.

Enzo. The boy he'd thought was helping him. The friend he'd trusted and would have done anything to protect. He was the last person Damian would have pinned as a threat.

Had he known anyone in this place at all?

"Your father was beginning to see through me, you know," Enzo said lightly, giving Battista's corpse a disgusted kick. He realized something was wrong. I was planning to get rid of him anyway, of course, but it would have caused some upset if I'd carried out the task too soon after getting rid of Leonzio."

Damian couldn't speak. And if he could, what would he say? His vision blurred around the edges, and he couldn't bring himself to look at the body Enzo had treated with such indignity. *Man to monster to meat.* Was he doomed to meet the same end?

"Why did you kill her?"

Damian didn't expect the snarl that tore free from Roz's chest.

He watched as the cracks in her mask fractured completely, and all at once she looked as if she were barely holding it together. He wanted to reach for her, but stopped himself, afraid to make any sudden movements in Enzo's presence.

Enzo blinked. "Excuse me?"

"Why did you kill Piera? Why did you kill *any* of the unfavored?" Roz hurled the words like individual barbs.

To Damian's bewilderment, Enzo appeared delighted to be asked.

"I intend to please Chaos, so that he'll return to help his children. And as you ought to know, he demands blood as payment. I'd already made my first two sacrifices—vellenium signifies to Chaos the sacrifice is indeed for him—and I was ready to make my third. Did you know the Shrine is the only place in Ombrazia where the likeness of Chaos remains? It was constructed long before the Palazzo, and not even the chief magistrate has the authority to change it."

"I altered my appearance so I could pose as a serving boy in the Palazzo, where I could eventually avenge my fellow disciples. I hoped I might even learn their fate. But one night I visited Chaos's statue in the dead of night, thinking I would be alone to present my offering to him. Eyes," he clarified, skimming his tongue across his teeth. "Eyeballs taken from my victims. A flesh offering is always appreciated, you understand. But I found myself with company. Leonzio Bianchi happened to walk in while I was praying to my patron saint."

"So you made him your next victim," Damian said quietly. "Didn't you?"

Enzo shrugged. "I didn't have much of a choice. He wasn't supposed to die yet, you see. I was choosing victims who wouldn't be missed. People whose murders wouldn't be looked into. Leonzio, your father, the chief magistrate...they were supposed to come later. A final hurrah, if you will, once I'd accomplished what I'd set out to do. But once Leonzio recognized my face, once he marked me as a heretic, I knew I was in trouble. I can make people see illusions, but unfortunately, I can't make them forget things.

"So I disposed of the disciple. I gave him a low dose of poison, one that would kill him slowly. He didn't go quietly. He fought against the madness vellenium brings, going so far as to create a shrine in his room to try to call upon the saints' protection." Enzo *tsk*ed, the corners of his mouth curving in amusement. "But he succumbed eventually. Of course, then I had another problem." He tapped his chin. "The chief magistrate was desperate to solve the murder. I overheard him suggest to Battista that you, Damian, needed a task force to assist you. Naturally, I had to kill him, too, though this time I managed to do so in secret. I took over the chief magistrate's role, posing as him, and told Battista you were to solve the murder alone. I must say, I never thought you would actually discover anything of note."

Of course Enzo was the killer. Of *course* he was. Now Damian thought about it, he'd never seen Enzo and the chief magistrate in the same place at the same time, had he? The last time he'd seen the real Forte, then, nearly two weeks ago. It was perplexing to consider.

"Wait," Damian croaked abruptly, remembering the night he'd seen the chief magistrate struggling to get into his office. "That night—that was *you*. That was why Forte's door wouldn't unlock. It didn't recognize you."

Enzo's smug expression was answer enough.

"You were at the Basilica too, weren't you?" Roz put in, cheeks still red with fury. "That was why Forte's—*your*—speech was so terrible."

Enzo adjusted the collar of his shirt, lips tight. His focus wasn't on any of them, but rather on the open-air ceiling. "I wouldn't have said it was terrible. I managed to fool everyone else, didn't I?"

He had, Damian thought, and that was the worst part. This whole time, he'd thought they were friends. They'd confided in one another. Had laughed so easily with Kiran and Siena. How could he not have known? At the same time, though, how *could* he have?

"Well, you underestimated Damian," Roz spat at Enzo, cheeks reddening. "You ought to have known he'd catch you eventually."

Enzo loosed a laugh that trailed off into a sigh. He spread his arms wide, indicating their group. "*Did* he catch me, though? It rather seems as though I've revealed myself to you."

"*You*—" Roz started forward, and Damian's heart skipped a beat. He lurched forward to drag her back.

"Roz, you can't," he said, even as fury pumped through his veins. There was no way to win where an illusionist was concerned, was there? Suddenly he was questioning everything he'd seen and heard over the past few weeks. No wonder disciples of Chaos were known for driving people to madness.

Roz's eyes were glassy. "He killed Piera, Damian."

"I know."

Enzo's gaze softened, becoming almost endearing as he stared at Roz. "Don't be sad, child of Patience. Your goals are aligned with mine, are they not?"

"How the hell do you figure?" she retorted.

"You hate the way this system treats people, and you want change. You don't feel as though you belong anywhere." He blinked long lashes, the corners of his mouth turning down. "I became interested in you, you know, after the day Damian got me to deliver that message to your apartment. The way you manage to be both disciple and rebel, and yet neither feels *quite* right, does it?"

Roz's lips parted ever so slightly. "What are you saying?"

There was a sheen of sweat on Enzo's pale brow, and excitement slunk into his voice. He took a step closer to Roz, fire in his black gaze. "You're probably wondering why I let you catch me tonight, instead of creating an illusion that allowed me to escape. Why would I reveal my secrets to you?" A single, eerie laugh. "The chief magistrate and his general are gone. The citizens of Ombrazia are angry. It's the perfect moment for the ascension of a new leader." Enzo lifted a hand in Roz's direction, as if he meant to touch her from a distance. "I didn't show any sign of being blessed by Chaos until I was much older. As such, before coming to the Palazzo, I went through life posing as one of the unfavored. I knew people who joined Piera Bartolo's rebellion." He twirled his gun, showing each and every one of his teeth. "Don't you see? Now that she's gone, the rebels will need a new goal. They can help us build a new system. Children of Chaos and Patience, working together—the way it was always meant to be."

"*What?*" Roz exploded, and Damian had to stop himself from stepping between them. "You killed Piera because you wanted the *rebels*? They'll never follow you, and neither will I. You're mad if you think we're on the same team."

Enzo drew himself up tall. When he did, he was nearly the same height as Damian. His eyes flashed. "We *are* on the same team. We want the same thing. And I have the ability to make it happen."

The terrible thing was, when he said it like that, Damian didn't doubt it.

Roz didn't back down. "To make *what* happen?"

"Anything." Enzo's voice was dangerous, smooth and alluring. "Anything you want. Chaos and Patience have always been a powerful combination. Imagine what we could do together. You can see it, can't you?"

Roz's lips trembled, and that was when Damian knew for certain: Roz *could* see it. She could see what it would be like to build the Ombrazia of her dreams, an illusionist at her side. Enzo could make things happen that she alone never could. He shared her deep-seated rage, and would understand her in ways Damian didn't. Couldn't.

It made him feel sick.

"*Roz.*" He heard the desperation in his voice, and hated it. "Don't listen to him."

But she didn't respond. She was fixated on Enzo, who stepped toward her through the blood.

"Say yes, tesoro," he murmured. "There's never been a better time for change. We can destroy all of this." Enzo waved a hand, gesturing at the Palazzo around them. "When Chaos returns, we will be greatly rewarded. No one will dare question us, for I think you'll find I'm quite adept at making people see things my way. I could convince you, you know, but I won't. I want you to choose this."

"Roz!" Nasim chimed in, finally shaken from her paralysis. "Remember why you joined the rebellion. It was because you believe everyone should have an equal say, right? Disciples and the unfavored alike. No matter what he tells you, you don't actually want the same things. You need to remember what we're fighting for."

Damian watched as Roz's eyes cleared, swiveling to focus on Nasim.

"You're right," she said eventually, then turned back to Enzo. "You're wasting your time. I want nothing to do with you. I *am* going to change Ombrazia, but not in the way you want."

The shift in Enzo's expression was sudden and frightening. "Is this because of him?" Enzo snarled the last word, jabbing a finger in Damian's direction. "You're not soft like him, darling. You're meant for more."

"I said no." Roz kept her voice very calm, for which Damian was thankful. He still had his gun aimed at Enzo, but if the disciple decided to shoot, Damian wasn't confident he would be fast enough to stop him.

"Fine," Enzo said softly. "Fine. But you *will* change your mind."

Then he was gone, disappearing between one second and the next.

"NO!" Roz screamed, whirling. Damian followed suit, pointing his gun around the Palazzo's entryway, but Enzo was nowhere to be seen. It was some sort of illusion—it had to be. He'd made them think he wasn't there, then made his escape.

"We need to find him," Roz said, cursing. "He can't have made it far. Nasim, can you warn the rebels? Damian, you search the top two floors. I'll search the ground floor and the cellar."

Damian nodded. He didn't have much hope they would find an illusionist who didn't want to be found, but he wasn't about to let Enzo get away without a fight. The last thing they needed was a disciple of Chaos loose in the city.

He didn't want to split up, but they didn't have much of a

choice. Nasim slipped outside, and as Roz made to follow, Damian grabbed her arm.

"Roz." His voice cracked beneath the strain. "Be careful. Please."

She gave a small smile. Tendrils of hair had escaped her ponytail and hung around her face in sweaty curls. But her eyes, blue as the summer sky, were determined. "You too, Venturi."

Then she disappeared down the hallway, the shadows swallowing up her lithe form and enfolding her into the dark.

38

Roz

Enzo was nowhere to be found on the main floor of the Palazzo.
Would he let her see him, Roz wondered, if by some miracle she
came across his hiding place? She didn't know. For all the good
her search was doing, she might as well have been walking around
blind. Enzo could be long gone by now. Perhaps on the other side
of the city, committing another murder.

Roz stumbled to the door of the council chambers, feeling like
an impostor in her own body. Like her skin didn't fit the way it
had moments ago.

Before she could enter, something in her periphery caught her
attention.

There were . . . *figures* at the far end of the corridor. Motionless,
strangely unsubstantial, but definitely human. Three of them.

"What do you want?" she called, her voice bouncing back to her. The echo sounded thin.

No response. The figures didn't so much as shift.

That was odd. Roz crept down the corridor toward them, keeping close to the wall, as if that might protect her should they decide to shoot. Though they were obviously standing, some macabre part of her expected them to be dead. But then, the ever-present concern: Was *this* an illusion? Something deliberately placed to distract her?

"Hello?" She detested her own wariness, and wished she had a real weapon. The knife in her hand was a comfort, but it wouldn't be much use against a trio of potential attackers.

Except, Roz saw as she finally drew close enough, these weren't attackers. They were security officers. She didn't recognize any of them, but she certainly had the time to look.

Because they were *frozen*, gazes fixed unblinkingly on something Roz couldn't see. It was unsettling, as though she were standing before a display of hyperrealistic statues. Their chests appeared to be rising and falling, however, so they weren't dead.

She shuddered, stowing her knife away and touching the nearest officer with an index finger. The man didn't react. Could you *feel* an illusion? Roz didn't think you could. So then what, exactly, was going on here? She snatched a pistola from the hands of a frozen officer. Still he showed no indication of having noticed.

Of one thing she was certain: Enzo had been here. Now that she focused, reaching out with her own magic, she could feel the prickling remnants of his. It was that same sensation she'd felt in Leonzio's room. Her body reacted immediately, and once she focused on the feeling, it became impossible to ignore. Breath catching in her chest, she let it guide her onward.

It didn't take her long to realize where it was leading her.

Of *course* Enzo would be in the Shrine.

Roz sprinted down the hall, urgency like a fever in her blood, until she reached the room connected to the Shrine's entrance. By now she'd snuck through this part of the building often enough to have committed it to memory.

The door was wide open.

Enzo wanted her to seek him out, didn't he? He may have disappeared, but she couldn't shake the sensation she was meant to find him.

That was fine with Roz. Because when she did, she wouldn't hesitate to shoot.

She raced down the narrow tunnels for the second time that night. Her heartbeat had come alive in her chest, beating out a relentless warning. She should have been afraid. She knew as much.

But she wasn't.

Her footsteps thudded against the stone as she calculated her earlier route in reverse, grip tight on her stolen gun. Perhaps it was better this way. Her against Enzo, one on one. In a way, Roz thought, Enzo appealed to the darkest parts of her. He was who she might have become, had she chosen a different path.

And that was why he needed to die. Because part of her *wanted* the picture he painted. Wanted it desperately. She was only lucky Damian and Nasim had been there to remind her what was truly important. She wanted to redeem herself in their eyes, and yet she feared she would never be good enough for either of them.

Everyone needed at least one redeemable quality, she figured, in order not to be considered *entirely* bad. Roz didn't have many redeemable qualities. She knew that. She held on to her sense of right and wrong like a lifeline. Perhaps it wasn't always flawless, but if she let herself slip, there was nothing stopping her from becoming the villain.

"There you are. It took you long enough."

Enzo's voice carried over to her as she burst into the belly of the Shrine. He didn't turn as he spoke. He stood before the covered statue of Chaos, hair gilded by the warm light of the candelabras. It was almost strange to think of him as handsome, given that she was accustomed to seeing him another way entirely, but his true appearance was unsettlingly good-looking. Or was that an illusion, too?

Roz halted, attempting to raise the gun, but her hands seemed to have frozen. *No, it's just in your head. Pull the damned trigger.* "I don't know why you let me find you, but I'm not going to change my mind."

Enzo made a noise in the back of his throat. He was wearing a black suit, Roz noticed, with the top few buttons undone. The white planes of his collarbones were distracting when he finally revolved to face her. Was that what he'd been wearing before? She couldn't remember.

The dark of the Shrine bore hungrily down on them, and Roz could see nothing beyond the semicircle of saints. The six she could see were cold and impassive. For the first time, she understood why people thought this place powerful. She felt it, too. But it was not a *good* kind of powerful.

It was a dangerous one.

"What is *that*?" Roz demanded, her stomach flipping over. There was something on the floor in front of Chaos. Something contained in a transparent jar. Something that looked horribly like—

"The eyes?" Enzo's voice was mocking. "Proof of the sacrifices I've made. They say he always knows when one of his followers kills with vellenium, but just in case..." He bent to pick up the jar, rotating it in his hands. Clear liquid sloshed against the sides, and the eyeballs bobbed against one another. "They sink when they're fresh, did you know that? But after a while..." Enzo gave the jar a shake. "Interesting, isn't it?"

Roz, who was not generally bothered by gruesome things, felt a bit nauseated. "You're deranged. I didn't come to watch your creepy little ritual." She tore her gaze away from the eyeballs, refocusing on Enzo's face as she rotated the gun. It would be so easy to dispatch him: He hadn't even bothered to pull his own weapon. For some reason, Roz knew, he didn't think she would do it. So she chose a different tactic.

"I understand why you're upset," she said softly, tracking his movements. "You've been vilified for no reason. All disciples of Chaos aren't inherently bad, no matter what the Palazzo says, and what they're doing to you is inexcusable."

"Oh, Rossana," Enzo mused, his voice a croon. One corner of his mouth slid up. "Do you really think you can disarm me with false empathy?"

Roz opened her mouth to argue, but before she could do so, the scene around her changed.

She was sitting in the council chambers, Enzo at her side. Sunlight streamed in through the window, leeching the color from the wall tapestries. When she glanced down at herself, she saw she was wearing the red coat and golden stars of a Palazzo disciple. Her rebels sat in a semicircle around the council table, each one focused intently on her face. Nasim. Dev. Piera.

Piera?

Enzo slid a sheet of paper across the polished wooden surface, his teeth flashing. Roz took it, unable to help herself, and saw that it was a list of policy recommendations.

Nearest the top were the words: *Withdraw from the war.* She stared at it for a long moment, not quite comprehending, until Enzo leaned close to her ear.

"Anything you want," he said, smooth as syrup. *"Name it, and I'll make it happen."*

Roz's heart swelled. If she could shape Ombrazia in whatever way she wanted, then she could do good. Having power wasn't wrong, as long as you knew how to use it.

But something pricked at the back of her mind. A wrongness began to seep through the cracks in the illusion, causing the scene to blur and fracture. The longer she stared into Enzo's eyes, the colder they became. Unease made her skin crawl.

"No," Roz heard herself say from somewhere between two places. "I told you, I won't be convinced."

She knew instinctively that the moment she said yes would be the moment she lost. Though she tried to ignore it, Roz had always known she would not be a good leader. A capable leader, perhaps, but not *good*. She and Nasim could lead the rebellion, but ruling a city-state was different. It could not be built on anger and vicious drive. Although she fought for justice now, she didn't trust herself not to be corrupted by power. She was not honorable. She was not merciful, or selfless, or careful. Roz wanted to change Ombrazia, but at the end of the day, she did not want to be the one to lead it.

In response, the illusion reformed around her. She saw herself in the streets of the city, decreeing that it would no longer be separated into sectors. She saw citizens bow as they passed her. One even morphed into her father, his eyes shining with respect.

It was everything she had ever dreamed of, parading by like a hard-won prize. Distracting and heart wrenching, drawing her deeper, it wore down her resolve.

What happened when the *want* became more important than all the rest?

Little by little, Roz felt pieces of herself begin to fall away.

39

DAMIAN

In the end, Damian decided to follow Roz.

He'd scoured the top floors of the Palazzo, discovering nothing of note, and returned to the main entrance to await her. The sky through the open ceiling was a black veil, punctuated by feeble pinpricks of light. The stars clung to the heavens as though something were trying to claw them down. Damian didn't know how long he stood there, drumming his fingers against his thigh, his pulse growing faster. Worry gnawed at him. Had Roz found Enzo? Had something happened to her?

Finally, unable to take it any longer, he made his way to the same shadow-plagued corridor where Roz had vanished like a phantom. He raced through the halls, checking every room on the west side of the main floor. Nothing. He felt as though he were in a dream—no, a nightmare—where the connection between his body and brain had begun to fray.

"Shit," Damian muttered under his breath. His grip on his gun was so tight he was surprised the weapon didn't shatter. Surely Roz wouldn't have left the building. Not without telling him.

His concern for her was a physical ache. But Damian couldn't deny that alongside it lay something colder: the deep-seated fear that Roz wanted what Enzo had to offer her more than she wanted justice. More than she hated the saints. More than she wanted *him*.

Needing to shake off his thoughts, to *move*, Damian bolted to the other side of the Palazzo, only to come to a grating halt when something stopped him in his tracks.

The door leading to the Shrine's entrance was open.

It was one of the last places Damian would have wanted to face an illusionist. There was an air of unreality to the Shrine that persisted without the addition of magical falsities. But if Enzo was to end his mad crusade anywhere, it was there. Beneath the earth at the last remaining statue of Chaos.

And so Damian ran.

He sprinted mindlessly down the tunnels, gun raised, braced for any kind of movement in the shadows. His heart throbbed like an open wound. Two scenes flashed in his mind. The first, Roz being hurt by Enzo. Suffering because Damian had waited too long and hadn't moved quickly enough. The second was Roz standing beside the disciple with a smile on her face. A smile that Damian knew meant he'd lost her.

Both were nightmarish possibilities. Enzo was a madman. A fanatic. He was determined to summon Chaos's return, no matter the cost. His belief in the saint was that strong.

Was Damian's? Did he really believe such a thing was possible? He didn't know. But he didn't particularly want to find out.

Damian skimmed his tongue over his dry lips as he rounded the last corner. The air in the Shrine was cold, eerily still, and heavy with memories of reverence. He shivered. Chaos may be down here, but so was Strength. So were Mercy, Patience, Death, Grace, and Cunning. He needed to remember that.

And yet, as usual, the thought of the saints brought little comfort. Especially once he saw them.

Roz and Enzo were standing close together, silhouetted by the candlelight. The statues of the saints were arranged around them, lending the impression they had gathered after the fact. Enzo had one hand on Roz's cheek. Her head was tilted, face angled toward the illusionist's, eyes wide and gold-washed. Damian couldn't fathom why she didn't appear bothered by his touch. Something vicious rose in the back of his throat, forcing a sour taste onto his tongue.

"I'm glad you changed your mind," Enzo was saying. "I knew you'd come around."

"*Roz*," Damian said loudly, and she glanced up, face whitening.

Enzo's hand dropped from her cheek. His lips stretched in an appalling grin. "Ah, Damian. Right on schedule."

Damian ignored him. "Roz, you were right the first time. Remember what Nasim said? You and Enzo don't share the same goals, no matter what he tells you. I know you're better than that."

"Damian...," Roz began, voice strained, but he wasn't finished.

"No. Listen to me. I'm on your side, now, remember? Ombrazia needs to change, and I'll help you. Just not like this. *Please*, not like this." He held her gaze, hoping she could see the sincerity in his eyes.

Enzo released a snarl, starting toward Damian. This wasn't the serving boy Damian knew from the Palazzo—not by a long shot. This was a man, powerful and enraged. And *desperate*. Damian knew from experience how dangerous people were when desperation took hold.

"My dear friend," Enzo purred, raising his pistola. "You're not going to hold her back. You're not going to hold *us* back."

"We are *not* friends. We never were," Damian spat. "And I know you're manipulating her. She would never choose you otherwise. I thought you said you weren't going to do that."

"I said I didn't *want* to do that." Enzo's tongue flicked over his top lip. "I didn't say I wouldn't." He sighed. "Both of you are so predictable, you know that? I knew Rossana would track me down without any trouble. And once she did, I knew you would come to find her. And look—here you are."

Roz seemed to be silently trying to communicate something. Her expression was serious, almost fearful. "Damian, I'm not being manipulated. You need to go. Please."

After their conversation in the dungeons, Damian knew Roz wouldn't let him down by truly siding with Enzo. A lump formed in his throat. She wanted him to leave, to save himself, and he wasn't going to take the bait.

Damian stood his ground, raising his own gun. "I'm not going anywhere."

"That's right," Enzo said silkily. The shadows clung to him like a second skin, blending with his inky suit. "You're not."

Something about the way he said the words flooded Damian with unease.

Enzo laughed. The sound was bone chilling, genuinely amused. "Seven saints, seven sacrifices. The girl they found dead

360

in the streets. The boy who washed up on the riverbank." He ticked them off on his fingers. "The disciple. The woman you discovered in the gardens. The chief magistrate. Piera Bartolo. Sadly I killed your father in haste, so he doesn't count as a sacrifice." Another laugh, this one inching up an octave. "Now tell me, Venturi, how many does that make?"

Damian didn't respond, though he counted in his head. Excluding his father, that made six.

Roz figured it out the same moment he did.

"*No*," she snarled, pulling away from Enzo and yanking a gun from her waistband. She pointed it at the illusionist, hands steady. "Damian will *not* be your final sacrifice."

"Ah, Rossana, I thought we were past this." The corners of Enzo's mouth turned down.

"I thought if I pretended to be on your side, you would leave him alone. I am *not* going to let you kill him."

Anger flared in the disciple's eyes. For a moment Damian feared he was about to find out who among them could shoot the fastest: him, Roz, or Enzo. His heart was pounding so fast, it felt like a single drawn-out beat.

Then Enzo disappeared.

Damian spun, pointing his pistola around the Shrine. It was a futile endeavor: Once more, Enzo was nowhere to be seen. This time, though, he hadn't left. His disembodied voice echoed from somewhere in the room.

"If that is how it is to be, Rossana, then I will let you decide between yourselves. Who will be my final sacrifice? You, or him? Don't worry— you'll never see death coming."

Roz was frozen, wild eyes flicking to lock with Damian's. Jaw tense, she fired a shot straight ahead. Then one to the left.

Damian flinched, ears ringing as she continued to pivot, emptying her pistola of bullets. He had half a mind to copy her, but somehow he didn't think it would be worth the effort. Their chances of hitting Enzo were slim to none. Especially when the disciple could see where they were aiming.

Roz flung her spent gun to the floor, cursing.

"Come now, Damian," Enzo crooned from nowhere. *"Surely you aren't going to let her die for you? I'll give you . . . Oh, shall we say, another minute to decide? Then I choose for you."*

Damian shuttered his eyes. Enzo would choose him. He knew that, and he was going to let it happen. There was no way both he and Roz were going to make it out of here alive. It was only a matter of time before the illusions layered on more thickly, one on top of the other, until neither of them knew what was real.

Enzo was right. Damian wouldn't see death coming. Because when it came, he would be looking at Roz.

"Don't you dare," she spat, voice rising across the room. It bounced off the stone and barreled into Damian with all the force of a physical blow. "I see that look on your face, Venturi. And there is no way in hell I'm letting you sacrifice yourself. If either of us deserves to die, it's me."

That simply wasn't true. It wasn't true at all. Damian was a murderer. He'd dealt death, he'd prayed for it, and now he was going to face it like a man. Not the kind of man who convinced himself he wasn't frightened, but the kind of man who understood it was okay to be.

"Roz," he said throatily. "It was always going to be me. Let it be me."

"No."

Damian couldn't let her die. Not for him. He needed to make

her understand, needed to make her see that he was cursed and unworthy and *wrong*.

"I've killed people who don't deserve it. I let Michele die, and I'm the reason your father never came home. Then I let you suffer alone, because I was too much of a coward to reach out. I'm not redeemable." His voice sounded tinny, far away, even to his own ears.

Roz was shaking her head, furious. "We're not going to list everything we've done wrong, Damian, or we'll go on forever."

He couldn't think of that, though. What Roz didn't understand was that, by doing this, he was only further proving how royally fucked up he was. Because he was being selfish, and knew he simply couldn't watch Roz die. After everything, he wouldn't be able to stand it.

"I deserve this," Damian said, barely a whisper now. "Don't you see? *Let it be me.*"

The candlelight flickered out.

The Shrine was nothing but chthonic darkness. Damian's hand shook on his pistola as he held it out before him. It made him feel better, having that firm metal in his grasp, but still he didn't dare shoot. Especially now that he couldn't see Roz.

Still she was silent. Good—it was right that she should hate him, and that it should save her life.

"Do it." Damian's voice was a growl flung into obscurity. "Do it, Enzo. Get it over with. I doubt it will bring your precious saint back, but I suppose you're going to have to find that out yourself."

There was no response. Not even the hiss of a breath.

"ENZO!"

Nothing. Ice spread through Damian's blood, starting in his chest and working outward to his extremities. Something in the Shrine shifted.

Then he heard Roz's harsh intake of breath.

"ROZ?" he hurled her name into the dark.

A single light flared back to life. One tiny pinprick against a wretched canvas. Damian blinked as his eyes readjusted, scanning the room wildly for a sign he wasn't alone. Had Enzo tricked them? Had he distracted Damian and escaped with Roz in tow?

A sound like a labored pant scratched the air. A sound that shook Damian to his core and turned him to stone as he glanced down.

Roz was crumpled on the ground, dark liquid trickling from the corner of her mouth. One arm was stretched out beside her. Her eyes rotated in their sockets to focus on the ink-black puncture wound, stark against the skin of her inner elbow.

Damian's mouth was bone dry. The seconds stretched taut, on the verge of snapping.

If his world had slowed before, he didn't know what it was doing now.

There was no world. There was only this—this *sensation*, whatever it was, and if the word *NO* could be a feeling, Damian thought this was what it would be like. Torture. A pain so great it felt like nothing at all.

Roz was dying.

Roz was dying, and Damian was pure rage. Or perhaps that was the vicious agony rising in his throat, choking him. He hadn't felt this way since he'd watched Michele die. It made him wild with an emotion he couldn't name. He felt as though he were on the front lines once more, ready to unleash all his pain and anger on the next thing that moved. His heart was an unrelenting drumbeat in his ears. He ripped his jacket off, draping it over Roz as if that might somehow lessen the effects of the poison in her veins. *Find a disciple of Mercy*, a voice in the back of his mind demanded, but Damian knew there was no point.

She had already stopped breathing.

There was nothing a disciple could do for her. Damian knew it, and the knowing was like a knife deep in his own chest. The pain was like—like—

He didn't know what it was like. There was no way to describe it. He wanted to keel over and die himself, just so it would be over. He wanted to cry, but he didn't have enough energy, enough breath. Roz's face was so perfectly still, her dark lashes casting crescent shadows on her cheeks, but the connection was gone. Damian could feel that *she* was gone.

Seconds passed, and it felt like hours.

Damian stood. He was a moon with nothing keeping him in orbit. The earth had imploded, and he was a rogue piece of rock hurtling aimlessly through space.

He was destruction.

For the first time, Damian thrust aside his desire for Strength. That wasn't the saint he needed. Not now. He had enough strength on his own.

Instead, he opened his heart to the darkness he'd been carrying for months.

He'd always interpreted it as the presence of Death, but now he knew it was something else. It filled him up like poison, eating away everything until only a deadly calm remained. It was gentle, but it was also hungry, and Damian felt something inside him shift.

He tore his eyes away from Roz, his love, his weakness, and rose.

"*ENZO!*" he bellowed, and the dual syllables were a tempest beneath the dome of the Shrine. The room screamed the name back at him, his anger emphasized a thousandfold.

There was nothing to see. And yet Damian did not stop looking, his gaze searing through the dark. Testing the pockets of shadow. He was not boy, but fury given form, and he picked up the jar in front of Chaos and hurled it to the stone floor.

It shattered, leaking fluid and sending fleshy orbs rolling wetly across the ground. *Eyes*, a distant part of Damian understood, but the realization was dull. He could feel Enzo's displeasure, somehow, as if it had become a tangible thing.

He inhaled deeply, unevenly, prepared to scream for Enzo to come and face him. To fight him. But through the haze of wrath and hysteria, his attention snagged on…something. Something in the middle distance between him and the other side of the Shrine. Still he *saw* nothing, and yet he found himself raising his pistola, hands suddenly more steady than they had ever been.

"Venturi?" Enzo's snarl drifted over to him, ghostly and agitated. "How—"

But Damian didn't hesitate. Not this time.

He racked a bullet into the chamber and fired it into the dark.

40

DAMIAN

Everything was dim orange light and marble stained with red. The hooded faces of the stone saints peered down in harsh judgment.

They watched as Enzo flickered into visibility, only to crumple to the ground.

The world turned on its head, then righted itself as something crucial shifted. Damian scarcely noticed. He stared down at himself. Shoes bloody. Shirt bloody. In his hand was the pistola, its handle warm, as if he'd been clutching it for hours. The room was a blur. His mind was a blur. He could do nothing but blink at the body on the floor in front of him.

Enzo stared blankly at the painted ceiling, expression contorted in eternal fury beneath the flecks of gore. His intricate robes, stitched by some skilled disciple, were dark with blood.

It had soaked into the fabric, already beginning to crust over in places. One of his hands was clawed, stretched futilely across the ground as if he'd made to reach for something in his final moments.

The bullet had gone straight into his skull.

Damian had *killed* Enzo. Had shot him like a soldier executing a deserter. He didn't know *how*—how he'd known where to aim, how he'd managed such a shot. Nothing made sense. Nothing made *sense*, and he was a murderer all over again. Panic swelled within him, and his head was abruptly full of death, the sounds of men dying, the look of horror on Michele's face as he crumpled in the mud.

Somewhere above him, Damian knew, his father had been executed the same way. A bullet to the brain, quick and efficient.

His eyes blurred, and he suddenly couldn't swallow. Battista was gone and his mother was gone and Michele was gone and Roz was *gone* and...and...

Damian sank to his knees. His pistola clattered to the ground as his hands went limp.

I missed you so much I was sick from it.

Sick from it

Sick

Damian had never felt so sick. He'd known grief before, but not like this. He felt like his whole body was shutting down. He wished it would.

He had nothing left to fight for.

Someone said Damian's name, though they sounded impossibly far away. Or maybe it was Damian who was far away. Too far to be reached, too far to be touched, too far to hear anything but his own thoughts slamming against the inside of his skull, again and again and *again* . . .

His hands began to shake. Furiously, uncontrollably, as though they belonged to someone else. Someone who couldn't remember how to be human. Or someone who didn't want to be, and no longer bothered trying.

"Damian?"

Perhaps he was more like his father than he'd thought. Battista was gone, a nothing-man, and Damian a nothing-boy. Infinitely hollow and empty.

Let it be over.

"Damian." A phantom touch on his shoulder. Someone breathed heavily near his ear. There was a hand on his cheek, and they moved into his line of vision, but he couldn't focus on them.

"*Damian.* What did you see?"

He heard the question, but it didn't make any sense. What did he see? He saw the dead. Nothing but blood and the dead, no matter where he looked.

Whoever had spoken knelt down beside him. Took his face in cold, cold hands. Lifted his chin.

Rossana's expression was broken.

Roz.

Roz.

Damian's lips parted, but no words came. She wasn't here. He *knew* she wasn't here. He had watched her die, curled against the floor of the Shrine. He'd finally shattered beyond repair, hadn't he?

He didn't even care.

"Damian." Roz's mouth moved as it formed his name, now

with a note of worry. "Damian, I don't know what you saw, but everything's okay. You killed him. He can't show you anything else."

Damian blinked in confusion. His lashes were damp. Should he have been embarrassed, even if she wasn't real? He didn't have the energy.

"Can you say something?" Roz's face was pale, strained. Her hair was a mess, a dark halo that tumbled to her ribs. "Are you hurt?"

The pieces began to fit together, slowly and in increments. *You killed him. He can't show you anything else.*

He'd killed Enzo. Enzo was a disciple of Chaos.

Now Damian really did begin to cry. He couldn't help it. The force of his sobs wracked his chest, and he shuddered like he was going to break. Roz was alive. She was alive, and she was here, and it had all been in his head. The slow horror of watching her crumple to the ground. The spreading black against her skin.

Roz's arms tightened around him, and she ran a soothing hand up and down his back. "Whatever you saw after Enzo disappeared, it wasn't real. He was toying with us, Damian. I don't know why, but I realized it when he showed me something that couldn't possibly be true. It was just an illusion. I promise it wasn't real."

She said it over and over again, more times than Damian could count, and each time it sunk in a little more. He'd never watched her die, helpless and fracturing on the inside. She tilted her head in the crook of his neck, and there was nothing but her scent, the heat of her body against his. Nothing else mattered.

"I thought you were dead," he rasped, barely able to force the words out. "Enzo disappeared, and when the light came back I saw—I saw—"

Saints, he thought she'd died. Had put herself forward as the final sacrifice.

It was the one thing that would have tipped him over the edge for good.

Somehow Roz seemed able to interpret his meaning. She angled herself so that she was blocking Damian's view of Enzo's body. Her eyes burned into his, blue as an afternoon sky, so fierce and alive.

"I would've, Damian," she said, pressing her lips to the palm of his shaking hand. They came away red. "If it were real, I would have."

Why? he mouthed, knowing she wouldn't hear. He cleared his throat. Tried to rid himself of the choking sensation as he said, "My father—"

"He's still dead," Roz whispered. "Damian, I'm sorry."

Damian shook his head. She wasn't, and it was fine. She had no reason to be. Not after what his father had done.

"It's true," Roz insisted, hearing his unspoken argument. "I've spent so long hating him. Dreaming of revenge. It kept me going, I suppose, but now..." She trailed off, shoulders slumping. "Seeing him dead, I realized I didn't feel any better. I still feel... broken."

Damian knew the feeling well.

"I think I need to accept that part of me always will be," Roz continued, still quiet, though no longer whispering. "And—" She made a gulping noise, and Damian realized she was crying. He squeezed her hand back as small tremors shook her body. Her spine seemed to curve in on itself. "I avoided grief by seeking retribution. I was so focused on that, I don't think the fact that my father was *gone* ever really sunk in. Not in the way it should have.

Not in a way that allowed me to move forward. I guess I just—" Roz's voice cracked, and she swallowed with some difficulty. "I just need to be sad, you know?"

"I do know," Damian murmured. Hell, did he ever know. Sadness lived in the very crevices of his heart. No matter what else he was feeling, no matter how the sadness swelled or shrunk depending on the day, it never left entirely.

He straightened as Roz softened into him. Holding her up the way she'd done for him only moments before.

Neither of them moved for a very long time.

41

Roz

Roz stared at the ceiling as dawn trailed searching fingers into the
bedroom at the Palazzo.

She hadn't slept. Had passed the hours staring at Damian,
watching the rise and fall of his chest as he navigated what Roz
could only assume were nightmares.

It had taken the arrival of Kiran, Siena, and Nasim to coax
them from the Shrine the night before. Free of Enzo's influence,
Kiran and Nasim had first come across Battista's body, then found
Nasim trying to get back inside the Palazzo. Together the three
of them had made their way down to the Shrine, where the pieces
began to fit together.

You didn't forget what had happened when you were under
a disciple of Chaos's control, Roz learned. You simply reframed
it once you came back to your senses. As such, Kiran and Siena

already knew exactly what had happened with the chief magistrate turned Enzo. They'd coaxed Damian to his feet, reassuring him he'd done the right thing by killing the disciple. Nasim had gathered Roz into a tearful hug, and Roz had even let her.

It was okay to know grief, she was realizing. It was okay to share it. That was what Piera had been trying to tell her all along, wasn't it?

You don't recover—you only grow stronger. You find a way to rebuild yourself, even with crucial pieces missing.

Once back in Damian's rooms, and once they'd been left alone, Roz had stripped Damian of his blood-soaked clothes and run a bath. He'd sat in it for a long while, watching the water turn to rust, gripping Roz's hand as she rested her back against the basin. She knew he wasn't merely suffering the loss of his father, but was struggling with what he'd done to Enzo. For Damian, it wasn't just murder. It was a reminder of the war. A memory of the last boy he'd seen shot dead, and now the finger that had pulled the trigger was his own.

Roz hadn't asked, and she hadn't needed to. She'd put Damian in his bed, sat beside him, and drawn her knees up to her chest, waiting for the dark to lift.

This wasn't what she'd thought it would feel like. Victory, that was. Battista Venturi was dead. So was Enzo, and the chief magistrate. None of this saddened Roz; their deaths were a sort of justice, she thought. She did not mourn them. She mourned Piera and Amélie. She mourned her mother's condition. She mourned her father, and the fact that his death was a weight on Damian's conscience. Roz knew Damian hadn't meant for it to happen. The world was cruel.

No—the world was only what people made it. Battista was cruel. The system he served was cruel.

But they were working on it.

The city was in turmoil, and the rebels had effectively emptied the prison. Roz would need to meet with them today. She and Nasim would tell them about the illusionist, and finally explain the murders. Dev would learn his sister's killer was dead, and hopefully that would bring him some peace. She longed to see him smile again. And if he needed longer to grieve—well, Roz would grieve with him.

Part of Roz despaired that neither Enzo nor Battista had been killed in the way she'd hoped: publicly and violently. She hadn't seen either of the two men meet their end. She supposed, in a way, they had paid for their crimes, but she'd wanted them to spend their last moments knowing *why* they were dying. Knowing it was penance for their evil.

Then again, Roz couldn't have killed Battista. She couldn't have done that to Damian. He'd made her show mercy whether she wanted to or not.

She'd made the choice that saved their relationship. But it wasn't a matter of choosing weakness over vengeance. It wasn't a matter of choosing Damian over the memory of her father. The choice, really, had been about the kind of life she wanted going forward. And Roz had chosen a life with Damian in it.

Her father wouldn't have begrudged her that. If she could find a corner of happiness in a bleak world, wasn't that a sort of justice in itself?

Roz gave herself a shake, pulling the sheets back. She needed to *move*. Needed to clear her head. The longer she sat here, the more likely her thoughts would drift to bigger problems. Like the fact that illusionists weren't extinct after all. Were there more like Enzo who had managed to escape detection? Were they living in secret among the rest of Ombrazia's citizens? Whatever the situation, Roz hoped they could eventually coexist peacefully.

She didn't know what the city would do otherwise.

Dragging herself out of bed, Roz staggered to the door and shoved it open. In the corridor, to her surprise, was Siena. The officer gave a grim smile as she stalked over. Her braids were pulled back, and the front of her uniform was spattered with blood. She wore it like a triumphant warrior. Roz didn't know what Siena had been told, and she braced herself for what might well be a slew of unpleasantry.

But Siena only said, "Roz. How is he?"

"About as well as could be expected."

Siena's gaze sharpened. "And you?"

Roz didn't know how to respond to that. "I'm alive," was what she settled on. It was enough, for now. "I just don't know exactly where we go from here."

"Yeah," Siena said with a hard laugh. "How do you rebuild a city?"

"I wish I knew." Although Battista and the chief magistrate were dead, Roz didn't delude herself that the rest of the city would accept any change in the status quo. The guilds, the disciples, would want everything back in place as quickly as possible. They'd elect new disciples to the Palazzo, and put someone else in charge.

Roz supposed that would be the rebellion's next challenge. After all, change happened little by little.

"Well," Siena said, "I've taken control of Palazzo security for now, with Kiran and Noemi's help. They spent most of the night herding protesters away from the grounds." She shook her head, jaw set. "The current story is that the chief magistrate and his general resigned as a result of the riots. I don't know how many will believe it, but at least the situation is under control for the time being." Her mouth twisted wryly. "Now that Battista's gone, everyone agrees Damian should be reinstated as leader of Palazzo security. If he wants the job. The saints know I don't."

Roz was taken aback. She'd known the other officers respected Damian, but she hadn't realized how much. Apparently Battista and Forte were the only ones who hadn't believed in him. Her chest tightened. "I don't know if he will or not." She didn't know if *Palazzo security* would still be a thing. In fact, if Roz had anything to say about it, it wouldn't. After all, it wasn't only the disciples who needed protection.

Siena nodded. "He can have as much time as he needs. We'd all be proud to follow him again. None of us know what things will look like from here on out, but I *do* know that Damian can handle whatever comes. Noemi's already said if he doesn't accept, she's joining the rebels."

Roz tried and failed to hide her smile. She didn't know much about Noemi, but she had no doubt the girl would be a formidable addition. "I'm sure they'd be happy to have her." There. That sounded like something a person who may-or-may-not-be-a-rebel would say. "I'll be back shortly."

Siena waved her away. "Take your time. I'll be on guard at least until Damian wakes."

Roz took the stairs two at a time. The rising sun cast the gilded stairwells of the Palazzo in dull gold. Someone had evidently cleaned the floors after last night: When Roz reached the main entrance, there was no sign of blood. Battista's body was gone. Above her head, the sky was various shades of orange, blue, and gray. But she left the dawn behind, making her way down into darkness. She had somewhere else she wanted to be.

The cold air of the crypt wrapped around Roz like an unwelcome cloak.

Her steps echoed across the stone floor as she navigated the tables. Someone had cleaned the bodies of blood, and she paused when she reached Battista Venturi's.

It felt wrong, staring down at the man responsible for her father's murder and feeling a fierce sense of triumph, when she knew Damian was suffering his loss. But she couldn't help it. The general's eyes were closed, his lips pressed together so he appeared displeased even in death.

"Your son was always a better man than you," Roz whispered into the darkness, each word edged like a knife blade. "And you never deserved him."

She trailed a finger along the frigid surface of the table as she turned away, heading for the man laid out at the far end of the room, arms limp at his sides. His face was relaxed despite the brutality of his death.

"Hello, Enzo," she murmured.

His clothes were as impeccable as they had been last night. If not for the damage Damian had wrought to his head, he might have been asleep. Roz rested her elbows on the table, studying the disciple.

"This is how you wanted things to end, isn't it?" Her soft voice was all but lost in the cavernous room. She flexed her fingers, tracing a line down the stitching of his jacket. "Just you and me."

The space between seconds seemed to lengthen. She thought

about what Enzo had shown her. The vision she'd been subject to while Damian had been watching her die. The memory trailed icy fingers along her cheeks, down the back of her neck, and brought her nerve endings to life.

She didn't understand how, nor what it had meant. In the illusion, she'd been standing in the Shrine, and everything looked the same as it had before the lights went out. Then her surroundings had disappeared, almost as though they were elastic. Scenes moved through her field of vision in a disorienting blur: scenes that didn't belong to her.

Enzo walking up a set of stairs, one hand on the railing.

Exchanging words with Battista, watching smugly as the general's gaze fogged over.

Gathering security officers in the main entrance of the Palazzo.

I am the chief magistrate, Enzo's disembodied voice had suggested from somewhere outside Roz's thoughts. *Bring them to me.*

He had shown her everything he'd done. And then, when he'd allowed her mind to return to the Shrine, he'd shown her his own death.

Before it had happened.

Across from where Roz was positioned, Damian had stood framed by the shadows. His pistola was aimed directly into the shadowed portion of the Shine, where Enzo supposedly waited, out of sight. Roz had been glad. Had stopped breathing, waiting for Damian to shoot.

But when he'd lifted the gun, his gaze had darkened in a way that caused Roz's heart to stutter in her chest.

She watched his face relax, watched his hand cease shaking. Saw the precise moment when he made his decision. His head tilted, irises depthless obsidian. It was…unnerving. Terrifying.

The edges of his mouth curved into an unconscious smile. It was a smile Roz didn't recognize. As if someone *other* had slunk into Damian's skin, just for a heartbeat, and taken over.

She hadn't been able to move. Hadn't been able to draw a single breath. Time stretched as she stood frozen in place, watching the boy she loved turn into something terrifying.

And that had been it. That was the whole illusion, up until the deafening sound of the real Damian's gun had dragged her back to reality.

She didn't know what it meant. Didn't understand why Enzo had shown her all that. Had he planned to die all along? Was Damian part of his final plan, somehow?

The uneasy sensation lingered, and Roz couldn't figure out why. None of it had been real. Damian certainly wasn't dangerous. What was she expecting to learn, sitting here staring at Enzo's body?

She stood, trying to shake off the cold settling in her bones, and made her way back upstairs.

DAMIAN

Damian woke to find Roz staring at him.

She sat cross-legged on the end of the bed, eyes sharp as they fixed on his face. He dragged himself up to rest his back against the headboard, feeling a sudden twinge of embarrassment.

"You slept the whole day," was all she said.

The events of the previous night barreled into him, sending a tremor through Damian's core. It felt vaguely like a nightmare, or something he'd watched happen to someone else. Agonizing emptiness still pulsed deep within him. It twisted his stomach into knots and formed a vise around his heart. But it had lessened ever so slightly, so that at least he could remember how to draw breath.

"Did you go somewhere?" Damian asked Roz, noticing she'd changed her clothes.

She inclined her head. "Nasim and I went to talk to the rebels. There was a lot of explaining to be done. And," she added, an afterthought, "I needed to let them know I wasn't dead."

Damian couldn't help wincing at that.

"Sorry," she said softly. "But you're not getting rid of me that easily, Damian. I endure out of pure fucking spite."

He laughed, once. A jagged sound. It was true, wasn't it? Roz kept herself alive through sheer force of will.

"I heard there's a meeting tomorrow," Roz said. She looked rather pleased at the thought; despite the exhaustion in her face, the corners of her mouth twitched up. "Representatives from the guilds are invited, of course, but apparently the unfavored can attend as well. It might be a disaster, but I suppose they've got to start somewhere. People need to learn the truth about the disciples of Chaos. They'll need a plan going forward—ideally one that doesn't involve murder."

"And the rebellion?" Damian couldn't help asking. "Where do you fit in with all that?"

Roz shrugged. "We wait, and see how things go. We'll be around if needed. Advocating for the unfavored will remain our focus."

The determination in her voice was stark, and Damian felt a twinge of pride. He'd always known Roz was the type of person who needed a goal, and now that revenge was off the table, she'd clearly latched on to a new one. A better one.

"That sounds great," he said, and he meant it.

Roz shuffled closer to him. "Siena also said the rest of the officers want you to head security again."

That gave Damian pause. He inhaled sharply, bewildered. They wanted *him*? The officer who'd failed to solve the murders, who had shattered time and time again for everyone to see?

It was all Damian knew how to be: a protector. Perhaps it was counterintuitive, but heading Palazzo security had given him meaning when he returned from the war. A purpose. A reason to carry a weapon that didn't involve senseless murder.

"Maybe," he said. "Would you *want* me to do it?"

"That's not up to me." A furrow appeared between Roz's brows. "But if you decide to take the role, things need to change. You can't exist only to protect the disciples. Not while there are unfavored children in the streets. Not while people are still being sent to war."

"I know." Damian nodded slowly. If he *did* lead the officers again, maybe they could focus on getting food, resources, to people in the outskirts who needed them. Maybe they could start bridging the gap between disciples and the unfavored.

He didn't know exactly how to go about it, but he knew things couldn't stay the way they were.

As his thoughts returned to the present, he saw that Roz was focused on his face more intently than usual. Damian wondered what she saw there. He forced himself to swallow. "Something's on your mind. What is it?"

"How'd you know that?"

"I know you, Roz Lacertosa."

A beautiful pink danced across her cheeks, and she shrugged. "It's nothing we need to talk about now." She reached out to brush a finger over his lips. "I just want you to know that...I see you, Damian. Even the dark parts. Okay?"

Damian stilled, lips tingling where she'd touched him. It wasn't what he had expected her to say. Did she know, somehow? Could she tell he was changed? Damian might have been inclined to dismiss it as part of the illusion, except that he had *felt* it—the flash of darkness right before he'd fired that shot in the Shrine. As if something had taken root in him. As if something had been waiting to take root in him for quite some time.

Maybe it was Death. Or maybe it was something deeper, more inherent. He didn't know. He didn't *know*.

Outside the window it began to rain. First in a light pattering of mist against the glass, then in a torrent. It echoed the roar inside his head.

Damian's eyes burned into Roz's. She stared back, gaze unwavering. Once they had been children, breathing wonder and trailing stardust. What were they now except two people touched by tragedy? Two pieces of a whole, hardened by pain and broken in places only the other could see. A rebel and an officer, trying to patch together a splintered world.

"I fear I have more darkness than you know, Rossana," Damian whispered.

She slung her arms around his neck, entwining her fingers behind his head. She was chaotic and lovely. A lighthouse at the edge of a sea that tried relentlessly to drag him under.

"Don't call me Rossana."

And she pressed her lips to his.

"Saints—" he breathed, but Roz snatched the words before he could finish.

"There are no saints here, Damian Venturi," she murmured against his mouth, soft and alluring. When she pulled back, her kohl-lined eyes were wicked. "There's only me."

For the first time in his life, Damian was fine with that.

Epilogue

Beneath the Palazzo, in a circle of unseeing faces, something shifted.

Seven saints, seven sacrifices.

A boy lay in the crypt, dead as his dream. But while boys might die, and saints might fall, magic always endured. Magic could wake where the dead could not.

Nobody felt a thing. Not even when the shadows themselves skittered into the corners, and that enduring silence held its breath.

Deep in the belly of the Shrine, the statue of Chaos cast off its shroud.

And a saint rose.

ACKNOWLEDGMENTS

Acknowledgments TK